30p

KT-493-485

Escape to the Little Chateau

WITHDRAWN

9030 00007 7155 2

Escape to the Little Chateau

Marie Laval

*Finalist for the RNA Jackie Collins Award
for Romantic Suspense*

Where heroes are like chocolate – irresistible!

Copyright © 2022 Marie Laval

Published 2022 by Choc Lit Limited
Penrose House, Crawley Drive, Camberley, Surrey GU15 2AB, UK
www.choc-lit.com

First published as *A Spell in Provence* by Accent Press in 2015
Edited and revised in 2020 by Choc Lit

The right of Marie Laval to be identified as the Author
of this Work has been asserted by her in accordance with
the Copyright, Designs and Patents Act 1988

All characters and events in this publication, other than those clearly in
the public domain, are fictitious and any resemblance to actual persons,
living or dead, is purely coincidental

All rights reserved. No part of this publication may be reproduced,
stored in a retrieval system, or transmitted in any form or by any means,
electronic, mechanical, photocopying, recording or otherwise, without the
prior permission of the publisher or a licence permitting restricted copying.
In the UK such licences are issued by the Copyright Licensing Agency,
Barnards Inn, 86 Fetter Lane, London EC4A 1EN

A CIP catalogue record for this book is available
from the British Library

ISBN 978-1-78189-472-9

LONDON BOROUGH OF WANDSWORTH	
9030 00007 7155 2	
Askews & Holts	
AF	
	WW21011358

Acknowledgements

I would like to thank my wonderful family, and my daughter Clémence in particular, for their support, patience and encouragements during the writing and editing of *Escape to the Little Chateau*. I know I'm not always very easy to live with, especially when my mind is hundreds of miles away, back in sunny Provence and trying to work out a tricky subplot or write the perfect romantic scene. I love you so much.

I would also like to thank the Choc Lit team for their support, including my brilliant editor for her great advice and suggestions, and the designers for another beautiful cover. Of course, thanks as always to the Choc Lit panel who liked the manuscript and made publication possible: Amy Nordon, Barbara Powdrill, Carol Orpwood, Carolina Castro, Deborah Warren, Gill Leivers, Honor Gilbert, Janice Butler, Jenny Mitchell, Karen Pimblett, Kathryn Whittaker, Kirsty White, Melanie Russell, Rosie Farrell, Ruth Nägele, Sally Pardey, Sharon Walsh and Sonya Alford. I am so happy that you enjoyed the story!

Merci beaucoup!

Chapter One

Amy turned the radio off and drove through the *bastide*'s rusty gates and into the cobblestone courtyard. The car hiccupped to a halt, files and books that were piled up high on the passenger seat crashed to the floor but she hardly noticed.

Bellefontaine, at last.

Forgotten was the long drive from Manchester and her aching neck and back. She was home. She flung the door open, sprung out of the car, and stood in front of the old house as church bells chimed the angelus in a nearby village and echoed in the quiet evening. With its stone walls glowing like pure gold in the winter sunset, its freshly-painted lavender shutters, and the windows reflecting the red ball of the sun setting behind dark hills on the other side of the valley, Bellefontaine was even more beautiful than she remembered. Was it only six weeks since she'd last been there?

She took a long, deep breath and smiled. The invigorating scent of pine from the nearby forest mixed with rich fragrances of earth, grasses and wild herbs. It may be late February, but here in Provence there was already a hint of spring.

A soft, cool breeze lifted strands of hair around her face. She pushed back the blonde tips that tickled her face, opened the car boot, and shook her head in dismay. Where to start? Like the passenger seats, the boot was packed with bags, suitcases and boxes. It was a wonder she'd managed to fit in so much, and an even greater wonder her old Clio hadn't broken down on the way.

She pulled out the crate closest to her. Filled with crockery, and with a bottle of champagne wedged on top, it was so heavy all she could do was toddle across the courtyard, stopping every few feet to catch her breath. She had almost reached the front door when a reddish brown dog appeared from nowhere and charged towards her, barking furiously. She only just managed to keep hold of the box.

'Where did you come from? Go home and leave me alone.'

The dog ignored her and ran in circles around her. Of course! It was a French dog. She repeated her instructions in French, with no more success.

A loud whistle cut through the barking, the dog stopped dead in its tracks, drew its ears back, and ran away with a yelp. Amy started towards the front door again, but her foot caught a loose cobble. This time she could do nothing to stop the box slipping from her grasp and crashing to the ground.

'Damn!'

Standing among a pile of broken crockery, she watched the bottle of expensive champagne she'd bought to celebrate her new life roll towards the front door. The bottle came to rest with a loud clank against a terracotta planter.

'*Tout va bien, mademoiselle?*'

She swung round with a gasp and squinted into the light. The dark figure of a man stood near the gates against the dying sunset. He was so tall and his shoulders so broad that he cast a huge shadow onto the cobbles.

Although the sun prevented her from seeing his face, she could make out that he carried a rifle and that a bag hung across his chest. Next to him, the silly dog who had caused her to trip whimpered and wagged its tail.

A hunter. She pursed her lips in distaste. She had been

warned that the surrounding hills, and especially the forest around Bellefontaine, were popular hunting grounds.

'*Oui, ça va,*' she replied in a cold voice.

'*Vous êtes sûre? Vous n'êtes pas blessée?*'

She darted an angry glance in his direction. Of course she was sure she wasn't injured.

'I'm fine,' she replied, 'but that's no thanks to you, or your dog. I suggest you keep it under control in future.'

It was unfair to blame the dog for the mess of broken crockery, since she had tripped on the cobbles all on her own, but she didn't care. She had no sympathy for anyone who wandered the countryside to shoot defenceless birds or animals.

'And by the way,' she added, 'hunting isn't allowed at Bellcfontaine. If you trespass on my land again I shall have to call the gendarmes and have you removed.'

Undeterred, the man gave his dog a command in a low voice and walked across the courtyard in a few long strides, his boots making crunching noises as he stepped on the debris littering the ground.

'You must be Mademoiselle Carter,' he said in English with just a trace of a French accent.

He bowed his head. 'Fabien Coste, *enchanté.*'

Her breath caught in her throat and her face felt like it had caught fire.

'Fabien Coste, from Manoir Coste?' She tilted her chin to look at him, taking in his tall, muscular frame, his faded jeans, patched up jacket, and green woolly jumper, which matched the colour of his eyes.

'That's right.'

Fabien Coste ... She recognised him now, even though she'd only ever seen him in glossy magazines, looking like a film star in a black dinner suit, and surrounded with politicians and celebrities who came from all over the world to the family chateau he had converted into a luxury hotel.

She swallowed hard. The man was probably the one business contact she needed to cultivate for her new venture, and she had just threatened him with the gendarmes!

So there she was, the new lady of Bellefontaine ...

Fabien looked down at the slim woman who barely reached up to his shoulders. Her long, light blonde hair shone like white gold in the dying sunlight. With her deep blue eyes, flushed cheeks and rosebud lips, she wasn't what he'd expected. Not at all. She looked young and fragile, and he didn't know whether it was a good thing or not.

No, he decided, hardening his stare. It had to be a good thing. She probably wouldn't stick around for very long, and Bellefontaine would once again fall into disrepair and lie abandoned and forgotten – the way it should. He'd never liked the place when it was empty and neglected, he liked it even less now it stood all spruced up.

A gust of wind blew the woman's fine blonde hair around her face. A strand flew across her cheek, touching her lips. Without thinking he lifted his hand to brush it aside, yearning suddenly to find out if it felt as soft and silky as it looked. He caught himself just in time, and gestured to the broken plates and glasses instead.

'I am sorry my dog frightened you. I will of course refund you fully for the damage it caused.'

Her cheeks flushed a deeper pink, she shook her head.

'Oh no, it wasn't really your dog's fault. I tripped. The crate was too big and I couldn't see where I was going.'

That she wasn't taking him up on his offer surprised him. He didn't know many people who would turn away the chance of getting money out of him.

'I do hope you have more crockery or you'll have nothing to eat your supper from tonight.'

She smiled, a genuine, sunny smile this time.

'I may not have any plates but I still have champagne to celebrate my first evening at Bellefontaine. It has to be a good omen that the bottle didn't smash along with all the rest, don't you think?'

'Indeed.' He bent down to pick the bottle up and frowned as he read the label. Deutz Brut. She looked young but she knew her champagne.

'It'll be dark soon, let me help you clear this mess and carry your things inside,' he offered, suddenly reluctant to leave her. Never mind that he was expected back at Manoir Coste for an evening function and that he'd taken far too much time off work already for a walk in the forest to clear his head.

He noticed the uneasy glance she cast towards his rifle and the bag where he'd shoved the dead rabbits he'd lifted from the poachers' traps in the forest, and remembered her earlier comment about hunters not being welcome at Bellefontaine.

'I'll leave those out here for now.' He slipped the bag off his shoulder and leaned the rifle against the wall of the house.

She was about to refuse his help when the sun slid behind the hills and blue grey shadows filled the courtyard. She felt the sudden chill in the air and shivered.

'All right then. That's very kind of you. I'll get the keys.'

'If I may say so, the logical way to proceed would have been to open the door before you carried your boxes out of the car.'

'Well, yes, I suppose you are right. I didn't think …'

She pulled her key out of her jeans pocket, slipped it into the lock with a tremor of excitement and pushed the door open onto the dark hallway. The house smelled of paint, detergent, and lemon wood polish, but most of all it smelled of old stones baked by centuries of sunshine and of the nearby cedar forest. It was wonderful. It was the smell of her new home.

She hadn't been inside the house since Paul Michon completed the renovation works. Her heartbeat quickened and she let out a gasp of delight as she switched on the light and took in the hall's terracotta walls and the smooth, shiny dark oak stair banister that ran to the first floor. All she wanted was to swirl across the red floor tiles and dance her way into the kitchen, but Fabien Coste was behind her, so she didn't.

'I'll check that everything is in order if you don't mind,' she said as she strode in.

With its almond green units, solid oak worktops, and old-fashioned wood-burning stove, the kitchen was warm and welcoming – and exactly what she'd hoped for. In the adjoining utility her brand new fridge, freezer, and washing machine were plugged in and whirred quietly.

She glanced into the lounge. Its bare stone walls and wooden ceiling beams, and the large fireplace gave it a warm, rustic feel, complemented by the old leather sofa and matching armchairs and the oak dresser she had found at a local *brocante* market. Leading on from the lounge was a formal dining room and a small study, empty for now.

Eager to explore the whole house, she retraced her steps back into the hallway and ran upstairs. There too Paul had worked wonders. Painted in shades of ochre, yellow and terracotta, every one of the seven en suite bedrooms had an authentic Provençal look. Bellefontaine was almost ready.

She smiled. All it needed now was the final touches. And paying guests, of course.

Fabien Coste waited in the kitchen, hands in his jeans pockets. He turned round, eyebrows arched inquisitively, when she came back down.

'Is everything all right?'

'It's more than all right. It's beautiful! Paul Michon did a wonderful job. Do you know him by any chance?'

A half-smile stretched his lips. 'I know most people around here.'

Of course, she sighed. He was the Duc de Coste, the lord of the manor. He must know everybody.

'Shall we make a start?' he asked, making his way back to the car. 'I'm sure you are eager to get settled before your staff arrives.'

'What staff?'

He grabbed a couple of large boxes from the car boot and started back inside. 'Your housekeeper, receptionist, and cleaner, a cook perhaps ... You are opening a hotel, aren't you, so you need staff.'

She laughed, pulled her duffel bag out of the boot and ran to keep up with him. He was already piling the boxes on top of one another in the hallway.

'I don't have any staff. I plan to run the place on my own.'

He turned to look down at her. 'Really? Then you must be very experienced. What kind of hotel did you manage back in England?'

'I didn't – I mean, I've never managed a hotel before. I worked in a bank, as a translator, until I was made redundant a few months ago.'

'So you have no experience at all?'

The glint in his green eyes made her cheeks heat up again.

'No, but I can cook and I'm good at organising things. I'm sure I'll be just fine.'

The way he stared at her made her nervous and she felt compelled to carry on.

'I fell in love with Bellefontaine on holiday last summer. I can't explain it but I knew straight away this was the place for me. I just had to buy it. Turning it into a guesthouse was the best way for me to earn a living.'

He shook his head and strode outside again to take more boxes out of the car.

'Running a hotel is hard work, Mademoiselle Carter. You'll soon find out that there is more to it than giving the walls a fresh lick of paint and putting a sign above the front door. It requires constant attention to detail, a great deal of time and commitment, and good business sense. You also need to find a niche for your hotel, something that makes it unique.'

His haughty tone of voice was like a slap in the face. Who did he think he was to talk to her as if she was stupid?

'Oh but I *do* have some idea about the hospitality business, monsieur,' she said, her cheeks no longer burning with embarrassment but with anger, 'and I know exactly what will make Bellefontaine unique, as you say – apart from its great location and the fact it's a wonderful old house.'

He arched his eyebrows. 'And what would that be?'

'I'm going to provide a friendly, welcoming and relaxing environment and offer home-made organic food.'

Her words tumbled out, and she took a deep breath, annoyed that she was letting the patronising man fluster her so much.

'I will dig a vegetable patch, grow fruit in the garden, make my own jam – everybody says I make the best raspberry jam ...'

He stacked up the last of the boxes in the kitchen and turned to look at her, a smile at the corner of his lips.

'This all sounds rather naive, bohemian and *hippy chic*. Home-made jam is very nice, but what you really need is a unique profile, a business plan, and turnover projections for the next three years.'

Heavens, the man was arrogant. Born the heir to a vast estate, he probably never had to work very hard at anything in his life and had an army of servants at his disposal to carry out his orders, do his business plan and his turnover projections!

'What I have or don't have is none of your business, Monsieur Coste,' she said, lifting her chin. 'I may be bohemian *and* an amateur, but if I want to establish a hippy commune where everybody frolics around naked, then it's my prerogative. I do own the place after all.' She was so angry she stammered the last words.

His lips twitched, his green eyes twinkled. 'Now *that* would definitely spice things up around here.'

Sobering up, he added, 'I'm sorry if I upset you. It wasn't my intention. The thing is, a lot of British people have opened guesthouses in the area these past few years. All of them had romantic and totally unrealistic expectations about life in Provence, and the running of a hotel.'

He didn't add 'just like you', but he probably wanted to.

He paused. 'And many failed after a couple of seasons, put their house back on the market, and went home.'

It was as if a gloomy shadow entered the kitchen. She shivered and crossed her arms on her chest.

'Well, this is my home now and I won't fail,' she replied with more assurance than she felt.

He didn't reply. Instead, he glanced towards the window and said, 'I'd better sweep up the courtyard before it gets dark.'

'No, thanks. I'll do it myself.'

Right now, she wanted him to leave. Never mind the mess of broken pots outside, she didn't need any more lectures about her naive outlook on life and lack of experience, or gloomy predictions about her chances – or not – of success. She'd heard enough of that these past few months from so-called friends, and from her sister Chris, back in Manchester.

Annoyance flashed in his eyes. 'I insist.' Even though his voice was pleasant, there was a steely edge to it. The man clearly didn't like being contradicted. Without giving her time to protest, he walked into the utility, came back with a tall, bristly broom, a dustpan, and a bin bag, and walked out.

No, she thought as she heard the scraping of the brush against the cobbles and the clanking of broken pots being emptied into the bin liner, the man could not be used to people standing up to him. She heard a muffled curse in French and smiled. He could not be used to sweeping up either.

She unpacked the few groceries she had brought, dug a couple of mugs out of a box, as well as soup bowls and some cutlery.

'I left the rubbish bag outside,' he said when he returned.

He combed back a lock of dark hair, and looked straight at her. Her heart made an annoying flip and thumped harder as his green eyes held her in their gaze. Fabien Coste might be haughty and patronising, but he was also the most attractive man she'd ever met.

He pointed to the bags, suitcases and boxes piled up against the wall in the hallway.

'Don't worry about unpacking these. I'll send a few of my staff later to help you settle in. They will have you organised in no time.'

His arrogance almost took her breath away, and once again her cheeks felt like they were burning.

'It's nice of you to offer but I don't need anyone to organise me, not even you, Monsieur Coste.' She didn't care if she sounded rude or if her voice quivered with anger. All she wanted now was to push him out of the door and send him on his way.

'Are you sure?' A doubtful expression appeared on his face.

'Positive. Let me show you out.'

He picked up his rifle and his bag. The bag gaped open when he slung it over his shoulder and she caught a glimpse of grey fur inside and repressed a shudder. A rabbit he'd just shot, no doubt.

She thanked him again, watched his tall, athletic figure disappear in the darkening shadows with the dog running excitedly around him, and closed the door with a sigh of relief.

At last she was alone to enjoy her first evening at Bellefontaine.

Even though Paul had set the central heating on, it felt chilly in the kitchen. She lit a fire in the stove with the old newspapers and wood Paul had left for her in a wicker basket, then hauled her bags and suitcase upstairs to her room. Located in the tower room at the far end of the corridor, the bedroom had a large window overlooking the garden and the forest.

She opened a bag, took out a couple of towels and some toiletries, and stepped into the en suite bathroom. After a hot shower, she put on navy tracksuit bottoms and a dark blue sweater, gave her hair an energetic towel dry and left it loose on her shoulders.

Back in the kitchen, she opened a tin of tomato soup

and a packet of crackers, and set a mug and the bottle of champagne on the worktop. Never mind that she'd lost half her crockery and had no decent wine glasses, she would celebrate her first evening in Bellefontaine in style, even if she had to drink champagne in a mug.

She was about to open the champagne when a loud knock on the front door made her jump.

'*Hello! Bonsoir!*' a man's voice called from outside. 'Delivery from Manoir Coste for Mademoiselle Carter.'

Puzzled, Amy walked over and opened the door. A man in jeans and fleece leaned against the door frame, a picnic hamper in his arms.

'There must be a mistake. I didn't order anything.'

The man stepped into the porch light and flashed a smile. With his dark hair and blue green eyes, he bore a striking resemblance to Fabien Coste. 'You are Mademoiselle Carter, aren't you?'

She nodded.

'Then there's no mistake. Where do you want this?'

She pointed to the hamper. 'What is it?'

'An offering from his lordship. Fabien can't resist helping a damsel in distress.'

'But I'm not a damsel in distress.'

'That's not what he said,' he snorted. 'So do you want it or not?'

She wanted to say that he could take the hamper back but delicious smells of roast onions, garlic, and herbs tickled her nose and made her mouth water. Whatever was in that hamper would be a lot tastier than tinned tomato soup and dry crackers.

'No, it's all right. Please come in,' she said, opening the door wider.

'I didn't introduce myself,' the man said as he followed

her inside. 'I'm Frédéric, the odd-job man at Manoir Coste, or the dogsbody depending on how you look at it.'

The resentment in his voice was so brief she thought she'd imagined it.

He put the hamper on the kitchen table, looked at her and whistled between his teeth.

'Very, very nice.'

She smiled. 'Thank you. I think it looks beautiful too.'

'I wasn't talking about the house, I was talking about ...' He pointed to her blue top. 'It's the exact colour of your eyes.'

'Oh ...' A little uneasy now, she opened the hamper and pulled out a business card with the coat of arms of Manoir Coste.

A short message written in a strong, masculine hand read 'Welcome to Bonnieux. Good luck with Bellefontaine. FC.' In the hamper were plates, a set of silver cutlery, a casserole dish, some cheese and a baguette, and a selection of tiny pastries. There was also a flask of coffee, a long-stemmed crystal glass, and a bottle of Côtes du Rhône. She took the lid off the casserole dish and breathed in with delight subtle aromas of garlic and herbs.

'His lordship mentioned that you were on your own and might want some jobs doing around the place.'

Once again, there was a hint of sarcasm in Frédéric's voice when he mentioned his boss.

'In fact,' he carried on, 'he said you'd need all the help you could get.'

Annoyed now, Amy crossed her arms and narrowed her eyes.

'Well, he got that wrong. I can manage perfectly well on my own.'

He chuckled. 'Fine. Then I'll show myself out. I hope you

13

enjoy your meal,' he said as he opened the front door. 'I'll call tomorrow for the hamper.'

'There's no need, I'll bring it back to Manoir Coste myself in the morning.'

'No problem. By the way, it's great to see that you're not put off by the stories about this place.'

'You mean the stories about the mysterious goddess and her bloodthirsty worshippers?' She shrugged as she recalled the odd tales the estate agent told her the first time she visited Bellefontaine.

'I found them rather … interesting.'

'Interesting? Most folk wouldn't dare set foot anywhere near Bellefontaine, never mind live in it,' Fred said with a crooked smile. 'You are very brave.'

'Brave? No, sensible, that's all. This place is wonderful. It's everything I always dreamt of and I'm not going to let a few old wives' tales put me off.'

'Let's hope you still think that way after living here for a few weeks,' he said before waving goodbye and climbing into a battered old Range Rover.

A shiver of unease crept down her back and she hurried to close the door on the dark winter night.

It didn't take her long to set the table for her solitary supper. She popped open the bottle of Deutz and poured a little champagne into the elegant crystal flute Fabien Coste had sent.

'To Bellefontaine!' she said aloud, raising her glass. Her voice echoed in the empty house, as if the walls were talking back to her.

No wonder Fabien Coste was arrogant, she thought as she put her dirty plate in the sink a short while later. His restaurant at Manoir Coste fully deserved its three Michelin stars. She had never eaten better food.

Stifling a yawn, she drank the last of the coffee. It was time for bed. Tidying the kitchen only took a few minutes. She locked the front door, closed the downstairs shutters, and went up to her room.

As she leaned out of the window to get hold of the shutters, small yellow lights dancing and flickering at the bottom of the garden caught her attention. They sparkled for a few seconds, then disappeared and the night was pitch black once more. Amy peered into the darkness for a while but the lights didn't come back, so she fastened the shutters and closed the window. Uneasy, she made the bed, and still in her jumper and jogging pants slipped between the cold sheets.

She tossed and turned for a long while after switching the light off, the house's unfamiliar sounds keeping her awake. The wooden stairs creaked, pipes gurgled, and the shutters rattled in the breeze. Outside, night birds called and the wind swished through overgrown grass and tree branches.

What if there were people out there – burglars, or poachers? Amy took deep breaths and tried to relax. She was being silly. The lights were nothing to worry about. It was probably only teenagers looking for a quiet place for a late night party.

At last she closed her eyes and drifted into a fitful sleep.

Loud banging on the front door woke her up with a start. Sitting up in the dark, her heart thumping hard, she switched the bedside lamp and checked her watch. 2:20 a.m. The banging stopped as suddenly as it started, and then there was only silence – a deep, thick, eardrum-bursting silence.

Should she stay in bed or go down and answer the door? Perhaps there'd been an accident and someone needed help ... Shivering, she got up, climbed down the stairs and switched on the hallway light. Her nerves taut with apprehension, she unlocked the front door and pulled the handle down. Something white, grey and furry flapped against the door as she opened it. Her hand flew to her mouth and let out a strangled cry as she realised what it was.

A rabbit hung, pinned to the door by a single nail through the throat.

Chapter Two

A fifteenth-century fortified castle, and the seat of the Ducs de Coste since the Middle Ages, the manoir stood at the top of a hill surrounded by a dense forest of cedar trees. With its high turrets and solid stone walls, it exuded pride and arrogance – rather like its owner, Amy thought, as she parked between two flashy sports cars.

She lifted the hamper out of the boot and started up the steps leading to the castle entrance, shivering in the chilly February breeze that seeped through her brown parka and blue jumper.

The glass entrance door led into a huge lobby and she hesitated a moment before stepping onto the shiny black-and-white chequered floor. With its rich brown wood-panelled walls and enormous crystal chandeliers hanging from the ceiling, the reception area spoke of power, heritage and wealth. Yet the fire burning in the massive stone fireplace and a few armchairs and coffee tables piled high with magazines and newspapers managed to give the place an inviting, cosy and intimate feel.

'May I help you, madame?' a woman asked from behind a modern, almost transparent glass counter discreetly tucked away in a corner.

'Yes … I would like to return this hamper to Monsieur Coste.'

'One moment, please. I'll see if he is available.'

While the receptionist made a call, Amy left the picnic basket on the counter and walked to the fireplace where a warrior in suit of armour stood to one side. With his helmet down and his gloved hands resting on the hilt of his sword, he looked about to spring to life. Carvings of knights in battle adorned the mantelpiece and right at the top, the Coste coat of arms proclaimed 'Coste

Vaincra!' like a battle cry.

'Coste will vanquish,' she whispered to herself.

'I'm afraid my ancestors were brutes who liked nothing better than gore and battles.'

Startled, she swung round to face Fabien Coste. Dressed in a navy suit that emphasised his broad shoulders, a white shirt with fine green stripes, and a dark green silk tie, today he looked every inch the successful businessman, and a far cry from the rugged hunter she had met at Bellefontaine the day before.

'Ah ... Good morning. I came to thank you for the lovely meal you sent me last night ... it was delicious but you really didn't have to.'

She paused and realised she couldn't remember a word of the polite but firm speech she had prepared on the way to make sure he understood she wasn't a charity case and didn't need his assistance.

He smiled. 'It was my pleasure. Listen, are you in a rush? I can show you around if you have time.'

Visiting Manoir Coste – the most exclusive hotel in the whole of Provence? This was an offer too good to resist and she forgot all about her resolve to have as little as possible to do with Fabien Coste.

'I'd love to.'

'Good.' He smiled again, and led her through a maze of long corridors and into a study where daylight flooded in from four French windows and reflected onto shiny parquet flooring.

A walnut desk covered with files and papers, and a sleek, widescreen computer dominated the room. Tall bookshelves lined the walls to the stuccoed ceiling and huge oil paintings of hunting scenes hung on either side of the mantelpiece. A couple of cream-coloured sofas and a coffee table stood in front of the fireplace which, like the one in the hall, was decorated with the Coste coat of arms and motto.

'Shall I take your coat?'

He leaned towards her from behind to help her out of her parka and she breathed in his subtle, and seductive sandalwood aftershave. His hands brushed against her shoulders; a shiver rippled over her body and her cheeks heated up. Fortunately he didn't seem to notice.

'Please take a seat.' He gestured to one of the sofas and sat opposite.

For a few seconds the silence in the room was only broken by the hissing and crackling of logs burning in the fireplace and the soft ticking of an antique clock on the mantelpiece.

Amy folded her hands in her lap, started to cross her legs and almost moaned aloud. Why hadn't she noticed how muddy her boots and the hem of her jeans were? Quickly she stretched to hide her feet under the coffee table. She could only hope she wouldn't leave any dirty smudges on the Persian rug.

'How was your first night at Bellefontaine?' he asked, breaking the silence.

She pulled a face. 'Not very good. I didn't sleep much.'

It would be more accurate to say that she hadn't slept at all. After removing the dead rabbit from the front door and stuffing it in the bin outside, she had sat in the kitchen, tense and scared, a blanket wrapped around her shoulders, jumping at every creaking or rustling sound inside and outside the house. It had been a long night, and rarely before had she felt so scared and so completely alone.

*

Fabien Coste arched his eyebrows and looked at the young woman in front of him.

'Any problems?'

She hesitated a fraction of a second too long before shaking her head. Her windswept ponytail swung from side to side, and tendrils of light blonde hair touched the slender curves of her neck.

'No problems at all. I must have been too excited to sleep.' She forced a smile but her deep blue eyes clouded over.

She was lying, he thought. Something had happened, and she didn't want to talk about it.

There was a light rap on the door and one of his assistants walked in and placed a tray with a silver coffee pot, delicate porcelain cups, and a plate of brioches on the table. Fabien thanked her and poured the coffee out.

'Would you like a brioche?' he asked, holding the plate out.

She smiled. 'I see you have a thing about feeding me.'

She took a small cake and bit into it with a little sigh. 'Hmm … this is delicious. I would love to ask your chef for the recipe.'

'He could probably be persuaded to let you have it … if you offer a swap for your raspberry jam.'

She glanced up, as if surprised that he'd remembered.

'I'm sure your chef has no need for any of my recipes.'

She ate the last of the brioche, reached out for her cup of coffee, and slipped two lumps of brown sugar in. Clearly Amy Carter was not the type to agonise about diets and calories.

'Actually, I'm glad you came by this morning,' he said. 'I would like to invite you to our annual Hunt Ball on Saturday evening.'

'Thank you, but … well, the thing is …'

Her cheeks turned bright pink once again.

'Let me guess,' he cut in. 'You don't approve of hunters – or of hunting – and the Hunt Ball is the last place on earth you'd like to be so you are wondering how best to decline my invitation without offending me.' He paused and smiled. 'Am I right?'

Her face turned an even deeper shade of red. 'Well … It is true that I don't find the idea of a room full of hunters very appealing.'

'And yet it would provide you with the ideal opportunity to meet people from Bonnieux and make useful contacts for Bellefontaine.'

She bit her lip, tucked a strand of hair behind her ear and frowned, as if unconvinced. He found himself holding his breath. He didn't usually have to insist when he asked a woman out and having to wait for Amy Carter to make up her mind disconcerted him.

'I suppose you're right,' she said at last. 'I do need to make myself known to the locals. I accept. Thank you.'

He let out a sigh and reclined against the back of the seat.

'Frédéric will come for you at eight. You met my cousin Frédéric yesterday, didn't you?'

A look of surprise flashed across her face.

'Yes, he brought the hamper over last evening. He didn't say he was your cousin, just that he worked for you.'

Knowing Frédéric, he must have complained about the way he was treated at Manoir Coste. His cousin never missed an opportunity to portray him as cruel, egotistic and a megalomaniac. Immediately, anger and guilt twisted inside Fabien, as it always did when he thought about Frédéric.

He rose to his feet. 'I'll give you a tour of the hotel now if you're ready.'

He showed her the downstairs reception rooms and drawing rooms, and his award-winning restaurant for which he'd chosen a strikingly modern decor that contrasted with the tall French windows overlooking the terrace and the park. He took her to the ballroom, and enjoyed seeing her deep blue eyes widen in front of the gilded mirrors, glittering chandeliers and the shiny parquet flooring.

She followed him to the first floor, commenting nonstop in a slightly breathless voice on the wallpapers, carpets and quirky combinations of antique furniture and designer pieces he had chosen personally. He had never noticed before how attractive an English accent was – so attractive he stopped paying attention to her words and only heard the inflexions of her soft, feminine voice.

'Now I understand why Manoir Coste has such an outstanding reputation,' she declared as they were walking back to his office. 'You must be very proud to own such a beautiful place.'

Although he had heard similar comments hundreds of times before, her spontaneity and sincerity made him smile. 'I am.'

It hadn't been easy to bring the estate back from the abyss and turn Manoir Coste into the successful business it now was, and he would do anything to keep it that way and protect its reputation and the Coste family name.

He gestured towards the window. 'Are you feeling up to braving the cold? There is something else I would like to show you.'

They went back to the study for her coat then walked out onto the terrace, which overlooked a formal parterre of topiary and a vast expanse of lawn. Further down, a gravel path wound its way to a fountain at the edge of the cedar forest.

'It looks ancient,' she said, lifting her hand to touch the thick carpet of moss that partly covered three lion heads spurting out water into a rectangular basin.

'It is very old indeed, one of the oldest fountains in the whole of Provence, I believe. But what makes it special is the water. This is our own spring – Manoir Coste and Bellefontaine's – flowing all the way from the top of the hill under the forest, my estate and your garden, then down into the valley.'

He dipped his fingers into the basin where the water reflected the grey clouds above and the dark green cedar trees swaying in the wind.

'Monsieur Chevalier, the estate agent, never mentioned a spring. He did tell me a horrible story about a goddess who was once worshipped near here. He said she is still supposed to haunt the forest, snatching unsuspecting travellers and butchering them. He even told me about the rather decadent carryings-on of her followers.'

She blushed, in a way he found surprisingly attractive, but her words made his heartbeat quicken.

What did she know? Had she found anything in the old house already?

'I'm afraid these stories are part of the local folklore,' he said, forcing a note of indifference into his voice. 'And so is the legend of the treasure buried near the goddess' lost temple.'

'Treasure? Monsieur Chevalier didn't say anything about that either.'

'The Romans are said to have hidden a vast treasure before fleeing in front of advancing barbarian hordes,' he explained. 'Many looked for it over the centuries, of course, but nobody ever found it. Ghostly stories or not, there are many people who wouldn't have contemplated buying a ruin like Bellefontaine. Especially when there are so many *bastides* for sale in the area which needed a lot less work.'

Her blue eyes were serious when she looked up. 'How funny, that's almost word-for-word what your cousin said last night ... By the way, isn't it him walking across the lawn over there?'

She pointed to the figure strolling towards them, a rake on his shoulder and a large bin bag in his hand.

Fabien masked his annoyance under a frozen smile and nodded. 'It's him all right.'

'*Chère* Mademoiselle Carter, how enchanting to see you again,' Fred said as he came nearer.

He bowed to Fabien with mock deference.

'Your lordship. Any new orders for your humble servant this morning?'

Fabien's eyes narrowed. He clenched his fists by his sides.

'Yes, actually. Mademoiselle Carter will be attending the ball on Saturday. You will pick her up from Bellefontaine at eight. Please don't forget.'

'How could I forget such a lovely assignment?' Fred exclaimed in a loud, cheerful voice.

Fabien frowned again. Surely his cousin wasn't drunk already, not at this time in the morning.

'I shall look forward to dancing with you,' Fred added, 'that is if I have any free time. No doubt I'll be running errands all night. For now, I'd better rake the lawn or I'll get in trouble with my lord and master.'

Fabien noticed the pitying smile on the young woman's face as Fred strode away and the coldness in her eyes when she turned to look at him. She didn't need to say anything, it was obvious she felt sorry for his cousin and found the way he treated him despicable.

'Shall we finish the tour?' he asked in a voice slightly sharper than he'd intended.

They made a detour to the tennis courts and the outdoor swimming pool – covered at this time of year – and visited the spa located in a wing of the chateau. By the time they came back to the study, Amy was even more impressed by Manoir Coste and the sleek, efficient way Fabien ran the place. He was attentive to every detail. He knew the names of all his staff and exchanged good-natured banter with every single one of them – all except his cousin, that is.

When they went back to the study, she was surprised to see a beautiful young woman dressed in a cherry red trouser suit, her black hair cut in a sharp bob, sitting on a sofa and flicking through a magazine with a bored expression on her face. On the coffee table was a laptop and a thick, glossy black file. The woman lifted her eyes from the magazine, gave Amy an appraising glance, and flung the magazine on the table.

'*Fabien chéri*, where have you been? It's not like you to miss a meeting.'

Fabien Coste's eyebrows drew in an almost imperceptible frown.

'I wasn't aware we had a meeting this morning.'

Turning to Amy, he added, 'This is Claudine Loubier, my PR. Claudine, meet Mademoiselle Carter, our new neighbour.'

'You are the new owner of Bellefontaine? How … nice.'

Somehow the surprise in Claudine's voice sounded forced, almost as forced as the smile that stretched her lips but didn't reach her dark brown eyes.

'I hope old Rosalie Bruni's ghost didn't tickle your feet during the night,' she said.

'A ghost? No, of course not.'

Amy shook her head and pulled the sleeve of her coat up to glance at her watch. 'I'm afraid I must leave. I have an appointment at the Tourist Office in Bonnieux.'

'Then I'll see you out.' Fabien Coste turned to Claudine and added, 'Please wait here. I'll be straight back.'

Dismissing Amy with a curt nod, the woman flipped open her laptop and started typing, her long red-painted nails making a clicking sound on the keyboard.

'Please don't hesitate to get in touch if you need anything,' Fabien offered once they stood on the Manoir's front porch.

There he was again, volunteering his help like a chivalrous knight to a … what had Frédéric called her? A damsel in distress. For a second she was tempted to take him up on his offer and tell him about the lights in the garden and the dead rabbit nailed to the door in the middle of the night.

The dead, pale grey rabbit.

An image of the rabbits Fabien Coste had in his hunting bag the day before flickered into her mind, filling her with unease. She drew in a breath and looked at the man standing in front of her, so businesslike and composed in his navy suit, his magnificent chateau behind him. Surely Fabien Coste wouldn't go nailing dead rabbits to her door in the middle of the night! The very thought was ridiculous. Still she resolved to sort out her own problems – whatever they turned out to be. 'I'll be fine, thank you.'

'Then I'll see you on Saturday.'

Even on a dull February day, Bonnieux looked stunning with its honey-coloured walls, rambling stone houses and narrow alleyways that climbed to the top of the hill. Amy parked and walked up a street leading to the main square. Lined with lime trees the square featured a large fountain with stone dolphins at its centre.

Fountains were the heart of every village here in Provence. Didn't an old local saying declare that '*Eici, l'aigo es d'or*' – 'Here water is gold'? And now it seemed Manoir Coste and Bellefontaine had their very own fountains too, even if Bellefontaine's was lost somewhere in the forest, next to a mystical old temple.

She walked across the square and pushed open the door to the Tourist Office. Monsieur Verdier, the director, was expecting her. Her point of contact during the long process of applying for an 'étoile' grading for Bellefontaine, he had helped her navigate the minefield of French bureaucracy.

The young man reading his newspaper behind the counter glanced up, let out a grunt, and carried on reading.

'Good morning,' Amy said, resisting the urge to pull the paper down. If Monsieur Verdier was helpful, the same wasn't true of Jacques, his part-time assistant.

'It looks like you've been redecorating,' she remarked, pointing at the bright red walls and a couple of battered paint tins pushed into a corner of the office.

He didn't answer, nor did he lift his eyes from his paper. He did however point his thumb towards a door at the back of the office.

'The boss is expecting you. He said you could go straight in.'

Amy bit her tongue. Jacques was the most unpleasant person she'd encountered so far – with the exception of Fabien Coste's beautiful PR, perhaps. Luckily Monsieur Verdier's friendly manners more than made up for his assistant's rudeness.

'*Mademoiselle Carter, quel plaisir!*' Monsieur Verdier stood up from behind his desk and gave her a handshake so firm her fingers felt numb for a few seconds afterwards.

'I just sent your dossier to our Paris office,' he said after spending a few minutes enquiring about her health and her move to Bellefontaine. 'I must apologise to have left it so late but several documents essential to your application went astray and I had to rewrite everything.'

He tapped his index finger against his forehead and added with a smile, 'I must be getting forgetful in my old age. Anyway, the next step is the visit from an inspector who will assess your guesthouse some time in the next few weeks. Don't worry, he will write to give me the dates of his visit, and you will have plenty of notice.'

He went on to explain about advertising in local and national hotel guides, offered to book a stall for her at a couple of forthcoming tourist fairs, and listed the steps she still had to take to make sure she complied with stringent health and safety regulations.

Her head fuzzy with administrative details, Amy left Bonnieux just before lunchtime. She was expected at Paul and Adèle Michon's house on the outskirts of the village.

Over the six months it had taken for Paul and his workmen to renovate Bellefontaine, he and his wife Adèle had become her friends, and Amy always looked forward to seeing them and their teenage son Stéphane. Today was no exception. Paul poured the drinks – a *pastis* for himself and two glasses of fragrant blackcurrant wine for Amy and Adèle.

'So, what do you think of Bellefontaine?' he asked as he gulped down his aperitif.

'I think that you have worked wonders,' Amy replied with enthusiasm. 'I'm so glad Monsieur Chevalier recommended you. He was right, no one else could have done a better job.'

Paul's hand shook and a little of his drink spilled onto the tiled floor.

'Marc recommended you? You never said.' Adèle glanced at her husband.

Paul coughed to clear his throat. 'I must have forgotten to mention it.'

Turning to Amy, he asked in a brisk voice, 'What do you want to do with the garden?'

'There is no way I can deal with it on my own. I need professional help to make it presentable before the opening. By the way, what do you know about a lost fountain and treasure in the forest?'

Adèle tightened her mouth. 'The fountain, the temple ... and the tragic love story between Philippe Coste and Rosalie Bruni. These old stories keep coming back, time and time again.'

'Rosalie Bruni? Wasn't she Bellefontaine's previous owner?'

Adèle nodded. 'She had a torrid and scandalous affair with Philippe Coste – Fabien's grandfather, which only ended when he died in a tragic accident.'

Paul interrupted her by slamming his empty glass down on the coffee table.

'That's all very well, ladies, but I have a business to run and no time to waste on idle gossip, especially when it concerns people who've been dead for decades.'

During lunch they chatted about her plans for the garden, then Paul left for his office in the village and Adèle and Amy sat in the living room to enjoy a cup of coffee.

Amy sank into the sofa and yawned.

'I do hope I can sleep tonight.'

She told her friend about the dead rabbit nailed to her door as a macabre joke.

'This is awful. I hope you reported it to the gendarmes.'

'No, I didn't want to make a fuss when I've only just arrived.'

'There are poachers in the forest, you know.'

'Poachers? So they must be the people who were hanging about at the bottom of the garden last night. I saw their lights in the dark – even though they looked more like candles than electric torches.'

Adèle arched her eyebrows. 'You saw lights in the forest? My auntie Lily would say they were spirits sent by La Bonne Dame.'

'La Bonne Dame ... who supposedly haunts the forest?'

'It certainly is. Who told you about her? Paul and I agreed not to speak about it. We didn't want to scare you.'

'Marc Chevalier, the estate agent, wasn't so thoughtful ... He told me so many horror stories about Bellefontaine I even thought he was trying to put me off buying the house.' She let out a chuckle. 'Which was silly, because estate agents don't frighten their customers off, do they?'

She expected Adèle to smile, but her friend let out a deep sigh.

'The thing is, I think you were right. Marc Chevalier didn't want anybody to buy Bellefontaine. His wife Serena was Rosalie Bruni's adoptive daughter. She grew up at Bellefontaine and always claimed the place was hers to inherit. She was furious when she lost her case to distant relatives of Rosalie's who immediately put the house on the market. I believe you came by only a day or two later and made an offer.'

'Why didn't she or her husband buy the house if they wanted it so badly?'

'They couldn't. A legal disposition forbids an estate agent or any of his relatives or associates to buy a property he is entrusted to sell for a whole two years. Marc probably planned to keep the house unsold for that length of time, then buy it for Serena. Your offer must have taken him by surprise.'

'Now I understand why Bellefontaine's photo was hidden in a corner of the agency's window and why he took me to view so many other properties "better suited to my needs". It also explains why he tried to scare me with silly stories.'

Amy drank the last of her black coffee and rose to her feet.

'I really must go back. I have so much to do before the opening I almost wish the mysterious goddess could step out of her lost temple to give me a hand.'

Adèle shook her head, and shuddered.

'You definitely don't want her around. Leave her in the forest where she belongs.'

Chapter Three

The rest of the week disappeared in a whirlwind of activity.

Amy cleaned the house from top to bottom, polished the downstairs floor tiles, and varnished the skirting boards and some of the woodwork. She drove to nearby Apt to buy furnishings and stacks of crockery, and to Marseille for curtains, blinds and bedclothes in sunny Provençal prints and to stock up on toiletries for the guest rooms.

Adèle gave her the address of a second-hand dealer where she acquired more furniture, including a desk, chair, laptop and printer for the study. At last, she thought, as she arranged her stationery and files in neat piles and connected the computer, she could print out the invitations to the open day and set up Bellefontaine's website.

She spent the evenings flicking through trade journals and gardening books or trying out new recipes, and collapsed into bed every night, her body exhausted but her mind filled with ideas, lists, and problems. However late it was, she always peered into the darkness from her bedroom window before closing the shutters and stumbling into bed. Fortunately, there had been no more lights flickering in the night and no more dead animals nailed to the door. At times she could almost believe that she had dreamt the whole incident.

On Saturday morning, a cold mistral wind blew the clouds away and the sky was a pure and brilliant blue. Amy tucked her jeans inside her boots, slipped a fleece and thick gloves on, and stepped into the outbuilding where Paul had left some tools and a collection of old paint pots. She came out pushing a rusty old wheelbarrow in which rattled a pair of shears, a hoe and a shovel, and stomped through damp, knee-high grass to the bottom of the garden where overgrown laurels, rampant junipers and gorse bushes formed a thick, dark hedge.

The lawn might be too overgrown for her to tackle on her own, but she would trim that hedge down before the day was over. She had enough of the place looking like Sleeping Beauty's abandoned garden.

By late afternoon, however, she had dropped her shears to the ground, taken her gloves off, and shaken her head in disgust. After hours spent cutting, hacking and snipping the thick bushes, the garden looked as wild as ever. She couldn't remember a time when her back and arms hurt quite so much, and it had all been for nothing. She ducked under the cedar trees to retrieve her shovel, and cried out in pain as she stubbed her toe on a stone sticking out of the ground.

What was this huge stone doing there? She knelt down on the fragrant carpet of pine needles and brushed the dirt off the exposed stone.

This was no ordinary rock, but a statue – or rather the head of a statue. She grabbed hold of the shovel and started digging around the stone, taking care not to chip it. She then heaved it off the ground and into the wheelbarrow to bring it back to the house.

Soil and damp needles still clung to the head so she spread newspapers on the kitchen table before placing it carefully on top. She stepped back to look at it. Large, empty eyes stared back from under a crown of carved leaves and entwined snakes. The statue's nose was missing but her mouth was fixed in an enigmatic smile. Apart from the hole where the nose should be, it was intact, and both beautiful and awe-inspiring.

Who was the statue of, and what was it doing half-buried in Bellefontaine's garden? Whatever it turned out to be, one

thing was certain. It was very old and she had to report it
to a museum. Shadows now filled the kitchen. It was getting
late, and she had to get ready for the ball at Manoir Coste.

Casting the statue one last look, she dragged her feet up
the stairs. Every inch of her body ached, her toe throbbed
where she'd stumbled on the stone. There was a line of dirt
under her fingernails, her hair was a mess of tangles, and
she couldn't stop yawning.

Why had she accepted Fabien Coste's invitation? Right
now, mixing in an elegant crowd and making conversation
was the last thing she fancied. Then again, it always was.
Maybe her sister was right when she said she was a timid
old maid at heart.

She kicked her boots off, unzipped her jeans, and pulled
her fleece over her head before walking into the bathroom
to fill the bath. She didn't want to think about Chris right
now, or the angry, bitter words she had thrown at her before
she left Manchester.

Amy took the rest of her clothes off, and poured a few
drops of her favourite bourbon vanilla essence into the bath.
She reclined against the tub, closed her eyes, and breathed
in the rich, soothing fragrance that enveloped her. Despite
herself her thoughts turned back to Chris.

'You are mad,' her sister had said. 'I can't believe you
sank your redundancy money and your savings into an old
house in a remote French village. And what on earth makes
you think you can run a hotel? You don't have the first idea
about business and accounts.'

Amy let out an impatient sigh and stepped out of the
bath. So what if she was a dreamer? She would make a
success of Bellefontaine. Therefore, like it or not, she would
attend the ball at Manoir Coste tonight, and all the other
social events she was invited to.

She dried her hair, put on a little make-up and dressed in the only evening gown she owned – a knee length, sleeveless black gown in slinky black jersey. She slipped her feet into high-heeled pumps, brushed her hair until it fell, shiny and smooth on her shoulders, so pale it almost looked white against the dress. Then wrapping a pink cashmere shawl around her, she went downstairs to wait for Frédéric.

He was late.

'I couldn't escape any sooner, sorry,' he said when he arrived at last.

His eyes glistened, dark and hot as they lingered on her. 'You look lovely.'

'Thank you.' Uncomfortable under his insistent stare, she forced a smile and opened the door to let him come in. 'I'll get my bag and keys.'

He followed her into the kitchen. 'What's this?' He pointed to the statue.

'I'm not sure. I found it today at the bottom of the garden. It looks very old.'

He rolled his eyes and said in a blasé voice, 'Another Roman statue, no doubt. I know someone who'll buy it from you.'

'Oh no, I can't sell it. I must take it to a museum.'

'Museums don't want any more Roman artefacts, they've far too many already. My friend is an antique dealer. She'll get you a good price for it, you'll see. I tell you what … I'll pick the statue up tomorrow and get her to ring you straight after.'

Surprised by his insistence, Amy put a protective hand on the statue and shook her head.

'Thanks for the offer but I think I'll keep hold of it for now.'

He shrugged. 'No worries. It's up to you. Shall we go?'

Frédéric drove fast – too fast – on the winding forest road. The tyres screeched at every turn, the headlights sweeping across the dark road in a mad dance. Images of her parents' crushed car flashed in front of Amy's eyes. Her nails dug into the leather seat and she squeezed her eyes shut, and forced long, calming breaths to fight the sickening feeling twisting her stomach.

'Here we are.'

Amy opened her eyes. Gravel flew as the car skidded on a bend of the road leading to the Manoir's car park. As soon as Frédéric stopped the engine, she flung the door open with a shaky hand, jumped out of the car, and took deep gulps of fresh air.

'Are you all right?' Frédéric asked, narrowing his eyes to look at her.

'I'm fine,' she lied.

'Good. I know I drove a little fast but I didn't want Fabien's guest of honour to be late.'

She turned to him, puzzled. 'Guest of honour? I'm not important enough to be anybody's guest of honour, especially not your cousin's.'

He tutted. 'His lordship has decided to be your knight in shining armour, rescue you in spite of yourself, and make you see the error of your ways.'

'What error?'

He shrugged again.

'I don't know. Buying that old wreck of Bellefontaine for a start, thinking you can open a hotel when you have no idea about the business … That kind of thing.'

So Fabien Coste had talked about her inexperience. No doubt he'd laughed at her too!

'What I do is none of his business,' she retorted as they made their way to the front of the chateau.

Frédéric turned to look at her, serious for once.

'That's where you're wrong, Amy – may I call you Amy, by the way?'

She nodded.

'Fabien is the Duc de Coste. He owns the place, and sometimes I think he believes he owns the people too. Everything that happens around here is his business. Everything and everyone.'

He sighed. 'Anyway, I'm afraid I'll have to leave you now. As usual, his lordship gave me a list of jobs to do as long as my arm.'

Shivering in the cold breeze despite her shawl, Amy joined the guests lining up to be greeted by Fabien, who in true lord of the manor style, stood tall and imposing at the top of the steps, with torches burning on either side of him.

He might wear a black dinner suit and a crisp white shirt instead of a suit of armour, but there was something untamed, fundamentally uncivilised and proprietary about the way he surveyed the crowd – as if he truly owned everything and everyone, like Frédéric had said, and Amy was seized by an irresistible, irrational and overwhelming urge to flee. Fabien Coste could keep his fancy chateau, his contacts and glamorous guests, she didn't need him. She would walk home. It wasn't that far.

She was about to step aside when he looked down and their gaze met. The torches hissed in the breeze, their flames shooting high in the air and reflecting in his green eyes, giving them a deep, dangerous glow. For the space of a heartbeat, the noise of conversations around her became distant and fuzzy, and all she could see was him.

He walked down, took her hand and lifted it to his lips. Even though his mouth barely touched her skin, a flash of heat reverberated through her body.

'Mademoiselle Carter – Amy, you're here at last.'

It was the first time he'd spoken her first name. He made it sound French, sensual and incredibly romantic. *Aimée*. Beloved.

'Shall I escort you inside and introduce you to a few people?'

Panic made her heart flutter and turned her brain to mush.

'Well, it's just that ...'

He arched a dark eyebrow, looked down, and smiled as if he knew exactly what she was feeling.

'You're here now. You might as well make the most of it.'

'Yes, of course, you're right,' she breathed out.

He put his hand around her elbow to guide her up the stairs and through the elegant crowd in the hall, where he scooped two flutes of champagne from the tray of a passing waiter.

'You look a little flushed.' A frown creasing his forehead, he handed her a glass. 'I hope it's not too hot in here for you.'

For the second time that evening she lied and said she was fine. She felt odd and unsettled, her feelings confused. Despite herself, she could not help being attracted to him.

And this was absolutely ridiculous!

She lifted the flute to her lips. Champagne bubbles fizzed on her tongue as she swallowed a sip of wine, then another. What was wrong with her? She must be more tired, or anxious, than she'd realised. Even if she was a hopeless dreamer, it wasn't like her to swoon at the sight of an attractive man, even a man as attractive as Fabien Coste.

This wasn't a fairy tale or one of those romance novels she loved. This was real life, and it was business. This would be her first contact with members of her new community, and she'd be damned if she'd let an inexplicable attraction for a man she didn't even like jeopardise everything.

She tilted her face up, took a deep breath, and followed him into the ballroom. The next half hour was a blur of new faces and names as Fabien introduced her to dozens of people. With him at her side, she smiled, shook hands, and tried to commit to memory people's names, titles and occupations. Surprisingly, she didn't feel as awkward as she'd feared.

She was almost enjoying herself when Claudine glided across the room, stunning in a long, tight-fitting silk cream dress, and diamonds sparkling at her ears. Was it possible to look any more glamorous? Amy wondered, as the woman approached, and whispered something into Fabien's ear.

He turned to Amy. 'I'm afraid I must leave you. It's time for my welcome speech. Claudine will keep you company.'

As soon as he left, Claudine looked down. 'How are you, Mademoiselle … Baker, was it?'

Amy narrowed her eyes. There was no doubt in her mind that Fabien's PR was being deliberately unpleasant.

'Carter – Amy Carter,' she replied, forcing a smile.

'Of course. Silly me.'

Claudine turned away and didn't speak again as Fabien made his way towards a stage which was scattered with musical instruments, microphones and cables. At the back stood several long-haired, bearded men wearing jeans and T-shirts, and holding glasses of beer – a far cry from the string orchestra she had expected to find at a ball tonight.

Fabien walked onto the stage, shook hands with the musicians. The conversations hushed.

'*Mesdames et messieurs, mes amis,*' he started, his voice deep enough to be heard throughout the huge ballroom without him needing the microphone. 'Thank you so much for being here with us tonight. It's always a pleasure to welcome you at Manoir Coste.'

He carried on talking about the success of the hunting season so far, and promised more excitement with Manoir Coste's famous boar hunts.

Around her people clapped and cheered. Amy shook her head, appalled. How could they be so excited at the prospect of chasing after poor, defenceless animals?

He went on to say that the restaurant was now serving food, that the ball started at ten and would be followed by fireworks in the park. When he finally raised his glass and said, '*Santé!*' everybody cheered.

'Another inspiring speech, *chéri*,' Claudine told Fabien when he was back at their side.

'I don't think it was particularly inspiring, but they seemed to like it.' He smiled. 'I'm taking Amy to the restaurant now.'

'But we always mingle together,' Claudine objected.

He shrugged. 'You'll have to mingle on your own for once. I'm sure you'll be fine.'

'It doesn't look as if I have any choice.'

Claudine threw Amy a venomous look and walked away.

Fabien led Amy to the restaurant and they sat at a table overlooking the garden. He poured out two glasses of red wine and gestured for a waiter to take their order.

'So, what do you think of the ball so far?' He looked at her as if she was the only woman in the room. The flame of the candle at the centre of the table cast a glow on his face and made his eyes a deeper, warmer green.

She picked at her bread roll to give herself something to do even though her throat was so tight she doubted she could swallow even a crumb.

'People seemed to be enjoying themselves. You must be pleased,' she remarked.

'I am. I would be even happier if you relaxed a little and told me about yourself.'

'About me?' she asked, genuinely surprised. 'There isn't much to tell.'

'I'll be the judge of that,' he answered. And as they ate he asked her about her job at the bank, about Manchester, which he'd never visited, and other parts of Britain he had been to. Surprisingly, she found that he was easy to talk to – maybe too easy – and that she could eat after all.

'You must be looking forward to your family visiting you at Bellefontaine,' he said after a waiter brought a selection of desserts over.

At once tears filled her eyes and her throat tightened.

'There won't be any visits, I'm afraid. My parents died in a car crash. A collision with a truck on the motorway, just over a year ago.'

'I am sorry,' he said in a deep, quiet voice as he held her in an intense, unwavering gaze. Her heart beat faster, so loud she was sure he could hear it.

She was the first to break eye contact. She picked up her spoon and dipped it into her pot of crème brûlée.

'You weren't to know. Their death was the catalyst for my buying Bellefontaine. It made me realise it was time I lived my dreams. My sister disapproved. She said I was mad to bury myself in a derelict old house in the middle of nowhere. I don't think she'll be coming here any time soon.'

She let out a half-hearted giggle.

'So for now I'm here all my own, and I actually quite like it – which is probably why Chris says I'm an old maid at heart.'

'An old maid, really?' Fabien said in a low voice. His eyes looked deep into hers, searched and probed her very soul.

'I find it hard to believe that there isn't a man in your life.'

'Well, there isn't.' And there hadn't been for quite some time.

Her cheeks red hot, she dropped her gaze, scooped a generous spoonful of crème brûlée and gulped it down, then ate another.

'Are you enjoying that dessert? I'll get the chef to give you the recipe along with the one for the brioche.'

Looking up she met his amused glance. What must he think of her? Not only did she babble like a scatterbrain and told him her life story in under fifteen minutes flat, but she ate like a glutton too.

She took a deep breath.

'It's delicious. I seem to have told you all there is to know about myself, but what about you? Does your family live here, at Manoir Coste?'

He leaned back in his chair. 'My mother lives in Paris.'

'Doesn't she like it here?'

He sighed. 'Not really. This place holds bad memories for her.'

'Does your father prefer Paris too?'

A shadow passed across his face.

'My father was killed in a hunting accident before I was born.'

He pushed his chair back, rose to his feet. Suddenly he looked as if he couldn't wait to get away.

'I have to leave you now. Some last-minute arrangements to make before the dance. Please take the time to enjoy your coffee and join me in the ballroom when you're ready.'

The ballroom was already heaving when she got there. She stood in the doorway, hesitant. There was no sign of

Fabien. A finger tapped her shoulder and she swung round to face Frédéric.

'I'm free at last, let's make the most of it!' He wrapped his arm around her waist and led her to the dance floor as the band started a fast-paced java.

The java was followed by several tangos and frenzied rocks. Frédéric guided her through the steps, leaving her every so often to fetch more champagne from the bar. After a few dances Amy's feet ached and she found that she needed fresh air and a rest.

'No problem. I'll come with you,' Frédéric said.

They were about to step onto the terrace when his phone beeped. He glanced at the screen and frowned.

'Sorry. An emergency. I'll be as quick as I can.'

Secretly relieved to be on her own, Amy followed the path that meandered across the lawn to the old fountain and sat on the edge of the stone basin. Myriads of stars glittered in the crisp night sky, and the moon cast a silver light onto the fountain and the grounds. Muffled echoes of music, conversation and laughter drifted across the lawn towards her, but she was far enough to enjoy the quiet and the crystalline sound of water trickling through the moss.

She bent down to dip her fingers into the basin, enjoying the feel of the icy water on her fingers. So this was her spring now – hers and Fabien Coste's.

Sounds of footfalls crushing the gravel broke the quiet of the night. She turned round, expecting to see Frédéric, and stiffened when she saw the tall, broad-shouldered figure standing in front of her, obscuring the moonlight.

It was Fabien. She must have drunk too much champagne because his very presence made her heart beat too fast and heat rushed through her veins.

'Is everything all right?' he asked. 'I'm sorry I had to leave earlier.'

'I was fine,' she answered as she rose to her feet. 'Your cousin looked after me.'

He narrowed his eyes. 'Did he now?'

She nodded. 'He was actually very kind, and dancing with him was fun. I was never one for discos and wild parties. In fact, I always used to make up excuses not to go out when I lived in Manchester.'

Stop babbling.

'Not that I didn't enjoy my friends' company but ...'

'Do you always talk so much?' he asked in a quiet voice.

'Well ... no ... yes. I mean, only when I'm nervous.'

He stepped forward and stood like a wall in front of her, so close she felt the warmth from his body and smelled the subtle scent of his aftershave. Trapped between his body and the stone basin that dug into the back of her legs, there wasn't enough air to breathe and her head started spinning.

'I hope I'm not making you nervous.'

His hands slid along her arms in a caress that made her shiver far more than the cold night.

'Not at all,' she answered in a quivering voice. This was the biggest lie she'd ever told. No one had ever affected her in the way Fabien Coste did.

His fingers wrapped around her wrists and he pulled her closer so that her body brushed against his. It was too dark to read the expression in his eyes yet as he leaned forward, slowly, and her heart drummed even faster against her ribs there was no doubt in her mind. He was going to kiss her. She should step away, right now. Instead she parted her lips and arched towards him.

His lips almost touched hers; she felt his breath on her face, tensed in anticipation ... And above them the sky exploded with colour and thunder. The fireworks had started.

She pulled away with a gasp as people ran out onto the lawn, clapping and shrieking excitedly.

What the hell did he think he was doing? She would avoid him like the plague from now on, just when he needed to keep a close eye on her and on Bellefontaine.

Next to him, the young woman looked at the display, her delicate profile chiselled against the skyline. Her hair shone like silver threads. He itched to run his fingers through it, bury his face in the curve of her neck and breathe in her intoxicating, vanilla scent until he was drunk on it.

Instead he leaned against the fountain's basin, shoved his hands into his pockets, and clenched his jaw. It wasn't like him to lose his head over a woman, but it seemed he couldn't keep Amy Carter out of his mind. He'd even dreamt of her, for God's sake, hot, sensual dreams that left him aching and frustrated, and unable to find sleep again. There was something about her, something rare and precious. She may not be beautiful, but she was genuine and candid, vulnerable yet determined ... and incredibly appealing.

He shrugged, shook his head. He wanted her, that was all, in the same way he'd wanted other women before. It wasn't as if he believed the old tale of a link – call it a curse or a spell in love and death between Manoir Coste and Bellefontaine – his father had written about. He remembered the papers he'd recently stumbled upon in the library. He may have destroyed them but the memory of his father's words were imprinted on his mind. Haunting him. Eating away at him. Nobody must know what his father did. Ever. He had to keep the secret, whatever the cost.

He was so lost in thought he hardly paid any attention to

the fireworks he had chosen with care and which had cost him a small fortune.

'It was beautiful,' Amy said after the last rocket thundered and left a starry trail in the sky.

He nodded. 'Indeed. Shall we walk back?'

His voice was cold, his manner indifferent. It was as if she had imagined the attraction between them. Yet he had been about to kiss her. Hadn't he? Perhaps it was all a game he was playing. Suddenly all she wanted was to be back in the silence and solitude of Bellefontaine.

'I am going to call it a night,' she said as they stepped onto the terrace. 'If you don't mind, I'll ask the receptionist to call a taxi for me.'

He frowned at her. Shadows danced on his face, in his eyes.

'I'll give you a lift back. Give me five minutes to sort out a car.' And he went inside before she could object.

She wrapped her shawl more closely around her shoulders and sat on a garden chair. The air was chilly but she'd had enough of people, noise and music for one night. She straightened her aching back, slipping her shoes off as pain lanced up the foot she'd stubbed on the statue earlier.

She waited but Fabien didn't come back. She hadn't been checking the time but she was sure it was more than twenty minutes since he had gone into the chateau. He must be busy. She rose to her feet and went into the lobby.

'Do you know where Monsieur Coste is?' she asked the receptionist.

The woman smiled apologetically. 'I haven't seen him for a while. He may have gone up to the Manager's Suite on the third floor. You could always try there.'

Although she wanted nothing more than ring a taxi and

go home, it would be rude to leave without saying goodbye, so Amy made her way up to the third floor. The thick red carpet muffled her footsteps as she followed a discreet sign to the Manager's Suite. She was turning round a corner when a door opened and Claudine came out, barefoot, holding her sandals in her hand, her black hair loose on her shoulders.

'Hurry up, *chéri*! I must get back to our guests, and you must take care of your little English *protégée*. I'm sure she'll be quite lost without you.'

A man's voice spoke from inside the room.

'You want more? You're a devil, do you know that?'

Claudine laughed and walked back into the room, closing the door behind her.

Her heart thumping, a sick feeling at the pit of her stomach, Amy ran down the stairs, and made her way across the crowded lobby and out of the chateau. She wouldn't stay one more minute at Manoir Coste, not even to call a taxi. She started on the road to Bellefontaine, her heels clicking on the tarmac in the silence of the night.

Fabien Coste was the most horrid, two-faced, cheating liar she'd ever met. How dare he ask her to wait while he made love to Claudine Loubier in his suite? Tears stung her eyes. She wiped them off in an angry gesture and walked faster. She wasn't crying because of him – of course not – or because for a few moments tonight she had been bewitched by the romance and sheer magnificence of Manoir Coste and its charismatic owner. She told herself this as she pulled her shawl more tightly around her shoulders. She was only crying because she was cold and exhausted, and had drunk too much champagne.

She was shivering with cold and her feet hurt so much she could hardly walk when she finally reached Bellefontaine.

As she pulled her key out of her purse, the roaring of a car engine made her swing round. A Range Rover turned into the courtyard at speed, and she stood blinking in the headlights, clutching her key in her hand.

Fabien pulled down the window and leaned out. 'Amy, thank goodness you're all right. I looked everywhere for you; I said I would give you a lift, so why did you walk back on your own?'

She gathered what was left of her pride.

'Surely you didn't expect me to wait while you were … engaged with Mademoiselle Loubier.'

A puzzled look crossed his face. 'While I was … what? And what does Claudine have to do with it?'

On second thoughts she'd rather not confess she'd been up to his suite and almost caught him and his lover in the act. Looking for inspiration, she took a deep breath, looked up at the starry night, and said the first thing that sprung to her mind.

'I wanted to walk and enjoy the moonlight. The stars are beautiful tonight, don't you think?'

Fabien stared at her as if she was some strange, demented creature.

'Well, I am glad you enjoyed the night sky,' he said at last. 'I take it you'll be all right now.'

She nodded. 'Yes I will. Thanks for your concern.'

'Don't mention it.'

He reversed onto the main road and with a screech of tyres, he was gone.

Chapter Four

By the end of March, the apricot, peach, and cherry trees in bloom painted splashes of soft pastels in the landscape, and on breezy days their pink and white petals flew around like confetti at a fairy tale wedding. The days got longer and brighter, and the garden party for Bellefontaine's official opening loomed closer. Amy was exhausted and increasingly distracted.

'I lose my keys,' she told Adèle while they were having coffee one afternoon. 'I forget to switch off the computer or the television. I leave the taps running in the kitchen all night. I think there must be something wrong with me.'

What she didn't say was that her forgetfulness had led to a more serious incident. She had been woken up in the middle of the night by the shrill beeping of fire alarms, and had rushed downstairs to find the living room filled with clouds of grey acrid smoke and the new rug on fire. She had been able to put the small fire out quickly with the extinguisher, but the incident had left her shaky and scared. The fire could have destroyed the *bastide*, she might have been hurt – or worse.

Since then, she stuck colourful Post-it notes all over the kitchen with reminders to turn off appliances, close taps and check the stove and the fireplace before going to bed. It was a strange, unpleasant feeling not to be able to trust herself and it made her restless and even more worried.

At last the day of the garden party arrived.

Like every morning, Amy woke up to the cooing of wood pigeons and the crowing of roosters in nearby farms. The sun filtered through the slits in the shutters and cast lines of golden light on the walls and the tiled floor.

She smiled and stretched, enjoying the contact of the soft cotton sheets against her skin, and the last few moments of tranquillity before the storm. Today was her big day. All she could hope now was that the people she'd invited came to enjoy themselves.

Well, maybe not all of them.

When Adèle had helped her draw up the guest list, she had been adamant that Fabien Coste should be invited.

'You can't leave him out. He is as close as it gets to being our lord of the manor. You must invite Mademoiselle Loubier too, of course.'

'I thought that the French had done with aristocrats during the Revolution. I don't see why I have to put up with Fabien Coste,' Amy objected, her cheeks getting annoyingly hot. 'I swear men bow their heads and women curtsy when they mention his name in the village. It's as if he owns the place.'

Adèle had laughed. 'That's because he does! Most of the land around here belongs to him. Did you not know that the whole forest is his?'

'Really?'

No wonder the man was arrogant.

'It's been in the Coste family for generations, but he doesn't mind people going in to hike or ride.'

Amy snorted. 'How very generous of him.'

Adèle had looked at her sideways. 'I thought you were rather taken by our dashing duc …'

Now Amy sighed and sat up against the bed head.

The problem was that she had been more than taken by Fabien, she had been positively smitten by him.

Her throat tightened every time she remembered standing in the corridor at Manoir Coste and listening to Claudine's throaty laugh as she called her 'his little English protégée'.

She pushed the memory to the back of her mind. She wouldn't let Fabien Coste ruin her big day. With any luck she wouldn't see him today. He must have much better things to do than attend the opening of Bellefontaine.

She got up, opened her window to let the sunlight and the fresh morning breeze in, and looked at the garden below. The landscape gardeners Paul recommended had cut down bushes, mowed the grass, dug out flower beds and resurfaced the terrace. A patch of land had been cleared for her fruit and vegetable plot and she couldn't wait to get started, even if she knew that taking care of a garden would be a lot harder than looking after the tubs she'd kept in the tiny courtyard of her Manchester terraced house. It would be worth it and she'd never been afraid of hard work.

'Hippy chic, indeed,' she mumbled, remembering Fabien's comments about her plans for Bellefontaine's organic vegetable and fruit garden.

The garden had revealed surprising secrets. Several stones carved with ancient inscriptions in Latin had been recovered from the edge of the cedar forest, near where she'd found the statue. She had emailed photos to the Antiquity Museum at Arles and a Professor Laurent Orsini had phoned a few days later to say that the site looked promising and that he'd be in touch to arrange a visit.

After a quick shower, she dressed in jeans and a long-sleeved red T-shirt, pulled her hair into a ponytail, and knotted a navy blue jumper on her shoulders. She would have time to change before the party. First she had to drive to Bonnieux to collect the organic meat Monsieur Lefèvre, the village butcher, had reluctantly agreed to order for her after muttering that there was nothing wrong with *his* sausages.

She ran downstairs and sighed impatiently when she came across the cellar door, partly open once again. She really had to be more vigilant ... She pushed the door shut, carried on into the kitchen and stepped into a puddle of water.

What had she forgotten this time? She glanced at the sink. The taps were closed.

She walked into the utility and let out a moan. The freezer door was ajar. All the food she'd prepared for the party had defrosted during the night and was now ruined, and the ice creams and sorbets she'd made were reduced to a sugary mush that leaked and congealed on the floor tiles. Right now, she wanted nothing more than to sit down and cry. Instead, she grabbed hold of a bucket, filled it up with water and started mopping the floor. Weeping wouldn't achieve anything. She had the house to get ready and a party to organise. What she should do however was to consult a doctor. She'd never been so distracted, so forgetful, even when working under pressure at the bank ...

It took her over an hour to empty and wipe the freezer and mop the floor clean. By the time she wrung the floor cloth dry and tucked the bucket in a corner of the utility room, there was no time left for breakfast, not even a cup of coffee.

She grabbed her car keys, opened the front door.

And gasped.

The Clio's tyres had been slashed, all four of them. A dead crow lay on the windscreen, its wings sprawled open and held into place by the wipers in a gruesome display, and bright red blood trickled from the bonnet and pooled on the cobbles.

'My God ...'

Her heart in her throat, she stepped outside, swallowing hard to fight a wave of nausea. There was so much blood – far too much for a single bird. She frowned, stepped closer, and realised with a sigh of relief that it wasn't blood but red paint on the car bonnet. Someone was determined to frighten her. This time, however, she wouldn't keep quiet. She would call the gendarmes.

An hour later a dark blue car drove into the courtyard and a stocky man in uniform with short hair and a moustache peppered with grey climbed out.

'Madame Carter? Lieutenant Bijard. Much obliged.' He pointed to the Clio. 'Is that the vehicle?'

A rather stupid question since it was the only car with slashed tyres and a dead crow pinned to its windscreen.

She bit back a sarcastic comment and nodded. 'Yes. The tyres were slashed, and they left this ...'

She pointed to the crow. 'It must have happened during the night. I didn't see or hear anything.'

She watched him examine the car, then walk across the courtyard, and finally write a few notes into a notebook.

'I'll make my report but I'm afraid there isn't much chance of us catching the culprits. You should ring the garage, get your tyres changed, and get rid of the bird.'

'Don't you want to keep the tyres and the crow as evidence?'

She was annoyed to see him smile.

'No, of course not. What would you suggest we do with that bird at the *gendarmerie*? Stuff it and put it on display?'

'The thing is, it's happened before,' she insisted. 'Someone nailed a dead rabbit to my door the night I moved in. There were people lurking in the garden too. I saw torchlights at the edge of the forest.'

He arched his eyebrows, lifted his *képi* and scratched his head.

'And you didn't report it?'

'I didn't want to make a fuss.'

'Well, there's not much I can do about that now, is there? Next time, phone us straight away,' he said.

'Next time?' Amy's throat closed in. 'You think there'll be a next time?'

'Who knows? Good day, madame.'

After a last shrug, he touched the rim of his *kepi* with his index finger and climbed back into his car.

Amy stomped back inside the house to phone the local garage. Well, that had been a waste of time. Lieutenant Bijard had shown no interest in her story whatsoever.

She had more luck with the mechanic who said he'd come straight away. In the meantime, she put rubber gloves on, disposed of the dead bird then washed her car, blinking back tears of anger and frustration. This wasn't how she had planned to start the most important day at Bellefontaine ...

True to his word, the mechanic soon arrived in his tow truck and changed all four tyres for her.

'I'm sorry I can't do anything about the red paint right now,' he said, wiping his hands on his overall when he'd finished. 'This is a bad business, mademoiselle. You should get yourself a dog, a big nasty one, preferably.'

She thanked and paid him, made sure all the windows were closed and the doors locked, and drove down to the village. Today, the drive did not bring a smile to her lips. Not even the blossoming orchard trees and yellow gorse bushes, or the vibrant new green leaves on the vines that ran in straight rows in the plain could make her forget that someone wished her ill.

Who hated her so much that they were ready to vandalise her car and kill animals to frighten her?

Saturday mornings in Bonnieux were always busy, and she had to park outside the village, a long way from the centre – which was just as well as she didn't want her car to attract too much attention.

Monsieur Lefèvre greeted her with a solemn face.

'*Mademoiselle Carter, c'est une catastrophe*! Jacques, my driver, just phoned. He broke down near Manosque and won't make it to Sisteron on time. I'm afraid you won't have your organic meat for your party today.'

Amy repressed a whimper. This couldn't be happening, not on her opening day! A French saying popped into her mind. '*Jamais deux sans trois.*' Bad things always happened in threes ... This was her third disaster of the day, so on a positive note, nothing else could go wrong now. Could it?

'But I've already paid for my order!' she objected. 'Never mind the delivery van, I'll go to Sisteron myself.'

Monsieur Lefèvre shook his head, looking genuinely sorry. 'It's too far, and as you can see, I don't even have enough left here today to help you out – and whatever's left isn't organic anyway. I know you're very particular about it.'

He gestured towards his counter, which like every Saturday morning had been cleared by eager shoppers and was by then almost bare. What was she going to do? The butcher stroked his moustache.

'Maybe we could hire a taxi or ...'

'There's no need for Mademoiselle Carter to worry, Monsieur Lefèvre,' a deep, calm voice spoke from behind her. 'One of my drivers from Manoir Coste will get the delivery done in time.'

Amy swung round, only to meet Fabien's deep green eyes. Her heart skipped a beat, then started again with a hard bump, and a hot flush burned her cheeks. It all came flooding back. The ridiculous but overwhelming attraction she felt for him. The shame and humiliation of the night of the ball. Right now, however, there was anger too. How dare he take charge and talk to the butcher as if she wasn't even there?

'I'll sort it all out for you,' he said. 'Just let me phone someone up and make arrangements.'

He pulled a sleek black mobile phone out of his jeans' pocket, flipped the cover open. 'Please give me the number of that place in Sisteron,' he told Monsieur Lefèvre.

'Here it is, Monsieur le Duc.' The butcher handed him a piece of paper then turned to Amy and smiled.

'You can relax now, mademoiselle, it looks like Monsieur Coste is saving your day.'

'I didn't ask him to do anything,' she snapped.

Fabien looked at her, then at the paper.

'Mademoiselle is right,' he said with a tight smile. 'I do have the bad habit of interfering in people's business. I presumed you needed my help, but if you don't, then let's talk no more about it. I'm sorry.'

He started closing his phone, and panic took over as the reality of her predicament sank in.

'No, wait!'

She didn't have much choice. She had to swallow her pride. He may be overbearing and she may not want his help but without him the barbecue would be a flop and she'd be forever branded as a failure by the locals.

'I'm the one who should be sorry. It is very kind of you to offer your help.'

Fabien nodded and phoned Claudine at Manoir Coste. After giving her brief instructions, he put his phone back in his pocket.

'All sorted. My driver is setting off as we speak. He will take your order straight to Bellefontaine this afternoon, just in time for your barbecue.'

He turned to Monsieur Lefèvre. 'I came to confirm the order for the hounds. Only the best cuts as usual. The dogs need to be on top condition for the hunt.'

'Of course, Monsieur le Duc, *cela va de soi*. I can't wait for Friday. You must see this, mademoiselle, it's a truly magnificent spectacle. The ladies and gentlemen in riding coats, the beautiful horses, the excitement of the blood hounds. And when the hunt master signals the start with the horn—'

'No, thank you, Monsieur Lefèvre,' Amy interrupted.

'It doesn't appeal to me at all.'

'Don't you like dogs?' He looked puzzled.

'I do like dogs. In fact, I was thinking of getting a dog to keep me company at Bellefontaine, but I'm afraid I don't agree with hunting, and even less with hunting with hounds and horses. It's a cruel, barbaric practice we thankfully banned in England.'

'Mademoiselle Carter, how can you say such things ... and in front of Monsieur le Duc too?' Monsieur Lefèvre gasped, his eyes opened wide in shock and his round cheeks turning the colour of beetroot.

She bit her lip. Maybe she shouldn't be so outspoken. Hunting was a way of life in France – there was even a political party dedicated to hunters' rights – and even more so in small rural communities like Bonnieux.

'I thought the whole ban was just a crowd-pleasing exercise,' Fabien said, 'and your politicians couldn't even be bothered to enforce the law.'

Amy shrugged. He was right but she wasn't going to admit it.

'It's only a matter of time before they do.'

'Then I take it you won't be at Manoir Coste next Friday to wish me *"Bonne Chasse"*.'

She shook her head. 'I'm afraid not. I don't condone hunting in any shape or form, and have no wish to take part in some brutal masquerade from bygone times.'

There was another strangled gasp from Monsieur Lefèvre but Fabien only smiled.

'I see you have very strong opinions on the subject,' he said, 'so I won't even try to change your mind.'

He opened the door. They stepped out into the bright sunshine and started walking down the cobbled street.

'By the way,' he said, 'thank you for inviting me to your open day. I have a couple of things on but I will come round in the afternoon.'

'Oh no, you don't have to come!'

The words were out before she realised and she felt her face grow hot with embarrassment.

'I mean, I will understand if you are too busy and have better things to do.'

He shook his head. 'I'm never too busy to wish someone well, especially when Bellefontaine is concerned.'

Now he was making her feel petty, as well as bigoted.

They stood face to face, close enough for her to notice how the bright sunlight made his green eyes sparkle. She gripped the handle of her bag so hard her nails dug into the palm of her hand.

He looked down and smiled. 'Is there anything else I can do to help?'

She took a step back.

'No ... I have everything under control.'

'Good. Then I'll see you later.'

After a curt nod, he turned to walk down the street.

As she drove back to Bellefontaine, she realised that she hadn't even thanked him properly. She didn't know what annoyed her the most – the fact that he assumed the role of the knight in shining armour to come to her rescue, or that she had actually accepted his help.

Chapter Five

Paul and Adèle were waiting for her when she got back, sitting in the sunshine and well away from the group of teenage boys who had taken over the courtyard for an impromptu game of football. Amy smiled as she parked the car. As promised Stéphane had brought his friends to help out at the party.

The boys stopped playing and stared, wide-eyed, at her paint-splattered car.

'Poor Amy! What an awful way to start your day.' Adèle gave her a hug after she explained about the morning's incidents. 'Don't worry, we're here now. Everything will be fine.'

It seemed that she was right. With everybody eager to help, it didn't take long to set up tables and chairs on the terrace, hang bunting between the trees, and put the finishing touches to the buffet. There wouldn't be as much as she had planned because of the freezer mishap, but there should still be plenty …

Shortly before one, Amy ran up to her room to change into a dark blue silk shift and matching pumps. Her tight ponytail had given her a headache, so she slipped the elastic band off and shook her hair loose and was about to go back downstairs when she caught her reflection in the mirror.

It was no wonder Fabien Coste had taken pity on her. With her pale skin and the mauve circles under her eyes, she looked as if she hadn't slept for weeks. Not that she cared about what he thought, of course. Annoyed, she searched through her toiletry bag for a blusher, mascara and lip gloss.

A few minutes later, she stepped back with a satisfied

smile. It was better, much better. She would never be as pretty as Chris, but at least she didn't look like an extra from a zombie film any more.

There was time for a last check around the house and the garden. She straightened the piles of plates on the long trestle table where nibbles, salads, and vegetable pies made a colourful display, wiped a smudge from a glass or two, and went over the instructions to her makeshift staff.

'There is to be no running when you are carrying food or drinks. Wash your hands every time you touch food ... or anything else, for that matter. Smile, and be polite. Understood?'

The teenagers nodded in unison.

'And boys, one last thing. Thank you! I couldn't do it without you.'

'People are coming!' Stéphane cried out excitedly as a car turned into the courtyard.

It was Monsieur Verdier and his wife. They gave Amy a bottle of chestnut liqueur, a local speciality, congratulated her on her big day, and went on a tour of Bellefontaine. As more guests arrived, the tension knotting Amy's shoulders loosened at last, and the visions of food going to waste and bunting flapping in the wind in a deserted garden that had haunted her nights started to fade away. People had come. The garden was full. The party was a success.

Soon the courtyard and the terrace buzzed with the sound of conversation. Children played hide and seek in the garden and their shrieks and laughter filled the air.

Marc Chevalier was one of the last to arrive. With him was a tall and strikingly beautiful red-haired woman wearing a long, fluid white dress. Amy presumed this was his wife Serena. She walked down the terrace steps to greet them.

'Good afternoon, Monsieur Chevalier, Madame, and welcome. Can I offer you a drink, or perhaps you would like me to give you a tour? I'm sure you will find Bellefontaine much changed.'

'Changed or not, this place was mine for long enough and I certainly don't need a tour,' the woman said in a slightly breathless voice. Her face was as white as her dress, with two red patches on her cheekbones, and if she was beautiful, her eyes were sunken and had a slightly haggard glint.

She pulled a gift-wrapped box out of her handbag and held it out.

'I almost forgot. This is for you, a moving-in present.'

'How nice! Thank you.'

Surprised, Amy opened the box. Inside was a large purple and white crystal that glittered in the sunlight as she lifted it out of the box.

'It's beautiful. What is it?'

'It's a local stone, a fluorite.' Serena Chevalier toyed with her necklace – a black ribbon snaking around her neck that emphasised the whiteness of her skin.

Her husband took her hand. 'Look, darling, Verdier and his wife are over there, let's go and say hello.'

Amy watched the couple walk away. What a strange woman. It was clear she resented her very presence at Bellefontaine, and yet she'd given her a lovely housewarming present …

By mid-afternoon, the pitchers of sangria, rosé and soft drinks had been refilled several times, as had the plates of crisps and nibbles. The noise of conversation and laughter was louder; couples twirled on the lawn to the accordion music playing from speakers on the terrace.

Paul pulled Amy aside. 'We should get the barbecue

going. Any news of that van from Manoir Coste? It should be here by now. Perhaps you could give Fabien Coste a ring and ask him what's happening.'

Indecisive, Amy bit her lip. Calling Fabien was the last thing she wanted to do, but Paul was right.

'I'll phone him right now.'

She went inside and retrieved his card from her address book. He didn't answer his office phone, so she tried his mobile. He picked up after a couple of rings.

'Coste.'

She could hardly hear him through the shrieks of children laughing in the background. It sounded as if he was at the local swimming pool. Surely not! Why would he go to a public pool packed with screaming children when he could enjoy the luxury of Manoir Coste's very own spa?

She explained that the van hadn't arrived. He promised to make some enquiries and call her back immediately.

'There was a misunderstanding, I'm sorry,' he said a couple of minutes later, raising his voice over the continuing noise. 'Claudine sent the driver on another errand, but it's all sorted. The driver will be with you any minute now.'

He was right. As she walked out of the house, a van pulled into the courtyard. Paul, Stéphane and a couple of his friends unloaded trays of meat, kebabs and sausages, and the barbecue got under way.

The party was still going strong when Fabien drove through the gates later in the afternoon. In the same faded jeans and rugby shirt he'd had on that morning, he opened the passenger door for Claudine and held out his hand to help her out. An unwelcome shard of jealousy pricked Amy's heart as Claudine, today in a sharply tailored white dress and matching jacket, slipped her arm through Fabien's, but she greeted her with a polite smile.

'So what exactly happened with your caterer – he let you down, didn't he?' Claudine asked in a loud voice that drew curious glances from people standing around. 'Lucky we had a spare driver and a van or your party would have been a fiasco.'

Amy stiffened. However much she hated to admit it, Claudine spoke the truth.

'I am truly grateful for your help,' she replied.

'There's really no need to dwell on it,' Fabien said then. 'Everything turned out all right in the end.'

He leaned towards Amy and added in a voice that only she could hear.

'But I hope it serves as a lesson in forward planning – namely, always have a plan B in case plan A goes wrong, and a plan C in case plan B doesn't work out.'

Amy's cheeks heated up. 'There was no way I could possibly foresee that the van would break down,' she protested.

'Maybe not … then again I suppose it's all down to experience.' His lips stretched in a condescending smile. 'Or in your case, inexperience. You will know better next time.'

Before she could say anything, a couple approached and asked him a question about the hunt. She stepped aside, reeling with anger. It took several deep breaths before she felt calm enough to join her guests again.

As the sun disappeared behind the trees and the sky lit up with glorious pink and orange, people started to leave. Everyone had kind words about Bellefontaine and the party – everyone except Serena Chevalier and her husband, who left without even saying goodbye.

Stéphane and his friends cleared the tables and would have stayed to wash up, but Amy paid them and insisted they went home.

Only a handful of people remained on the terrace as the garden filled with blue and grey shadows. A cool breeze rustled through the bunting as stars appeared in the sapphire blue sky. Amy shivered, but not with cold. Soon everybody would leave and she would be alone. For some reason, the thought filled her with dread.

'Would anyone like a coffee or a liqueur?' she offered.

Claudine stifled a yawn. 'No, thank you. We must go home.'

Fabien pulled his car keys out of his jeans pocket.

'I think I'll stay a while longer. You take the car. I'll walk.'

Claudine and Amy looked equally surprised.

'I've hardly seen you all day,' said Claudine. 'There are things we need to discuss, and I have a stack of papers on my desk which need signing.'

He smiled. 'You work too hard, Claudine. Relax, and take the evening off. After all, that's what I'm doing.'

She snatched the car keys off him, muttered a farewell, and left.

A few people joined them in the house, among them Adèle's elderly aunt, Lily, who had come with a neighbour late in the afternoon.

A small, wiry woman in her eighties, Lily usually dressed in black and arranged her steel-grey hair in a tight bun pinned on the top of her head. She paused in front of the statue that Amy had found in the grounds and was now placed on top of a cabinet in the hallway.

'La Bonne Dame,' she whispered with awe as she raised a hand to touch the stone face.

'You think this is the goddess who guards the forest?

The one I have heard so much about?'

Amy looked at the statue with renewed interest.

Lily nodded. 'You must put it back where you found her. It's bad luck to have her in here.'

'Bad luck? Why?'

'Tatie Lily, please don't start with these old stories again,' Adèle interrupted. 'You don't want to scare Amy, do you?'

She put her hand on the old lady's arm and ushered her through to the living room, where she settled her into an armchair near the fireplace. It had gone cooler so Amy decided to make a fire. When she rose to her feet she found that there was only one seat left, on the sofa next to Fabien. Taking care not to brush against him, she sat down and accepted the small glass of Monsieur Verdier's chestnut liqueur Paul handed over.

'My wife is curious about that statue you found in the garden,' Monsieur Verdier said.

'She's beautiful, isn't she?' Although Amy didn't touch Fabien, the proximity of his body sent prickles all the way down her. She sipped the liqueur. Its earthy taste burned a path down her throat and made her eyes water.

'I emailed pictures to the museum in Arles,' she said.

'They are sending a team to investigate.'

Lily sat up in her chair.

'They won't dig up the forest, will they?' She turned to Fabien. 'Monsieur Coste, you must stop them. La Bonne Dame will be angry.'

'How can a statue be angry?' Amy was amused.

'It's not the statue. It's the goddess,' the old woman replied.

'Lily believes that even though they were destroyed over two centuries ago, the Roman fountain and the temple are still cursed.'

Fabien lifted his glass to his lips.

'The temple may be lost, but it still belongs to La Bonne Dame,' Lily protested, 'and anyone profaning her sanctuary is doomed for generations. You more than anyone should know that this isn't just a tale. Your family suffered from the curse over generations. Look what happened to your grandfather when he tried to find the temple. He paid for his arrogance with his life, and the life of others. He wasn't the first Coste, and won't be the last, to die violently.'

Her words echoed in the living room.

Amy cleared her throat. 'I don't understand what this curse is about.'

'It was one of my ancestors who ordered the temple to be destroyed some time in the nineteenth century,' Fabien explained. 'Since then, my family has been doomed ... or at least that's what some people believe.'

He sounded rather casual for someone who was supposedly victim of a deadly curse.

'Then I hope La Bonne Dame, if it's indeed her, won't be angry with me.' Amy forced a smile.

He shook his head. 'I wouldn't worry too much about that.'

'What about the people from the museum?' Lily asked.

'I have no intention of granting anyone the authorisation to dig in the forest,' Fabien said.

Lily closed her eyes briefly, let out a breath and muttered, 'Thank goodness for that.'

Opening her eyes again, she turned to Amy.

'Adèle said that you saw lights in the garden.'

'Please, Lily, you're not going to talk about the lights now,' Paul said as he put down his empty liqueur glass on the coffee table. 'Every time we get together we have to go through the same old tales.'

'I saw them once, when I was little,' Madame Verdier joined in. 'My father had taken me for a walk in the forest. It was getting late and we cut through Bellefontaine's garden to reach the main road. I had the strangest feeling that someone was watching me, and when I turned round I saw a light flicker in the trees. Then more lights appeared. My father pulled my hand and we ended up running. I'm sure he was scared, too, even though he never talked about it afterwards.'

'People always used to say the forest was haunted,' her husband agreed.

'Will o' the wisps, that's what the lights are,' Lily explained. 'The goddess' guardian spirits.'

'Here we go again.' Paul shook his head. 'The goddess and her fancy lights ... Next, you'll mention the people who disappeared or got hurt in the forest. There are far too many stories going round about spirits, the goddess and the—'

'The cult?' Lily darted her piercing brown eyes towards Paul. The lines on her face appeared harder in the light of the fire. 'We all know it's true, you included.'

'Aunt Lily, please stop now. You're making Amy nervous,' Adèle remonstrated. 'She's already had a couple of nasty shocks since she arrived.'

Fabien turned to her. 'What nasty shocks?'

Amy shrugged, embarrassed.

'Tell me what happened,' he insisted.

She sighed. 'On my first night at Bellefontaine, there were lights in the garden, and later someone nailed a dead rabbit to my front door.'

Fabien put his hand on her arm. It was warm and made her skin tingle.

'You didn't say anything the next day when you came to Manoir Coste.'

She shrugged again.

'Did you call the gendarmes?'

'No, but I did call them today.' She pursed her lips.

'For all the good it did.'

'Why today?'

'During the night my car tyres were slashed, and a dead crow was left on my windscreen and red paint sprayed all over my car. The gendarme who made a report treated it like a nasty joke.'

Fabien frowned.

'This sounds like a lot more than a nasty joke.'

'It will probably be all right now I reported it,' Amy remarked with forced optimism before diverting the conversation on to the safer topic of gardening. She didn't want to be reminded of the incident, and of her vulnerability alone at Bellefontaine.

It was late by the time Monsieur Verdier and his wife left, followed by the Michons and Lily. When Amy walked back to the living room, she found Fabien poking at the logs in the fireplace. Ribbons of sparks flew up the chimney, the fire popped and crackled.

'I would love another coffee if you have any,' he said, standing up. 'It's been a long day.'

'Sure. No problem,' she replied, surprised that he was making no move to leave.

He followed her into the kitchen, glanced at the brightly coloured notes she had stuck all over the cupboard doors and smiled.

'What's with all the Post-its? Are you trying out a new colour scheme already?'

She laughed. 'Oh no! I've been getting forgetful over the past few weeks so I write myself reminders to check that everything is turned off and all the doors closed before I go to bed ... although it didn't work last night. I left the freezer door open and all the contents melted away.'

He read a couple of notes and shook his head.

'You ought to be more careful. Something nasty could happen to you or the house.'

It already had, she thought, remembering the fire in the living room.

When the coffee was ready, she handed him a cup, and they went back into the living room. She sat opposite him, and sipped her hot coffee whilst he stared, silent, at the flames.

'You must let me know if there's anything – I mean anything – troubling you,' he spoke at last. 'And please don't let these silly tales about vengeful goddesses and curses frighten you. Old ladies like Lily like to dig out stories, especially when members of my family are concerned. We Costes were always a favourite topic of gossip.'

'Are you referring to your grandfather?'

Fabien nodded. 'Finding the temple and the fountain became his pet project, his obsession. Personally, I suspect he was really after the treasure. He gathered extensive research material, journals and sketches, and even paid a team to investigate the forest.'

He paused.

'In the summer of 1935, there were torrential rains here. The Durance and the Calavon overflowed, the plain was flooded, but my grandfather forced his workers to carry on excavating anyway.

'The dig in the cedar forest collapsed. My grandfather and three of his men drowned in the mudslide.'

Amy gasped.

'So that's why Lily talked about the goddess' curse.'

His face hardened, and in the light of the dying fire, his eyes looked very dark with a speck of red glowing at their centre.

'There was no curse, just greed and stupidity. My grandfather knew nothing about archaeology. He was a deluded fool who caused his own death and the death of innocent men by not following basic safety rules.'

'Was your father interested in finding the temple too?'

His jaw clenched, making his face look even more uncompromising.

'My father … Yes, I believe he was. Amongst other things.'

He glanced up and their eyes locked. Amy grew tense and warm. Her chest tightened, and her heart beat fast, too fast.

There it was again, the indefinable attraction between them. The air seemed to sizzle around her. Her whole body tingled. She held her breath, parted her lips.

The phone ringing in the hallway made her gasp. Her heart still pounding hard, she jumped to her feet and ran into the hall.

'Laurent Orsini, from Arles Museum here,' said the man's voice on the line. 'Sorry to ring so late but I have just returned from a dig in Italy and I wanted to tell you the good news straight away. My boss at the Historic Monuments Department is giving me the go-ahead for a ground survey. My team and I will be with you a week on Monday.'

The archaeology professor booked three rooms, promised to confirm the details by email in the next couple of days, and put the phone down.

'I have my first hotel guests. Archaeologists from the Arles Museum,' she announced proudly when she returned to the living room.

Fabien stood up.

'So they're going ahead with the dig at Bellefontaine?'

'That's right. Isn't it exciting?'

'I suppose so.'

Somehow he didn't look in the least excited or even pleased.

'It's late, I should leave,' he said. 'Would you like any help tidying up?'

'Thank you but no. It was my party, I'll deal with the mess.'

She locked the front door behind him and heaved a deep sigh. It was over. After a disastrous start, the day had been a success in the end. The party had been well attended, and now she even had her first paying guests.

Piles of food, empty bottles, dirty plates and glasses awaited her in the kitchen and utility. Her shoulders sagged a little but she cleared everything up. It was well past midnight when she finally went upstairs. She put her pyjamas on, opened the window to reach for the shutters, and froze.

They were back.

At the bottom of the garden, a few shimmering lights danced in the darkness.

Chapter Six

'Patricia, look at this *salinum*!' Ben called across the dig site, holding a small object above his head.

A young woman stood up, her short red hair vibrant as a flame in the sunlight.

'Prof will be pleased,' she said. 'With the *patellas* and fragments of oil lamp we've found, it'll confirm his theory about the Roman temple. Give me a moment, I need to finish tidying up here.'

Amy turned back to the pink geraniums and sunny marigolds she was planting along the terrace. It looked like another good day for Laurent Orsini and his two assistants. In the short time they'd been at Bellefontaine they had unearthed several carved stones, a collection of potsherds and some oil lamps.

'If we managed to find all that in four days,' Laurent had said, his eyes shining with excitement the previous evening, 'think how much we'll dig up once we extend into the forest.'

When he had jumped down from his van, Amy had at first been a little disappointed. Far from the rugged, weather-beaten adventurer she had pictured, Laurent Orsini was tall and skinny, with floppy brown hair. He wore corduroy trousers and old-fashioned checked shirts, and there wasn't a leather jacket, hat, or whip in sight. Then again, she didn't need an Indiana Jones lookalike, just a competent historian to shed some light on Bellefontaine and its hidden treasures.

And competent Laurent was, as well as relentless.

Every day, he and his team were out from seven in the morning through to lunchtime. In the afternoon, Laurent worked on his laptop or catalogued the potsherds and artefacts unearthed that day, whereas Ben and Patricia carried on outside until after six, when they had a review meeting.

Amy checked her watch and wiped her hands on her jeans. The preliminary stage of the ground survey was now complete, and Laurent had invited her to his last briefing. He and his team were driving back to Arles in the morning and taking all their finds with them, including the statue.

She rose to her feet and went into the house to make tea and coffee.

'I believe there is a major pre-Roman religious site around Bellefontaine,' Laurent started when his team gathered around the table.

'We found relics indicative of the cult of Bona Dea and possibly an earlier goddess – a Gallic goddess.' His voice became dreamy, his brown eyes thoughtful.

'Ben said he found some kind of container this afternoon,' Amy said as she placed a tray of home-made lemon biscuits, a pot of tea, and a cafetière on the table.

Ben handed her a rectangular container. 'This is it,' he said, 'a *salinum*, in perfect condition. It was used to keep salt, a substance which in ancient times was considered powerful, magic even, and was used in religious ceremonies to purify both the victims and the temple before a sacrifice.'

'You don't mean a human sacrifice?' Amy winced and her fingers gripped the metal container more tightly.

Ben nodded. 'I do. You see, although they were outlawed by the Roman senate sometime around 200 BC, human sacrifices carried on in remote provinces of the empire for much, much longer. This *salinum* bears the mark of the Emperor Severus, whose reign ended in 211 AD. Therefore it is likely that sacrifices carried on around here until then. Maybe later …'

A shiver crept along Amy's spine. She gave the *salinum* back to Ben.

Laurent turned the screen of the laptop.

'This is an enhanced photo of the Latin inscription on one of the garden stones we found today. It's fascinating. The reference to a fountain is clear ... *NITIDUS FONS* translates to 'pure spring water'. So this place was associated with a fountain for a long, long time.'

Laurent's finger pointed to the letters on the screen.

'This one is more intriguing.' He clicked on the mouse and another photo appeared. '*Lucus erat* ... The sacred wood ... *quem medium ex opaco specu fonsperenni rigabat aqua* ... in which flowed an eternal, sacred spring ... *Quo quia se persaepe* ... coming out of the dark cave ... *at congressum deae inferebat* ... where you meet the goddess.'

He narrowed his eyes and read on. 'And listen to this. *The spell flows with the spring, binding hearts together until death tears them apart.* A love charm, how romantic...'

'There is a spring between here and Manoir Coste,' Amy remarked.

Laurent glanced up and smiled. 'Really? Then you'd better watch out or you and Monsieur Coste could get entangled in that love spell I just read out.'

She shook her head. 'I don't think so. He is an arrogant, big-headed, patronising boor.' He was also impossibly attractive and he made her heart beat wildly every time he was near. She breathed in and looked at the ancient writing on the screen again. A love spell between her and Fabien Coste? Not in a million years.

'The reference to the eternal sacred spring does surprise me,' Laurent mused. 'I would expect to find such a religious reference in sites like Entremont or Glanum, but here?'

'Where is Glanum?' Amy asked.

'Near St-Rémy-de-Provence, about fifty kilometres to the west. It's one of the most important Salyen settlements in France,' Patricia answered. 'I worked there for a few months last year.'

'I've never heard of the Salyens. Who were they?'

'A powerful Gallic tribe who established important settlements in Provence in the seventh century BC. Glanum was built around a sacred spring and dedicated to the earth mothers and their god Glan – hence the name. It was taken over by the Greeks, then the Romans who built temples and villas, enclosed the sacred spring in a *nympheum* and renamed all the Salyen earthen mothers. One of them became Bona Dea – the goddess dedicated to women.'

Amy frowned. 'Didn't the Romans have their own gods?'

'They did, but they often adopted the local divinities of the territories they conquered,' Laurent explained.

'This Bona Dea, could she be La Bonne Dame? An elderly lady from the village said that was the name of the goddess of the lost temple.'

'Yes, that sounds about right,' Laurent agreed.

He lifted the statue's head from a padded crate.

'Here she is. Our beauty. Bona Dea.' As always when he touched – or even looked at the statue – his voice was hoarse with emotion.

'Be careful, Prof,' Ben said then. 'You know that we men aren't supposed to say her name.'

'Technically, it's her secret name you males are forbidden to say,' Patricia interrupted.

Amy stared at the statue's empty eyes. 'She has a secret name?'

Patricia nodded. 'Yes, it's Fauna.'

'Now you've lost me. Why did she need two names?'

Laurent smiled. 'Probably because like all women, she

is a complicated creature. No, seriously, Bona Dea was the goddess of life and fertility and Fauna was her dark alter ego, and the goddess of sex and prophecy. Both are the opposite sides of the same goddess. We academics think that the Romans found the original Gallic earthen mother too complex, so they divided her into two distinct deities who would be easier to worship.'

He stroked the statue's smooth stone face. 'Our beauty here wears a crown made of oak leaves – a symbol of fertility for the Gauls – together with snakes which represent sex, and Fauna. I think this is a representation of the first, original earth mother. The one who came before all other representations of Bona Dea ever discovered.'

Patricia tapped her fingers on the tabletop. 'If it's the case, then this site is of huge importance for the whole of Provence.'

'I don't understand why all the writing is in Latin,' Amy said then. 'Didn't the Salyens have their own writing?'

Patricia shook her head. 'If they had, we haven't found it yet. We only know about them from their art, ceramics, and statues, and a handful of accounts by Roman and Greek writers. That's why these engraved stones are so fascinating. It's the first time we have some written account of a Salyen cult.'

Laurent switched his laptop off, flipped the cover down, and tidied up his files and photographs into piles.

'I have to make a case to my boss at the museum for more funding. Like everything else, our budget is being squeezed, but with all the evidence we found, I'm sure it won't be a problem.'

He looked at Amy. 'I hope you won't mind having a hotel full of hungry and muddy archaeologists.'

'Not if it means finding out what exactly is out there –

the sanctuary to Bona Dea or Fauna, or whatever her name is, the ruins of the Roman fountain … or the treasure.'

He laughed. 'You never said anything about treasure!'

'Fabien Coste said the Romans hid a treasure trove before retreating in front of barbarian hordes. It's supposed to be somewhere in, or near, the lost temple.'

Laurent closed his eyes a moment.

'Imagine if we were to discover a treasure as well as a new goddess,' he said in a dreamy voice. 'Now that would make us as famous as our colleague Professeur Dupré who found the greatest Roman hoard ever in the bed of the River Rhône in Arles a few years ago.'

He stood up.

'I must speak to this Fabien Coste tomorrow morning before we leave for Arles. I need his authorisation to extend the excavation site.'

Amy let out a sigh. 'I think you're in for a challenge there. He said he'd refuse anyone the authorisation to dig in the forest.'

Laurent smiled, rubbed his hands together.

'Don't worry, I'm used to dealing with these stuffy, old-fashioned aristocrats. For now, I'm taking you all out for a pizza tonight, and that includes you, Amy.'

'We don't need to go out,' she protested. 'I will make pizzas here, if that's what you want to eat.'

'Oh no, you won't.' He gestured to the door. 'You're coming with us, whether you want to or not.'

And why not, she thought as she watched him carefully lift Bona Dea and place it into the padded box before gathering his files into a tidy pile on the table. It would be nice to go out. Not only did Laurent, Patricia and Ben have a great sense of humour, but their stories of digs all over the world were captivating.

A short while later, they pushed open the glass door of Bonnieux's only pizzeria, a small restaurant tucked away in a winding cobbled streets. As they made their way to a table, she spotted Frédéric and a woman who looked like an older version of Claudine Loubier sitting in an alcove at the back. She waved, he smiled and waved back. She had just sat down when he walked over.

'Good evening. It's nice to see that work doesn't keep you from enjoying yourselves. How is the dig going?'

'It's going well, thank you,' Laurent replied, unfolding the menu in front of him.

'Did you discover anything interesting?'

Laurent nodded enthusiastically. 'More than we could ever have expected. It's a shame we must leave tomorrow, but we'll soon be back. It shouldn't be too hard to secure a grant. My boss will take one look at all the artefacts and the files we've compiled and he'll sign the cheque straight away.'

Ben and Patricia laughed.

'And then, we'll find the temple and the treasure.'

Laurent shrugged. 'I'll be happy with just the temple.'

'I see …' Frédéric looked at Amy. 'Are you coming to the hunt at Manoir Coste tomorrow morning? It should be a grand occasion. Breakfast, mulled wine, genteel company … and his lordship himself doing the honours.'

His voice dripped with sarcasm.

Amy shook her head. 'No, I'm keeping well away. I'm not keen on hunting.'

'Shame,' Frédéric said before gesturing towards his table. 'I need to go back to my friend, who by the way is Anne Loubier, Claudine's mother. She owns an antique shop in rue Marceau. She was the one who would have bought your statue if you had wanted to sell.'

He said goodbye and went back to his table.

'I for one am glad you didn't sell Bona Dea off to some shady back street dealer,' Laurent remarked as he cast a disapproving glance towards Claudine's mother. 'Far too many treasures disappear into private collections.'

They ordered pizzas and a bottle of red wine and talked about Glanum and the Gauls again. Amy was so engrossed in their conversation that she didn't even see Frédéric and his companion leave. It was well after eleven when they paid and drove back to Bellefontaine.

Amy knew there was something wrong as soon as she drove into the courtyard and the Clio's headlights swept over the house's gaping door. She switched the engine off and jumped out of the car.

'Someone has broken in!'

The front door swung on its hinges, and she caught a glimpse of a mess of papers in the hall.

'Stay here with Patricia.' Laurent pushed her to one side and ran in, followed by Ben.

But Amy didn't want to wait outside. She followed the two men into the hall and trod over the papers and tourist brochures littering the floor. The burglars hadn't ransacked the kitchen or the living room, but in the study the desk drawers had been pulled out, and their contents strewn around. Her laptop lay smashed on the floor.

The dining room too had been turned over, the dresser's contents emptied, its doors almost ripped out.

A sick feeling gripped her stomach and tears pricked her eyes as she walked across the broken pieces of a vase she'd just bought and the burglars had smashed to the ground. Laurent and Ben stood next to the table, aghast.

'They took my laptop, my USB sticks and all the files,' Laurent said, pointing to the table where he'd left his computer and the site survey reports earlier on.

His face turned deadly white, he muttered a curse.

'Bona Dea!'

He ran out and Amy followed him upstairs, praying that the burglars hadn't caused too much damage on the first floor.

Her room was a mess. Clothes, shoes, cosmetics were strewn around, and the jewellery box she kept on top of a chest of drawers was gone. That hurt. Her mother's favourite brooch and pendant had been in there, and now they were gone, perhaps forever.

Laurent emerged from his room. He raked his fingers into his brown hair and squeezed his eyes shut.

'They took Bona Dea.'

Amy put a comforting hand on his arm.

'I'll call the gendarmes. Hopefully they'll be able to do something.'

She went downstairs, made the phone call, and prepared some coffee. Keeping busy may help fight back the tears.

'It's my fault,' she told Laurent when he came into the kitchen.

'Of course not. Why do you say that?'

She poured black coffee into four cups.

'If I'd stayed here tonight, there would have been no burglary.'

'You can't be sure of that. A woman on her own isn't much of a deterrent to a gang of thieves. Actually, I'm glad you were with us. The burglars may have hurt you.'

She forced herself to take long, calming breaths but her hands shook so much when she lifted her cup that hot coffee spilled on to the table and she had to put it down.

'We need to make a list of what was taken before the gendarmes arrive.'

She took a pad and a pen and they sat at the kitchen

table. For the next twenty minutes they endeavoured to draw up a complete inventory of what was stolen. All in all, it was a very strange one.

The gendarmes were of that opinion too when they arrived.

'Not your common burglary,' the man in charge, a Capitaine Ferri, stated as he read through the list.

'Why take old stones and paperwork but leave the television? And why not take both laptops?'

He instructed his men to inspect the forced door and went inside the outbuilding from where all the potsherd and Roman artefacts had been stolen. Even though the gendarmes dusted the door handles for prints, Capitaine Ferri wasn't hopeful as he gave Amy a card.

'That's your reference number. We'll be in touch if there is any news, but there are too many prints, all of them smudged, so they'll be no use for identification purposes. As for the jewellery and Professeur Orsini's laptop, I doubt whether you'll see them again. If it's any consolation, at least we were able to fix your front door, so you don't have to call the emergency locksmith tonight.'

After they left, Laurent, Ben, and Patricia offered to help tidy up but Amy was adamant. She would deal with the mess. It was her responsibility.

As Laurent went upstairs, nursing a headache, he sighed, 'I can't believe we lost Bona Dea, and pretty much everything else too. All this work, all for nothing.'

Patricia put her arms around his shoulders.

'It wasn't for nothing, Prof. We now know that there is something extraordinary at Bellefontaine, and we will find it. It's just going to take us a little longer, that's all.'

Clearing up the mess took hours. After sorting out the papers and folders in the study, Amy picked up pieces of the broken laptop and put them in the bin. She then swept and mopped clean the whole of the downstairs floor. The idea that thugs had violated her home made her stomach heave. She would make sure no trace remained of them.

As she walked into the hall, Serena Chevalier's crystal glittering under the hallway light caught her eye. She picked it up, took it to her room, and put it on her bedside table. It was lucky the thieves hadn't smashed it to the ground.

It was well after two when she finally took a shower, slipped a thin cotton nightshirt on, and stumbled into bed. Even though weariness made her body heavy and achy, her mind raced and raced, and sleep eluded her, so after a while she got up, walked to the bathroom and drank some cool water straight from the tap before slipping into bed again. This time she fell into a fitful and feverish sleep, filled with shadows and whispers, and the horrible sensation of being smothered by a wet cloth pressed against her mouth.

As nightmares went, this was one of the worst she'd ever had. She felt as if she was lifted up and carried through a long tunnel carved into rock lit with flaming torches, which cast shifting, breathing shadows.

She was hot, so hot sweat stuck her hair, face and neck and made her nightdress cling to her body. Then she was in a round chamber where dozens of candles flickered and incense filled the air with scents of rose and jasmine.

Men and women clad in long, white robes stood still around a stone slab at the centre of a white triangle painted on the floor. She was placed down on the cold slab, and a woman started chanting nearby in a language she didn't understand.

A man stood close to her, and even though he was wearing a mask and she couldn't see his face there was something familiar about him. Maybe it was his tall stature and broad shoulders, the way he moved or the deep ring of his voice.

He took out a pinch of a white substance from a silver *salinum* which had lions and snakes engraved on the sides.

Terror made her heart beat faster. As the man threw the white powder over her and held the *salinum* close to her face, something shone into her eyes – his oval blue ring with letters engraved in gold. It looked like a C and a V, but she couldn't be sure.

The man put his hands on her shoulders, and his fingers slid along to her throat. He unfastened her nightdress and held the sides apart as she lay naked and helpless. She closed her eyes, desperate to escape but unable to move. The drums were louder, faster and echoed her heartbeats. She gasped as the man's hands slid on her skin.

Please, no. Not this.

'I want her now,' he whispered to someone standing next to him.

'Not tonight,' a woman said nearby. 'You can't risk it just yet, I just want her scared and confused.'

'You said she was mine,' he protested.

'We've done enough for one night. There are others here tonight who can satisfy you. Leave her be.'

'Too bad.' The man's hand travelled back to her throat and pressed hard.

Chapter Seven

The ground beneath her shook and resonated with the beat of drums. Every part of her ached. Her head pounded, and her throat was so dry she could hardly swallow. She opened her eyes onto a patch of grey sky peeping through a canopy of dark green branches. How odd ... She was dreaming of the forest.

She blinked, expecting to see the familiar ceiling of the room at Bellefontaine, but the grey sky and tall cedars were still there. Tentatively she spread her fingers by her sides, touching pine needles, pebbles and damp soil.

This was no dream. She *was* in the forest.

She sat up straight and gasped. No wonder she was shivering with cold. She was barefoot and her only clothing was her white nightdress, now dirty and ripped, with its sides hanging open. She tried to do the buttons up, but her fingers were numb with cold and she gave up.

Wrapping the nightgown around her as best she could, she pulled herself to her feet. A spasm of pain gripped her stomach, a wave of nausea overtook her and she just had time to bend down before being violently sick.

She wiped her mouth with the back of her hand. How had she got here? And how was she going to get back to Bellefontaine when her legs were so weak she could hardly stand?

The ground shook again. The sound of dogs yelping excitedly echoed in the forest, followed by the thunder of galloping horses. It was the hunt from Manoir Coste, and it was coming her way! In a panic, she glanced around for somewhere to hide. There were only trees and a couple of boulders. The dogs would find her straight away. She might as well stay where she was.

She hardly had time to comb her dishevelled hair back with her fingers before the pack of hounds appeared between the trees and charged towards her. Two dozen riders followed after the dogs. The man heading the hunt pulled the reins of his black horse metres away from her.

It was Fabien.

He jumped to the ground, dispersing the dogs with the slicing of his whip.

'Amy! What are you doing out here, in such a ...'

His eyes widened as he took in her ripped nightdress and bare feet.

Without giving her time to reply he slipped off his black jacket, and stepped towards her.

'Put this on,' he said, covering her shoulders with the jacket.

It was still warm from the heat of his body and smelled faintly of leather, horse and sandalwood aftershave.

'What on earth happened to you? Has anyone ... hurt you?'

Concern darkened his eyes. His hands were strong and warm on her shoulders, pulling her close and she could hardly resist the temptation to lean against him.

'I'm not sure,' she replied. 'I think I may have been sleepwalking.'

'Have you done it before?'

She thought about the incidents of the past few weeks. The taps running, the television and the radio turned on at night ... Maybe she had sleepwalked in the house all this time without ever suspecting it.

'I don't know, I may have,' she replied, hesitant.

Still standing between her and the riders, he put his arms around her.

'You're shaking with cold.'

He started rubbing her back, his hands leaving a warm trail along her spine.

'Don't worry, I'll take you home.'

'What's going on?' A man called behind him. 'Is she one of these crazy hunt protesters?'

A few people laughed.

'Never mind who she is, the woman is clearly deranged – or drunk,' someone else urged. 'Let's carry on. We're losing the scent.'

'Isn't that Amy Carter, from Bellefontaine?'

Amy recognised Claudine's voice and bit her lip. Today, she would have preferred if the woman had forgotten her name.

Still holding Amy tightly against him, Fabien called to one of the riders at the back of the pack.

'Fred, will you lead the hunt for me? I'm taking Amy back home.'

'You can't do that,' Claudine cried out. 'A Coste never abandons the lead.'

Fabien shrugged. 'There's a first time for everything. Go ahead. I'll meet you later.'

Frédéric rode past, followed by the handler of the hounds who urged the dogs back on the path with a few shouts and whistles, and the rest of the hunters followed. Claudine looked down at Amy with a pitying smile. Others grinned or made suggestive comments about her state of undress.

It was a nightmare. Soon the whole village would hear about Bellefontaine's landlady wandering half naked in the forest. They might even suggest she was crazy or on drugs. She held her head high, and fought back her tears. She wouldn't give the hunters the satisfaction of seeing her upset. She had been sleepwalking, that was all. These things happened.

'Don't worry, Bellefontaine isn't too far,' Fabien said once they were alone. 'We'll ride Pacha.'

He took her hand and led her to his horse, but Amy shook her head. There was no way she was going to be able to climb onto the horse dressed as she was.

'I'll walk, just point me in the right direction.'

'You are not walking,' he replied in a steely voice. 'You are barefoot, in shock, and hypothermic.'

Without leaving her time to protest, he put his hands around her waist and lifted her up on to Pacha so that she sat side-saddle. He swung himself up behind her, took hold of the reins and urged the horse on. The horse's slow pace and the heat of Fabien's body soon lulled Amy into an exhausted torpor.

Cradled in his arms, she felt safe at last. Her cheek rubbed against the soft linen of his shirt and the regular beating of his heart echoed her own. She heaved a sigh, closed her eyes, and let herself be rocked to sleep.

'We're here.'

The rumble of his voice woke her up.

She opened her eyes to see that they had reached the bottom of Bellefontaine's garden.

'I see your archaeologists have been busy,' he said dryly as they rode past the excavation site and across the garden towards the house.

'They have. Although I'm afraid it's all been for nothing.'

Before he could ask her to explain, she added, 'Here they are, loading up the van. They're leaving today.'

Laurent, Ben and Patricia were in the courtyard, and turned at the sound of Pacha's hooves on the path.

'Amy! My God, did you have an accident?' Laurent stepped towards her as Fabien helped her dismount.

'No. Yes. I don't know.'

In a few words she explained she'd been sleepwalking and had woken up in the forest.

'Monsieur Coste was kind enough to bring me home,' she finished.

'To think that you went out during the night and we didn't hear a thing,' Laurent said, shaking his head in dismay.

'Actually, we were just saying that the three of us slept remarkably well, considering last evening's events. We only just got up, and when we found the house empty we thought you'd gone to the gendarmes in Bonnieux.'

'What happened last evening?'

Fabien frowned as he looked down at her.

Amy had no choice but to tell him about the burglary. His lips tightened but he didn't make any comment.

'By the way, I'm Laurent Orsini, from the Arles Museum,' Laurent said, turning to Fabien. 'I was hoping to see you later today.'

'So you're the one responsible for the mess in the garden,' Fabien said, the hard look in his eyes belying the casual tone of his voice.

Laurent laughed. 'You call it a mess, I call it a job well done. The artefacts we unearthed all point to the existence of a major Roman, and possibly protohistoric Gallic site – or rather, they did before they were stolen. I would like to extend the excavation site into the forest if you will give us the authorisation.'

Fabien remained silent for a brief moment and when he did respond his voice was curt.

'I'm afraid I must decline. Sometimes, things are lost for a reason. If there is anything to find in the forest, I'll find it myself – or not. Right now though, Amy needs to go inside and get warm.'

Patricia put her hand on Amy's shoulder and gave a light squeeze.

'Monsieur Coste is right. Come on, sweetie, I'll help you.'

Amy looked up at Fabien.

'Thank you for your help. If you don't mind waiting, I'll return your coat as soon as I've put some decent clothes on.'

He shook his head. 'Don't worry about the coat. I'll drop by this evening. You can give it back to me then.'

He mounted his horse in one swift, fluid move, nodded to Amy, and rode out of the courtyard onto the main road.

'Wow! What a hunk, I think I'm in love,' Patricia exclaimed, squeezing her hands against her heart and rolling her eyes. 'I wouldn't mind if he rescued me from the woods.'

'Well, your hunk just denied us access to the forest,' Laurent said mournfully. 'Now it's going to take ages to apply for a compulsory order with the *Préfet*.'

Amy slept until lunchtime. Her aches and pains may have subsided by the time she woke up, but her humiliation hadn't. The second she opened her eyes, everything came back with sickening clarity: the hunters sniggering at her; the horrified look in Fabien Coste's eyes as he covered her up with his coat and lifted her onto his horse. She pulled the covers over her head. What must he think of her? She'd never be able to see him again without feeling ashamed.

She had never sleepwalked when she lived in England – not that she knew of anyway. The exhaustion and excitement of her new life in France and the shock of last night's burglary must have triggered the episode.

She swallowed hard. There had been that dream, too. The images, sensations and smells were still fresh in her mind, vivid and disturbingly real: the chamber, the men and women dressed in white robes, the man who had undressed and touched her, his sinister mask and breathless voice.

No doubt Laurent's stories of ancient rituals and Lily's tales of goddesses and curses had preyed on her mind. She could only hope now that time would erase the dream from her memory.

The bed felt like a protective cocoon. Resisting the temptation to fall asleep again, she got up, took a long, hot shower, dressed in a pair of black corduroys and a cream cable-knit sweater and went downstairs.

She found Patricia in the kitchen, flicking through a history publication, a cup of steaming black coffee on the table in front of her.

'Hi! You're up already. How are you now?' Patricia lifted her eyes from her magazine and smiled.

'Much better, but I still feel stupid, and ashamed.'

Amy took out a cup and poured herself some coffee.

'It was awful in the forest with all those hunters staring at me.'

Patricia shrugged. 'So what? You gave them something exciting to talk about.'

Amy drank a sip of coffee and shuddered.

'They thought I was drunk, or crazy. One of them even thought I was an anti-hunt saboteur.'

'Your saviour, Fabien Coste, didn't seem to think you were crazy.'

Patricia cast her a knowing look.

'Quite the opposite in fact, he seemed very protective of you.'

She sighed and leaned back on her chair. 'I found him very handsome.'

Amy blushed and she quickly drank a sip of coffee to hide her face, but it was too late.

Patricia laughed. 'It looks like I'm not the only one who fancies the handsome Duc de Coste.'

Amy didn't answer. Fabien had once again come to her rescue. Rarely before had she felt so safe and well cared for than when she'd nestled in his arms to ride back to Bellefontaine.

She put her cup down on the worktop. He may have been kind today, but she would do well to remember the night of the ball when he had made a pass at her, then left her waiting on the terrace while he made love to Claudine.

'Let's have some lunch,' she said to change the subject.

She wouldn't waste one minute more thinking about Fabien Coste or his deep green eyes. Instead she would concentrate on what was needed – buying a new computer and phoning the gendarmes to check on the progress of the investigation.

Straight after lunch Amy and Patricia went to buy a new laptop and Amy checked her emails as soon as she got it set up.

'It looks like I have a booking for next week,' she said. 'A newly-wed couple from London are planning to tour the Luberon.'

Patricia gave her a hug. 'That's excellent news. I'm sure they'll love it here.'

It was late afternoon when Laurent and Ben returned from their survey of the forest. They offered to stay until the following morning, but Amy shook her head.

'I know you have a million things to do at the museum. I'll be fine. Really.'

She managed to keep a brave smile on her face until the three archaeologists piled up their van with tools, bags and equipment and waved goodbye, but the moment they had disappeared in the distance, silence and emptiness seemed to engulf her, and tears filled her eyes.

For the first time since moving into Bellefontaine, Amy looked around her with a heavy heart. What if she walked out into the forest at night again, set the house on fire, or even tried to drive her car and ended up causing an accident? Who would be there to keep her safe – to keep Bellefontaine safe? There would from now on always be a gnawing doubt in her mind that she couldn't trust herself …

She put the radio on in the kitchen for company, and took out a mixing bowl, flour and yeast. There was nothing like baking to keep worries at bay, she thought, as she twisted her hair into a rough plait, fastened the ties of her apron, and started making a tomato and basil loaf. By the time she had kneaded the dough into a velvety smooth lump, her arms and hands ached but she was singing along to the radio.

The roaring of an engine in the courtyard startled her. She turned the radio down and opened the front door just in time to see Fabien Coste get out of his Range Rover, holding what looked like a bundle in a blanket against his chest.

'You look a lot better.'

'I feel a lot better,' Amy agreed, forcing a smile to hide her embarrassment. Not only had the man seen her practically naked, but she had fallen asleep in his arms as they rode back through the forest.

She looked down. 'What do you have there?'

The blanket in his arms wriggled and the white and ginger head of a Poitevin puppy peeped out.

Fabien smiled.

'This is Michka,' he said. 'She's yours, if you'll have her. I have far too many pups at Manoir Coste and you'd do me a great favour if you took her in.'

'You mean, you're giving her to me?'

'You did say you were thinking of getting a dog, didn't you?'

Amy took the little animal from him. Michka was adorable, her eyes a milk chocolate brown and her silky smooth coat a mix of white and ginger.

'She'll be a good guard dog in a few months. In the meantime, she'll keep you company when you're alone.'

Amy held the dog to her chest, ruffling her soft fur, and smiled. This was one of the nicest things anyone had ever done for her.

'Thank you. I promise I'll look after her.'

'Hang on, I brought her things.'

He came back from the car with a wicker basket and a plastic bag.

'Here you have a lead, bowl, some food, her favourite toys and her veterinary record.'

He took everything into the hall.

'Goodbye then, little one.'

He tickled the puppy's head, laughed as she yelped and licked his fingers. For a minute he looked young and carefree, and Amy felt a yearning so strong it took her breath away. If only she could nestle in his arms once again, if only she could trace the outline of his face with her fingers and …

The dog wriggling in her arms brought her back to reality. She took a step back.

'Do call me if there's anything troubling you, Amy. I mean it,' he said, serious.

'I will, I promise. Wait! You mustn't forget your jacket, it's in the hall.'

With one hand she unhooked his black riding jacket from the coat rack and handed it to him. Their fingers touched, giving her a jolt.

She stood in the hall for a long while after he left. No man had ever affected her so much. She'd had a few boyfriends before, of course, but even when she tried hard to please them, her body remained frustratingly cool, her heart remote, and her senses unresponsive.

Until now …

Every time she was with Fabien Coste, it was like standing on top of a cliff and being pulled closer to the edge by an irresistible force, with no fear or regard for the dangers that lay ahead. For the first time she understood that desperate desire to touch and be touched, to kiss and be kissed that she'd thought she would never experience.

Chapter Eight

'Bellefontaine's sleepwalking beauty sabotages hunt!' by Armelle Capitelli.

'Amy Carter, Bellefontaine's new English landlady, was found wandering scantily clad in the cedar forest early on Friday morning by Monsieur Fabien Coste as he led one his famous boar hunts.

Mademoiselle Carter, who is known locally for her strong anti-hunting feelings, claimed she was sleepwalking in the forest when she inadvertently wandered into the path of the hunt. Monsieur le Duc had to take the distressed lady home, thereby abandoning for the first time ever the lead of the Bonnieux hunt, and causing thirty-five riders to return to Manoir Coste disgruntled and empty-handed after hours of chasing after an elusive boar.

Could this be an unusual, and successful, attempt at sabotaging the hunt? We will have to wait until the next hunt of the season, scheduled for Thursday 7th April, to see if any more sleepwalking beauties appear on the hillside ...'

Amy threw the copy of the *Journal du Luberon* newspaper across the kitchen table.

How could they print such rubbish? Even a local gazette should have standards. Someone must have overheard what she'd said in the butcher's shop and reported it to the journalist. The last thing she wanted was to spark a campaign about hunting and attract hunt saboteurs and anti-animal cruelty activists to the village.

'Good morning, Amy.'

A brown-haired young woman, very pale and with dark circles under her hazel eyes, peeped into the kitchen.

'Good morning, Eva. Are you feeling any better today?'

'No, I'm tired, again. I kept Justin awake most of the night.' Eva sighed. 'I don't know what's wrong with me. It's been four nights now I've had these horrid nightmares and I can't sleep …'

'You should have breakfast outside,' Amy suggested. 'The sunshine, the blue sky, and the fresh air will do you good.'

'Good idea. I love your garden.'

Eva bent down to scratch Michka's back. The dog wagged its tail in response.

'And I love your dog, it's just so cute.'

Amy smiled. She too had grown fond of her puppy. In the space of a few days, the little dog had become an integral part of Bellefontaine and of her life. She had decided to throw a thank you dinner party for Fabien on Saturday evening and had even invited Claudine – she felt she had to – as well as her friends the Michons, and her English guests Eva and Justin Barlow.

She set a coffee pot and a cup on a tray, together with warm home-made crusty bread and a pot of raspberry jam and took it outside.

'Where are you off to today?'

'Aix-en-Provence,' Eva said. 'I want to see the Cézanne exhibition, visit the old town, and do a bit of shopping. We'll eat there tonight, I think, so don't wait for us.'

A tall and lanky man walked out onto the terrace and let out a loud yawn.

'Blimey, that sun is bright. I need my shades.'

Eva glanced up and chuckled.

'Poor darling, you look frightful.'

'I feel it too. I need coffee, and lots of it.'

He sunk into the chair, combed his hair with his fingers and rubbed his stubbly cheeks.

'Coffee coming right away!'

Amy prepared another tray and left the exhausted newlyweds to enjoy their breakfast and the garden, already fragrant with scents of rosemary, thyme, and basil.

The postman's moped backfired loudly in the courtyard as it did every morning, making Michka growl and bark. Would she have any new bookings today? Amy wondered as she went to the letterbox. Sadly, there were only a couple of bills that she put down without opening them. Bad news could wait …

As soon as the Barlows left for Aix, she took Michka for a walk into the forest. It was empty and quiet. The pine needles crunched under her feet, releasing their invigorating scent. She let the dog off the lead, and it leapt ahead, sniffing the ground and running in and out of the trees.

Twenty minutes of brisk walking later, Amy was deep into the forest and Michka was nowhere to be seen. She called, clapped her hands and whistled, but the puppy didn't come back, too busy chasing after rabbits or birds. Amy left the path and cut through the undergrowth, following the barking that echoed among the trees.

The forest was different here: the trees no longer cedars but oaks, their trunks twisted and gnarled. Arrows of sunlight shot through the thick canopy and bathed the ground in dappled green and gold. A clear stream snaked between mossy rocks. It was like stepping into a forgotten world, an oasis inside the cedar forest. Could this be the ancient wood and the sacred spring Laurent had referred to? If so, the ruined fountain and the lost temple might be nearby.

Not far away, she caught a glimpse of Michka's ginger and white coat. The puppy was tearing at a piece of white fabric, which was caught on a branch.

'What are you doing, you silly dog?'

Amy pulled the fabric loose. It felt like linen and gave off a very faint scent. Her throat tightened, her hand started shaking. She knew that scent. It brought back memories of a dark, enclosed space lit by candles that flickered and cast shadows on rocky walls, of sounds of ancient chanting, but most of all it brought back feelings of terror and helplessness. The fabric slipped out of her fingers.

She drew in a long breath and stared at the white linen on the ground. This was silly. She'd had a bad dream, the product of an overactive imagination, inflamed by Laurent's tales of ancient cults and dead civilisations. That piece of fabric had nothing to do with it.

Yet she couldn't help but cast uneasy glances around, as if robed silhouettes were about to appear amongst the trees. She should leave. Bending down, she clipped Michka's lead on and urged the dog on to the path and back to Bellefontaine.

She spent the rest of the day baking shortbread biscuits, sticking labels she had designed on to miniature jars filled with home-made jam, and checking through her publicity material for the fair Monsieur Verdier recommended she attend the following day. By the time she loaded everything into the car, the sun was slipping behind the hills, mauve shadows were gathering around the *bastide* and she had almost forgotten about her incursion into the ancient woodland.

As Eva and Justin were eating in Aix-en-Provence, she warmed a pan of tomato and basil soup she ate with some bread and cheese in the kitchen. Afterwards she settled down to read a book about the history of Luberon. Michka stretched out at her feet and started snoring.

She flicked through pages of photos and drawings, hoping to find depictions of Bona Dea, of her darker, wicked twin sister Fauna, or other Gallic earthen mothers. Nothing looked remotely like her statue – Bellefontaine's La Bonne Dame.

Where was it now? Capitaine Ferri believed it had already been sold on the black market. In fact, he was pessimistic about the chances of recovering any of the stolen items.

Her mobile phone ringing drew her back to reality. She looked at the number displayed on the small screen and let out a resigned sigh before taking the call.

'Hi, Chris.'

Amy's voice was tired and strained but as usual her sister didn't notice and launched into a torrent of recrimination against her boyfriend Toby. For the next ten minutes, Amy only spoke to punctuate her sister's monologue with the occasional 'really?' and 'he didn't,' or 'that's terrible.' She didn't care for Toby and there was much more she wanted to say, but she knew from experience she'd be wasting her time. Chris was madly in love with him – or so she claimed – and not ready to acknowledge that he cheated on her.

When Chris finally ran out of steam, Amy asked about Peter. As always when she thought about her seven-year-old nephew, guilt and sorrow tightened her throat. She missed the quiet, serious little boy, and often felt like she'd abandoned him by moving to France.

'Why don't you two come over for the Easter holidays?' she suggested. 'I'd love to see him – well, both of you – and I'm sure it would do you good to be away from Manchester.'

And from cheating Toby, she finished silently.

Chris promised to think about it. As an afterthought she asked Amy how she was doing. Amy made a joke about sleepwalking in the woods and being rescued by the lord of the manor, and actually succeeded in making her sister laugh for once.

She didn't say anything about the horrible first night she had spent at Bellefontaine or about Eva Barlow's nightmares. Nor did she mention her vandalised car or the burglary. It wasn't so much that she didn't want to worry Chris, more that she didn't want to hear her say that buying Bellefontaine had been a terrible mistake and she should come home.

Her throat was tight when she hung up, and not for the first time she wished she and Chris were closer. It was nobody's fault if they were often at odds, they were too different. Chris was impulsive and dramatic, whereas Amy was quiet – or as Chris said, aloof, cold and boring – and hated being the centre of attention.

She closed the shutters, locked the front door, and made her way up to her room. Eva and Justin had a key so she didn't need to stay up to let them in. She read in bed until she heard them come back some time after midnight, then switched her bedside lamp off and fell asleep.

A blood-curdling scream woke her up in the early hours. Heart thumping, she jumped out of bed and ran out of her room into the corridor. Light showed under Eva and Justin's door. She heard Eva cry out and knocked on the door.

'Eva, are you hurt?'

'No, it's just another bloody nightmare,' Justin's grumpy voice answered. 'Sorry, Amy, we'll be fine. Don't worry.'

Justin declined her offer of a hot drink and she went back to bed heavy-hearted. Something was definitely wrong with Eva. Having so many nightmares night after night wasn't normal.

It was just before seven when Amy left for Apt the following morning. The hospitality fair was being held in the town hall. Amy parked her paint-splattered car, piled up her boxes filled with brochures and postcards, biscuits and jam, and tottered across the square into the building.

'I'm sorry but there isn't any booking in your name,' the receptionist said after she'd put her boxes on the counter and introduced herself.

'Please look again, I booked a stall weeks ago,' Amy insisted.

The young woman flicked the pages of her register, and frowned as she pointed a finger to her list.

'Carter, you said? Now that's odd. Your name was crossed out and your pitch reallocated. I don't know what happened. Anyway, you're in luck. There are still a few stalls left over there.'

She gestured to the back of the hall.

'But I paid for a good pitch at the front, not a stall hidden at the back.'

The young woman shrugged. 'I'm sorry but there's nothing else I can do. You will probably be able to get a refund if you complain to the Tourist Board in Bonnieux. They're the ones who handled your booking.'

Arguing further was pointless, so Amy picked up her boxes and carried them across the hall, past the elegant stalls of restaurants, shops and local hotels, including Manoir Coste. There was no mix up with *their* booking, she fumed as she caught a glimpse of a couple of smartly dressed hostesses arranging displays of complimentary chocolates and luxury toiletries, with large, glossy black and white photographs of Manoir Coste as backdrop.

She found a vacant stall at last and started to set up. Not bad, she thought when she stepped back an hour later. The tins of biscuits and miniature jam jars made the stall homely and welcoming, and if her own photos of Bellefontaine in the sunset were too amateurish to compete with Manoir

Coste's stunning display, they perfectly captured the mysterious atmosphere of the place.

As church bells rang nine o'clock, Monsieur le Maire officially opened the fair. Wearing his tricolour ribbon across his chest, he proceeded to visit every stall and exchange a handshake with exhibitors.

'Ah, Bellefontaine in Bonnieux,' he bellowed after glancing at Amy's brochures. He didn't offer Amy his hand.

'You must be the infamous Mademoiselle Carter. I read all about your exploits in the newspaper. I hope you're not planning another silly protest to ruin Monsieur Coste's next hunt.'

There were a few sniggers from the mayor's entourage. Amy fought to control her breathing.

'The newspaper article was wrong, monsieur,' she replied in a shaky voice. 'I may not agree with hunting but I never set out to sabotage Monsieur Coste's hunt.'

The mayor snorted and walked away.

An attractive blonde woman in a smart navy suit approached.

'May I ask what you're planning to do to stop the Coste hunt on Thursday?' she asked, her small, inquisitive dark brown eyes gleaming.

'I have no plans to stop anything,' Amy snapped.

'Yet it would be a good publicity coup for Bellefontaine if you did,' the woman went on. 'I can just picture it. You in a flimsy nightdress once again, throwing yourself across the path of Fabien Coste. He scooping you into his arms ...'

'For the last time, I have no intention of protesting against anything, and certainly not against Monsieur Coste. He has been very good to me.'

The woman's thin lips stretched into a slow smile.

'Has he really? So you are his *protégée* then? How interesting.'

Amy gasped as if she'd been slapped

'I am nobody's *protégée*,' she retorted. 'I don't believe we have been introduced. Who are you?'

The woman pulled a business card out of her handbag.

'My name is Armelle Capitelli, I'm a reporter for the *Journal du Luberon*. Call me any time.'

Amy let the card drop on to the table and folded her arms across her chest.

'I won't call you, and I suggest you check your facts before you print anything next time, Mademoiselle Capitelli, or I might sue your paper for libel.'

The journalist shrugged. 'You wouldn't be the first one to try – and fail. I'm sure we'll talk again before long,' she said.

The morning wasn't starting at all well, Amy thought as she picked out a biscuit and bit into it. Not only was she relegated to the back of the hall because of some unfortunate mix-up, but she had been singled out by the mayor and made an enemy of Armelle Capitelli when she desperately needed good coverage in the local press.

Biscuit crumbs fell on to the front of her blue dress.

'I almost didn't see you back there … Was this the only stall you could afford?'

This time it was Claudine who stood in front of her, stunning today in a cream trouser suit and black silk shirt. Amy flicked the biscuit crumbs off her dress impatiently. As usual, Claudine made her feel frumpy and gauche – and extremely bad-tempered.

'There was a mix-up with the booking, and this was the only place left,' she replied.

'Really? That's a shame. Oh, by the way, Fabien and I won't be able to come to your little dinner party tomorrow night. We're far too busy. Fabien's mother is arriving from

Paris in the morning, then there's the hunt to organise for next Thursday.'

She leaned towards Amy, as if she wanted to tell her a secret. 'Between you and me, I don't think Fabien wants to be seen in your company at the moment ... He was furious about the article in the paper. He hates having his name mixed up with sordid stories in the press.'

Before Amy could speak, Claudine pointed to the display of jam pots and biscuits.

'Did you make those? How ... quaint.'

And she walked away, leaving a trail of perfume behind her and Amy in an even worse mood.

As the hours ticked by and the hall filled up with visitors, Amy forgot about Claudine, the mayor and the reporter. The sun shone through the hall's high windows and made the place hot and stuffy, and by the end of the afternoon, her head ached and she yearned for a breath of fresh air.

Thankfully packing up didn't take long, since all her biscuits and jam jars – quaint or not – had been snapped up. On the drive home she rolled the window down and enjoyed the breeze playing with her hair, and she felt better by the time she got back to Bellefontaine.

'Hi, everybody, I'm back.'

Michka ran towards her and leapt against her legs, with Eva close behind.

'Hello, sweetie.' Amy crouched in the hall and scratched the Poitevin's head.

'How did it go?' Eva asked.

'Fine. Apart from a mix-up with my booking and an argument with the mayor and a journalist about my anti-hunting sympathies.'

She looked up. Eva bit her lip. Her eyes were red, as if she'd been crying.

'Is there anything the matter?'

Eva nodded. 'I don't know how to say this ... our bags are packed and in the car. We're leaving tonight. I'm sorry, Amy. I know we booked our room until next Tuesday, but we can't stay. I can't stay ...'

The young woman burst out crying.

Amy stood up and put her arms around Eva's shoulders.

'Don't cry. Come on. Let's sit down.'

'It's the nightmares,' Eva explained once she sat at the kitchen table and the tears had stopped. 'I just want to go home. I want to sleep, and forget all about those horrid dreams I've had every night since we arrived.' She bowed her head.

'They feel so real, and they're getting worse. I'm sure they'll stop once I leave Bellefontaine.'

'Why should they? I mean, what do they have to do with Bellefontaine?'

Eva let out a shaky sigh. 'I can't explain. It's something to do with this place.'

She shuddered.

'The nightmares always start the same way. I am in the garden, it's getting dark, I see lights flickering in the forest.'

Amy stifled a gasp. 'What kind of lights?'

'Flames, candles. I don't know.' Eva shrugged. 'I follow them. It's like a force drawing me in. I walk deeper into the forest until *they* come and take me.' Her whole body shook and she whimpered.

'Who are *they*?'

'They're evil, they hurt and kill people, right there in front of me and I can't do anything to help. There's blood – blood everywhere.'

She put her face in her hands.

Amy tried to think. Eva's dreams sounded like the stories about the goddess and her cult that Marc Chevalier had told her the day she first visited Bellefontaine. How could Eva know about them?

'Has anyone spoken to you about a goddess that used to be worshipped around here, a long, long time ago?' she asked.

Eva nodded. 'Yes, actually, there was a woman in the village antique shop we talked to the day we arrived.'

'An antique shop?'

Justin walked into the kitchen and stood behind Eva.

'It was a quirky little shop in the village. We told the lady there that we were spending our honeymoon at Bellefontaine and she started talking about a lost temple in the forest and what used to go on there in the old days.'

Eva shivered. 'I know these are only old stories and the nightmares are caused by my vivid imagination, but I can't help the way I feel.'

'That lady was quite nice, if a bit intense,' Justin added. 'Before we left, she gave us a crystal to wish us luck because we were newly-weds.'

'What kind of crystal?'

'I can't remember its name, but it made me think about toothpaste.'

Eva smiled at last. 'It's fluorite, silly!'

Fluorite? Wasn't that the name of the crystal Serena Chevalier had given her?

'Hang on a minute.'

Amy jumped to her feet and rushed to her bedroom upstairs. The crystal was lit by the last of the sunset pouring through the open window. She took it downstairs and put it on the kitchen table.

'Is this like the stone you were given?'

Eva nodded, touching the shimmering white and purple stone.

'Almost the exact same one. The lady said it would give Justin vigour for ... you know...' Her face coloured. 'She said I had to put it under my pillow every night of our honeymoon.'

Justin let out a groan. 'At least we can now confirm that crystals don't work for ... that. However, Eva wondered if the crystal might be causing her bad dreams so we've thrown it away.'

Eva turned to Amy. 'We'd better leave before it gets too late. I'm so sorry, Amy. I find this place amazing but ...'

'I understand.'

Amy went into the study to print the couple's invoice. Justin offered to pay for the full week but Amy wouldn't hear of it.

'I'm so sorry your honeymoon was such a disappointment,' she said, giving Eva a hug. 'Have a safe journey back and take care of yourself.'

The young woman looked back with haunted eyes.

'It's *you* who should take care,' she whispered.

After they'd left, Amy sat down to think. If word got out that guests had to leave Bellefontaine because of terrifying nightmares, nobody would ever want to come and stay – nobody except lunatics in search of thrills.

So she had failed already. She might as well forget about the guesthouse business, get in touch with translating agencies and ask for freelance jobs or she'd never be able to pay her bills and keep this place. Hadn't Chris predicted that she would fail before the year was over? She heard again a deep, cutting French male voice, calling her naive and ill prepared.

Pride made her stiffen her spine. She wouldn't wallow in

self-pity and give up her dream, not yet anyway. She would show her sister, Fabien and everybody else that she was a fighter.

She took a large slice of leek and onion tart out of the fridge, reached for a bottle of white wine, and poured herself a glass.

'I think I've earned it after the day I've had, don't you?' She winked at Michka and drank a sip of wine.

The dog wagged its tail in response.

She carried her meal into the sitting room and picked up her history book, but she couldn't concentrate on the words or the illustrations tonight. The accounts of Eva's nightmares preyed on her mind and made her restless.

Outside night was falling. It felt like darkness was closing in on Bellefontaine.

Chapter Nine

'You should have let them pay for the full week,' Paul muttered as he poured himself another *pastis*. 'I never heard such rubbish in my life. Cancelling a holiday because of bad dreams.'

Adèle frowned as she watched her husband drain his third *apéritif* of the evening.

'I must say it does sound a little far-fetched,' she said, turning to Amy. 'Maybe they just wanted an excuse to go home.'

'I don't think so. Poor Eva was genuinely terrified. I only hope no one else hears about this, especially not that newspaper reporter, or I'll never have any more guests.'

It was nice to have her friends around tonight, even though Paul seemed short-tempered and jumpy. He kept drumming his fingers on the arm of the sofa and darting nervous glances around the room. Adèle too seemed preoccupied and toyed absent-mindedly with her long pearl necklace. She had dressed in a smart blue dress, probably because she knew Fabien and Claudine had been invited. She and Paul had looked relieved when Amy had announced that the couple weren't coming and it would just be the three of them for dinner after all.

'I have nothing against Monsieur le Duc,' Paul had remarked, 'he's all right, I suppose, even if I don't know what we could possibly talk about over dinner. Mademoiselle Loubier, however, is another matter. Between you and me, I think she fancies herself as the next duchess.'

Probably because she soon would be, Amy thought.

Michka ran in from the garden, yelping and barking.

'You never said you'd bought a dog,' Paul said as he bent down to stroke her.

'She's a present from Fabien,' Amy explained. 'He brought her over the day after the burglary.'

Paul whistled through his teeth. 'He gave you one of his prize-winning hounds? Well, well ... That was mighty nice of him. The dog will keep you company. You must be a little worried out here on your own, especially after the break-in and that sleepwalking incident.'

Amy shook her head and let out a sigh.

'I made such a fool of myself that day.'

'Of course you didn't. It wasn't your fault you were sleepwalking,' Adèle said kindly.

'I take it you're not planning a repeat performance for the next hunt?'

'Not if I can help it ... It's so scary to think that I opened the front door, walked into the forest at night and I don't remember any of it.'

Thoughtful, Amy bent down to scratch Michka's head. 'I hope this little dog will wake me up if it happens again.'

The noise of a car engine in the courtyard, followed by a door slamming caused Michka to bark and run out of the room. Who could it be at this time? Amy wondered as she followed the puppy into the hallway.

It was Fabien, dressed in dark grey chinos and a white shirt, and holding a bottle of champagne.

'Oh? Good evening. I wasn't expecting you. Claudine said you were too busy to come.'

His eyes narrowed to dark green slits.

'Claudine was wrong.'

He handed her the champagne.

'I hope I'm not late.'

'Not at all. Please come in.'

She opened the door wider, feeling absurdly happy to see him, and even happier that he was alone.

He followed her into the kitchen where Adèle was busy taking warm plates out of the oven.

She looked surprised. 'Good evening, Monsieur le Duc.'

He smiled. 'There's to be no Monsieur le Duc from now on. Please call me Fabien.'

If Paul and Adèle were a little tense to start with, Fabien soon put them at ease with anecdotes about Manoir Coste's celebrity guests. He sympathised with Paul about the slump in the building trade, exchanged village gossip with Adèle, and complimented Amy on every single dish she served.

'That was the best tarte aux pommes I have eaten in a long time,' he said as he pushed his empty plate away.

Amy laughed. 'I find that hard to believe. Your chef at Manoir Coste is exceptional.'

'Actually, I almost forgot ...'

Fabien fumbled in his shirt pocket and pulled out a piece of paper, which was covered with fine, spidery writing.

'The recipes – for the brioche and the crème brûlée you liked so much,' he explained, 'with the compliments of the chef.'

She met Fabien's gaze. He wasn't smiling any longer.

Like the night of the Hunt Ball, he looked at her as if they were alone in the room, as if she was the most beautiful woman in the world and no one else mattered.

Yet, she knew very well that wasn't the case. Fabien had a girlfriend, and Claudine was a hundred times more attractive than she could ever be. It was silly, immature and plain wrong of her to get so flustered. The man wasn't looking at her in any particular way, she was imagining things. And if he was, he had no right to do so. Annoyed with herself, she pushed her chair back and said she would make some coffee.

'Good idea. I'll get the fire going in the living room,' Paul said. 'I hope you still have some of that chestnut liqueur Verdier gave you.'

Adèle frowned at her husband, whose face was already flushed with too much drink, but said nothing.

'How has your season been so far?' Fabien enquired when Amy brought the tray with the cafetière and cups into the living room.

She couldn't repress a sigh.

'Not very good. The only guests I've had until now were the archaeologists from Arles and an English couple who left yesterday.'

She didn't mention Eva's nightmares. The fewer people who knew about them, the better.

'Don't worry too much,' he said. 'It takes time to establish a business. You have to make yourself known, advertise, plan events, attend trade fairs. The most important thing is to have a marketing strategy.'

She pulled a face and fiddled with the ties of her dress.

'I suspect that my marketing strategy so far has been a total flop.'

She told him about the fiasco at the tourist fair and her altercation with the mayor and the reporter.

'All people are interested in are my anti-hunting views and the fact I ruined your hunt last week.'

He drank some coffee and stared into the fire.

'You didn't ruin anything,' he said softly. 'By the way, do you know when Orsini and his team are coming back to Bellefontaine?'

'Laurent won't be back for a while. He needs to get

funding first, which will take longer now the statue and all the other artefacts have been stolen.'

'Have the gendarmes recovered anything yet?' Adèle asked.

'I'm afraid not.'

'They won't,' Fabien said. 'The antiquities black market is thriving, and anything with any supernatural connotations like La Bonne Dame of Bonnieux will fetch a fortune with collectors. I wouldn't be surprised if the burglars acted on behalf of an organised gang who found out about the dig at Bellefontaine.'

'Then they might come back when Laurent finds the temple,' Amy said.

'If he finds it,' Fabien said in a very low voice.

'He will. Actually, I think I know where it could be.'

She went on to describe how she had found the ancient wood within the cedar forest and what she believed was the sacred spring mentioned on the carved stones.

'If it is the sacred woodland Laurent talked about, then the ruined fountain and temple can't be far from there.'

Adèle put down her coffee, a look of alarm on her face.

'You shouldn't go into the forest on your own, Amy, and certainly not steer away from the path. I dread to think what would happen if you fell or got lost ...' She lowered her voice. 'Or if you stumbled into the cult followers.'

'There are no cult followers,' Paul snapped. 'I am sick to death of these stories about that damned temple.' He poured himself another glass of liqueur.

'My aunt Lily isn't the only one to claim that the cult of La Bonne Dame is still alive today,' Adèle remarked, 'and that it's been linked to cases of rape and missing persons over the years.'

Amy was shocked. 'Rapes and missing persons? You

mean those terrible stories Marc Chevalier told me could be true after all? I know that Laurent and his team think human sacrifices were carried out here long after they were banned by the Roman Empire, but surely that was a long, long time ago.'

'Of course it was,' Fabien said curtly. 'The good people of Bonnieux made everything up and it's high time they stopped spreading silly rumours.'

'Then maybe you should allow Laurent to search the forest for the lost temple,' Amy suggested.

'I'm not going to give him the opportunity.' Fabien's voice was suddenly hard. 'If there is anything worth finding, I'll find it myself.'

'He said he would apply for an injunction to grant him access to the site whether you agreed or not.'

Fabien's jaw clenched, then relaxed and his lips stretched into a tight smile.

'He can always try.'

Adèle drained her cup of coffee and rose to her feet.

'It's time to go home, Paul. I don't want to leave Stéphane alone for too long.'

Paul staggered as he walked across the room, and cursed under his breath as he bumped against the dresser.

Adèle put a steadying hand on his arm. 'Give me your car keys, I'll drive.'

Amy showed her friends out. When she came back, Fabien was standing in front of the fire, his back to her, his hands in his trouser pockets.

'I hope Paul doesn't have a sore head tomorrow morning or he won't be able to attend the Palm Sunday procession,' she said as she started to gather empty coffee cups.

Fabien said nothing so she carried on talking about the celebrations planned in Bonnieux for the following morning, aware of her voice sounding increasingly breathless in the quiet room. When he turned around, shadows played across his face and her empty words died on her lips.

'You really do talk a lot. Not that I mind. I love the sound of your voice.'

He stepped towards her and took the tray from her.

'What are you doing?' she asked in a whisper.

He didn't answer but touched his finger lightly to her cheek. Lifting his hand to her hair, he curled a strand around his finger.

'It's just as silky as it looks – and so is your skin.'

His fingers stroked the sides of her throat, slow and light, and so warm they made her body shiver.

She had to step back, push him away or she was lost.

Instead she tilted her head back to look at him, and her breath caught in her throat. Never had a man looked at her like that before.

Her heart drummed hard and loud, her chest was so tight it hurt. He held her in his gaze as he bent his head slowly towards her. The light dimmed, the room blurred and she only saw his eyes. They were dark, and as mysterious as the cedar forest. He hesitated a second or two, probably to give her the chance to step back. But she didn't want to step back. She wanted him to kiss her …

She shuddered when his lips touched hers. His hands slid to her waist, then down to her hips. His chest rubbed against her breasts. His scent made her dizzy. She wanted to get closer, she *had* to get closer. She arched against him, digging her nails into his shoulders, parting her lips.

He let out a soft growl, his hands cupped her hips and pulled her closer. This time when his mouth claimed hers, his kiss was deep and urgent. All she could hear was her own ragged breathing, the drumming of her heart, the rustling of their clothing as they moved against each other.

Her body sizzled, vibrant and alive in his arms. Her fingers clasped the back of his neck, tangled into his hair, traced feverish patterns on his back where she could feel the ripple of hard muscles under his shirt. More. She was burning for more. She'd never felt like that before.

As if he knew exactly what she yearned for, his hands glided along hers and he pulled up the hem of her dress. The contact of his fingers on her bare skin gave her a jolt of pleasure so sharp she cried out and gripped his shoulders tightly.

She wanted to touch him. Wanted him to touch her.

To take her. Here. Now.

She could forget the world, forget Claudine …

But – she forced her mind to work – this wasn't right. Fabien wasn't hers to touch, to kiss. However unpleasant she was, Claudine didn't deserve to be cheated on. Fabien was probably toying with her – and she was stupid enough to fall straight into his arms.

She put her hands flat on his chest and summoned what was left of her pride to push him away.

'What's the matter?'

'I think you'd better leave,' she said, breathless.

'Leave? Now?'

'Yes. I don't want … this. I don't want you.'

Anger flashed in his eyes.

'Is that right? You could have fooled me.'

She crossed her arms and took another step back. 'I want you to leave, and we'll pretend nothing happened.'

He frowned. 'Nothing bloody well *did* happen.'

'Please go now.'

Her heels clicked on the tiled floor as she almost ran to

the hall. She had to unlock the door, show him out, forget that moment of madness and the temptation she'd almost succumbed to. She managed to put the key into the lock but her hand shook too much to turn it.

'Let me do this.'

He reached from behind to slide the bolt open and she caught his scent again. For a second her desire came rushing back.

He pulled the door open, stepped out and turned to look at her. This time there was only puzzlement in his eyes. Raking his fingers into his dark hair, he let out a long breath.

'Listen, I'm sorry if I overstepped the mark. I would never have taken the liberty to … I mean I really thought you and I both wanted the same thing.'

'You were wrong, now please go,' she said, quickly pushing the door closed behind him.

She leaned against it, her heart pounding hard and blood roaring in her veins until she heard him start his car and drive away.

Her lips were still swollen from his kisses. She could still taste him, feel the heat of his hands on her body. She was seized with a longing so strong it took her breath away and she had to squeeze her eyes shut to fight back the tears.

An overwhelming feeling of shame washed over her. How pathetic to be attracted to a man like him – a man who had no qualms about cheating on his girlfriend, a man who probably collected one-night stands. No wonder he had tried to get her into bed. She had been so naive and transparent. She blushed, babbled and stammered like a teenage girl every time he was near. Tonight he only had to look at her for her to throw herself at him.

Chapter Ten

Mont Ventoux stood out, tall and proud against the cloudless blue sky, its limestone tip shinning like a snow cap in the bright sunshine. Amy walked briskly along the main road, one hand curled around Michka's lead, her ponytail swinging from side to side. The cold wind that whipped her cheeks helped clear the unpleasant memory of her heated confrontation with Fabien the previous evening.

It got busy as she approached Bonnieux, with cars parked on either side of the road, people chatting and laughing excitedly as they brought branches of olive tree and made their way into the centre of the village. She walked down to the church at the bottom of the village, where she had arranged to meet Adèle and where the procession would start before making its way up to the medieval chapel at the top of the hill.

'Amy!'

Adèle waved. Next to her stood Lily, dressed in black, her face serious as usual. Not for the first time Amy wondered if the elderly French lady ever smiled. She'd never met anyone more solemn. The two women were alone. Paul was nowhere to be seen.

'He couldn't get up this morning, I'm afraid. Too much wine and liqueur.'

Adèle sighed, then looked at Amy. 'You look tired. What's up?'

'Nothing,' Amy lied. 'I stayed up late.'

Church bells rang, loud, fast and melodic in the clear blue morning and the crowd hushed. The church's wooden doors opened. A priest dressed in a red and gold cassock over a white alb and holding a golden cross came out, followed by a dozen altar boys. He said a few words in Latin and the procession started up the street.

Adèle and Amy linked arms with Lily and followed at a slow pace. By the time they reached the top of the hill, the service had started. The old chapel was full, so they sat on a bench in the shade of a lime tree and listened to the singing drifting through the open doors.

After the service, the priest came out on to the square, followed by Fabien and an attractive blonde woman who clung to his arm.

'That's Fabien's mother, Céline,' Adèle said. 'We don't often see her around here. She lives in Paris.'

'Fabien said that his mother didn't like Bonnieux.'

'That's right, which isn't surprising really, since her husband was killed in the forest only a few weeks before Fabien was born.'

'What happened to him?'

'He was shot during the hunt. It was a terrible accident and Céline couldn't bear to stay at Manoir Coste after that. She gave birth to Fabien here but brought him up in Paris.'

'Who looked after Manoir Coste?'

'Frédéric's father. Although it's fair to say that he didn't look after the estate so much as ruin it. The man was a notorious gambler. When Fabien took over the family affairs ten years ago, he discovered that the family fortune was almost gone. That's when he decided to turn the chateau into a hotel. The easy way out would have been to sell up what was left and return to Paris – that's what people around here expected him to do – but he worked hard and made a success of it.'

So Fabien wasn't an idle, privileged aristocrat; Amy had got that wrong.

Lily pointed to Fabien's mother.

'She doesn't want him to stay here. She knows that Coste men die young. It's the curse, the goddess punishing the Ducs de Coste for destroying her temple and leaving it to rot in the forest.'

The old woman's words made Amy shiver in spite of the bright sunshine and the festive atmosphere in the church square. She looked at Fabien as he bent down to talk to his mother. He must have felt her eyes on him because he swung round and stared at her. The smile died on his face, and he gave her a sharp nod.

Adèle frowned and shot her a puzzled glance.

'Oh dear, he looks grumpy this morning. I wonder why.'

'How should I know?'

Amy feigned indifference but the night had done nothing to dispel the raw yearning that his touch and his kisses had awakened inside her, and her humiliation at being used to satisfy a passing fancy.

Frédéric came to stand near Fabien and his mother in front of the church.

'They are so much alike,' she remarked to divert Adèle's attention. 'They are cousins, but they look more like brothers.'

'Which is surprising given the fact that they are only distant cousins,' Lily muttered. 'He's a bad seed, that Frédéric, just like his father, and his grandfather before him.'

They followed the crowd down to the market square where smells of freshly baked bread, coffee and chicken roasting in *rôtissoires* outside the butcher's shop drifted. Together they strolled around the market square, and sampled fragrant olives, slices of garlic sausage and dry, hard goat's cheese. The gentle peeling of wind chimes attracted Amy to a stall selling jewellery, tie-dye clothing and crystals. On an impulse she walked over to the middle-aged stallholder and asked if she knew anything about fluorite crystals.

'Fluorites? They're unusual these days, especially the white and purple ones,' the woman said. 'People prefer green fluorites which promote calm and harmony, whereas white and purple stones are said to unleash dark forces and induce prophetic dreams.'

Her fingers toyed with the rows of coloured beads hanging around her neck.

'Which is why in many ancient religions, high priests and priestesses used them to get in touch with their gods.'

She leaned closer and winked.

'I've read that it works wonders for your libido if you put it under your pillow.'

Amy thanked her and walked away, thoughtful.

'I didn't know you cared about crystals,' Adèle remarked.

She shrugged. 'I don't.'

Nevertheless, she couldn't help finding it unsettling that Eva had suffered so many nightmares after being given a fluorite crystal. Were the lights, the evil and the blood the young woman dreamt about really linked to Bellefontaine? And did her own nightmare have anything to do with Serena Chevalier's housewarming present? She had heard from Eva that she hadn't had any more bad dreams since returning home from Bellefontaine.

No, this was impossible. Crystals didn't hold any magic power!

She said goodbye to Adèle and Lily and started on the walk back home.

The woman's voice on the answerphone was hesitant.

'This is a message for Mademoiselle Carter. My name is Sophie Dessange. I really need to speak to you. I'll phone again later.'

Amy played the message again. The woman hadn't left her number or a reason for her call, so she would have to wait for her to phone back to find out what she wanted. There were other messages too, enquiries about vacancies for the Easter holiday. One couple, the Ducros, wanted a double room for five nights and a Monsieur Garnier from Paris booked a single for Saturday night.

Feeling considerably more cheerful, she wrote their names down in her reservation book. Things were looking up at last! She had forgotten all about the other message when the phone rang.

'Is this Mademoiselle Carter? My name is Sophie Dessange. I called earlier. I wanted to talk to you about an article I read about Bellefontaine recently, and about you sleepwalking in the forest.'

Amy's fingers gripped the phone more tightly.

'I am sorry but I really don't want to talk about it. If that was all you wanted, I'm afraid I'll have to—'

'No, please don't hang up,' the woman cried out. 'You don't understand. You see, the same thing happened to me at Bellefontaine, years ago.'

Amy drew in a breath. 'You stayed at Bellefontaine? When was that?'

'Over twenty years ago, but I would prefer to talk to you face to face about it. Could we meet? I live in Avignon.'

'Can you not tell me on the phone? Or maybe you could come here.'

The woman gasped. 'Oh no, I couldn't possibly come back to Bellefontaine. It's difficult enough for me to talk about it. Please.'

Amy hesitated. 'Listen, if it's about these old stories about the temple in the forest, I really don't think—'

'There are things you need to know,' the woman interrupted in a more forceful voice. 'Believe me, I wouldn't ask to meet you if it wasn't important.'

Amy thought carefully, then sighed. 'Very well. Where we can meet?'

Sophie Dessange suggested the garden of the Palais des Papes on Tuesday morning.

'It will be quiet,' she said. 'The Palais is closed on Tuesdays.'

Amy put the phone down, uneasy. Was it wise to drive all the way to Avignon to meet a woman who claimed she'd been sleepwalking in the cedar forest and had important information? Sophie Dessange might be deluded, or deranged. It was an odd coincidence, after all.

After lunch she sat in the study to sort out her mail. Buried under a pile of papers was an invitation to a cocktail party she'd forgotten about. It was organised by the local Chamber of Commerce and would take place at Manoir Coste the following Saturday evening.

She stared at the elegant golden lettering. She dreaded seeing Fabien again. Talking to him, or just being in the same room as him, would be torture. On the other hand she had a business to think about, and Bellefontaine had to come before her bruised ego and immature crush on her wealthy, handsome neighbour. Furthermore, there would be lots of people at the cocktail party and she may not even have to talk to him at all. She typed an email accepting the invitation and sent it before she had time to change her mind.

Later in the afternoon, she took Michka out for a walk along the main road, which overlooked the plain. In the distance was a group of riders. She could just about make out a dark-haired man riding a huge black horse in the lead. Fabien and Pacha. He was probably exercising the horses for the hunt the following week. She was almost glad to be reminded of yet another side of him she didn't like. Together with his arrogance, his love of hunting and his womanising, there was really little to like about the man. No, she corrected. There was *nothing* to like about Fabien Coste, and she would do well to remember it the next time she met him.

Chapter Eleven

A flight of stairs next to the Palais des Papes led to a secluded garden overlooking the river Rhône and the Pont Benezet, the original Pont d'Avignon. Annoyingly, the tune of the nursery rhyme crept into Amy's mind as she made her way along the gardens' empty lanes and sat on a bench to wait for Sophie Dessange. She didn't have long to wait.

'Mademoiselle Carter? I'm Sophie.'

A brown-haired woman, smartly dressed in a blue linen trouser suit and white shirt, stood in front of her.

Amy smiled and stood up.

'Shall we walk?' Sophie suggested.

They strolled in silence for a moment.

'I wasn't sure you'd come ... Are you happy at Bellefontaine?' Sophie asked.

Amy nodded. 'I am. Bellefontaine is a wonderful old house. It's a new start for me ... a new life. You said that you'd been there. When was that?'

Sophie leaned against the stone wall and gazed at the fast flowing waters of the Rhône.

'It was in 1983. I was a student teacher here in Avignon, and decided to travel to the seaside during the Easter holidays. I went to Cannes, Nice and Hyères, and ended up in Marseille where I met an English boy. He was called Mike and was on the last leg of a journey around Europe. He was kind, funny ... and gorgeous.' She paused and turned to Amy.

'We decided to hitchhike our way back to Avignon and stopped in Bonnieux one night. It was warm, so we thought it would be fun to sleep under the stars. We found an empty farmhouse – Bellefontaine – made a fire, had a few beers and something to eat, then we fell asleep.'

Sophie's face crumpled, her voice shook.

'I had the most horrid nightmare that night. I was in some kind of cave, or a temple. People wearing masks and long white robes surrounded me. They seemed to be performing a ceremony. They were … doing things to me. I couldn't fight them off. I couldn't move, I couldn't even scream.'

Amy gasped, and her fingers gripped the rough edges of the stone wall. It sounded disturbingly like her dream. How could two people have the same dream, over thirty years apart?

'Before I lost consciousness completely, I heard the most terrifying scream. It was Mike, I'm sure of it. When I woke up in the early hours of the morning, I was alone in the forest. My clothes were torn, I was bleeding and in pain. I managed to find my way back to the garden of the old house. Mike had left, all his things had gone. I knew straight away that something dreadful had happened, so I changed into clean clothes and walked to the gendarmerie in Bonnieux.'

She paused, took a deep breath.

'The gendarmes listened to my story, but I knew they didn't believe me. One gendarme even said that we'd been drinking or taking drugs, and implied I was … easy, since I was travelling and sleeping with a boy I knew nothing about.'

She bent her head.

'It was true, the only thing I knew about Mike was his surname. I didn't even know where he was from in England, or if he had any family. We were in love, and it hadn't seemed important at the time. One of the gendarmes made fun of me, and said I'd better leave before he charged me for trespassing on private property and wasting police time.'

Her eyes shone with tears and anger.

'I'll never forget his name. Bijard.'

Amy remembered the stocky, grey-haired gendarme who had come to Bellefontaine the morning of the garden party. He hadn't been particularly sympathetic to her either.

'He still works in Bonnieux,' she said. 'I met him just a few weeks ago.'

'He said that Bellefontaine's landlady had died recently and that nobody lived there any more. He told me to go home and forget about the whole thing. Mike had left me and moved on, that was all. He more or less bundled me in a police van and drove me to the train station.'

She looked at Amy and her face was hard.

'I was young, scared and alone. I was hurt. I did what he said and I will forever regret it. I was raped that night. And that scream I heard ... I know it was Mike, and that he was murdered.'

Amy was chilled to the core. 'Did you tell anybody else about this?'

Sophie shook her head. 'What was the point if the police didn't believe me? I couldn't talk to my parents, I was too ashamed. After a while, it seemed as if it had just been a dream, I convinced myself that Mike had really left me behind.'

She looked at Amy.

'Now would you mind telling me what happened to you? The reporter mentioned that you were sleepwalking and woke up in the forest.'

However reluctant she was about talking about her own experience, Amy felt she owed the woman the truth, so she told her about the long corridor, the room lit by torches, the stone table in the middle of the geometric figure of a triangle painted white on the ground. It seemed that the more she talked, the more she remembered.

'There was music, ancient music,' she said, 'lute, zithers and drums. One of the masked men undressed me and … touched me. Thankfully it didn't go any further. I hope.'

She would have known if like Sophie she'd been sexually assaulted. Wouldn't she?

'Then you were lucky,' Sophie said. 'Now I've told you about me, are you going to report what happened to you to the gendarmes? They're bound to reopen the case of Mike's disappearance.'

Amy put her hand to her forehead, took a deep breath.

'I'm sorry for what happened to you and your friend, but I'm not ready to believe that anything actually took place the other night. As far as I'm concerned, I had a nightmare, a very vivid and unpleasant nightmare and nothing more.'

She saw the hurt and disappointment in Sophie's eyes.

'I understand,' Sophie said in a soft voice. 'It's a lot for you to take in, but maybe one day you'll remember more and—'

Amy let out an impatient breath. 'To tell you the truth, what I really want is to forget about the whole thing.'

Suddenly in a hurry to be back at Bellefontaine, far away from Sophie and her bizarre story, she opened her handbag and dug out her car keys. The similarities between Sophie's experience and her own nightmare were troubling, but for all she knew, the woman could have made the whole thing up after reading Armelle Capitelli's article, and Mike never even existed.

Sophie nodded. 'Of course. Well, thank you for coming and for listening to me.'

The two women agreed to keep in touch, but deep down Amy hoped that she'd never hear from Sophie Dessange ever again.

She grew increasingly uneasy on her way back to

Bellefontaine. Was her home the safe haven she loved or did it hide a dark and sinister secret?

It was just after seven in the morning but already over a hundred people had gathered in the grounds of Manoir Coste to watch riders and hounds depart for the last hunt of the season.

The dogs could be heard yelping and barking from the kennels. On the lawn long tables held urns, stacks of cups, and plates with cakes and sandwiches. Hotel staff in smart navy and white livery served coffee laced with brandy, tea with lemon and rum, or mulled wine to the hunters and to the crowd of onlookers and villagers.

The morning was cool and crisp. The rising sun bathed the chateau in a hazy, golden light that softened its lines and gave it a dreamlike quality. Amy stood apart from the crowd, a cup of tea in her hand, but she kept checking her watch, and wondering when she would be able to make her escape.

'You don't look as if you want to be here, my dear,' a man said behind her.

Amy turned round to face Monsieur Verdier and his wife, both holding plates piled high with cakes and sandwiches.

She smiled. 'You're right. I'd much rather be at home.'

The couple staying at Bellefontaine had been desperate to attend the hunt that morning but their car wouldn't start, so they asked Amy to drive them to Manoir Coste. The Ducros had now disappeared into the crowd and she was waiting for them.

'You are not planning a grand gesture of protest, are you?' Monsieur Verdier asked. 'Something like throwing yourself under Monsieur le Duc's horse, or waving anti-hunting banners?'

Amy shook her head. 'No, don't worry. I shall keep my opinions about hunting to myself.'

'Good ... Actually, I'm glad I bumped into you.' Monsieur Verdier was serious now. 'We've had a few computer problems at the Tourist Office and I noticed yesterday that Bellefontaine's details had been erased from our database. We have sorted it out now of course but it might have cost you a few bookings. I don't understand what happened and I do apologise. The database is Jacques' responsibility and he has promised to be more vigilant from now on.'

Amy almost replied that mishaps would be unavoidable with lazy Jacques in charge.

'Look! The scouts are back.' Madame Verdier pointed to a couple of men striding out of the forest with dogs on a lead. 'It's time for the hunt report.'

Fabien walked out of the chateau and on to the terrace. Imposing in his black riding jacket, cream breeches and leather boots, he spoke to the scouts before shaking hands with both of them.

'Good morning all.'

His deep voice could be heard across the lawn.

'We're riding towards Lacoste where the dogs picked up the scent of a boar. The riders are setting off in a few minutes, but everyone please feel free to stay and enjoy the refreshments provided.'

He surveyed the crowd, and his eyes became fixed on Amy. Heat spread across her face. Her body tensed. Her chest hurt. Once again, the strength of her response to the man took her by surprise.

'I'll try and find my guests now,' she told the Verdiers, now in even more of a hurry to leave.

'Wait, my dear. Monsieur Coste is coming this way,'

Madame Verdier said. 'I think he wants to speak to us – to you.'

Amy's heart fluttered in panic as Fabien strode across the lawn towards her. She didn't want to talk to him, or even to be anywhere near him.

He was soon by her side and exchanged a few words with the Verdiers before turning to her.

'I didn't expect to see you here.'

She explained once again about the Ducros' car failing to start.

Looking preoccupied, he asked if he could speak to her alone.

'This way.' He took hold of her elbow and led her towards the old fountain.

'Is everything all right at Bellefontaine?' he asked. 'You haven't had any more incidents?'

She shook her head. 'No. Everything is fine.'

'Good. You will let me know, won't you, if there is anything worrying you?' He put a hand on her shoulder, and bent down slowly towards her.

She stiffened, held her breath. Surely he wasn't going to kiss her now, in front of the whole village?

'Fabien *chéri*, are you ready? Everybody's waiting for you.' Claudine's sharp voice startled them both.

Amy stepped back. Claudine didn't acknowledge her but tapped the lash of her whip to the side of her black leather boots. Tall and slim in her riding outfit she looked the perfect match for Fabien – the perfect new duchess.

Fabien let out a sigh. 'I'm coming.'

He looked down. The light of the rising sun played on his face and made his green eyes seem deep and warm. Time slowed. The noise from the crowd became muffled and distant, and all she could hear was the crystalline spring water trickling in the old fountain. The spring that ran through the forest between Manoir Coste and Bellefontaine and bound hearts and lives together, or so the spell said … Her heartbeat slowed, or maybe it stopped altogether. It was as if Fabien and she were alone. Desire, fear and another feeling she didn't recognise overwhelmed her and made her dizzy.

'Well then, goodbye,' he said in a low voice.

And he was gone, striding alongside Claudine to the stable lads who held the horses. Most hunters already sat in the saddle. Dog handlers brought the hounds over from the kennels and took their place at the front of the hunting party. Fabien and Claudine mounted their horses and the hunt lined up behind them. A man blew into a horn, Fabien raised his arm in the air, pointed towards the forest and said something she didn't hear.

'*Bonne chasse*, Monsieur le Duc!'

People all around shouted their good wishes for the hunt. It was a scene from bygone days. The lord of the manor leading his men through the forest and despite herself she felt a stir as the riders disappeared into the forest in a thunder of hooves.

Suddenly all she wanted was solitude, quiet and peace of mind. Or rather peace of heart, if there was such a thing. The realisation of what she felt for Fabien hit her. It wasn't a crush, not even a strong physical attraction. It was a million times more potent, overwhelming and devastating. She was in love with him.

She closed her eyes for a moment, but all she could see was Fabien. She could almost breathe in his scent, feel the heat of his touch, the strength of his body against hers.

Her eyes flew open. This was all wrong. How could she be in love with him when there were so many things she disliked about him? Nothing good could ever come out of it. She had to fight it. She would fight it. And anyway, it wasn't love she felt for him. It couldn't be. It was infatuation. Chris was right. She was an old maid indeed – an old maid who'd been lonely for so long she was prepared to throw herself at the first attractive man who'd shown her a crumb of interest – and believe herself in love.

She sighed and turned to look at the fountain. For the first time she noticed something peculiar about the lion heads. They were in fact half man, half lion, and that each looked in a different direction. The portico above the basin displayed carvings of Latin words and Roman numerals. Remembering the Latin inscriptions on Bellefontaine's stones, she took a piece of paper and a pen from her handbag and scribbled the words down.

Ibant obscuri

Geminae sorores ... The rest was too worn to be decipherable.

Pervigilo templum subterras

Oblivione obruere

She walked around the fountain and bent down to examine the carvings on the lower part of the basin. Although very chipped, they featured soldiers kneeling down with their hands tied behind their back, several of them missing their heads.

She took a few pictures with her mobile phone.

'Are you interested in our fountain, mademoiselle?'

She looked up. Céline Coste stood in front of her, elegant in tan corduroy trousers, a silk blouse and a cream cardigan. Her blonde hair was held in a ponytail by a Hermès scarf.

'Yes, indeed. I find it fascinating,' she answered, rising to her feet. 'Do you know how old it is, or what the inscriptions mean?'

Céline Coste shook her head. 'I don't, but there are plenty of records in the library that could give you an answer. My father-in-law, Philippe, developed an obsession with local fountains and gathered an impressive collection of sketches and documents – an obsession I am afraid to say both my late husband and my son seem to share.'

She smiled and extended her hand. 'I'm Céline, by the way. And you are Amy Carter, Bellefontaine's new lady. I heard about you.'

Amy's face heated up. 'If you are referring to the incident in the forest, I can assure you that I never intended to disrupt the hunt.'

Céline laughed but her eyes were hard.

'My dear, you can disrupt the hunt any time you want. If I were in charge, I would get rid of that hateful tradition and ban hunting, here at Manoir Coste and everywhere else.'

Of course, Amy remembered. She must be thinking about her late husband's hunting accident.

'Would you like to come to the library with me and have a look at Philippe's portfolio?' Céline asked. 'We could have coffee and a chat. It's not every day I get to meet one of Fabien's friends.'

'I'm not exactly a friend,' Amy protested, 'although Fabien has been very … kind to me since I moved in.

He even gave me one of his puppies.'

Céline raised her eyebrows. 'Then he must consider you a friend indeed. His hunting dogs are his pride and joy.'

The two women walked towards the chateau. People milled around, drinking and eating, but the Ducros were nowhere to be seen. They must have made their own way back to Bellefontaine.

Manoir Coste's library had shelves stacked up with

books all the way up to the ceiling, and a table at the centre disappeared under books, papers and an artist's portfolio.

'Fabien seems to be spending a lot of time in here at the moment.' Céline sighed. 'He had become so protective of these old papers he even forbade me to step into this room.'

She opened the portfolio and flicked through pencil and charcoal drawings of the Coste fountain. 'These were Philippe's sketches. As you can see, he was a good artist.'

There were over twenty drawings, most of them of fountains in villages around Bonnieux. The name of each place and the dates were carefully recorded.

The last drawing was different, since it was the charcoal portrait of a woman. Amy bent down to look at it more closely, and the woman appeared to stare straight back at her with dark, almond-shaped eyes. Her nose was straight, her cheekbones sharp and prominent, and her full lips slightly parted as if waiting to be kissed. Her curly black hair was loose and brushed her naked shoulders, and around her neck a black ribbon slithered like a snake. It looked like the same necklace Serena Chevalier wore ...

'Who is she? She's beautiful.'

'Rosalie Bruni,' Céline Coste answered. 'One of the infamous ladies of Bellefontaine. She and Philippe are said to have had a torrid affair that carried on even when he was married. Then he became obsessed with finding the temple, the fountain and the treasure, and died in a terrible accident shortly before his son Armand – my husband – was born.'

Amy could well believe that a man would go wild for a woman like Rosalie Bruni. She seemed so confident, brazen and sexual. Yet she had never married. She never had children, except for her unofficial adopted daughter Serena, much later in life. Maybe she had loved Philippe Coste so much that she could not form any other attachment after his death.

'Would you like to borrow the portfolio for a few days?' Céline suggested. 'Fabien won't mind.'

Amy hesitated. 'Are you sure? You said he was protective of his family papers.'

Céline gathered all the drawings in the portfolio and tied it with a leather bind.

'To tell you the truth, I don't want him spending any more time thinking about ancient temples and Roman fountains. Philippe's obsession cost him his life. My husband was about to resume the search when he was killed.'

She looked up and there were tears in her eyes.

'You may find me silly, but some old women in the village have talked of a curse and I have come to agree with them. I want to keep my son safe – and keep him away from this family fixation for that goddess and her temple.'

She handed the portfolio to Amy. 'I want you to have it. Don't worry about Fabien. I'll tell him that I was the one who gave you the papers.'

She smiled, as if a weight had been lifted off her shoulders.

'What about that hot drink? I'm sure you've had enough of this dusty old library.'

'Thank you but I must go back to Bellefontaine,' Amy said. 'I'll look through the portfolio and bring it back tomorrow ...'

'Keep it as long as you want,' Céline insisted.

Back at Bellefontaine, Amy found the Ducros enjoying a rest in the sunshine after walking through the forest from Manoir Coste. Monsieur Ducros said that the village mechanic had towed their car back to the garage and that it wouldn't be ready before the following Tuesday at the earliest, so Amy offered to drive the couple to Cavaillon so that they could hire a car for the weekend.

She made a potato gratin, mixed a vinaigrette and tossed some green lettuce in a salad bowl, then checked her emails while the gratin baked in the oven. It was good news. Now the computer glitch had been fixed, the Tourist Office had taken over a dozen bookings for Bellefontaine in the coming weeks.

Next she sent an email to Laurent about the Coste fountain, attaching the photos of the carvings and the Latin inscription, and mentioned that Philippe Coste's portfolio was now in her possession. Hopefully, this would entice him back.

After lunch, Amy drove the Ducros to Cavaillon. It was mid-afternoon by the time she came back to find Stéphane sitting in the courtyard alone. He seemed upset.

'You're a nice surprise,' she said as she unlocked the front door. 'Come in. I'll get us something to eat.'

She made a pot of tea, took some chocolate cake out of the fridge, and brought a tray outside on the terrace. While he ate she talked about the dig at the bottom of the garden, about Michka and the hunt. The boy was clearly worried about something, but there was no point rushing him.

'It's my dad,' Stéphane said at last. 'He's acting weird at the moment ... and he's drinking too much. Mum is trying to hide it from me, but I'm not a kid any more and I can see there's something wrong. He keeps talking about sending me away to some boarding school too, but I don't want to go. Would you have a word with him, please, Amy? Every time I try to tell him I don't want to go he gets mad at me.'

'Me? I'm afraid your parents' decision regarding your education is nothing to do with me.'

Stéphane looked so dejected, she sighed. 'But I can try to talk to him …'

She couldn't understand why Stéphane seemed so frightened of his father. Even if Paul was a little tense lately, she'd never seen him bad-tempered with his only son.

'Would you? Please.'

So Amy took Stéphane home. A red-faced Paul opened the door. His shirt was partly unbuttoned, his hair stuck up, as if he'd just woken up. He seemed reluctant to open his front door, and when he finally let them in, Amy understood why.

An empty bottle of whisky stood on the coffee table, next to a tumbler filled to the brim.

'So what's it about?' Paul asked, slurring his words.

She told him about Stéphane being upset at the idea of boarding school, and that it would be hard for him to leave his school in the middle of the academic year and start somewhere new where he didn't know anybody …

Paul's face twisted in anger. 'What has this got to do with you?'

Amy sighed. 'Nothing, I know, but I hate to see Stéphane so upset.'

'Well, mind your own business.' Paul took his jacket and his car keys. 'I'm going out,' he announced.

Amy shook her head. 'Surely you're not thinking about driving, are you?'

'Why shouldn't I?'

'You've had far too much to drink.'

'Once again, Amy, do me a favour and mind your own business.'

He slipped his jacket on and walked out.

'It's all my fault,' Stéphane said in a small, shaky voice. 'Dad hates me.'

'Of course he doesn't.'

She gave him a hug, and said she'd stay until his mother came home.

When Adèle returned, she told her about her argument with Paul.

'Actually, there is something else.' She hesitated. 'I don't quite know how to say this, but he had an awful lot to drink before he left.'

Adèle buried her face into her hands and started crying.

'He is angry with everybody these days. I don't know what's wrong with him. He says he has money worries, but I've never seen him like this.'

Amy stayed with her friend most of the afternoon, but eventually she had to return home to serve the Ducros' evening meal.

'Give me a ring, or better still, come round tomorrow,' she told Adèle before leaving,

She made a tomato and basil soup and defrosted several home-made bread rolls. Tonight, however, she felt tense and jumpy after her argument with Paul, and cooking did not calm her nerves.

She cast a glance at the window. It was still daylight.

A walk would soothe her, she decided. She called Michka, clipped the lead on, and walked across the garden and into the forest. Once on the path she gave the lead some slack. The dog raced ahead and they were soon deep amongst the cedar trees. The forest was empty, and eerily quiet. Suddenly the dog froze, its nose in the air, its ears pulled right back. It gave a low growl that gave Amy goosebumps.

'Come back.'

She pulled on the lead. The dog growled again, its small body tense and shaking.

Two men, both wearing dark clothing, were walking

at a fast pace towards her, waving their arms as if they were arguing. Her chest tightened with apprehension. She stepped closer to Michka, ready to scoop her into her arms, when she realised one of the men seemed familiar. She let out a sigh of relief.

'Paul? What are you doing here?'

'I could ask you the same thing,' he said, a startled look on his face.

His companion lifted the rim of his black hat, and Amy recognised Marc Chevalier.

'Mademoiselle Carter, it's not a good idea to wander into the forest on your own. Shall we put you back on the right track?'

His lips stretched into a thin smile. It must have been the dimming light and the shadows that surrounding trees cast on his face, but there was an almost sinister look in his eyes.

'Thank you, but I can manage,' she said, taking a step back.

'Hurry, Amy, it'll be dark soon,' Paul said, casting a worried glance towards Marc Chevalier. He didn't seem drunk or angry any longer, she thought, but afraid.

She nodded, called the puppy and turned back on the path, but for a long time her neck prickled and an uneasy sensation burnt her back, as if the two men were watching her.

Chapter Twelve

Amy squeezed the Clio between a rusty white van and an ancient-looking 2CV on Buoux's village square. She still hadn't got round to getting the bonnet re-sprayed, and the splodges of garish red paint often attracted comments and stares. Today, however, the landscape in front of her was so magnificent she didn't care if passers-by remarked on her car's scruffy bodywork.

The Saint-Symphorien bell tower rose majestic above the village, its stonework golden against the dark green hills. In the background the white cliffs, which attracted rock climbers from all over the world, gleamed in the sunshine.

She scanned the village's red-tiled roofs and pretty houses, and focused on the fountain that stood across the square. It looked exactly as Philippe Coste had drawn it, over seventy years before, with a plain stone pillar and a cast iron pipe spurting water into a rectangular basin.

The inscription above the pipe made her smile. '*Abreuvoir, défense de se laver dans la fontaine*'.

As if anyone would want to wash in such a small basin and in full view of villagers! Then she noticed the date carved in the middle of the pillar '*1835*'. Bending down, she saw the words carved at the side.

Pulchra fons

Terracula pervigil

They sounded Latin. On the side of the basin was another, smaller carving – this time a Greek word Ρσκλίσίᾱ in the centre of a crown of oak leaves.

She read the Latin words aloud. In Latin, *fons* meant spring or fountain, but she couldn't make sense of the rest.

She wrote them down anyway and took several photos. The late morning sun began to burn her neck and face and the sound of fresh water trickling into the fountain made her thirsty, so she decided to have a drink at the little café on the square.

An old man came to take her order as soon as she sat down at the zinc table. She ordered a *diabolo menthe* –mint cordial and lemonade – pulled her guidebook out of her bag and flicked through the pages to find the entry on Buoux.

Like many hilltop villages, Buoux, she read, was built on a prehistoric settlement. The area had been taken over by Gauls before being conquered by the Romans some time during the second century BC. Laurent's assistant Patricia had said that the original Gallic tribes in Provence were the Salyens who had established strongholds in the region, the most notable places being Entremont and Glanum.

The guide gave a brief outline of the tribes' belief in earth mothers and sacred springs, in their cult of the dead and predilection for human and animal sacrifices. The Salyens believed that severing and preserving the heads of defeated enemies or tribal heroes would make them invincible and give them special powers.

The author mentioned Glanum's miraculous spring and the deities worshiped there – among these was the 'Good Goddess' who the Romans later adopted under the name of 'Bona Dea'. This was exactly what Laurent, Ben and Patricia had talked about.

Bona Dea, Amy whispered, *here we are again*. La Bonne Dame. How strange she should have such a benevolent name when the belief system was quite the opposite, with human sacrifices and severed heads. She remembered the empty glare of the Bellefontaine statue and wondered how many sacrifices she had witnessed in her now lost temple.

The elderly man brought Amy a tall glass filled with the sparkly, bright green drink.

'These guidebooks are all the same,' he grumbled, after peeping at the book over her shoulder. 'It's all about Glanum and Entremont, but what about Buoux, or Bonnieux? I could tell you a thing or two about this area and where to find traces of the old people.'

'Do you mean the Gauls – the Salyens?'

He nodded. 'They left traces all around us, you know – underground, in the hills and the caves.'

She frowned. 'Underground?'

'*Mais oui,* mademoiselle. Many hills around here are riddled with tunnels and caves, even if most of them have now collapsed.'

Amy felt uneasy. Every time someone mentioned tunnels or underground chambers, the memory of her dream and of Sophie Dessange's story came flooding back.

'What do you think about the claim that some people around here still worship the old gods?'

The man snorted. 'Are you talking about *La Bonne Dame* and what's been going on in Bonnieux's forest by any chance?'

She nodded.

He squinted at her, examining her face. 'You're not a journalist, are you?'

'Oh no. Not at all! I've just bought a house in Bonnieux and I heard a few scary stories about the forest. I was wondering if—'

'If *La Bonne Dame* would come and get you?' He smiled, uncovering a row of uneven and tobacco-stained teeth. 'Let me give you a few words of advice, young lady. Don't go wandering alone in the forest, especially not in the evenings, and if you ever see any lights, run in the opposite direction as fast as you can. Many young women got caught because they were in the wrong place, at the wrong time.'

'Caught? What do you mean by that?'

He laughed. 'Just do as I say, and you'll be all right.'

Sensing that he wasn't going to tell her anything else, she pointed at the fountain across the square.

'Do you know anything about the fountain?'

'Not much. It was rebuilt after the 1835 earthquake by a stonemason from Bonnieux. My grandmother used to say it was cursed because the man used parts of an ancient temple to build it. Didn't stop her from drawing water from it though, even though she used to cross herself before doing so.'

A woman's voice called from inside the café and the old man said he had to go. Amy sipped her drink. Now she understood why Philippe Coste had drawn the fountains from Buoux and nearby villages. They must all have been built from the temple in the forest. She would have to take a look at them all. Who knows, maybe she would be able to find clues to the location of the lost forest temple?

She finished her drink, slipped her book in her bag, and got back to the car. She had time to look at another fountain before going home.

The road to Saignon meandered through orchards, vineyards and fields of lavender. The village appeared at a turn of the road, perched on top of a cliff like an impregnable fortress.

The village was quiet, the only shops open that Easter weekend were an old-fashioned café, which doubled up as a Bureau de Tabac, and a bakery. Amy flicked through Philippe Coste's portfolio and selected a sketch of the fountain she was after. A smaller version of the one in Buoux, it featured a basin surmounted by a rectangular pillar, with water pouring out from a cast iron spout. Music playing on the radio drifted from the open doors of the café on the square, next to an elaborate fountain shaded by huge elm trees in the village square. This wasn't the one she was looking for.

Hesitant, she looked at the streets winding their way up to the top of the village, picked one at random, and climbed up the steep lane among stone houses covered with ivy, passiflora, or fragrant wisteria.

She found the fountain at the top of the village. There too, the date '1835' was carved on the pillar, together with a long inscription in Latin.

> *Templum sub terra habitare*
> *Margo Sub fons In Silva est*
> *Jubemus te salvere mater Gallia*

Underneath was the same oak leaf crown as in Buoux and the Greek Ροκλίσίᾱ.

She felt a rush of excitement as she wrote the words down. Wasn't the inscription about an underground temple near a fountain in the forest? She was sure *mater* meant mother, and *Gallia* meant earth. This must be a reference to an earth mother, a Gallic goddess.

So she had been right in thinking that the fountains had been rebuilt by the same stonemason, with parts of the lost temple in Bonnieux's cedar forest. She couldn't wait to share this latest information with Laurent Orsini.

She needed to get back to Bellefontaine. The reception at Manoir Coste was this evening, and she had some cleaning to do before her next guest arrived during the afternoon.

Back home she changed into a pair of faded jeans and an old cotton pink shirt, and tied her hair up with a scarf. She caught her reflection in the hall mirror and let out a bitter laugh.

She bet Claudine Loubier never wore scruffy old clothes, even when doing her cleaning. Come to think of it, Fabien's glamorous PR probably didn't do her own cleaning either.

When she had finished tidying up, Amy worked on her accounts for a while but her thoughts kept wandering back to the fountains and the Latin inscriptions. She opened her notebook and typed the words into an online translation site.

The inscription at Buoux translated roughly into 'Beautiful spring/fountain. Forever wakeful ghost.' The one at Saignon read, 'The temple remains underground. Its entrance lies near the fountain/spring in the forest. We salute you mother/goddess.'

She sent Laurent another email, asking him to research the possibility that both fountains had been rebuilt sometime after an earthquake in 1835. Maybe he could find out the name of the stonemason. Whoever he was, he'd had access to stones from the temple.

Her new guest, Monsieur Garnier, arrived in a navy BMW late in the afternoon. A tall, severe-looking man in a business suit, he carried a travel bag and a laptop case. He seemed disconcerted by Amy's clothing and she realised she still wearing her old jeans and faded shirt. He said he wouldn't require an evening meal because he was invited to a cocktail party.

'Are you going to the function at Manoir Coste by any chance?'

He nodded. 'That's right. A business event.'

'I am invited too. I'll drive if you want,' she offered.

They agreed to leave for the reception at eight. Amy took Michka for a walk, but was reluctant to venture into the forest and risk meeting Marc Chevalier again, so she stayed on the main road.

The sky was pink, with traces of fire where the sun set

behind the hills. It cast long shadows that slid like giant fingers towards her, as if to pull her into the forest. She knew she was being fanciful, influenced no doubt by the Latin references to ghosts and underground temples, and what the old man in the café had said, but tonight the forest looked darker, deeper and more mysterious than ever. She cut her walk short and turned back towards Bellefontaine.

She fed the dog, took a shower, and washed her hair before slipping into the same black jersey dress she had worn for the Hunt Ball. She tied her hair in a high ponytail, leaving a few locks of hair to fall onto her bare shoulders.

Monsieur Garnier came down at eight o'clock sharp and they set off for the short journey to Manoir Coste. He wasn't the talkative type – in fact he rebuffed all her attempts at making polite conversation, and Amy was relieved when she saw the entrance to the castle, lit once again by torches.

'I always find this place most impressive,' he remarked as they got out of the car.

'You've been before?'

He nodded silently and they gave their invitation cards to a receptionist in the lobby and proceeded towards the ballroom. They agreed to meet at ten and parted company.

Amy took a deep breath and made her way through the crowd towards a group of shop owners from Bonnieux she recognised from the garden party. Now wasn't the time to be shy. She had come here to talk to people, to network – as business people said. Even if she intensely disliked both the word and the idea, that's exactly what she would do.

'How nice to see you again,' a local businessman she had met at the Hunt Ball said. 'How are things shaping up for you at Bellefontaine?'

Amy answered that business was improving and that she was now taking a number of bookings.

'My season has been pretty slow so far,' a woman commented. She was an interior designer and owned a fabric shop in the village. 'I blame it on the property market, of course. Nobody can afford to buy a house around here any more.'

Turning to Amy, she added ruefully, 'You were lucky to snap up Bellefontaine last year – although some people might disagree with me.'

'What do you mean?'

The woman smiled. 'You must know by now that Bellefontaine always had something of a sinister reputation. The Bruni family were a strange lot. They didn't have many friends in the village. Mind you, they may not have had many friends, but their women weren't short of lovers.' She lowered her voice. 'Some of them from the very family who are hosting us this evening.'

'Leave it, Carla, Mademoiselle Carter can't possibly be interested in such old gossip,' the man objected before steering the conversation onto the benefits of advertising.

The woman glanced towards the door, put her hand on her heart and remarked in a dreamy voice, 'Look at them. Don't they make a lovely couple? I wonder when they'll announce their engagement. The man has kept poor Claudine waiting far too long already.'

Amy swung round in time to see Fabien walk into the ballroom with Claudine at his side. Once again she had to admit that they were indeed well suited. They were both tall, dark-haired, and glamorous – Fabien in a black dinner jacket and Claudine in a red silk dress that shimmered with her every step.

Claudine whispered something into Fabien's ear and he laughed wholeheartedly. A stab of jealousy pierced Amy, so painful she gasped. Muttering an apology, she turned round and walked away. She should pity Claudine, not envy her. Fabien was a philanderer, and no self-respecting woman would want such a man for boyfriend or husband. No self-respecting woman would feel that deep, overwhelming love she felt for him either ...

She picked a glass of orange juice and a couple of canapés from the buffet, though she wasn't hungry.

'Amy, over here,' Céline called and waved from across the room.

'At last, a friendly face,' Fabien's mother exclaimed, slipping her arm under hers. 'I hardly know anyone here tonight. Let's go out on to the terrace to look at the sunset. The sky is enchanting this evening.'

Outside, Amy put her glass of orange juice on a garden table and leaned against the stone balustrade to gaze at shadows that now shrouded the park and forest.

'The woods look so dark,' she remarked. 'I wouldn't like to walk back to Bellefontaine that way, especially at night.'

'In the old days, there would have been a quicker way to go back to your place,' Céline said, pointing to the ground under their feet.

'My husband told me his ancestors had dug tunnels in the hillside that they used as escape routes when under siege. He mentioned some very old plans which showed how tunnels linked Manoir Coste to Bellefontaine. No doubt they collapsed a long time ago.'

Once again Amy's throat tightened as she remembered her dream.

'Do you know where the plans are?'

'In the library probably, but you've seen the place, it would take days, or weeks, for me to find them. And I can't give you any more of our family papers after the way Fabien reacted when I told him you had Philippe's portfolio.'

149

She shook her head sadly.

'I've never seen him so angry. I fear he is getting as obsessed with the temple as his father and grandfather were, and that can't be a good thing.'

Amy stared at a couple making their way across the lawn towards one of the summer pavilions in the distance. The man was tall, dark-haired, and the woman blonde and very loud. His arm was wrapped around her waist yet she staggered, unsteady in her high-heeled shoes. As she kissed him, her shrill laughter reverberated into the night. Right into Amy's heart. Fabien had found another woman to make love to …

'Like father, like son,' Céline said, pursing her lips. 'I'm afraid Frédéric will never change, no matter how many chances Fabien gives him.'

The grip on Amy's chest relaxed as she realised her mistake. So it was Frédéric, and not Fabien, who was walking across the lawn. Once again she had to admit that from a distance the men looked identical.

'There you are, Maman, I've been looking all over for you.'

Fabien's voice behind her made Amy jump.

'Darling, you know I don't like crowds,' Céline answered with a smile. 'I'm much happier chatting to Amy out here.'

Fabien looked down at Amy and bowed his head in a formal greeting before turning to Céline again.

'You have a telephone call, in the study. A friend of yours from Paris, I believe.'

'Thank you, darling. Will you keep Amy company for me? I won't be long.'

Céline smiled and patted Fabien's arm.

'There's no need, really,' Amy protested after Céline disappeared into the Manoir. 'You must be busy, and I'm perfectly all right on my own.'

Fabien ignored her, and came to stand close by. The solid strength of his body formed a wall between her and the other guests on the terrace. It felt like they were alone in the darkening evening.

Sensations and feelings she couldn't ignore flooded her. Her face on fire, she folded her arms and took a step sideways.

'Are you cold? Maybe you would prefer to go inside.'

He looked at her bare arms and shoulders, his slow, insistent gaze almost a caress that made her breath hitch in her throat once again.

'No, I'm fine.'

'Listen, Amy, I wanted to talk to you about my grandfather's portfolio. I'm really not happy about you having it. My mother was wrong to give it to you. These are family papers and they belong here, with me.'

She looked up, meeting his stern gaze.

'Of course, I understand, but your mother practically begged me to take it home with me. She seemed dreadfully worried about ... I don't know what exactly – about you spending too much time searching for the temple and the fountain, I think.'

He stared into the distance, towards the shadowy edge of the forest.

'What she is really worried about is the infamous curse we Coste men are supposed to fall victim to.'

'The one Lily talked about the other night?'

'That's right. My mother fears I will end up like my father and grandfather, and all the other Costes who, like them, suffered a premature and violent death. She must have listened to too much of Lily's gossiping. She's starting to believe the goddess is punishing us for destroying her temple and not protecting what's left of it.

It's complete nonsense, of course.'

He turned to her and asked, 'What do you make of the portfolio? Do you have any idea why my grandfather drew fountains over and over again?'

'Well, I do actually. I drove to Saignon and Buoux to take a look at two of the fountains he sketched and discovered both had Latin and Greek inscriptions relating to the goddess and the temple. In fact,' she added, unable to hide the excitement in her voice, 'I believe both fountains were rebuilt with stones from the forest temple.

'There must be records in local libraries about the 1835 earthquake which destroyed the village fountains and the stonemason who was commissioned to rebuild them,' she carried on. 'I think we now need to find out when and why the temple was destroyed.'

'It was Renaud Coste who was responsible for the destruction of the temple and the fountain back in 1813,' Fabien said. 'I came across his diaries in the library a few days ago. He was a prolific chronicler and reading through his journals will take time – unless we join forces.'

Amy's heart beat faster.

'Shall we put our heads together and see if we can come up with something?' He leaned closer and gazed at her expectantly.

She swallowed. Spending time alone with him wasn't a good idea. She was all too aware of the strength of her feelings for him. Yet she wanted to read his ancestor's journals and find out more about that mysterious temple. She would be able to relay information to Laurent ... That, surely, was a sensible reason to agree.

'All right. I'll help you.' She paused. 'By the way, I would like to know more about these underground passages linking Manoir Coste and Bellefontaine your mother mentioned. Do you know where they are?'

This time he smiled.

'I wish I did … When I was a boy here on holiday, I made it my mission to explore the chateau's cellars and discover the secret tunnels, but I never found anything. The castle was altered over the centuries, and the entrance to the tunnels must have been blocked a long time ago.'

Frédéric's slurred voice behind them interrupted him.

'Here you are, cousin – or should I say, my lord and master …'

'Damn,' Fabien cursed under his breath.

Frédéric was holding a bottle of champagne. His bow tie was undone, his hair dishevelled, his face flushed.

'And here is our lovely Amy too, of course.'

Frédéric carried on in a loud voice as he raised his glass in her direction. 'You won't make any useful contacts hiding out here in the dark, Mademoiselle Carter, unless a grope from my wealthy cousin is the only contact you're after.'

Amy felt embarrassed, as people on the terrace stared.

Frédéric carried on, undaunted. 'Here's to you, your lordship.'

He lifted the bottle in a mock salute and drank a long gulp.

'Why don't you take Amy to your suite and put the girl out of her misery? It's obvious she's pining for you. Of course, she's not your usual type but somehow I don't think it'll stop you.'

'That's enough.' Fabien's cold voice cut through the night like a steel blade. 'You're drunk.'

'So what if I am? I fancy her too, you know.'

Frédéric raised his hand to touch Amy's bare shoulder. She stepped back with a startled cry. Fabien grabbed Frédéric's arm and pulled him away with such force the man staggered and bumped against a table.

'I said that's enough.'

The two men faced each other as if they were about to fight. Suddenly Frédéric laughed.

'All right, you can have her. For now. She is tasty, you'll enjoy her.'

'I'm warning you for the last time. Stop insulting my guest and making a fool of yourself.'

'Don't worry, I'm going. Any jobs you'd like me to do, sir? Scrub the kitchen floor, empty ashtrays ...'

'Just go, before I lose my temper.'

Fabien's face was set in stone, his eyes glittered in anger.

'All right, all right. I may be only a servant these days, but this was all mine once. Before you killed my dad.' Frédéric opened his arms as if to embrace the whole of the castle and the park. 'And it'll all be mine again one day.'

With this, he staggered away.

'Are you all right?'

Fabien put his hand lightly on Amy's shoulder and she shivered under his touch.

'I'm sorry about Frédéric's outburst. It was unforgivable of him to talk to you – about you – in such a way, but he is a very troubled man.'

He paused, took a deep breath. 'And somehow I am responsible.'

'Why do you say that? It's not your fault he had too much to drink,' Amy protested, but the incident had shaken her more than she'd realised.

'I'm afraid it is. You see, it was Frédéric's father, Henri, who was in charge here when I was growing up in Paris. Henri didn't do a very good job of managing the estate. Quite the opposite, in fact. He almost ruined us. I was so angry when I found out I sent him away and threatened to have him arrested if he ever showed his face around here ever again.'

He looked at Amy and there was sadness in his eyes.

'He got drunk and committed suicide two days later. So you see, Frédéric is right. It was my fault his father died, and the least I can do now is make amends by providing my cousin with a job and a home.'

He sighed.

'I'd better check that he's not creating any more havoc. Will you be all right on your own for a little while?'

'Of course. Don't worry about me.'

He gave her a tight smile and went after his cousin.

So she'd had the relationship between Fabien and Frédéric all wrong too ... She had been aware of the tension between them before, but had always felt sorry for Frédéric and annoyed at the way Fabien was treating him. Frédéric wasn't the fun and harmless character she once thought, and she would from now on do her very best to avoid him. The way he had talked about her, the way he'd looked at her and the touch of his sweaty palm on her skin had been revolting.

'Bonsoir, Mademoiselle Carter.'

Amy turned, startled. She hadn't heard Serena Chevalier approach.

Serena looked striking tonight again, her alabaster skin contrasting with her dark green dress and the plain black ribbon that curled around her neck, and that she had seen in Rosalie Bruni's portrait.

'I'd like to offer you some advice,' Serena carried on.

'Leave Bellefontaine. Now. Before things become unpleasant, or dangerous. You were never meant to live there. The place belongs to me.' Once again, she sounded breathless, as if even talking was too much of an effort. The woman really didn't look well.

'Are you threatening me, Madame Chevalier?'

Serena didn't answer but the hatred in her eyes made Amy's heart beat faster.

'You are wrong about Bellefontaine,' she said, trying to stop her voice shaking. There was no way she would show Serena how deeply her hostility affected her. 'It's mine now, and nothing you can do or say will change that.'

Aware of the woman's gaze following her every move, Amy took her glass from the table, stood as tall as she could, and walked towards the ballroom.

Pausing a moment at the doorway, she drained her orange juice and left the glass on a nearby table. As her eyes swept over the crowd, she spotted Monsieur Garnier talking to Claudine on the other side of the room. Loud dance music played through the speakers, the rhythm of drums and bass guitar echoed inside her body, beating in unison with her heart. Faster and faster, harder and harder. Her body felt warm, her skin clammy. Dizzy suddenly, she swayed and bumped into someone.

What was happening? She couldn't even walk straight any more.

The man turned, surprised.

'I'm sorry,' she said. 'I'm not feeling very well.'

He smiled. 'Enjoyed too much champagne, have you?'

What champagne? She'd only had orange juice. A waiter walked past her and she grabbed hold of his arm.

'Please, could you take me somewhere quiet? I fear I'm going to faint.'

'Of course, madame. We'll go to the drawing room. There's no one there.'

She was aware of people's eyes staring at her as the waiter helped her across the room, but their faces and the room soon became a blur.

Claudine laughed as she walked past her and Monsieur Garnier.

'It looks like your landlady is a little bit worse for wear. I don't think she'll be able to give you a lift back to Bellefontaine tonight.'

Amy held onto the waiter's arm more tightly. Everybody thought she was drunk. She didn't care. She was too busy trying to reach the drawing room before passing out. Thankfully the small drawing room was empty. The waiter helped her sit down on a sofa, stuck a couple of cushions behind her head.

'Would you like a glass of water, madame?' he asked.

'Please.'

The room spun so badly she had to close her eyes. She must have fainted for a few moments. The next thing she knew she heard the faint tapping of footsteps on the parquet flooring, and felt the weight of someone sitting on the sofa next to her.

The waiter must be back with her water.

'Good evening, my lovely.'

Even though it was only a raspy whisper, Amy could make out it was a man's voice. Who was this? She tried to open her eyes, but her eyelids felt too heavy.

'Do you remember me? Do you remember when I touched you here ... and here?'

A hand tickled the side of her throat, slid down onto her breast. In a panic, Amy tried to move away. Her body didn't respond. She parted her lips to shout for help. No sound came out.

The man breathed heavily against her ear.

'I can't wait to finish what we started. Don't worry, I'll make sure you enjoy it too.'

There was a movement against her as whoever had been there stood up.

Then there was silence.

'Your water, madame.'

This time she recognised the waiter's voice.

'I think I'd better call Monsieur Coste. You really don't look well,' he added.

The next thing she knew, Fabien was talking to her, urging her to wake up and speak to him, but she was a prisoner in her own body. She couldn't speak or move. All she wanted to do was to drift away and sleep.

Fabien scooped her into his arms, held her tightly against him.

'I'm taking you to a room,' he said as he carried her into the lobby. Amy heard him ask the receptionist which room was free.

'*Chambre douze*, monsieur. I'll open it for you.'

She was dimly aware of Fabien settling her on a soft bed, of her shoes being taken off. The last thing she remembered before losing consciousness was Fabien ordering a member of his staff to ring an emergency doctor.

Chapter Thirteen

'How are you, darling?' Céline asked, sitting on the bed.

Amy blinked and looked around the spacious room decorated in shades of cream and aubergine. Muslin and brocade curtains partly obscured two large French windows and fell in gracious drapes from the moulded ceiling down on to the parquet floor. Her fingers brushed over the bedclothes. The sheets were of the softest Egyptian cotton. She was in one of Manoir Coste's luxury suites. But what was she doing in there, and why did her head hurt so much?

'You gave us such a fright,' Céline carried on. 'The doctor said that there was nothing he could do and that we should let you sleep. He said your symptoms were consistent with your drink being spiked with some drug called gamma ... something, I forget the name. It's commonly called the date-rape drug.'

Amy tried to sit up. Her head throbbed. Her mouth was dry. Sketchy memories of the previous evening spun in her head like a kaleidoscope.

'A drug? But who ...? I don't remember anything after Fabien's argument with Frédéric, talking to Serena Chevalier, and feeling dizzy. People were looking at me as though I was drunk.'

She lifted a glass from the bedside table with a shaky hand, drank a long sip of cold water, then massaged her forehead, but she knew it would take a lot more than that for the migraine to go away.

Céline rose to her feet. 'I'll leave you to rest.'

Amy started to protest. What about Bellefontaine, and Michka? And what about her guests? Monsieur Garnier must have been furious with her, especially if along with everybody else, he believed that she had overindulged on champagne.

Tears welled up in her eyes. 'I have to go back, yet I don't think I can move.'

Céline patted her hand. 'Everything is being taken care of. Don't worry.'

Too exhausted to ask Céline what she meant, Amy leaned back on the pillow and drifted into sleep.

The next time she woke up, she was alone. Her migraine had eased off, and she didn't feel quite so dizzy. She pulled the bedclothes down and sat up. She only had her underwear on, but some of her clothes were on a chair near the bed. Somebody had been to Bellefontaine and brought back a white T-shirt, a grey jogging suit, some underwear and a pair of trainers. Slowly she swung her feet over to one side of the bed, got up, and walked to the bathroom.

She stayed a long time in the shower, letting the steaming hot water glide over her body and revive her. Afterwards, she wrapped herself in a fluffy white robe and looked through the toiletries placed at the side of the sink. As she brushed her teeth and rubbed some lemon-scented cream into her skin, questions swirled in her mind. What happened last night? Had somebody really spiked her drink, and if so, why? Was it deliberate or a mistake?

She put her clothes on, slipped her feet into her trainers, and glanced at her watch on the bedside table. It was already two in the afternoon. Time to leave.

There was a knock on the door, and Céline walked in.

'What a relief it is to see you're awake! Poor darling, you still look dreadfully pale. How are you feeling?'

Amy combed her damp hair away from her face with her fingers and smiled tentatively.

'Better, thanks. I really must go. It's late.'

'Not before you have something to eat. I don't want you fainting on your way back to Bellefontaine. You'll have something to eat in the garden.'

Without leaving Amy time to object, she slipped her arm under hers and led her outside. It was a warm, sunny afternoon. Deckchairs scattered the lawn and hotel guests were making the most of the garden, swimming pool and tennis courts. They walked to a small table under the shade of a lime tree, near the mossy old fountain.

'Are the clothes all right?' Fabien's mother asked. 'I wasn't sure which ones to choose, but I thought that you would prefer something comfortable.'

'They are perfect, thank you. I put you to a lot of trouble.'

'Not at all.' Céline waved her hand dismissively. 'Fabien and I were very concerned about you. Actually, he reported the incident to the gendarmes last night, straight after the doctor's visit. He blames himself for what happened.'

'He shouldn't. It's not his fault someone put some drug in my drink.'

She couldn't think of who would have done that, and why, and could only hope the gendarmes soon caught the culprit. A waitress put plates of sandwiches and a bowl of mixed salad in front of them, as well as a pitcher of fresh water.

'I fear my reputation took a serious setback last night,' Amy said as she poured water into her glass.

Ice cubes tinkled against the sides of the crystal tumbler.

'I remember people said I had drunk too much champagne.'

She tried to smile, but anxiety tightened her stomach in a knot.

'What happened to Monsieur Garnier?'

161

Céline snorted. 'Him? What an unpleasant character! It's fortunate you won't have to suffer his sour mood when you get home. According to Maurice, he left Bellefontaine early this morning.'

Amy looked up. 'Who is Maurice?'

'Maurice is one of the managers here. Fabien sent him to look after your guests last night.'

So Bellefontaine hadn't been abandoned after all.

'It was very kind of him,' she said, her voice a little shaky. 'Please thank him for me.'

'You can do that all by yourself right now. Here he is.'

Céline turned towards the terrace and waved at Fabien.

His face lit up when he saw Amy and he walked across the lawn in long strides.

'I'm so glad you're up at last,' he said, pulling a chair next to her. He looked at her with searching eyes for what felt like a long time, then relaxed into a smile.

'You look a lot better.'

He, on the other hand, was pale, with dark circles under his eyes. He had a nick on the side of his throat, probably where he had cut himself whilst shaving. He looked tired, exhausted even. Overwhelmed by a rush of tenderness, Amy yearned to lean closer, touch his cheek, and kiss the line by the side of his mouth. She swallowed hard and gripped her glass of water more tightly.

'I hear you sent someone to look after my guests,' she said. 'Thank you.'

'It was the least I could do. I only wish I could lay my hands on the bast—'

He took a deep breath.

'I mean the person who drugged you last night. It was terrible to see you so ill. Can you remember anything at all?'

'Only that I spoke to Serena Chevalier on the terrace after you left.' Amy paused. 'She was very hostile, as usual.'

'Serena? What did she say?' He glanced at his mother, but Céline was eating and didn't seem to be listening.

'She warned me that things were about to get unpleasant for me, and that Bellefontaine was hers.'

'I can't see Serena slipping some drug in your glass, but then I can't imagine anyone who would do such a thing. And you don't remember anything after that?'

'No, it's like a kaleidoscope of distorted images and sounds.'

Shivers crawled all over her skin. She was cold suddenly, cold and frightened.

'I never want to feel that way again. All I want is to forget about it.'

She finished her glass of water and stood up. 'I really must go back.'

Fabien rose to his feet too. 'Then I'll drive you home.'

'There's no need. My car is still here, and I'm feeling much better. Once again, thank you, for everything.'

Céline kissed her cheek and said she was taking the train back to Paris later in the afternoon but would be back soon.

'We'll meet up and have a good, long, girly chat, shall we?'

Amy nodded uneasily and glanced at Fabien. Although she liked Céline very much, she wasn't sure getting too close to her was such a good idea. She had the distinct impression that Céline could see right through her where Fabien was concerned.

'The offer of looking at my grandfather's papers and Renaud Coste's journals still stands, if you're interested,' Fabien said a few moments later as they reached the car park where Amy had left her Clio the previous evening.

She took a deep breath. However fascinating it would be

to delve into Manoir Coste's and Bellefontaine's past and find out what happened to the temple, she wasn't sure it was worth the torment of being in Fabien's presence.

As if sensing her hesitation, he added. 'It would mean a lot to me to have your input.'

'Then I will help you,' she said before letting herself into the car. 'I'll phone you tomorrow.'

She closed the door and started the engine. When she checked her rear-view mirror, Fabien hadn't moved. He was still standing in the car park, watching her.

Once Amy's car had turned onto the main road, he walked back to the Manoir, stopping to exchange a few words with hotel guests or members of staff when all he wanted was to be on his own.

'I'm not taking any calls – unless it's the gendarmes or Mademoiselle Carter,' he told the receptionist before going into his study and closing the door.

He sank into the black leather chair behind his desk, and stared blindly at the computer screen in front of him but the words and the figures didn't make any sense. He raked his fingers in his hair and let out a deep sigh.

He'd hardly slept, had been unable to concentrate that morning or take any decisions, even the most trivial and mundane ones. His thoughts kept going back to Amy and the puzzling events of the night before. Once again, as he remembered how lost and scared she had looked, anger made a cold, hard, tight fist inside him and he had the urge to punch something – anything. Or anyone.

Another memory pushed its way into his mind, tormenting him again. The feel of her soft body in his arms, and the sweet, intoxicating vanilla scent he could breathe on her skin and hair as he took her upstairs.

He let out a ragged breath. That evening at Bellefontaine, she had responded to him, she had yielded under his touch, his kisses. She may deny it but she was attracted to him, and he found it more and more difficult to stop thinking about her. To stop imagining how it would feel to kiss her again, explore her body, caress her with his hands and mouth, and taste every inch of her skin.

But he was completely out of order! The woman had just been poisoned while under his roof – with a date rape drug of all things – and all he could think of was making love to her instead of finding the bastard who had drugged her!

At least she had agreed to look through his family papers with him. He may not like the idea of getting her involved any more than she already was, but he needed to keep an eye on her, and what better way to do so than suggest they worked together? This way too, if Orsini got in touch, or found anything worthwhile when he came back to Bellefontaine, he would know about it straight away.

For the hundredth time, he wondered if he should change his mind and grant the archaeologist and his team access to the forest. Orsini was a professional. He knew how to decipher clues, follow trails, and translate Latin or Greek or any other ancient inscriptions. If anyone could find the fountain and the lost temple, it was probably him.

Fabien got up and looked out of the patio door and on to the park. Orsini may be the man he so desperately needed. On the other hand, he couldn't risk him, or anyone, exposing his family's dirty secrets.

Maurice had the most beautiful moustache she'd ever seen. Long and bushy, it curled at the tips and gave Fabien's manager the air of a warrior right out of an *Asterix* comic.

'Monsieur Garnier left just after nine,' Maurice said as

he wiped the cooker and the work surfaces in the kitchen, despite Amy's protests that he'd done enough already.

'He complained about just about everything, from the scented soaps in the bathroom to the colour of the bedclothes – he even criticised the tomato and red pepper omelette I made for breakfast.'

He pulled a face and clicked his tongue. 'The Ducros, however, are charming. They said they were spending the day in Aix and won't be back until late this evening.'

He dug inside the breast pocket of his white shirt and gave her a piece of paper.

'You had two phone calls. One from a Laurent Orsini, the other from your sister.'

Amy smiled at him. 'You were very kind, staying at Bellefontaine last night and taking care of my guests. How can I ever thank you enough?'

'I was only doing what Monsieur Coste asked, mademoiselle,' he replied. 'I hope you're feeling better and the gendarmes catch whoever did that terrible thing to you. You hear that this kind of thing goes on in nightclubs in big towns but I certainly wouldn't expect it around here, and especially not at Manoir Coste.'

Once alone, she made a pot of tea and sat at the kitchen table. As if sensing that she needed comfort and affection, Michka put her head on her lap.

Amy scratched gently behind the dog's ears as she dialled Chris' number but there was no reply. She tried Laurent's mobile number. He picked up immediately. He sounded very excited about Amy's emails.

'You can join my team any time, Amy. You'd make a great historical detective. Your translations of the Latin inscriptions are correct. The Greek inscription translates as "The Good Listener". Patricia said that she came across the same inscription in Glanum. It refers to the Gallic earth mother who became known as Bona Dea under the Romans. So once again it seems we're back to good old Bona Dea.'

'Why is it in Greek?'

'The whole of Provence had strong ties with Greece,' Laurent explained. 'In fact Marseille was founded by the Greeks in 600 BC – they called it Massalia – and many Gallic tribes adopted Greek writing. Later, when the Romans ruled the region, Latin replaced Greek as the official language.'

Amy asked him if the inscriptions on the fountains referred to a lost temple.

'They do indeed refer to an underground sanctuary, near a fountain, and in the woods, but I find the mention of ghosts and spectres very confusing.'

He paused. 'Listen, I'm not going to wait for my boss to approve my application before coming back to Bellefontaine. I am due some time off so I'll carry out my own research. I'll be there on Sunday, that's if you have room for me, of course.'

'I did have quite a few bookings for next week,' she said. 'Just let me check my emails.'

Disappointment awaited her when she opened her mailbox. All the bookings she'd taken the day before from the Tourist Office were cancelled, all without explanation. Was it due to another computer problem? She would have to phone Monsieur Verdier and ask him.

Letting out a sigh, she confirmed that Laurent could definitely have a room.

'In fact, it looks like you'll be the only guest at Bellefontaine,' she told him.

The Ducros came back early in the evening. After enquiring after her health, Madame Ducros declared that her sightseeing day in Aix had exhausted her and that she was in need of a good rest.

She started up the stairs but paused halfway.

'By the way, I'm sure there were people in the garden last night. I saw some lights near the trees when I closed the shutters.'

Amy's heart missed a beat. If the lights were back, it meant that someone was lurking out there at night again.

'Don't worry about it,' she replied, doing her best to sound insouciant. 'They were probably tourists enjoying a late walk through the forest.'

As soon as the Ducros had gone up, she made sure she locked all doors and windows securely. As an afterthought, she even locked the door to the cellar before going up to bed.

She could hear water dripping. The sound, repetitive, annoying and getting louder, was soon impossible to ignore. It reverberated inside the room, echoed inside her head. She sighed, glanced at the digital clock on her bedside table. The luminous display indicated that it was after 2 a.m.

She must have forgotten to turn a tap off again. Shivering, she got up to check the bathroom. All the taps were safely turned off. She opened her bedroom door, tiptoed barefoot into the corridor, and stopped at the top of the stairs. The noise got louder. It came from downstairs. From the cellar.

Reluctantly, she unlocked the door and flicked the switch before making her way down the steps and into the basement. She halted halfway across the room. A trap door that she never knew existed gaped, wide open.

A blue light glowed faintly from below the ground. Amy's hair pricked on the nape of her neck. Sensing danger, she swirled round but it was too late. Two hands grabbed her throat and squeezed harder and harder, until she could no longer breathe.

'Amy! Are you all right?' Someone was shouting and banging on the door. A dog barked nearby.

She sat up and put her hands to her forehead. Where was she? What had happened? She looked around her, disoriented to see that she wasn't in the cellar but in bed, with Michka yelping and growling next to her. It had all been a dream. Yet, the pain in her throat had seemed so real swallowing was almost impossible.

'Open up, Amy,' Monsieur Ducros said from behind the door.

Amy pulled the sheets down, got up and made her way across her room to unlock the door.

'Thank God you're all right.' Madame Ducros stood in front of her in her nightdress, with her husband in stripy blue and white pyjamas next to her. 'You screamed so loudly we thought someone had broken in and ...'

Amy rubbed her face with her hands.

'I'm sorry I woke you. I had a nightmare.'

Madame Ducros recommended a cup of hot milk laced with honey.

'Hot milk? What the girl needs is brandy,' her husband objected.

Amy thanked them for their concern and they returned to their room, debating the pros and cons of brandy versus hot milk. She was about to go back to bed when a white, luminescent gleam on top of the dresser caught her eye. The fluorite crystal. It almost seemed to be mocking her. Suddenly the thought of having it in her room was unbearable. She plucked it from the top of the dresser, rushed down the stairs, and pushed it to the back of a kitchen drawer. She knew she was overreacting, but right now it didn't matter. She wanted nothing more to do with it.

Since she was downstairs she decided to take Monsieur Ducros' advice and pour herself a large cognac, which she sipped slowly whilst sitting at the kitchen table, a glossy magazine in front of her. When she could no longer focus on the printed pages, she dragged her weary body back up the stairs. She slipped into bed, but despite snuggling up against Michka, sleep eluded her for a long time.

She woke up with a headache and a sick feeling at the pit of her stomach. So she'd had another, terrifying, nightmare. The hands gripping her throat had felt so real. She'd really believed she was choking to death.

Throwing open the window and shutters she gazed for a long while at the fresh blue sky scattered with wispy white clouds. In the garden, wild flowers glistening with morning dew swayed in the breeze. Melodic trills and whistles of blue tits, finches, and thrushes filled the air. Wood pigeons called from the forest. It should be an idyllic picture, yet even the caress of the rising sun on her skin failed to soothe her. Her eyes were drawn time and time again to the shadows lurking deep inside the cedar forest.

She showered and dressed quickly, and went downstairs to prepare breakfast for the Ducros who planned to travel to Avignon to see the Easter parade.

Tidying the house and sorting out her papers and accounts didn't help with her restlessness. Images and sensations from her nightmare kept coming back, vivid and disturbing. She didn't want silence, or to be alone at Bellefontaine today.

An insidious doubt wormed its way into her mind. Céline and Fabien had talked about underground passages under the forest – passages linking Manoir Coste to

Bellefontaine. What if there was indeed some sort of tunnel under Bellefontaine? What if there was a trap door in the basement?

She pulled Fabien's card from her address book. Today was as good a day as ever to research his family's past, read the journals he said he had found, and look at his grandfather's drawings. Perhaps they would find a mention of the underground passages.

She rang him and he suggested she come over straight away.

'I'll get the diaries and letters together,' he said. 'You bring the portfolio back.'

She locked the house up, drove to Manoir Coste, and introduced herself at the reception, expecting to be directed to his office or the Manager's Suite. Instead the receptionist instructed her to walk across the walled garden to the gatekeeper's cottage.

'Monsieur Coste isn't working at the Manoir today,' the woman explained.

The gatekeeper's cottage was an old stone house with dark green shutters and a façade covered with ivy. It looked old and romantic, and not at all the kind of house she imagined Fabien would choose for himself.

The door was ajar. She knocked.

'Come in,' he called from inside.

He was sitting on a battered cream-coloured sofa, a laptop on his knees. As soon as she came in he put the computer on the coffee table, pushed aside piles of old papers, files and books and stood up to greet her. He looked casual in a white cotton shirt with the sleeves rolled up and a pair of faded blue jeans.

'I'm sorry if I am early,' Amy said.

'Not at all,' he replied, combing his dark hair back with

his fingers. 'I was finishing some accounts. I always bring too much work home.'

She frowned. This little house was his home? What about the Manager's Suite on the third floor of Manoir Coste? She looked around. The whitewashed walls were bare except for one large landscape painting and a modern wrought iron piece of wall art. Persian rugs with muted brown and reddish tones covered the tiled floor. A huge, flat screen TV hung on the wall, a sleek hi-fi with tall, slim speakers stood in the corner, together with a well-stocked compact disc tower.

'Please sit down.' He gestured to the sofa, and asked if she wanted a drink. She said no.

'So you don't live in the chateau then?' she asked.

'Not any more. It was like being at work all the time. I moved in here a couple of years ago. I keep a suite on the third floor at the Manoir. It's handy for meetings.'

For meetings and lovers' assignments, no doubt. Amy opened the portfolio and kept her head down to hide her disappointment. For a brief moment, she had been filled with the absurd hope that it hadn't been Fabien who had been with Claudine in the manager's room the night of the ball.

'Are you all right?'

He leaned across towards her and put his hand lightly on her arm.

'I'm fine,' she snapped, and shuffled away from him before pulling drawings of the fountains at Buoux and Saignon out of the portfolio.

'Did you say you transcribed the inscriptions on the fountains?' he asked as he looked at the drawings.

She nodded and searched inside her bag for the notebook in which she'd copied down the Latin inscriptions out and their translations.

'They refer to an underground temple and a sacred spring, to a female deity and to spectres or ghosts ... The other fountains may have similar inscriptions. Laurent seems to think they'll help discover where the temple is. I wonder why this ancestor of yours didn't keep some kind of record of its location.'

'He wanted it that way. He wrote that he wished the temple to be lost, forgotten, hidden. Almost erased from the surface of the earth.'

He turned to Amy and handed her a journal.

'The cedar forest was planted by Renaud Coste. He bought a whole cargo ship of saplings from a famous botanist who had collected them during an expedition to Tunisia. Renaud had ordered the temple to be destroyed. This is what he wrote in May 1815:

'Destroying the temple wasn't enough. This time, I believe the villagers' claims about evil doings in the woods and I have decided to cover the hill with a cedar forest. It will take many years to grow but then the infamy will be hidden forever.

It is with a heavy heart that I leave Manoir Coste to join my emperor's army on the northern border. My only consolation is that I will be leaving treachery and wickedness behind.'

Fabien looked at Amy.

'Napoleon was defeated at Waterloo in June 1815, and Renaud was killed on the battlefield.'

'Is there anything in the journal about why he so wanted to erase the temple from the surface of the earth?'

Fabien read several entries of the diary silently, turned a few brittle, yellow pages, and shook his head.

'I need his earlier diary, the one for 1813 and 1814. I think it must still be in the library. I'll get it later.'

'I wonder what he meant when he wrote about evil doings,' Amy said.

Fabien didn't answer but pulled a couple of drawings out of Philippe Coste's portfolio. Checking his watch, he turned to her.

'Shall we drive round to Ménerbes and Lourmarin this afternoon and have a look at the fountains? I'd like to put your theory to the test.'

When she agreed that it was worth a try, Fabien took his car keys out of his jeans pocket.

They were walking across the walled garden towards the car park when his mobile rang.

He looked at the screen and frowned. 'I need to take this. Sorry.'

He turned away to talk on the phone, then came back and looked at her. 'I'm afraid something has cropped up, and I'm wanted at Maison Espérance. One of their youth workers phoned in sick and they have nobody to take the kids to the swimming pool.'

She frowned, puzzled. 'Maison Espérance? Isn't that the children's home?'

'That's right. I'm one of the sponsors, and I try and help out once or twice a week. I take the children to the zoo or the safari park, and we go rock-climbing or to football matches in Marseille when I can get tickets.'

She couldn't help but smile. 'That's very generous of you.'

He shrugged. 'I know what it's like to grow up without a father, and I can afford both the time and the expense.'

Amy remembered the background noise of children laughing when she'd phoned Fabien on his mobile the day of the garden party. So that's what he was doing that day, taking the children from Maison Espérance out. The man was decidedly full of surprises. She would have thought him more likely to indulge in expensive hobbies such as motorboat racing, water-skiing or shopping in designer boutiques in Cannes or St Tropez.

'I need to hurry and get my swimming trunks ... I am sorry. We'll have to go to Lourmarin and Ménerbes some other time.' He finished.

She tried not to look and sound at disappointed as she felt. 'Sure. No problem.'

Perhaps it was for the best ...

Chapter Fourteen

The Ducros left the following morning. They promised to recommend Bellefontaine to friends and family.

'Your cooking alone would justify a visit, dear,' Madame Ducros said before waving goodbye.

They had just left when the postman made his usual loud arrival on his moped and slipped a letter into her letterbox. She carried it into the kitchen. It was from the *Fédération des Offices de Tourisme*, the National French Tourist Board. At last there was news about her application for a star grading!

Her heart sank as she read the first few lines. The Board's inspector concluded that she had failed in her most basic duties of care towards her guests. Even a single star was out of the question until Amy showed an improved level of service. The letter finished by stating that she was more concerned with consuming alcohol than with fulfilling her responsibilities and was signed Arthur Garnier.

So Garnier was the board inspector who had played the mystery guest. Why had Monsieur Verdier not warned her of his arrival in advance like he'd promised?

Amy steeled herself. This was a bitter blow, but she would appeal. Fabien, Céline and the emergency doctor could all testify that her indisposition had nothing to do with drinking too much alcohol. She sighed and closed her eyes. She could remember seeing Monsieur Garnier talking to Claudine in the ballroom. Claudine had pointed at her and laughed.

She tried to concentrate on the broken film her mind was playing. The waiter's face. The empty Petit Salon. A voice whispering in her ear. Perhaps her memory of the evening was coming back at last.

Amy's eyes flew open. There had been someone there with her, someone who had frightened her, even though she couldn't remember their exact words. Someone who had touched her.

Blood pounded in her ears. Sweat beaded on her forehead. Who had been there with her? Perhaps it was the very person who'd drugged her drink?

Her dark thoughts were interrupted by Fabien ringing to say that he was going away on business for a couple of days but would call her on his return so that they could resume their investigation into the temple and Renaud Coste's diaries. Even though Amy doubted that spending time alone with him was a good idea, she replied that she was looking forward to it.

She couldn't concentrate on her paperwork. Lily's stories preyed on her mind and all she could think of was the underground chamber of her dreams and the mysterious trap door opening in her cellar. She pushed her files away and dropped her pen on the desk. Worrying was pointless. It was time to investigate Bellefontaine's basement.

She unlocked the cellar door, switched on the light and went down, followed by Michka. Metal shelves and empty wine racks stood against the walls. She pulled them all away and slid her hands along the smooth, even walls to feel for any concealed door or opening. There was nothing there.

It had been a bad dream, that was all, she thought with relief. She was about to turn back when Michka started sniffing the bottom of the wall with excited whimpers and wagged her tail furiously, and Amy went over to investigate. The ground sounded different there, almost as if it was made of wood instead of stone or concrete.

177

She knelt down to touch the floor. Although it was perfectly camouflaged and painted the same grey colour as the rest of the basement floor, the faint outline of a trap door was visible. She couldn't find a catch or handle to open it. It was as if the trap door could only be opened from the other side.

She piled crates on top of it, and never mind if she was being paranoid. When the trap door was entirely covered with metal shelves and boxes, she climbed the cellar stairs and locked the door. In the hall, her eyes focussed on the wooden chest. Perfect, she thought. Filled with books and knick-knacks she'd bought at flea markets and second-hand stores, it was so heavy she was panting by the time she'd dragged it across the tiled floor and pushed it against the door.

She didn't care if she was overreacting. Nobody would sneak up from the cellar and into her house now.

Chapter Fifteen

In the Middle Ages, the ridge-top village of Ménerbes was reputed to be impregnable. It wasn't difficult to see why. Even today the half-ruined walls of its fortress rose high above the hillside, and its belfry shot up like an arrow towards the sky. Amy liked its old buildings, winding streets and archways, and the two chapels at either end of the village.

Philippe Coste's sketches were still with Fabien so she relied on her memory to find the fountain. She remembered it to be taller and more ornate than the ones at Buoux and Saignon. She started from the central square and walked up one street to the castle, then back down another lane, exploring the village for the best part of an hour.

She finally reached a belvedere at the west end of the village, and there it was, in front of her. Her heart beat a little faster as she came closer.

There was no carving on the wide pillar except for a coat of arms and a date:'1835'. The same date as the other two fountains.

There must be something else. Some Latin or Greek writing, she thought, as she walked around. She bent down to examine the basin but the stone was worn and smooth. She stood up again and then she saw it, under the carved lion head into which a pipe was inserted.

The inscription was faint and partly hidden by the running water.

Res divina sacrificium
Hominess pro victimis immolare
Terricula pervigil
Pulchrum fons

The last two verses were familiar. She'd seen them on the other fountains. *Beautiful spring/fountain. Spectre forever awake.* As for the rest, it didn't take an expert in Latin to understand the words 'sacrifice' and 'victim'.

She wrote the lines down, took a few photos, and walked back to the car, mapping out in her mind the route to Lourmarin, the last village in her 'fountain trail'.

Who was the stonemason who had rebuilt the fountains, and why did he use the temple's stones? Was it his way of making sure the cult wouldn't be forgotten, or was he saving money by reusing materials nobody would touch because they were supposed to be cursed?

Lourmarin, a busy market town roughly eleven kilometres south of Ménerbes, wasn't as picturesque as other hilltop villages. It was still popular with tourists, though, who came for its sixteenth-century castle, Roman church, antique shops and the cemetery where the graves of Albert Camus and Jean Giono, two of France's best loved twentieth-century writers were found.

She walked to the fountain which stood in a small square shaded by an old lime tree. It looked like a miniature Roman temple, with columns and a classical portico above its central pillar. Unfortunately, the carvings were far too worn and she was unable to decipher even one word.

So the Lourmarin fountain would keep its secret. Disappointed, Amy headed back to the car park. She took her time, looking at shop windows as she wandered through the narrow streets. Her attention was attracted by a large terracotta vase in the window of a *bric-à-brac* shop. It would look beautiful in Bellefontaine's living room and would replace the one the burglars had smashed. One look at the price tag however was enough to discourage her.

Etchings were propped up among chipped plates,

wooden toys and old-fashioned railway annuals. One of them featured a chateau that looked just like Manoir Coste.

She pressed her nose against the windowpane. It was Manoir Coste! Intrigued she pushed the door open and walked into the shop.

A man was sorting out sets of playing cards on a table. He looked up.

'Bonjour, madame.'

Amy pointed to the window and asked to see the etchings.

'*Certainement*. These are mid-eighteenth century,' he explained as he lay the pictures flat on the table.

Altogether there were five etchings of Manoir Coste, each of them drawn from a different perspective. Two, however, were different and Amy's pulse raced as she leaned over them. One depicted a semi-circular fountain adorned with statues in the middle of a wood. Behind the fountain, she could just about make out the outline of a construction with square pillars and steps, standing in the shadows of the trees.

Amy pointed to the fountain.

'Do you know where this is?'

'I don't, but it's what we call a monumental fountain, or a *nympheum*,' the man replied. 'They were built by Roman senators. The most famous one is at Glanum, near St Rémy, but I believe there is another one in Nîmes.'

Amy stared at the last etching, which showed a close-up view of the temple. It was a primitive construction, with square pillars, a portico, and two statues on either side of the entrance, standing guard like sentinels. The statues looked identical to the one that had been stolen from Bellefontaine: her Bona Dea, wearing the same headdress of oak leaves intertwined with snakes. 'Where do these prints come from?'

The man looked uneasy. 'I'm not sure, sorry.'

Why was he so evasive? Could the engravings be stolen?

'How much are you asking for them?'

'Two hundred euros. They're very old, you know.'

'That's far too much, especially if you can't establish their provenance. I'll give you forty euros.' She tried to sound indifferent when in reality she was shaking with excitement. These were prints of the fountain and the temple, she was certain of it, but there was no way she could spend the amount of money the shopkeeper was asking for.

'Sixty,' the man bartered.

'Fifty.'

'*D'accord*, but I only take cash.'

Amy went to a nearby cash dispenser, paid the shopkeeper, and left with the etchings secure in a large envelope. She couldn't resist taking a look at them again as soon as she sat in the car. If the lost fountain was impressive and beautiful, the temple looked mysterious. It was no wonder the villagers had been afraid of it.

It was time to drive back to Bellefontaine. A Monsieur Dubois had booked five rooms for himself and his family for the night, and she could only hope they would decide to stay longer. She had no other bookings before Laurent on Sunday, and the balance of her bank account was getting dangerously low. Her savings were now almost completely gone, and bills were piling up.

Monsieur Verdier had been most apologetic about the cancelled bookings, blaming them on yet another technical problem. He had also apologised for not warning Amy about Monsieur Garnier's inspection, and said he hadn't known about the inspection himself. He had however written to Monsieur Garnier to ask him to change the conclusion of his report, and had testified that Amy was a most competent and welcoming host who had been the victim of a shocking crime.

Once back at Bellefontaine, she scanned the etchings into her computer and attached them to an email she sent to Laurent before running upstairs to change into her old grey cotton shirt and faded jeans. When she was ready, she tidied up the house, put a bunch of fresh flowers in a vase in the five rooms Monsieur Dubois had booked, straightened up the towels in the en suites, baked a cake, and went outside to mow the lawn with the antique petrol-powered mower she had bought at a flea-market.

It took determination and the best part of two hours to complete the task and by the end of the afternoon, her arms ached, her sweaty shirt clung to her body and her face and forearms were speckled with bits of grass. She switched off the engine and was about to go into the kitchen and pour herself a large glass of water when she heard a car pull up in the courtyard. She breathed a sigh of relief. She was just in time to welcome her new guests.

Fabien grabbed hold of the journals, pushed the door of the Ranger Rover shut, and looked up to see Amy appear in the doorway. Her cheeks were flushed. Her tousled hair shone like spun gold in the sunlight. She looked so damned adorable his throat tightened and a rush of heat flashed through him. All he could do to stop himself from reaching out and pulling her to him was to tighten his grip on the diaries.

'I brought Renaud Coste's journals as promised,' he said as he stepped nearer. 'I hope it's not a bad time. You look busy.'

She smoothed her hair self-consciously and shook her head.

'Not at all. I've been mowing the lawn. Actually, I'm glad you came. I was going to phone you. I have something incredible to show you.'

He followed her inside, noticing the wooden chest against the cellar door. He didn't remember it being there last time he had called.

'Won't this make it hard to open the cellar door?' he asked.

'That's the idea,' she replied, her shoulders lifting in a delicate shrug.

She pointed to the open patio doors before he could ask her to explain.

'Please take a seat outside, I won't be long.'

As soon as he stepped onto the terrace, Michka rushed to greet him. He made a fuss of her, ruffled her ears and stroked her brown-and-white coat while he waited for Amy.

'I found this set of prints this morning in a *bric-à-brac* shop in Lourmarin,' she said when she joined him on the terrace.

She spread four etchings out on the garden table.

'What do you think?'

'That's Manoir Coste and the old fountain.' He pointed to two of the prints. 'And these look like …'

'The Roman fountain and the temple,' she finished, a glimmer of excitement in her eyes. 'The statues are identical to the one I found in the garden.'

She pointed to the statues that stood on either side of the temple entrance. He bent down to examine the prints closely. It was the first time he'd seen a representation of the temple his father and grandfather had searched so long for.

'I think you may be right,' he said at last. 'Look at the signature in the far right corner. The prints are by the same artist – a Denis Piquot. And both are dated 1755. I wonder where they come from.'

Amy said the shopkeeper had looked shifty when she enquired about their provenance.

'He must have cut them out of an art book or a travel journal. Dealers make more money when they sell individual prints.'

'Then I'll do an internet search to locate Denis Piquot's books,' Amy suggested. 'I'm curious to find out who he was and why he drew pictures of your chateau, the fountain, and the temple.'

She glanced at the two leather-bound volumes on the table. 'Are these the diaries you were looking for the other day?'

He nodded. 'They are. Do you have time to read a few pages now or shall I come back another day?'

She leaned closer, tormenting him with the warm scent of her skin.

'Oh no, please do read.'

They sat down and he opened one of the diaries.

'Very well. I'll start in 1813, when Renaud decided to destroy the temple.

'*15 March 1813. Father Chabot came here this morning. Madame Lignac, the baker's wife, claimed she had seen Magali Bruni lead a ghostly procession through the woods last night. She estimated that there were over a dozen men and women, all clad in long white robes, holding lanterns, and chanting the devil's song as they walked to the temple.*

The curé crossed himself several times as he talked. "The temple must be taken down, stone by stone," he urged, "and the Brunis must be sent away without delay."

How can I argue with these ignorant, superstitious fools? I know the rumours surrounding the Bruni family. People were always suspicious of them, just because they keep themselves to themselves.

In the end, however, I had no choice but to agree to demolish the temple and so I asked my estate manager to

185

gather around fifteen of our strongest men and ask them to bring any tools they could find. An hour later, there were more than thirty of us heading into the woods as men came en force from the village, eager to destroy the temple once and for all. On my signal the men started pulling the building down, knocking the pillars to the ground, wrecking the statues and the stonework. We saw the entry to an underground passage which a few men called "the gaping mouth of hell" and which I ordered to be blocked.

Unfortunately, the men's frenzy of destruction did not stop at the temple. They turned to the fountain and I regret to write that it too, was brought down. Yet I thought it better for them to take their anger out onto old statues rather than the Brunis. When there was nothing left but ruins, I sent everybody home and promised to deal with the Brunis myself.'

Fabien interrupted his reading and looked at Amy. 'This is where things get ... interesting.

'16 March 1813. I met my love tonight. How can I believe those who claim that she is an evil witch? I have done what I could to protect her but she is no longer safe in Bonnieux, so I gave her some money and persuaded her to leave for Lyon with Gaston, her brute of a husband. She will come back when people have calmed down in a few months' time. I am not sure, however, that I can survive without her until then.'

'So Renaud and Magali Bruni were lovers, just like your grandfather Philippe and Rosalie!' Amy exclaimed. Immediately her eyes opened wide, her cheeks flushed a deep pink, and she bit her lip.

'I'm sorry, that was rude of me. I didn't mean to repeat gossip.'

Fabien smiled tightly. 'It's all right. I already knew

about my grandfather and Rosalie Bruni. Their liaison was common knowledge in my family. I must say, however, that I was taken aback by the revelation that Renaud and Magali were lovers too. It's rather odd – almost as if there is a connection between Manoir Coste and Bellefontaine, isn't it?'

He looked away, towards the cedar forest, which in the late afternoon light was filled with shadows.

A connection. A spell binding his ancestors to the ladies of Bellefontaine. He may not believe in magic, but Renaud wrote about Magali as if he was infatuated and she had cast a charm on him. His grandfather Philippe had been just as obsessed with Rosalie. He thought of the letters he had found in his father's old papers a few months back which revealed the secret of another, altogether closer and more upsetting connection between his family and the ladies of Bellefontaine ... Nobody, however, was likely to find out about that. He'd make sure of it.

And what about him? Wasn't he becoming just as obsessed with Amy?

Focusing on Renaud's diary, he flicked through the thin pages.

'There are no further mentions of Magali, the temple, or any "evil" incident for a few months. Until this.

'*28 August 1813. Summer storms have caused havoc in the fields and orchards. As I walked the dogs yesterday, I was once more drawn to Bellefontaine, so forlorn and desolate without my love.*

I was most surprised to see that the shutters were open and that there was a horse and carriage in the courtyard. At last, she was back from Lyon. I could hear women's voices inside. I knocked on the door and she came out, looking even more beautiful than I remembered. I would have taken

*her in my arms there and then were it not for the maid who
I could see in the kitchens.*

*She explained that she'd had enough of Lyon, but that
her husband would stay there for some time, having been
appointed master stonemason to build a new church. My
heart leapt at the news and I left after promising to visit
very soon.'*

'Gaston Bruni was a stone mason?' Amy cried out. 'I
wonder if he was the one who rebuilt the fountains around
Bonnieux. Please carry on ...'

Fabien nodded.

*'That night, as a mighty thunderstorm shook the whole
hillside I went back to Bellefontaine, and my love and
I made up for all our months apart. She is the most fiery
creature I ever possessed. She burns my whole being. She
burns my soul ...'*

Fabien's voice turned a little hoarse as he read the last
lines and the melodramatic passion in Renaud's last words
echoed around.

He cleared his throat, turned a couple of pages.
'Anyway ... I'll carry on.

*'31 August 1813. The thunderstorm was devastating.
Some people in Bonnieux saw a sign that God was angry
that Magali Bruni had returned to Bellefontaine.'* He
glanced up.

'There are several entries after that about estate business
here, a few mentions of Gaston Bruni visiting his wife at
Bellefontaine every so often.

*'30 October 1813. My love is with child. She says it will
be a girl. This time, when I talked to her about leaving
Bellefontaine, she agreed. For the safety of the baby, she
said. She left today for Lyon, where she will stay with her
husband until the baby is born. Is the child mine?'*

'Magali came back a few months later,' Fabien said.

'*25 May 1814. She has returned, with her husband and the child. It is as she predicted, a girl. She is named Béatrice.*'

'The two lovers seem to carry on pretty much as before Béatrice's birth, until this:

'*15 July 1814. I was blind. I was tricked by an enchantress. I saw them together tonight at Bellefontaine through the half-closed shutters.*

They betrayed me, made a fool of me, she and that scoundrel who lives under my roof. Did he know that Magali was mine? Did he seek to spite me by seducing her? Is it his revenge for having to remain in my household as my servant and not being able to inherit the estate and the title? I cannot help but wonder how long they have been deceiving me and whose child Béatrice really is.'

'Who is he talking about?' Amy interrupted.

'His cousin, Arsène Coste, I think. According to my family charter, even though both branches of the Coste family have the right to live on the estate, the title can only belong to one bloodline – mine. I looked up old family papers. Arsène was about the same age as Renaud. He must be the one who was having an affair with Magali Bruni.'

Amy frowned. 'Is Frédéric related to Arsène Coste by any chance?'

'Yes. That's Fred's side of the family.'

He had no intention of talking about Fred right now. He'd given him an ultimatum after his outburst at the cocktail party. Sort yourself out or leave. And above all keep away from Amy Carter. Never before had he had to struggle so hard to stop himself from smashing his fist into a man's face. Fred must have seen the hard resolve in his eyes and heard the threat in his voice, because for the first time in ten years, he'd actually apologised for his behaviour.

'What happened to Renaud after he found out Magali was unfaithful to him?' Amy asked, breaking the brooding silence.

Fabien turned a few pages.

'After wallowing in self-pity for months, he finally married in November 1814. He joined Napoleon's army in May 1815, and was killed at Waterloo a few weeks later, a few weeks only before the birth of his son ... that's how the legend of the curse was born, I suppose. Anyway, something happened a few weeks before he left that changed his mind radically about Magali and that cult local people accused her of leading. He doesn't say what he saw but it scared him so much he decided to have the cedar forest planted.

'*10 May 1815. I have decided to cover the hill with a cedar forest, hide this infamy and make sure it is lost forever ... destroying the temple was not enough. The goddess' worshipers have other ways of going underground to carry out their wicked acts. This time, I do believe the villagers' claims about evil doings in the woods for I have witnessed myself the awful truth. Magali will be judged by God. May she be tormented for eternity.*'

Fabien's words died in the quiet evening.

'I wonder what he saw.'

Amy's deep blue eyes were deadly serious. As she leaned forward to gather the prints, her arm brushed against his. His throat went dry, his blood pumped hard. The hell with being patient and waiting for the right time. The need to touch her, kiss her, was too strong.

He put his hand on hers, turned it over. She gasped but didn't pull away.

'What is it between the ladies of Bellefontaine and the lords of Manoir Coste?' he asked in a low voice. 'And why do the men in my family always seem to fall for the women who live here?'

They locked eyes.

'Laurent claims that there is some kind of enchantment between Manoir Coste and the *bastide*,' she replied. 'It goes like this. "The spell flows with the spring, binding hearts together until death tears them apart." It was written in Latin on one of the stones he found in the garden.'

'I don't usually believe in spells,' he said.

And yet right now he was held captive by the power of her deep blue eyes.

Slowly, his fingers stroked the inside of her wrist, the palm of her hand. She looked at him, and parted her lips. He felt her whole body shiver under his touch.

Suddenly, she yanked her hand out of his grasp, pushed her chair back and rose to her feet.

'You'd better go,' she said in a breathless, panicked voice. 'I am expecting new guests any minute. I need to tidy up and get changed.'

Fabien took one long, deep breath, then another. It didn't help much. It would take a lot more to keep his body under control.

His voice was a little raw when he spoke next.

'Would you like to keep the journals for a few days?'

She nodded, serious. 'Yes, thank you. I'll show you out.'

She was already rushing down the terrace steps and into the courtyard where his car was parked. It looked like she couldn't wait to be rid of him.

He drove back to Manoir Coste too fast, anger, desire and frustration seething inside him. He must have read too much into the way she blushed and always seemed flustered around him. The new lady of Bellefontaine had made it very clear she wasn't interested. He should stop behaving like a love-struck idiot and making a fool of himself.

Chapter Sixteen

Amy peeled her shirt and jeans off, stepped into the shower, and turned the water on. As she washed bits of grass out of her hair and let the hot water soothe the ache from her shoulders and back, the same questions swirled endlessly in her mind. Was Fabien genuinely attracted to her or did she just see what she wanted to see? How could she love a man who had no sense of honour? A man who was prepared to cheat on his girlfriend, his almost fiancée, if the rumours were true – love him so much she lost all sense of self and was reduced to a weak and helpless creature every time he was near? She could pity Chris as she clung to her cheat of a boyfriend and refused to face the truth. She was just as pathetic as her sister. That served her right for being so judgemental and self-righteous where Chris and Toby were concerned.

She put on a white cotton summer dress with tiny pearl buttons at the front, slipped her feet into sandals, and ruffled her hair dry. There, she thought as she glanced at her reflection in the mirror: she may not compete with Claudine's designer clothes but she was a little more presentable for the arrival of her new guests ... whenever that may be.

A couple of hours later, she started to wonder if the Dubois family would ever arrive. She had no way to get in touch with them because the booking had come through the Tourist Office and the office was now closed for the night. What if they had an accident, or if they'd changed their minds and no longer needed rooms? The phone rang, and she answered straight away. It wasn't the Dubois but Adèle, who sounded sad and upset about Paul.

'He gets drunk every day, and has now locked himself in the spare room and won't speak to me. I have a hospital outpatient appointment in Apt tomorrow – nothing major, but I was hoping that he would come with me. Now I doubt he'll be in a fit enough state to do so.'

'Text me if you need a lift, or just company,' Amy said. She tried to comfort her friend but there wasn't much she could say.

After putting the phone down, she sat at the kitchen table and flicked through Renaud Coste's journal, eager to read once again the words that had moved her so much when Fabien read them. What wouldn't she give to hear him talk about her with such passion?

She pressed a hand against her chest. Her heart ached, her whole being ached. She loved him. Yet she must forget him, and the sooner the better. He was only playing with her and it was destroying her.

She would give him the diaries back, tell him she wasn't interested in investigating the temple any longer then keep well away from him.

She stood up. She would go to Manoir Coste right now. It was after eight – probably too late for Monsieur Dubois and his family to arrive – but just in case she pinned a note on the front door, explaining that she would be back shortly.

She grabbed her car keys, slipped Renaud Coste's diaries into her bag and went out. The roads were quiet and the drive only took ten minutes.

As she arrived at Manoir Coste she wondered briefly if she should leave the books at the reception for Fabien, but decided against it. It would be the coward's way out. She would talk to him and make sure he understood that she didn't want anything to do with him from now on.

Fairy lights lit the way to the cottage. Sweet, heady scents of herbs and flowers filled the air, blue shadows shivered in the light breeze as she walked across the empty walled garden. At last she arrived in front of Fabien's house. Light shone through the half-closed shutters, a piece of piano music could be heard through the open window. He was in. Her throat tight, she knocked on the door and waited.

A couple of minutes passed.

He must be busy. Perhaps he wasn't alone, and Claudine was there.

The door opened just as she was about to leave.

He must have just come out of the shower. His hair was wet, droplets of water speckled his chest and he was barefoot. All he wore were a pair of jeans and a white towel around his neck.

'Aimée?'

He had a way of saying her name which was almost a caress and made her heart beat faster.

She pulled Renaud Coste's diaries out of her bag and held them out.

'I'm sorry to trouble you at home. I know it's late, but I'd like to give these back to you.'

He looked confused. 'I thought you wanted to read through them.'

'I did. Well, I read enough anyway. The thing is … I also wanted to tell you that I don't think we should carry on with our … investigation. I'm going to be far too busy with Bellefontaine, and Laurent is coming back in a few days. He is far more qualified than us to carry out the research, don't you agree?'

Once again, she realised she talked too much, too fast.

'Why the sudden change of heart?' he asked in a cold voice.

'Pardon?'

'Am I so insufferable you can't stand the idea of spending any more time with me?'

Confusion and embarrassment made her face burn. He sounded hurt and angry. She swallowed hard, shook her head. 'No, of course not.'

'Then why are you cutting me off? I thought we made a good team.'

'We do,' she replied weakly. 'But I'm sure you'll have no problem finding someone else to help you.'

How she wanted to run away and be as far from him as possible ... No, that wasn't the truth! She wanted to touch him, wanted to feel the heat and the strength of his body against hers. She wanted him to kiss her like he had that evening at Bellefontaine.

'I don't want anyone else,' he said. 'I want you.'

She let out an anguished whimper.

'Please, don't say that. I have to go. Good night.'

'*Aimée*. Wait.'

He stepped forward and pulled her to him, trapping her hands against his chest.

'What are you doing?' she asked in a breathless whisper as she lifted her face up.

'What I should have done a long time ago. What I think you want me to do despite everything you've just said. I am right, aren't I?'

She nodded. The feel of his arms around her, the scent of his bare skin, still damp from the shower, was making Amy dizzy.

'But ... What about Claudine?'

He frowned. 'What about her?'

'How can you forget her so easily, how can you suggest that we ...'

He looked puzzled. 'Wait a minute. Surely you don't

think I'm involved with Claudine. Whatever gave you that idea?'

'Everybody seems to assume that you two are as good as engaged.'

He shook his head. 'Claudine works for me, that's all. And before you ask, there's nobody else either. You're the only woman I want, and it's been driving me insane for weeks. *Aimée*. Look at me.'

He ran his fingers through her hair. His mouth touched hers, hard, impatient, demanding. She parted her lips under the pressure, and he deepened the kiss. His hands slid up and down along her back, branding her through her thin cotton dress.

Overwhelmed by a molten surge of desire, she gripped his shoulders and let herself be swept away.

'Come with me.'

He pulled her inside the house and kicked the door closed. Her bag slipped off her shoulder and thudded to the floor. Fabien pinned her against the wood with his body.

'I've wanted you for so long,' he whispered as his lips trailed down the side of her neck. The stubble on his cheek rasped against her tender skin, creating an explosion of sensations that made her body tense and tight and shivery. The music, loud inside the room, played a dramatic soundtrack to the ache and the yearning in her heart. Her fingers dug into his shoulders. He looked down.

'Now is the time to walk away.'

He sounded hesitant, a far cry from his usual proud and confident self.

'I don't want to walk away.'

'So now you want me?'

'I always did.'

His eyes darkened. He pulled her close and bent down to

kiss her, his mouth in turn tender and hard, until she burned with the wild, primitive need to give, take, and be taken.

He let out a ragged breath.

'I think we'd better go up.'

She nodded and he took her hand. He led her up the stairs, and into a large bedroom. Their shadows danced on the walls as he pulled her into his arms again and started caressing the side of her throat, the swelling of her breasts through her light summer dress. His hands settled on her hips and he drew her closer. She threw her head back, breathed out a sigh. This was torture, sweet, beautiful torture.

'I want you, so much,' he said as he struggled to unfasten the buttons of her dress.

She helped him. Her dress parted open.

'I can take care of the rest,' he said in a raw voice. He pulled the dress down. It billowed as it fell to the ground. And then she stood in front of him in her white lacy underwear.

His hands gripped her hips as he kissed the hollow at the base of her throat, the swelling of her breasts just above her bra. She linked her fingers in the nape of his neck to pull him closer, and a moan escaped from her lips as her body writhed, hot and pliant in his arms.

He unclasped her bra, which slipped from her shoulders, and the contact of his bare skin sent shockwaves through her body. 'Fabien.' She whispered his name over and over again as he cupped her breasts, circled the small, hard tips with his thumbs, and bent down to kiss her.

Spreading her fingers on to his chest, she stroked random patterns until his breathing was harsh and his heart drummed fast and hard against the palm of her hands.

'Come.'

His eyes were hooded as he motioned her towards the bed, helped her lie down on the dark covers. He undressed swiftly, lowered himself down to the bed, and covered her body with his. He was hot, heavy, and strong. His hands, his mouth stroked and possessed her, relentless, and when he entered her pressure built and coiled, tighter and tighter until a bright, white light exploded behind her eyelids. She opened her eyes as he started moving, hard and fast, his gaze never leaving hers for a second. Wave after wave of pleasure made her body tighten and fly. She heard her own voice whisper and cry out, and then he followed her on the other side of the storm. Time stopped. She was his, now and forever.

Hours later, after they dozed off and made love again, she curled up against him, rested her head on his chest, and listened to the beating of his heart. He stroked the nape of her neck where her hair was tangled.

'You know what? I think I have developed a certain fondness for old maids.' His fingers trailed along her back. 'Especially English old maids.'

She took a deep breath and closed her eyes. This was a dream, a wonderful dream.

'Would you like something to drink?' he asked. 'A glass of champagne or white wine, perhaps?'

'Just water for me, please.'

He got up and ran downstairs. She heard the clinking of glasses on a tray, the gushing noise of a tap being turned on and off. The fine cotton sheets were smooth against her skin. Her whole body was more sensitive, her senses sharper. She stretched, smiled and let out a sigh. Never before had she felt so elated, so content – so whole.

She glanced at the objects displayed on the shelves at the other end other room. Even though she had noticed them before it had been too dark to make out what they were, and she'd had other things on her mind. Her eyes were used to the dim lighting now and she could see the objects were vases, or containers of some kind.

The blood drained from her face.

No. It wasn't possible. It couldn't be!

She got up and walked to the shelves. In front of her was the same object she'd seen in her dream of the secret ritual – the rectangular silver container Ben called a *salinum*. In her dream, the man carrying out the ceremony had taken some white power from it and sprinkled it all over her body. She lifted the *salinum* off the shelf and towards the light to study the engravings. Two lions, sitting opposite each other, with snakes writhing out of their manes. Like the one in her dream.

What was it doing on Fabien's bedroom shelf? How could she have dreamt of the very same object when she'd never seen it before?

Fabien came back into the bedroom with a tray that he placed on the bed.

'Here is your glass of water, Amy ... I see you are admiring my Roman collection.'

He walked towards her and took the object from her hands.

'I believe this is called a *salinum*, and was used to carry out religious ceremonies.'

He put it back on the shelf and turned to her.

'Listen, I'm going to pop out to the hotel kitchen for a few supplies. I'll make us something nice for breakfast. It'll soon be daylight.'

He pointed towards the window and Amy saw that indeed, the sky was lighter to the east. Already, goldfinches and thrushes were singing their dawn chorus.

'It's a good idea,' she said, although her throat was so dry, so tight, she had no idea how she could speak.

He got dressed quickly, slipped some trainers on, and rushed down the stairs.

As soon as she heard the front door slam shut, she dressed, ran downstairs and opened the front door. Once outside, she ran towards the car park. *Faster. Faster. She had to leave before Fabien came back.* Her hands shook so badly that she struggled to unlock her car door. She sat behind the wheel, slipped the key into the ignition and almost cried with relief as the engine roared to life. With a last look at the dark silhouette of Manoir Coste, she reversed her Clio and drove down the road towards Bellefontaine.

She managed to hold back the tears until she was home. Her note for the Dubois was still pinned to the door. She had forgotten all about them the moment Fabien had kissed her, so if they had come, they must have tired of waiting and found another guesthouse.

Michka greeted her at the door. As she walked through the empty farmhouse it felt that her whole world had come crashing down.

The discovery of the *salinum* changed everything, She sat at the kitchen table, stroked the puppy's head, tried to think.

She had to try to be rational about this. What did it really mean that Fabien had a *salinum* identical to the one in her dream? Could it be that it wasn't a dream after all and that, like Sophie Dessange, she had been subjected to some kind of ritual in an underground temple?

That would also mean that people had sneaked into Bellefontaine, drugged her, and carried her out without leaving a trace, perhaps using the underground passage and the trap door she was now sure existed in the cellar.

A shiver of fear ran down her spine, a sick feeling

weighed down at the pit of her stomach. Had Lily been right all along?

There was a darker, deeper fear she now had to confront, even if it could destroy her.

Was Fabien involved? Was he the man she'd seen in the temple? Had he been using the *salinum* she'd seen on his shelf during the ceremony?

Amy put her head in her hands and let out a cry of anguish. He'd been sceptical, angry almost, every time people mentioned the cult. He had even forbidden Laurent and his team to dig in the forest, and said that sometimes it was better for things to remain lost. Was it because he was involved and didn't want anyone to find out? His mother had said he'd been fiercely protective of his grandfather's papers, so much so he'd even forbidden her access to the library and had been enraged when he'd found out Céline had lent her the drawings.

She shook her head. No, he couldn't be involved. He had shown her Renaud Coste's diaries when he didn't have to. He wanted to work with her, and said they were a good team. He had made love to her with a passion that still resonated inside her whole body. Maybe he was just pretending to need her help. Was he also pretending when he made love to her? Was it his way of keeping her close ... controlling her and keeping her quiet?

The phone rang, strident in the silent house. It must be Fabien. He must be back at the cottage by now and wonder why she left so abruptly.

She'd better answer. She didn't want to run the risk of him coming to Bellefontaine. She needed time on her own to figure out what to do, what to think.

'Allo?' Her voice was faint, shaky.

'Amy! What's wrong? Why did you leave?'

Her mind raced. She had to come up with a convincing answer.

'I felt ill suddenly. I needed to go home.'

'How are you now?' he asked in a slightly more mellow tone of voice.

'Not very well, I'm afraid. I don't know what the matter is … I'm sure I'll feel better after a few hours' rest.'

'Would you like me to come over?'

'No!' she cried out. 'No, thank you,' she said more calmly. 'I'll be fine.'

There was a short silence.

'All right then. Let me know if you want anything. I'll call you later.'

'Sure. Goodbye.'

She put the phone down. Fresh tears welled up in her eyes. After the night she spent in his arms, she couldn't switch off her feelings for him so easily.

Never had she felt so utterly alone. And there was no one she could confine in. Adèle had her own worries, and so did Chris, who was miles away anyway. Besides, the last thing she wanted was to make wild accusations against Fabien without proof.

No, she would have to wait. Laurent would be here soon. Together, they would make sense of what – if anything – was going on. For now she would try to get some sleep. She undressed and slipped between her cold sheets.

Chapter Seventeen

The reference section at Apt library was empty, except for the librarian sorting out books and files behind the counter. Amy sat down, put her bag at her feet, and set Denis Piquot's journal on the table. The title was so faded it was barely visible on the dark green leather cover.

She bent down and breathed in the book's musty scent. *Récits étranges d'un voyageur dans le Luberon, 1755 (The Strange Tales of a Traveller in the Luberon, 1755)*. It was an intriguing title for what seemed a collection of tales and legends. She flicked through the yellowed pages and found copies of the prints she had bought at Lourmarin at the back, together with other engravings of Bonnieux and surrounding hilltop villages.

Fabien was right. The shopkeeper in Lourmarin had cut the prints out of another copy of the book to sell them separately. No wonder he'd looked uneasy when she had asked about their provenance. According to the librarian, Denis Piquot's books were very rare. So rare Amy had been very lucky to find a copy after running an internet search. Would she be lucky enough to find the answers to the questions which now haunted her? After seeing the *salinum* at Fabien's house, she believed that the ceremony hadn't been a dream after all. Who were the people involved, why had they taken her and, more importantly, was Fabien one of them?

She skimmed through the table of contents and found three entries about Bonnieux: 'Will-o'-the-wisp in Bonnieux'; 'The devil's mouth'; and 'The forgotten virgins'.

She was just about to turn to the first story when the librarian came over.

'I am sorry, madame, but we are closing for lunch.'

'I've barely had time take a look at the book,' Amy said. 'Can I not take it into the main library downstairs and read it there?'

'I'm afraid not. All books from the *service de documentation* must stay here,' the librarian answered. 'We are short staffed today, that's why we have to close the reference section for a couple of hours.'

Amy had no choice but to pick up her bag and leave. Once outside, she switched her mobile back on. She had two missed calls from Fabien and a text from Adèle. Her friend reminded her that she was in Apt for a hospital outpatient appointment today and texted that Paul had refused to come with her.

She called her voicemail, listened to Fabien's first message.

'I hope you're feeling better. Would you like to come over for lunch? Or maybe I could come and see you at Bellefontaine and bring a picnic. Please call me when you get this.'

He had left the second half an hour earlier, and his voice was noticeably colder.

'It's me. I hope you're better. Please call.'

She deleted both messages. She didn't want to talk to him. Not just yet. Not until she had more facts about the goddess and her cult – and she had found out whether or not he was involved.

On an impulse, she decided to meet Adèle at the hospital, which was only a short walk away. The receptionist directed her to the outpatient floor and as she walked across the atrium to get to the lift, she saw two familiar figures coming her way. Serena and Marc Chevalier.

She steeled herself for another hostile confrontation. When their paths crossed, however, Marc Chevalier nodded at her but Serena didn't even glance her way. Her feet shuffled on the floor like an old woman, and she leant heavily on her husband's arm. She seemed to have aged twenty years since the last time they had met on the terrace of Manoir Coste.

Amy found her friend in the waiting room, and Adèle rose to her feet, beaming. 'Amy! I am glad to see you.'

'I thought I would take you for lunch after your appointment and give you a lift back home,' Amy said.

Adèle was soon called in to see the doctor and to pass the time Amy flicked absent-mindedly through a magazine. As she turned a glossy page, her heart felt it had stopped.

A photo of Fabien stared out at her. Just looking at him now made her tremble, every inch of her body remembering his touch, his kisses and the fevered words he whispered against her skin.

Her fingers lingered on the photo, on the line at the side of his mouth that she had kissed again and again. If only she knew for sure, if only she could trust him ...

'I'm ready.'

Adèle, popping her head through the doorway, interrupted her thoughts.

'How are you?' Amy asked her.

'The doctor seems to think it's nothing serious, thank heavens ... and right now, I'm famished!' Adèle laughed.

'That's wonderful. Let's have lunch. My treat.'

Amy slipped her arm under her friend's to walk to the restaurant, a traditional brasserie near the market square, where red and white parasols provided welcome shade in the midday sun, and terracotta pots filled with oleander bushes screened the terrace from the busy street. They ordered salads, sandwiches and cold drinks.

After coffee, Adèle suggested a spot of shopping but Amy declined.

'I have work to do in the library.'

'What kind of work?'

'Research. I found an old book about Bonnieux. To cut a long story short, I need to find out more about these ancient rituals, about the goddess and her curse. I have to know what is real and what is fantasy,' she lowered her voice, 'and if I am safe at Bellefontaine.'

'Are you afraid the burglars will come back?'

'I am, but there's something else too.'

Amy hesitated, then decided it was time to tell her friend about her dream and the terrible story Sophie Dessange had told her in Avignon.

In a shaky voice she described the underground temple, the men and women in long white robes, and especially the man with the gold and blue ring.

'I found a trapdoor in the cellar. I can't help thinking that's the way people can get in and out of the *bastide*.'

Adèle frowned. 'I thought Paul resurfaced the floor in the cellar when he renovated Bellefontaine.'

'He did.'

'Then he must have found that trap door – if indeed it is one. I'll ask him about it tonight … if he wants to talk to me,' she added in a sad voice.

She paused, put her hand on Amy's, and gave a light squeeze. 'As for your dream, it does remind me of my Aunt Lily's stories – people in robes, strange music, an underground chamber.'

'You think my subconscious made it all up?'

Adèle shrugged. 'I'm sorry to sound so dismissive but it's the only rational explanation, isn't it? The woman you met in Avignon might be mentally unstable, or have invented the whole thing. If the stories about the cult murders and rapes were true, why did the culprits go unpunished for so long? Surely the ring leaders would have been found out and apprehended at some point.'

'Maybe they are important people – people with connections in high places, like ...'

Like Fabien, she finished silently. As the head of the region's leading aristocratic family, powerful landowner and businessman, he would be practically untouchable.

As if she heard what she was thinking, Adèle smiled and shook her head.

'You don't seriously believe Fabien Coste is mixed up in any of this, do you? If anything, I think he's in as much danger as you are.'

'I thought you didn't believe in the goddess and her curse on Coste men.'

Adèle shook her head. 'I wasn't thinking about the curse, more about human passions. There's another explanation to the premature death of the ducs de Coste, you see. A more rational, down-to-earth one.'

She leaned closer to Amy.

'I'm not the only one around here who thinks that the legend of the curse provided a convenient explanation to cover up deliberate killings.'

Amy's eyes opened wide. 'You think the ducs were murdered? Who would have killed them?'

'Think about it for a minute,' Adèle started, her voice almost a whisper. 'Someone had to look after the estate after the duke's death, at least until the Coste heir was born and came of age, and who was better placed to do so than another Coste – a cousin from the poor branch of the family – the branch which were never going to inherit?'

'Frédéric's side.'

Adèle nodded. 'Exactly. They must have profiteered from their position as estate managers.'

'Surely that's all in the past. You don't think Frédéric would harm Fabien to inherit Manoir Coste, do you?'

But as she spoke Frédéric's spiteful words on the evening of the cocktail party came back to her. How hateful he had sounded when he said Manoir Coste belonged to him, and that it would be his again one day.

Adèle shrugged again. 'Probably not. You're right. Paul would say I'm being fanciful, like my auntie Lily.'

She picked up her handbag and stood up.

'I tell you what … I'll come with you to the library and help you with that book you found, shall I?'

The two women linked arms and walked across the square. The bells of Saint Anne Cathedral chimed half past two as they climbed the library steps to the top floor, only to be greeted by a closed door on which a handwritten sign was pinned. '*Le service de documentation est fermé cet après-midi.*'

'The librarian did say they were understaffed today,' Amy remarked, disappointed. 'I hope they keep Piquot's book for me.'

So that their afternoon wouldn't be entirely wasted, they decided to go into the main library to check old newspapers. With any luck they would find references to the rebuilding of the village fountains Philippe Coste had drawn.

'Your best chance is to look at the local newspapers,' the librarian told her. 'The first one was founded in 1832 in Aix-en-Provence. It was called *Le Petit Journal*. We have most issues here on microfiches.'

She directed Amy and Adèle to a microfiche reading machine at the back of the library and said it would take her about half an hour to locate the microfiches in the archives.

Adèle sat down behind a machine that looked like a large computer.

'What exactly are we looking for?'

'Anything about the Brunis or the Costes, and the rebuilding of fountains around Bonnieux.'

They didn't have to wait too long. The librarian came back with a box of card-shaped pieces of photographic film, explained how to insert them into the machine, and wished them good luck.

A four-page publication, *Le Petit Journal* consisted mainly of local news about markets and fairs, and court judgements. It was interesting at first to read all about life in the area, but after a while Amy realised it could take hours, days even, before she found anything about the fountains and her enthusiasm started to wane.

'The print is so tiny, it's making me cross-eyed,' Adèle complained as she inserted yet another new microfiche in the reader. 'Wait a minute! I think I have something here.'

She pointed her index finger onto the screen and started reading.

'This is dated 23rd March 1835. "Monsieur Louis de Coste generously offered to commission new fountains in the villages of Saignon, Lourmarin, Ménerbes, and Buoux, which are still without public fountains after last January's devastating earthquake. Gaston Bruni, a reputed stonemason from Bonnieux, was appointed to carry out the works. It is hoped that the fountains will be completed by the summer."'

Gaston Bruni was Magali's husband, Amy thought, and Louis must be Renaud's son – the son he'd never met since he died at Waterloo. She would have to check the Coste and Bruni family trees. The two families were linked, generation after generation.

'Is there any mention of Gaston's wife Magali or their daughter Béatrice?' Amy asked.

'I'll check the paper for the following summer. There might have been some kind of ceremony to inaugurate the fountain.'

She gave Amy a curious glance.

'You seem to know an awful lot about the Brunis … How come?'

Amy told her friend about Renaud Coste's diary and the tumultuous liaison between him and Magali Bruni. 'So the ducs de Coste have had affairs with the Bruni women for a long, long time,' Adèle said when she finished. 'This is getting really strange.'

She wound the microfiche down, narrowed her eyes to peer at the screen, and let out a long breath.

'You were right. There is something about a Béatrice Bruni attending the inauguration ceremony in July 1835.

'"Today marked the formal inauguration of the newly restored Buoux public fountain … Monsieur Louis de Coste was in attendance, together with his mother the duchess, the mayor Monsieur Raymond and …"' Adèle read a few more names, '"and Monsieur Gaston Bruni, still in mourning after the passing of his wife last month. His charming daughter Béatrice did the honours and cut the ribbon. A reception at the town hall followed … etc … etc …"'

'There's something else. "Unfortunately a distressing incident spoilt what should have been a convivial event. A mob gathered outside the town hall and hurled insults and rotten fruit at Monsieur Bruni and his daughter as they were leaving the reception. Monsieur Coste offered the pair the safety of his carriage for the ride back to Bonnieux. Several of the troublemakers were arrested by the gendarmes, and we understand they meant to protest against the building materials used by Monsieur Bruni which they claimed were cursed and would bring ill fortune to the village."'

That was exactly what the old man in the café had told her.

Adèle turned to Amy. 'What is all that about?'

'Gaston Bruni used the stones from the temple to rebuild the fountains destroyed by the earthquake,' Amy explained.

She searched the paper for items in the autumn that same year. Scrolling down the screen, among headlines of local fairs and harvest festivals was a short article about the disappearance of a young man named Barnabé Dujean, who had come to Bonnieux as an apprentice and had not been seen for over a week after leaving the tavern where he'd spent the evening. In the following issue was a report about a young woman molested and left for dead in the forest. A group of hunters had stumbled upon her and taken her to the local dispensary. It was feared that shock had altered her mental faculties so much she would not be able to identify or name her attackers.

Amy scrolled down the next few issues.

'There it is ...' she whispered as she read the headline she had been expecting. "*Headless corpse found at the bottom of a pit.*"

In a few lines, the journalist confirmed that the mutilated body of Barnabé Dujean had been found near the old village of Bories. '"In the absence of any clues leading to the perpetrators, the local magistrate recorded a verdict of unlawful killing by one or several persons unknown. This reporter, however, heard several disgruntled comments in the audience to the effect that it wasn't the first time a young person was killed and savagely mutilated in Bonnieux, and that the culprits were known but that the gendarmes were too scared or too corrupt to investigate the case properly.'"

A young man and a girl ... A murder and a rape. She was reminded at once of Sophie Dessange's tale. She had to come back and read more old papers to search for similar incidents. Next to her, Adèle yawned and rubbed her eyes.

'I think we'll call it a day,' Amy said.

'Good idea. I'm getting a migraine,' Adèle agreed.

They handed the microfiches back to the librarian and walked out of the building.

They didn't talk much on the way back to Bonnieux.

'Try not to worry about the cellar,' Adèle said when Amy dropped her off in front of her house. 'I'm sure there is a simple explanation for that trap door, and for your nightmare.'

But questions still swirled inside Amy's mind as she drove back to Bellefontaine. Was Adèle right and she had indeed dreamt the ceremony? Was there even a secret cult or was it only the product of local gossip and legends? Adèle seemed pretty sure that the stories were pure fabrication, yet the newspaper reports about the young man disappearing and the girl being molested were troubling indeed. It reminded her a little too much about Sophie Dessange's story. If there was indeed a cult, then was Fabien involved, or was he in danger – whether from the goddess' curse or from his cousin's greed and hatred?

She left the main road and turned into Bellefontaine's courtyard to find herself face to face with the man she had sought to avoid all day, the man she couldn't stop thinking about.

Fabien was sitting behind the wheel of his Range Rover. His door was open, as if he was ready to pounce out at any moment. It was too late to drive away. It looked like she would have to talk to him, even if she wasn't ready.

As she parked, her hands shook so much she drove into one of the plant pots and knocked it over. She turned off the engine, and tried to compose herself before he swung open her door.

'Are you going to tell me what you're playing at?' His eyes were searching. His broad shoulders and tall, muscular frame filled all the space. He must have realised he was being overbearing because he stepped back to allow her to come out.

'It's too hot to talk outside,' she said. 'Let's go in.'

He followed her into the kitchen where Michka gave them both a rapturous welcome. She patted the dog's head, stroked her soft coat, and opened the patio door to let her out into the garden, trying to gain time.

When she turned back, Fabien was leaning against the door frame, his arms crossed on his chest.

'Would you like a drink?' she asked as she turned the tap on and filled a glass of water.

He shook his head. 'No, thank you.'

She drank half the water, and put the glass down and walked towards the fridge.

'Would you like some fruit salad? A piece of apricot tart, maybe? I made it with organic fruit from the market ...' Her voice sounded too high-pitched and she talked too fast.

'I don't want anything to eat or drink, I want an explanation. I'm not in the habit of chasing after women, and yet that's exactly what I feel I've been doing since dawn this morning. I was worried about you. You said you were ill, you didn't return my calls, but you weren't ill at all. Were you?'

An awkward silence fell between them.

Amy cleared her throat. At least she could speak part of the truth. 'No, I wasn't.'

'Are you avoiding me?'

'Well, I ...' She closed the fridge door and turned round.

How could she possibly explain her fears? Should she take a risk and tell him everything? Her heart was telling her to trust him. He was a good man, he took orphans on trips, gave his drunk of a cousin a job and a roof over his head.

Yet something held her back. They stood only a few metres apart, but although every fibre in her body screamed for his touch, the distance between them seemed insurmountable.

'Why did you run away from me, why did you not return my calls today? Damn it, Amy, what's going on?'

'Where did you get that small Roman container that was on your bedroom shelf?' she asked.

Fabien raised his eyebrows. 'The *salinum*? What has that got to do with anything?'

'Just answer me. Please.'

'It was a present from Claudine for my birthday a couple of years ago. Her mother owns an antique shop in Bonnieux and specialises in Roman antiquities.'

'Did she tell you what it was used for?'

'I told you. It was a salt container used in religious ceremonies. Why?'

'Did you lend it to someone recently?'

'Why would I do that? It's not exactly the kind of thing people ask for, like "by the way, I'm having a Roman-themed party, can I borrow your *salinum*?"'

He smiled, his face softened, and his eyes became the deep, warm shade of green she loved so much. She felt suddenly weak, so weak she had to lean against the fridge door for support.

'Why are you so interested in the *salinum*, and what on earth does it have to do with you running away from me?'

It had everything to do with it, but she couldn't tell him that.

'Did Claudine's mother say if it was a common design?'

Fabien frowned. 'If you're that interested in Roman antiquities, I suggest you pay Anne Loubier a visit and ask her all about it yourself.'

He walked across the kitchen floor and stood right in front of her, so close she could touch him.

'Look at me.'

She raised her face towards his. All she yearned for was to feel the strength and warmth of his arms around her, his lips on her mouth, his skin under her fingers. But there were too many questions that needed answering.

'Have you changed your mind about us?'

She decided to lie. He was offering an easy way out. She would take it.

'Yes, I have. I'm sorry if I misled you. The thing is, I realised I didn't want to be involved in a relationship right now. I have too many obligations. I want to focus on this place. On Bellefontaine.'

She forced her lips into a half-smile. 'I told you, I'm just an old maid at heart.' Even to her, it sounded a lame excuse.

In a swift movement he pulled her towards him. She didn't resist when he kissed her slow and deep.

Her heart beat so wildly it hurt, and she couldn't help but respond. Her lips moved against his, her body sought closer contact. Then, as suddenly as he had started, he pulled away.

'The things I loved the most in you were your honesty, your determination and lack of artifice,' he said in a hoarse voice. 'It seems that I was wrong on all counts. You can rest assured I won't be bothering you again.'

Amy heard the front door slam shut, the revving of an engine. Then there was silence.

All she wanted was to rush out after him, drive to Manoir Coste, and tell him she loved him. But her doubts and fears were too strong. So with tears streaming down her face, she went out onto the terrace, sat on the stone steps, and looked at the garden bathed in golden sunlight, with the dark green cedar forest behind.

It was beautiful as always but all she felt in her heart was loathing and rage.

'Whatever you're hiding, I'll find it,' she said aloud.

Chapter Eighteen

Saturday was another gloriously hot and sunny day – far too hot and sunny for April, according to the news reporter on the local radio she listened to whilst nibbling at a piece of toast on the sun-drenched terrace. The unseasonable weather was now a cause for concern for farmers who complained that the lack of rain put their crops and orchards at risk. The ground was so dry any sudden downpour could cause flash floods as the water would run down the hills and pool onto the plains without soaking through.

There would be no rain today, Amy thought as she clipped the lead on Michka's collar and started on the road to Bonnieux. The sky was bright blue, without the wisp of a cloud. It was hot already but she reckoned some exercise would do her good. Who knew, if she felt tired enough, she might even sleep tonight instead of tossing and turning in bed, torturing herself about Fabien …

It was market day in Bonnieux and the village buzzed with locals and tourists. Shopping, however, had to wait. First, Amy wanted to pay a visit to Anne Loubier. Her antique shop was in the rue Marceau, one of the larger streets winding around the heart of the village.

Amy studied the eclectic mix of antiques on display in the window – oak furniture and intricately embroidered linen, vases and jewellery. There was also a collection of crystals together with books entitled 'Crystal energy' or 'Lithotherapy, curing ailments with crystals'. She was definitely in the right place. She felt for the fluorite in the pocket of her blue jacket, tied Michka's lead to a lamp post, and pushed the door open.

The bell rang in the empty shop. Inside was more furniture, crockery, bronze and marble statues. She stood for a few minutes looking at walls covered from floor to ceiling with paintings and etchings.

She could hear a woman speaking at the back of the shop.

'You have to give me more time. I'll have the money by the end of next week ... yes, I told you. I have a buyer in Russia. No questions asked. No, don't do that! Soon, I'll have enough, more than enough, to repay you in full.'

The woman lowered her voice and Amy couldn't hear any more. She walked to a cabinet to look at the emerald-encrusted brooches, diamante watches and ruby earrings on display. All the prices were far too high for her.

'I'm so sorry to have kept you waiting. How can I help—' Anne Loubier's voice faded as she recognised Amy.

In her smart grey suit and crisp white shirt, and with her silky smooth black hair and heavy make-up, she was the spitting image of her daughter.

Amy forced a smile. 'I was admiring your beautiful jewellery. Are they antiques?' She pointed to the pair of ruby earrings.

Anne Loubier nodded. 'Mid-eighteenth century. Probably Spanish. The rubies are exceptionally clear. Would you like to try them next to your face? Although I don't think they would suit your colouring. You have to be a brunette, like my daughter, to wear rubies.

'I believe you met Claudine at Manoir Coste. She is Fabien Coste's public relations assistant. He would like her to be more than that, of course. Maybe I shall advise him to get the earrings as an engagement present.'

The woman was lying. Fabien had said he wasn't involved with Claudine, or anyone else. Then again, if he lied about being a member of the cult he could also have lied about his affairs too.

'Unfortunately, I couldn't afford rubies even if they suited me.'

'No, I didn't think so,' Anne Loubier said, a smug look on her face.

Amy took the crystal out of her pocket and pointed to the display of books and stones in the window.

'I see you're something of an expert in crystals and wanted to ask about this one.'

'Fluorite.' Anne Loubier held the stone in her manicured hand.

'I was told it was used in ancient religious ceremonies.'

The woman looked surprised. 'People usually mention their aphrodisiac qualities, but yes, you are right. This is a "dream stone" – one that can induce prophetic dreams. Roman priests used them to get in touch with their gods.'

'Where does it come from?'

'Several quarries around here still produce fluorite, but mainly the green and yellow crystals which are more in demand.'

She gave the stone back to Amy. 'Have I satisfied your curiosity?'

'Partly ... One of my guests, a young English woman, visited your shop with her husband a couple of weeks ago. She said you gave her a fluorite just like this one and told her gruesome old stories about Bellefontaine. She suffered such horrific nightmares after that she cut her holiday short and went back to England.'

Anne Loubier shrugged. 'I have seen quite a few English women these past few weeks. I don't recall giving any of them a crystal. Why would I do that? I sell crystals, I don't give them away, even to newly-weds.'

She stepped forward and stared straight into Amy's eyes. Her scent drifted towards her, heady and sickeningly sweet, a blend of rose and jasmine. Amy stepped back with a gasp and bumped into the glass display cabinet.

The woman wasn't going to acknowledge she'd given Eva Barlow the crystal, and there was no way Amy could prove otherwise. Better leave it for now.

She placed the stone onto a small table next to her. 'You can keep it. I don't want it any more.'

She paused. 'There was something else I wanted to ask you. You specialise in ancient Roman artefacts, don't you?'

Anne Loubier stroked the fluorite stone, scraping her long, red nails on the surface.

'I do indeed. What are you after?'

'A *salinum*. It has to be silver, with engravings of lions sitting opposite each other and snakes coming out of the lions' manes.'

Anne's fingers stopped stroking the crystal. She looked up.

'You are very specific about the type of *salinum* you want. Have you seen one of them before?'

'Yes, at Fabien Coste's house. He said your daughter gave it to him.'

Anne's fingernails started scraping the surface of the stone again.

'Do you think there are any similar *salinums* around? I particularly like that design.'

Anne put the stone down hard on the console table.

'I have no idea. Now if you'll excuse me, I have work to do.'

There was nothing else to do but leave. The visit had been a waste of time, but then what had she really hoped would happen?

Amy went out into the hot, bright sunshine. She untied

Michka's lead from the lamp post and followed the winding street towards the market square, trying to shake the feelings of unease her encounter with Anne Loubier had caused and the headache the woman's perfume had triggered.

She went into the Tourist Information office next, and smiled despite her headache when she saw Monsieur Verdier behind the counter instead of his grumpy assistant. Amy asked about the malfunction of the booking system and the cancelled bookings she'd had through his office.

Monsieur Verdier looked puzzled. 'I don't understand. You are the first hotelier to complain about this. Jacques said he'd fixed our computer. Between you and me, that boy has been rather distracted lately. I've stopped counting the times he's come in late.

'He has another part-time job now – as courier for Manoir Coste – on top of his driving job for the butcher, and I strongly suspect he has a serious crush on Mademoiselle Claudine. She could ask him to jump from the top of the cliff at Buoux and the silly boy would do it!'

'Jacques works for Monsieur Lefèvre too?'

Monsieur Verdier nodded. 'I suppose that's why the boy is so grumpy all the time. He is exhausted. Anyway, don't you worry about these glitches with the bookings, mademoiselle. It won't happen again. I'll look into it myself. Or at least I'll try. I'm no expert, as you well know.'

After leaving the Tourist Office Amy headed for the market to purchase lettuces, tomatoes, green beans, and new potatoes. Hopefully in a year or two she would grow her own vegetables and would pick everything she needed fresh from the garden. She also bought some goat's cheese and creamy Saint Félicien before paying a visit to the bakery for bread and croissants. Laurent was due the following day, and she remembered his healthy appetite.

Her bag hung heavy from her shoulder as she started on the main road. Michka pulled on the lead and sniffed tuffs of grass and tree trunks. The midday sun was so hot a hazy brume rose from the tarmac. There wasn't a breath of wind, and sweat soon ran down her spine and stuck her hair onto the nape of her neck. She paused at the side of the road to tie her hair up and take her linen jacket off. It was going to be a long walk home.

As she started to walk again, she heard a car stop behind her and Céline's voice called out. Amy turned and saw Fabien's mother wave from the Range Rover.

'I'm sure you could do with a lift home,' Céline said. 'Fabien darling, what are you waiting for? Go and help the poor girl with her bag.'

Fabien got out. From the look on his face, it wasn't hard to guess that he wasn't pleased to see her and had only stopped at his mother's suggestion. He held out his hand to take her shopping bag but she stepped away.

'Thank you but I'd rather walk,' she said.

'Nonsense,' Fabien retorted in a cold voice. 'I know people say that only dogs and English people can stand the midday sun, but you'll get heatstroke if you walk all the way back to Bellefontaine, especially carrying this bag. It's far too heavy.'

She was annoyed that he should talk to her as if she was a silly child.

'I'll be fine.'

'If you don't care about yourself, at least think about Michka,' he added even more coldly. 'She's far too young for long walks in this heat. Dogs get heatstroke too, you know.'

She glanced at the little dog who sat down in the shade of a pine tree, breathing fast with her tongue sticking out.

She didn't like to admit it but Fabien was right. Her puppy looked tired. Reluctantly she handed him her bag. He put it in the boot of the car, and she slid onto the back seat with the dog on her lap.

'It's lucky we bumped into you,' Celine said. 'I've just arrived from Paris and I was going to invite you for dinner tonight at Fabien's cottage.'

Fabien glared at his mother. 'You never said anything about this before. I have important business tonight.'

Céline laughed. 'Don't be silly, darling! You always have important business. However, being the boss means you can delegate and take the evening off.'

Amy liked Céline very much, but there was no way she could spend a whole evening with Fabien, especially at the cottage where there would be so many reminders of their night together. She glanced at him but he seemed totally focussed on the road.

Céline turned to her. 'Shall we say eight o'clock?'

'I'm not sure I can come,' Amy said. 'I am expecting a new guest tomorrow ...'

Knowing what Fabien thought about the dig, she was reluctant to mention that it was Laurent she was expecting.

'Oh.' Céline let out a disappointed sigh. 'I have something rather exciting to show you both. After my last visit, I remembered where I had seen old plans of Manoir Coste. They were in a box, in the study of our Paris apartment. I must have filed them in there after the ...' her voice faltered '... after the shooting accident. I believe you will find them very interesting. I promise it won't be a late night.'

Amy couldn't refuse a second time without being rude.

Fabien pulled into Bellefontaine's courtyard, and got out of the car. He opened the back door and lifted her shopping bag out of the car. They brushed against each other when she got out. She felt the warmth of his skin against her arm, breathed in his aftershave.

His face was unfathomable.

'I'll pick you up at eight,' he said.

The evening promised to be awkward, she thought as she watched the Range Rover drive away, but with any luck, she wouldn't have to stay too long.

She was in the middle of mopping the downstairs floor when the phone rang. She cringed as she recognised the self-assured voice of Armelle Capitelli, the journalist from the *Journal du Lubéron*.

'I want to write something about Bellefontaine and its mysteries,' the woman announced.

'What mysteries?' Amy combed her tangled hair back with her fingers.

'I understand one of your guests suffered nightmares so horrific while staying at Bellefontaine that she left early. Has this happened to any other of your guests?'

Amy's fingers tightened on the receiver.

'Who told you about this?'

The journalist chuckled at the other end of the line. 'I'm sorry, but I am unable to divulge my sources. Do you confirm that the young English bride had to cut her honeymoon short?'

'I won't confirm or deny anything, Mademoiselle Capitelli.' Amy slammed the phone down.

How did the reporter find out about Eva when only Adèle, Paul, and Lily knew about her? No, that wasn't true ... Someone else knew. She had told Anne Loubier that very morning. She must be the one who had contacted the journalist.

Amy frowned. One thing was odd. Armelle Capitelli knew that Eva and Justin were on honeymoon. Come to think of it, Anne Loubier did mention English newly-weds, yet Amy was certain she hadn't said that Eva and Justin had just got married. That could only mean one thing. The antique dealer had lied. She was the one who had given them the crystal.

The evening came far too quickly for Amy's liking. She stood for a while in front of her wardrobe, deciding what to wear. There was no point getting dressed up. Dinner at Fabien's cottage would be informal. She picked another white cotton dress with a pretty gathered neckline, left her hair loose and slipped on a pair of pumps.

Fabien was right on time. As soon as she heard his car, she draped her pink shawl loosely on her shoulders and opened the front door. Like her, he had dressed casually, in a pair of jeans and one of the stripy blue and green rugby shirts he seemed to favour. They looked at each other without saying a word. Amy's throat was dry. She was aware of a dull ache in the region of her heart.

For a second, she wanted to touch him so much it hurt. Fabien broke the silence. 'Shall we go?'

They were both quiet in the car on the way to Manoir Coste. The evening sky was beautiful, pale blue with a few wispy orange and pink clouds.

They still weren't talking when they arrived at Manoir Coste, and she followed him to the cottage. Tonight even more fairy lights than before lit the path around the walled garden.

'As you can see, we are gearing up for our *Fête des Lumières* at the end of April,' Fabien explained.

'Is it a local tradition?'

He nodded. 'It started when people of Bonnieux offered thanks to the Virgin Mary for sparing the village from the plague in the Middle Ages, but some say the tradition is much older and dates back to Roman times or before.'

'Do you think it has anything to do with the lights in the forest – the goddess' lights?'

'Maybe. Anyway, we always hold a ball and have fireworks in the park that weekend. That's why my mother came back from Paris. No doubt she'll invite you. She seems to have the wrong idea about us and I didn't have the chance to explain that you weren't interested.'

Once again, her heart pushed her to tell him that she had lied, that she loved him. And once again her head held her back.

Inside the cottage, Céline gave Amy a hug and a kiss on the cheek.

'Here you are, darling, just in time. The chef just delivered our supper.'

There were crystal flutes on the coffee table. A bottle of champagne stuck out of an ice bucket. Nibbles and canapés were artistically displayed on a silver platter.

Fabien poured the champagne out and gave Amy one of the tall, delicate crystal glasses.

'I think we'd better eat,' he decreed. 'I must prepare for my trip to Paris tomorrow. Claudine is already there.

She emailed me some papers I need to look at.'

'How long will you stay?' Céline asked.

'Only until Monday evening. I promised to take the boys from Maison Espérance rock-climbing on
Tuesday.'

The three of them sat around the oak table to eat the selection of seafood dishes, salads, terrines and fresh fruit pastries the restaurant staff had delivered.

Over supper, Amy couldn't help looking at Fabien. It was difficult to believe that he could be involved in something as evil as murders and rapes.

Their eyes kept meeting across the table. His were cool and indifferent, and gave nothing away.

'Let's look at the plans now,' Céline announced after they'd had coffee.

She asked Fabien to tidy up the dishes as she fetched a leather satchel and unrolled the plans on the dining table. There were half a dozen thick parchment papers. Even though the drawings had faded, it was still possible to recognise the front elevation of the castle.

'These date from 1690.'

Fabien pointed to the date at the bottom of one of the plans. 'That's the one we want – the plan of the basement.'

The three of them leaned forward. The basement of the chateau was divided into over twenty cellars. Fabien indicated the lines going off from four cellars to the west, east and north.

'These lines must represent the tunnels. The west tunnel goes towards Bellefontaine, the east tunnel goes to Bonnieux, and the north passages towards the old village of Bories.'

He traced the outline of the basement area with his finger. 'This is the central staircase leading to the main larder area. The west tunnel starts from the tenth basement room.'

He looked up. Excitement shone in his eyes. 'I'm going down there now.'

Céline gasped. 'Not tonight!'

'Why not?'

'It might be dangerous.'

'I'll come with you,' Amy declared.

'No, you will not,' he said. 'It'll be cold and dirty. There might be mice or rats.'

'I'm not afraid of a few mice. All I need is an old shirt or jumper to wear over my dress. Please,' she insisted.

'Very well, if you're sure. I'll get you something to cover up with.'

He went upstairs and came back with a blue shirt. It was so big it almost covered her white dress down to her knees.

Celine said that she would wait for them at the Manoir. It only took five minutes to walk through the gardens to the service entrance at the side of Manoir Coste.

'The staircase is this way.'

The corridors and the kitchen were busy with hotel and restaurant personnel. All greeted Fabien and looked at her with undisguised amusement as she had to run behind him to keep up with his long strides, his blue shirt flapping around her.

He grabbed a couple of torches from a utility room near the kitchen, pushed a huge wooden door open, and flipped an electric switch.

'There is electric light in the first five cellars because that's where we keep our wine, but after that it will be pitch black,' he explained as they went down the stone staircase.

'Switch your torch on and watch your step,' Fabien instructed when they walked past the last wine cellar.

The temperature dropped as they walked into the darkness. She followed him closely as he lit the way, shining his torch onto the alcoves on each side.

Each time there was a junction, he counted how many pillars they had passed before carrying on.

He turned to the right.

'This is it. Cellar Number Ten.'

He shone his torch onto the stone walls from the floor to the low, vaulted ceiling.

'This is the west wall. Can you see anything? An opening, or a door?'

She walked along all the way to the far corner. Shadows of cobwebs, as delicate as lace, moved upwards on the wall under her torch's yellow beam.

'There's a draft blowing from behind here,' she said.

He put down his torch, and started to push against the stones. At first nothing happened. Then a section of wall shifted with a grinding sound. Fabien kept on pushing until the wall revealed a dark passage. A gust of frigid air blew into the cellar, raising goosebumps on Amy's skin.

'This is the entrance to the west tunnel, and it's not even blocked. It's almost as if it's been used recently. I'll leave it open and return with a couple of lads in the morning. Let's go back.'

'What's that, over there?' Amy asked as she saw something glittering near the tunnel opening.

Fabien picked it up and shone his torch on it.

'I don't believe this.'

Amy stared at the gold and blue signet ring in his hand, with two gold letters – CV.

She had seen it before. Images flashed in her mind. A man's hand. Strange, hypnotic music. Torches on the wall. Herself, lying down, almost naked, helpless and terrified.

'It's my ring' he said.

Amy stared at him in horror.

So it was true! He was the man in the underground temple. The man who had performed the ceremony, who had thrown the white substance all over her, who violated her …

'It was you in the temple,' she said in a hoarse whisper. 'It was you all along.'

He walked towards her. The torchlight threw menacing shadows on his face. She stepped back but her legs were shaking and she stumbled. The darkness came closer, surrounding her.

She put her hand to her throat and would have collapsed to the ground if Fabien had not caught her in his arms.

Chapter Nineteen

Amy stared bewildered at the ornate moulded ceiling. Her gaze trailed down to the heavy bronze-coloured curtains drawn against the night, and the oil paintings of hunting scenes hanging on the walls. A sleek designer desk lamp shone a dim, warm glow onto neat stacks of files and papers. She recognised the room. She'd been here before.

This was Fabien's study. The question was why was she lying on the sofa with a cushion under her head and a soft, warm blanket on top of her? A subtle sandalwood scent she recognised only too well filled the air. She frowned, looked down. It was no wonder she could smell Fabien's aftershave. She was wearing his shirt!

Memories of the evening came rushing back. Céline had found maps to the basement. Fabien had led the way down into the cellars. Together they had found the entrance to one of the tunnels. And then …

Then she had seen something on the ground. His ring – the proof he was one of them!

She jumped to her feet, peeled the shirt off, and threw it into a heap on the Persian rug. Her heart felt like it was breaking.

What else had Fabien done? Had he arranged the burglary, nailed that dead rabbit on her door the first night she'd arrived at Bellefontaine, slashed her tyres, and left the dead crow on her car in a gruesome display to scare her? Had he drugged her drink at Manoir Coste too?

Whatever Fabien was up to, she had to get out before he came back to check on her.

Too late! She heard footsteps in the corridor and froze in terror as the door knob turned and the door opened slowly

Thankfully, it wasn't Fabien, but Céline.

'Amy darling, are you alright?'

Her eyebrows drawn in a worried frown, Céline took Amy's hand.

'You must lie down and rest.'

'No.' Amy pulled her hand away. 'I don't want to stay here a minute longer.'

'Now you're being unreasonable,' Céline retorted in a stern voice that had the same authoritative note as her son's. 'You shall have a nice hot drink, then I'll get a member of staff to drive you back. I knew it was a bad idea to go down to the basement tonight. Fabien said it was so cold down there you passed out. He tried to revive you but in the end had to carry you back up.'

How could Amy tell Céline that it wasn't the cold that caused her to faint, but the realisation that her son was involved in some kind of cult?

'Where is he now?'

'He set off for Paris while you were sleeping. I don't know why he had to leave so fast but he was in a terrible mood.' She cocked her head to one side and looked at Amy.

'But of course! How silly of me not to realise before. You two argued, didn't you? That's why you're crying and why he left so suddenly. Oh darling, don't worry. Everything will be fine. It's plain to see you two are very much in love.'

'We're not,' Amy cried out. 'You have it all wrong. He doesn't love me, and I certainly don't love him.'

Céline smiled, made a tutting sound and pointed to the sofa.

'Sit down, wrap the blanket around your shoulders, and wait for me. I won't be long.'

She walked out, leaving Amy to gaze at the half-open door. For a moment she was tempted to sneak out and make her way back to Bellefontaine on her own, but decided against it. Now Fabien had gone, she was safe at Manoir Coste. So she sat on the sofa and as she was shivering, she pulled the blanket tightly around her shoulders.

Céline reappeared a few minutes later, followed by a waitress carrying a tray with a teapot and two cups.

She sat on the sofa next to her. 'Tea? Milk and sugar?'

Amy nodded. Céline poured out two cups and placed one on the table in front of her.

'I think I know what you're going through,' she started after Amy swallowed a few sips. 'Coste men aren't easy to understand, let alone to love. They are so very proud, so intent on having their own way they often come across as cold, haughty tyrants. In that respect, Fabien is very much like his father. Manoir Coste, this land, it's everything to them. I didn't think Fabien would be so attached to this place since he was brought up in Paris, but I was wrong. Every time we came back for holidays, it was as if he was exactly where he belonged. Here. And when he was of age to take the place over and realised what a mess Frédéric's father had made of things, I hoped he'd sell. But it only made him more determined to live here and bring Manoir Coste back from the brink of ruin.' She smiled faintly.

'My son is a very proud man, Amy. Some of his business associates would no doubt call him stubborn and ruthless too ...'

She put her porcelain cup down.

'But I've seen the way he looks at you, and heard the way he talks about you. He is crazy about you, even if he doesn't quite understand it yet.'

Unable to listen to another word, Amy stood up.

'And I say you are wrong. Thank you for the tea, but I'll leave now. Could you phone for a taxi please?'

'There's no need.'

Céline rose to her feet, walked to Fabien's desk, and phoned the reception for a driver and a car.

'I left my bag at the cottage,' Amy said. 'My keys are inside.'

'I'll send someone for it.' Céline phoned through to reception again and asked for Amy's bag to be picked up. They didn't speak as they walked out of the office and into the lobby, where a driver handed Amy her handbag.

'I can't help thinking that I am somehow responsible for what happened tonight,' Céline said as she turned to say goodbye. 'If only I hadn't shown you the plans of the basement, you wouldn't have gone down to the cellar and then you and Fabien probably wouldn't have quarrelled.'

There were tears in her eyes, and Amy felt a pang of guilt.

'It's not your fault. Not your fault at all. Good night, Céline,' was all Amy could manage before following the driver out.

Back at Bellefontaine. Michka greeted her at the door, as usual, and Amy stroked her silky coat absent-mindedly.

What should she do now? Capitaine Ferri would probably laugh at her and think she was insane if she told him she suspected Fabien of being involved in a criminal cult. After all she had no proof.

Ferri had been in touch a few times about the burglary, and he had also been kind and understanding when she had made her statement at the Gendarmerie after her drink had been spiked at Manoir Coste. She had tried to be objective and only mentioned Serena Chevalier's name as a possible witness, even though the woman had a motive for wanting to hurt her, since she hated her, and wanted her gone from Bellefontaine ... But the gendarme had come up with no suspect and no lead in either case ...

The phone's shrill ringing echoed in the silence. She glanced at her watch and saw that it was almost eleven.

'Thank God you're there,' her sister breathed out at the other end.

'Chris? What's the matter?'

'Can you pick Peter and me up at Marseille Airport?' Chris paused. 'I've left him, Amy. I've left Toby and I'm not going back. You were right about him.'

There was no point asking for more details right now. She told Chris to wait in the terminal, ran upstairs to slip a jumper over her dress, and grabbed her car keys. As an afterthought, she lifted Michka in her arms, clipped her lead on, and put her on the seat at the back of the car. The dog might provide a welcome diversion for Peter.

The drive took her onto dark country roads to Aix-en-Provence where she joined the motorway to Marignane Airport. It was half past midnight when she parked near the arrival terminal. It was almost empty, so she had no difficulty spotting her sister, sitting on a bench with Peter curled up at her side, his head resting on her shoulder.

Chris hugged her.

'Thanks for coming to get us,' she said. 'I'm sorry for being a nuisance, but I didn't know where else to go.'

Amy looked at her, puzzled. That was new. Chris was usually self-centred and rarely took other people's lives and feelings into account.

'Don't worry about it. It's great to see you both.'

Behind Chris, Peter blinked, stifled a yawn and straightened up.

'Hi, Aunt Amy.'

'Hi, sweetie,' she said as she helped him to his feet.

'What happened to your car?' Chris asked, pointing to the bonnet of the Clio. In the crude electric light of the car park, the red splodges of paint looked even more garish than usual.

Amy sighed. 'I'll tell you about it later.'

Michka leapt out with loud yelps and Amy handed Peter the lead. 'You can hold her lead while she runs around, and if you want, it'll be your job to look after her at Bellefontaine.'

'Cool. I've always wanted a dog,' he said with a beaming smile.

Half an hour later, Amy checked her rear-view mirror and saw that Peter had fallen asleep with the dog on his lap. She smiled.

'I think he'll love it at Bellefontaine. You will too ... although there are a few things I need to tell you—'

Chris interrupted. 'Same here. You were right about Toby. I ignored the signals for too long. I was stupid. The thing was, I didn't want to see what he was really like ... that he was cheating on me with half of Manchester and never cared for me or his son. He didn't even care when I said I was leaving him.' Chris heaved a shaky breath. 'I hope you can put us up for a while.'

'Of course, as long as you need,' Amy agreed. Now wasn't the time for lectures or taking big decisions about the future.

'I hope you've worked on your French,' she added. '*Moi? Bien sûr.*'

The sisters exchanged a smile. Chris rested her head on the window, closed her eyes and fell asleep.

It was almost three in the morning when they reached Bellefontaine. Amy warmed up some milk for Peter and while he sat at the kitchen table drinking it, she helped Chris haul their suitcases up the stairs.

'It's a beautiful house,' her sister whispered a short while later after having put Peter to bed. 'You must be very happy here.'

'I am, but ... well ... there have been a few problems,' Amy started.

Chris rubbed her eyes and stifled a yawn. 'Really? What kind of problems?'

'I'll tell you about it in the morning. First you need to sleep.'

'Thanks for taking us in, sis.' Chris kissed Amy on the cheek. 'Good night.'

When her alarm rang at seven, Amy tumbled out of bed and headed straight for the shower. Her eyes were gritty with lack of sleep, her body ached, and her head pounded. That morning, even the steaming hot shower didn't revive her.

She wrapped a towel around her and opened her shutters and window onto another clear blue sky. The shower may not have managed to wake her up, but the fresh, scented breeze did.

She threw on a pair of jeans and a red and white embroidered tunic, towel dried her hair, and slipped her feet into a pair of canvas shoes. Downstairs she opened the shutters and the patio doors to let Michka out and started making breakfast. Soon, coffee was brewing in the percolator and croissants were warming up in the oven. She took a brand new jam jar out of the cupboard.

Going through her daily routine helped her focus on the day ahead. First, breakfast. Then, she would prepare Laurent's room and make lunch. She would ask Chris to join them as she told him what she had discovered so far – including the revelations about Fabien. It was only fair that her sister knew Bellefontaine may not be the safe haven she had hoped for.

Chris came out onto the terrace as Amy was pouring her second cup of coffee. She stretched in the sunshine before sitting down and helping herself to coffee.

'This is paradise!'

'Well, maybe not quite. Is Peter still asleep?'

Chris nodded. 'Poor kid.'

Tears filled Chris' blue eyes, her chin started to tremble. 'Why was I so blind where Toby was concerned? And do you know what – I am quite sure I didn't even love him. I just didn't want to be alone like …'

'Like your old maid of a sister?' Amy finished with a smile.

'Sorry. Well. You know me. You may be the old maid, but I've always been vain and shallow and deep down I've always envied you,' Chris said.

Surprised, Amy put her hand on her sister's. 'At least it's over, now. '

'I'll wake Peter up,' Chris said. 'He can always have a nap in the afternoon if he's still tired.'

Laurent arrived before lunch, as promised. He had borrowed the museum's van and some equipment to carry out his own private investigation into Bellefontaine's garden.

It was like seeing an old friend again. He was wearing one of his checked shirts, but because of the warm weather his sleeves were rolled up and his collar unbuttoned. Amy kissed his cheek, showed him into the kitchen, and introduced him to Chris and Peter who were setting the table for lunch.

'Don't talk too fast,' she instructed. 'My sister's French is rusty.'

After lunch, Amy sent Peter outside with Michka and asked Laurent and Chris to sit down and listen to what she had to say. With hesitation, she told them everything she knew about the Brunis, the secret ceremonies and the forest temple. She told them about Renaud Coste's account of his liaison with Magali Bruni and the destruction of the temple. Then she spoke about the ceremony she thought she had dreamt, and all the old stories she had heard about rapes and murders, secret rituals and mutilations.

Lastly, and with a choked voice, she mentioned Fabien and how she now believed he was involved in the cult.

'I don't believe this is happening for real.' Chris shook her head. 'It sounds like a horror story.'

'Exactly,' Laurent said, smiling at her in approval, 'therefore the first thing we must do is to eliminate all the supernatural elements – goddesses' spirits, will-o' the-wisps, curses, or spells – and focus on the facts.

'We know that a Roman fountain and a temple once stood in the woods. We also know that there are underground passages under the hilltop.'

He turned to Amy.

'Did you say there were three tunnels on that plan of the castle you saw yesterday?'

Amy nodded. 'Yes, to the west, north, and east of Manoir Coste. Fabien opened up the west tunnel, the one that is supposed to lead all the way to Bellefontaine – perhaps even to the trap door in the cellar.'

'I will look at it later. I have some equipment in the van, including a hand-held GPR. That's a ground penetrating radar to survey the basement floor.

'Talking about tunnels, there is something that doesn't add up in your theory about Fabien Coste. If indeed he was involved in the cult – whatever that turns out to be – then why did he take you down to the cellar and show you the entrance to the tunnel? Surely the last thing he'd want would be to reveal its existence – especially to you.'

Amy had thought about that very question earlier.

'Maybe he had no alternative after his mother showed us the plans. If he had gone down on his own, like he wanted to at first, he probably would have reported that the tunnels didn't exist anymore. When I insisted on coming with him, he had to fake the discovery of the tunnel. He could always pretend later that the tunnel was blocked or didn't lead anywhere.'

'Hmm ... I'm still not convinced,' Laurent said, shaking his head. 'But let's go back to the temple for now and get our facts straight. I asked Patricia to look through the Museum archives for information about Bonnieux. She also went to Glanum to do some research there. This is what she found.'

He opened his notebook and flicked through a few pages.

'The topography of this hilltop is very similar to other Salyen settlements in the region. Here in Bonnieux, we have Manoir Coste, which was probably built on the location of the original hill fort where the chief of the tribe and his men lived. Then we have the old village of Bories on the hill for the rest of the tribe, and a temple somewhere in the forest ... what is missing is the sanctuary, the priestesses' dwelling and the temple.'

'The village of *what*?' Chris asked.

Laurent looked at her. 'The *bories* are stone huts that date back to the Gauls. The whole hilltop used to be a Gallic settlement, with Manoir Coste being built on the location of the ancient fort. The village was where the tribe lived, and was still used by shepherds until the middle of the twentieth century. It's completely abandoned in thorns and brambles nowadays.'

He paused.

'From the evidence we unearthed when I was last here, I think we can safely assume that the sanctuary was located here at Bellefontaine. It would explain why underground passages link Manoir Coste, Bellefontaine and the old village, as you saw on that map yesterday. There will also be a tunnel leading to the temple. It's exactly like the other settlements with their old tunnels linking the different areas of the site.'

Panic constricted Amy's throat. 'You see, it's true. It's all true ...'

Laurent laid a calming hand on her arm. 'Not necessarily. We still have a lot of digging around to do.' He pulled a face. 'Literally and figuratively. We also know that back in the 1810s Renaud Coste was involved with Magali Bruni of Bellefontaine, whom some people in Bonnieux accused of leading evil practices in the temple – basically of being a priestess or cult leader. Renaud later seemed to agree with this and ordered the temple to be destroyed and the cedar forest to be planted.

'What we have after that is pure gossip. Since the destruction of the temple, a so-called malediction has affected the ducs de Coste, most, or all of whom, suffered fatal accidents.'

Laurent grabbed a pen and wrote down a few notes.

'I will draw the Coste family tree to establish exactly when and how the ducs died and trace the Bruni family too. I can do that by checking the registry office and the local archives at the public library in Apt.'

'So what do you think about the sect, the ceremonies, the rapes, and murders?' Chris asked, sounding frightened.

'Here we are leaving the facts for local folklore. I am not denying that people got murdered or hurt around here, but there could be lots of explanations for it, such as muggings or revenge killings. The same goes for rapes, unfortunately. These things do happen without the involvement of an evil cult.'

He glanced at Amy.

'I'm sorry if I sound dismissive, but is it possible you dreamt the ceremony? The mind is a strange processing tool. It can store images, sounds, or information for years. You may have watched a programme or read a book about Roman religion years ago. You may have seen the photo of a *salinum* and believed it was the same one Fabien Coste had in his bedroom.'

He gave a little embarrassed cough and Amy felt her cheeks heat up. She hadn't explained why she'd been in Fabien's bedroom but Laurent and Chris must have drawn their own conclusion.

'You had a nightmare,' he resumed after a few seconds of silence, 'a very vivid nightmare, and you sleepwalked into the forest. It is odd, but not unheard of at all. Sleepwalking can occur when people are under a lot of stress.'

'There was something else,' Amy said in a quiet voice. 'Something I haven't told you. I don't know if it has anything to do with the cult or the burglary ...'

'What is it?' Laurent asked.

Amy told him about her drink being spiked during the reception at Manoir Coste.

'What did the police say?'

'They still don't know who did it, or why, and neither do I,' Amy answered.

'If there is indeed a so-called cult,' Laurent carried on, 'it could be just a group of people seeking to re-enact old ceremonies to get cheap thrills. You only have to search the internet for Roman religion or Roman sects to realise that there is everything and anything out there, ranging from the fairly innocuous to the frankly bizarre, complete with dominatrix priestesses and orgiastic rituals.'

'So you're saying that there might be some kind of kinky sex club around here?' Chris grinned.

Laurent glanced at Chris and a bright pink flush crept up his neck, all the way to his cheeks.

'Well … who knows?'

Serious once more, Chris looked at Amy.

'You must have been so worried all this time, and yet you never said a word. Every time I phoned, you said everything was fine. Has any of this got anything to do with the red paint on your car?'

'I'm not sure. Maybe it was just a prank, along with the dead crow and the slashed tyres.'

'What dead crow and slashed tyres? What on earth has been going on here? Poor Amy, you've been through so much and all on your own, and I've been so selfish, as usual!'

Chris gave her a hug, then burst into tears and ran out into the garden.

Laurent looked at Amy enquiringly. 'Is she all right?'

'She will be. She just split up from her boyfriend.'

Chris had changed. It was the first time ever she admitted to being wrong or self-centred. Maybe they had a chance to become friends after all.

She turned to Laurent. 'I'll show you the engravings I bought in the shop at Lourmarin.'

'The temple is Gallic – early Salyen, I'd say,' he remarked later as he studied the prints. 'The statues look exactly like the one you found in the garden. The fountain however is unmistakably Roman.'

'The shopkeeper called it a *nympheum*.'

'That's right. It's a monumental fountain, like those erected by Roman patrician families on the site of a spring or above a sacred cave. This one is a beauty. There aren't many like it left. It's a great shame it was destroyed.'

He raked his fingers in his brown hair. 'I want to put together all the inscriptions you transcribed from the fountains. If the temple pillars were really used to rebuild the fountains in Buoux, Saignon, Lourmarin and Ménerbes, they will give me a better understanding of the cult celebrated there. I made a copy of all your emails.'

He turned over a few pages.

'Do you remember the first stones we found here at Bellefontaine? The engravings were fascinating. One was about *"The sacred wood in which flows an eternal spring coming out of a dark cave, where you meet the goddesses."* Then there was that one about the enchantment. How did it go? Ah yes, *"The spell that flows with the spring, binding hearts together until death tears them apart."*'

He glanced up and smiled. 'I can't help it, I still find it incredibly romantic, in a tragic kind of way.'

'It's more a curse than a spell, and there's nothing romantic about it,' Amy said.

Romantic was mild and flowery, safe and gentle. What she felt for Fabien was at once dark and fiery, overwhelming and all consuming, filled with uncertainty and pain. It wasn't romantic to love so much – to hurt so much.

'There are references to the sacred spring on every single fountain you looked at,' Laurent went on. '"*Pulchra fons, Terracula pervigil*" translates into *"Beautiful fountain or spring, vigilant spectre forever standing guard."* The inscription on the fountain in Saignon tells us that *"The temple lives below ground, its entrance under the spring in the forest."*'

'Then we have the Greek name of the goddess, which predates the Latin since the Greeks arrived in Provence earlier – Ροκλίσίᾱ, which means "The Good Listener" or "The Wish Granter" and was Bona Dea's Gallic name – her ancient name.' He paused to turn a few pages.

'We also know what kind of ritual took place in that underground temple, thanks to the inscription on the

Ménerbes fountain. "*Res divina sacrificium, Hominess pro victimis immolare.*" A sacrifice for the goddess. A human sacrifice.'

He put his pen down, leaned back on his chair, and linked his fingers at the back of his neck.

'You said you didn't believe in the stories of young men being killed and mutilated by having their heads cut off and of young women being raped in the temple,' Amy said.

Laurent didn't answer straight away.

'Well, I only said I didn't believe that there were ritual killings and rapes as late as the nineteenth century, but the beheading of enemies or heroes was certainly a typically Gallic custom. Heads were embalmed and displayed in special niches, on hooks in temples or in private homes as a mark of respect and to ensure the power and strength of these special people would be preserved forever.'

'Wait a minute … This reminds me of something I saw at Manoir Coste.'

She took her mobile out of her bag and showed Laurent the photos she'd taken of the old fountain. 'Look at the carvings of warriors.'

Laurent scrutinised the photos.

'Yep, you're right … This is a depiction of a Salyen ceremony. I really do think what we have here at Bellefontaine is the original Gallic, or Salyen, goddess, the one the Romans watered down with Bona Dea and Fauna everywhere else in their empire – everywhere else but here. Somehow the original cult survived in Bonnieux.'

'And may still carry on to this day,' Amy finished. Laurent shrugged. 'That's unlikely.'

'What if I told you that I found a reference to a murder and mutilation in a local newspaper from the 1830s,' she insisted. 'Who knows how many more I would find if I dug deeper?'

Laurent got up.

'I'd say I need to go to the library at Apt and do a bit of research myself. In the meantime, I'll get my equipment out of the van and do a GPR survey in your cellar since you said you were worried about that trap door. Do you think your nephew could give me a hand? I'm sure he'll be interested in all my gear.'

They called Peter who squealed with delight at the prospect of helping Laurent.

'You do geo-phiz, like on the television programme? Cool!'

Laurent smiled. Although he didn't speak much English he still managed to explain the basics of his GPR equipment to Peter. Together they pulled the chest in front of the cellar door away and went down into the basement. Once they'd removed the shelves and crates Amy had piled on top of the trap door, Laurent knelt down and examined the floor.

'This is indeed a door. However, for all we know it could just be an old coal or grain storage box.'

He connected his GPR to a laptop, switched the computer on, and asked Peter to keep an eye on the screen before methodically scanning the whole surface of the cellar.

'It'll take a while to process the results,' he said an hour later as he tidied his instruments away. 'Let's put the crates back.'

The three of them were gathering Laurent's equipment when Chris appeared at the top of the stairs.

'Two gentlemen from the police would like to speak to you,' she said, her voice tight. 'I asked them to wait in your office.'

Amy ran up the stairs, wondering if the gendarmes had found out who had drugged her at Manoir Coste, or perhaps they had news about the burglary ...

'We're here to ask you about a woman called Sophie Dessange,' Capitaine Ferri started.

Amy opened her eyes wide. 'Sophie Dessange? Has anything happened to her?'

'Do you know the woman?' Bijard asked.

'I wouldn't say I know her. I only met her once. What is this about?'

'On Thursday, Madame Dessange made a statement at the *commissariat* in Avignon to report a rape and the disappearance of a young English man, here at Bellefontaine almost thirty years ago,' Capitaine Ferri said slowly.

'In her statement, the lady claimed you suffered a similar assault on your person a few weeks ago.'

Lieutenant Bijard interrupted. 'Is this true? And if so, why didn't you report it?'

Capitaine Ferri frowned at him but said nothing.

Amy remained silent as anger and embarrassment swelled inside her. Sophie had no right to tell anyone about her and her dream, no right at all.

'Mademoiselle Carter, is Sophie Dessange speaking the truth or not?' Capitaine Ferri asked.

'I don't wish to talk about it,' Amy answered at last. She wasn't ready to make accusations about Fabien or a mysterious cult. She needed proof. Tangible proof.

Capitaine Ferri coughed to clear his throat.

'Very well. There is something else. We are expecting Madame Dessange later in the week and will require access to Bellefontaine and the garden. In the meantime, if you remember any detail which might be important, please get in touch either with me or with Lieutenant Bijard at the gendarmerie in Bonnieux.'

'Yes, of course.'

Amy walked the gendarmes to the front door and watched them climb into their blue van and drive away.

Chapter Twenty

'Why don't you sit on the terrace, order us a drink, and enjoy the sunset?' Laurent suggested. 'I'll take a look at the fountain and join you in a few minutes.'

He walked across the village square, which was a lot busier that evening than when Amy had been there first. Men played pétanque, girls practised their skipping and boys passed a football around. A group of teenagers stood near the fountain, talking and watching clips on their mobile phones.

Amy found a table on the terrace of the café overlooking the square. A young woman came to take her order. Tonight there was no sign of the elderly man who had served her last time she came. Amy ordered a kir for herself and a pastis for Laurent, and watched the archaeologist kneel down to take a closer look at the fountain, oblivious to the teenagers making fun of him.

She took a sip of her drink, enjoying the blend of fruity blackcurrant liqueur and cool white wine.

'*Aimée*? What are you doing here?'

The glass almost slipped from her fingers onto the zinc table.

Fabien was dressed in a long-sleeved grey T-shirt that clung to his chest, and tight black running pants which stretched over his muscular thighs. Next to him, a couple of teenage boys wearing sports clothes carried shopping bags full of sweets and biscuits, chocolate and cans of pop.

She pointed to the archaeologist across the square.

'I came with Laurent. What about you?' She tried to keep her voice cool but she was shaking inside.

'I've been rock climbing with a group of kids from Maison Espérance. We just bought a few supplies to keep everyone happy at the youth hostel where we're staying tonight.'

He turned to the boys and told them to go to the minibus.

'Tell Frédéric to drive to the Bergerie without me. I'll make my own way back.'

Before she could protest, he pulled a chair out to sit down, waved to the waitress, and ordered a *demi* of lager.

Amy looked to Laurent across the square but he was still engrossed in his examination of the fountain and wasn't about to rescue Amy.

'We need to talk,' Fabien said in a quiet voice.

'No, we don't.'

His gaze was so intense it made her heart thump.

'Yes, we do. You owe me an explanation, don't you think?'

The waitress arrived with Fabien's beer. Fabien drank some and turned to her.

'I want to know what I've done to make you so scared of me, and why you reacted the way you did in the Manoir's cellars. I saw fear in your eyes that night. No, more than fear. Terror. And those words you said. That it was me in the temple. You spoke of a ceremony. What the hell were you talking about?'

His eyes were so earnest, his voice so sincere she didn't know what to believe any more. Was he innocent or a consummate actor? Was he telling the truth or did he just want to check what she had discovered about him and his associates? He leaned forward. Their arms brushed against each other, the contact sending heat all over her body.

'*Aimée*, what is it? Speak to me.'

'You said the blue and gold ring was yours,' she started in a shaky voice. 'How do you explain its presence down in the castle's cellars, next to the entrance to the underground passage?'

'The ring was my father's, and his father's before that. It bears our family's coat of arms. *CV* for "*Coste Vaincra*". I keep it in a trinket box. I haven't seen it for years and had no idea it was missing. Now will you tell me what this is really about?'

Once again she was struck by the sincerity in his voice.

Laurent seemed to have finished with the fountain. He stood up, wiped his hands on his jeans and walked towards them.

'Monsieur Coste, this is a nice surprise,' Laurent said, extending his hand.

'Did you find anything interesting?' Amy asked him.

He grinned, excitement twinkling in his eyes. 'Yep.'

'I see you're still searching for clues on the fountains,' Fabien remarked. 'Are you any nearer to finding the location of the temple?'

'I believe so. Actually I need a favour. I would like access to your estate and the chateau, especially that tunnel Amy said you found on Saturday evening. I'd really appreciate it if you could let me explore it with you.'

Fabien looked in the distance. He took hold of his glass and swirled the amber liquid inside. Amy held her breath. If he refused now, it would be another proof that he didn't want the mystery of the fountain and the temple to be solved. A further proof of his involvement in the cult, despite what he'd just told her about the ring.

He put the glass down. 'All right. I'll give you and your team free run of the Manoir, the park and the forest. You can search the library, the grounds, dig holes anywhere you want – within reason, of course. I was too arrogant to believe I could figure things out on my own. I was wrong.'

He gave Amy a long, hard look that made her heart flip.

'I don't know what you think I've done,' he said in a low voice meant only for her, 'but I don't want you to be afraid of me.'

He finished his beer in one long gulp, stood up, and turned to Laurent.

'I'll give my assistant at the Manoir a ring so that they know to expect you tomorrow. Now, I must set off or I won't make it for the evening meal. The staff at La Bergerie are very particular about punctuality.'

'There's no need for you to walk. We'll give you a lift back. Won't we, Amy?' Laurent said.

She nodded, still torn between hope and doubt.

Laurent drained his pastis aperitif and the three of them walked back to the Clio.

'I see you still haven't had time to get your car painted,' Fabien remarked.

'The red spots are growing on me,' she replied. 'I think I might keep it that way.'

He smiled and she had to make a conscious effort to keep her hands from shaking on the wheel. The road meandered down the hills into the wild vale of the Aiguebrun river. Fabien gestured to the right at a junction. The road became a narrow, bumpy track. Finally, they reached the youth hostel, a one-storey farmhouse standing at the foot of white limestone cliffs that rose to three hundred feet above the valley. A dozen boys were playing football on a patch of grass at the front.

Laurent whistled through his teeth. 'Do you actually climb up these cliffs?'

Fabien nodded as he opened the door. 'We do. There are *pistes* for all abilities so you don't have to be an expert to go all the way to the top.'

He jumped out and was quickly surrounded by the children.

'Fabien! Where were you? You promised us a game of football!'

He laughed, ruffled a little boy's unruly dark brown hair. 'I'll be with you in a minute, guys. Keep practising.'

He leaned into the car to speak to Laurent. 'You can go to Manoir Coste tomorrow. I should be back early afternoon. We'll explore the tunnel then. Feel free to look at my family papers in the library before that.'

He turned to Amy, nodded briefly, and without another word he walked away towards the children waiting for him on the makeshift football ground.

Laurent got out of the car and sat in the passenger seat next to her. They didn't speak for much of the drive back to Bellefontaine but after a while he coughed to clear his throat.

'I find it hard to believe that Coste is mixed up with the cult, Amy. It's just a gut feeling, of course, but he seems an OK guy to me. Plus, there are other things I need to tell you, things I found out at the registry office about his family. Your friends Lily and Adèle were right. All the heads of the family since Renaud Coste died relatively young, and all of them before the birth of their sons. That's actually rather spooky. No wonder there are rumours of a curse. I wouldn't sleep too soundly if I were Fabien.'

Amy wanted to ignore the warning in Laurent's last remark – a warning she had heard before.

'You said you found more inscriptions at the fountain in Buoux?'

Laurent flipped his notebook open. 'There were two inscriptions at the bottom of the pillar, hidden away on the other side of the fountain. The stone was worn, it was no wonder you missed them. Listen to this.'

He closed his eyes and recited in a slow, dramatic voice. '"*Ex matris ut filiadea phasmatis mos ago dea mos sermo per cruor hominum*" Which I can roughly translate to, "The goddess will live, from mother to daughter and she will speak through the blood of men."'

'What does it mean?'

'It's another reference to the reading of oracles. The goddess demands a blood sacrifice to tell the future. A man's blood.'

Laurent must have sensed Amy's fear because he clapped his hands on his thighs and smiled.

'Anyway, enough about that horrible goddess. I hope your sister is a good cook. She said she was making dinner tonight – spaghetti – and I'm ravenous.'

Amy drew in a mock shocked breath. 'Oh dear ... Chris is a disaster in the kitchen. She always cooks her pasta far too long and it ends with up a gooey mess.'

She smiled at the look of genuine horror on Laurent's face.

'Just joking. If there's one thing Chris can cook, it's spaghetti Bolognese. She used to cook it all the time ...'

When their parents were alive, she finished silently, and they used to have Sunday lunch together as a family – without Toby, who was always far too busy, or hungover, to join them.

Perhaps her sister wanted to impress Laurent. She had noticed that Chris sat at the kitchen table every evening while Laurent worked through his notes, and, and was keen to listen to Laurent's patient explanations about his work. They may only just have met but it seemed that romance was blooming between the pair, and why not? Laurent was a nice man, a good man, who had become a friend.

'About time you two came back,' Chris said when she opened the front door, a huge smile on her face.

An appetising smell of meat, garlic and tomato sauce

drifted through the house from the kitchen. Peter was sitting in front of a generous helping of his mother's pasta.

'I was too hungry to wait,' he apologised, shovelling spaghetti into his mouth.

Amy shook her head when Laurent offered her wine with the meal Chris served. She didn't want to muddle her thinking as she tried to decide about Fabien.

She remembered his concern when he'd found her shivering in the forest. How fast he'd jumped down from his horse to cover her with his riding coat. The passionate words he'd whispered as he made love to her. The way he'd made her feel, as if she was the only woman in the world he really wanted.

She pushed her plate away.

'I know I'm out of practice with my cooking but I didn't realise it was that bad,' Chris remarked. 'What's the matter, sis? Are you sick?'

'We met Fabien Coste in Buoux,' Laurent told Chris, and the two exchanged a meaningful glance.

'Oh, I see ...'

Chris took Peter's empty plate off the table.

'Darling, why don't you watch the television in the living room? I'll bring you some ice cream in a minute.'

Laurent waited for Peter to be out of earshot before opening his notebook.

'It's time I told you about my day in Apt at the reference library and the registry office. I'll start with Denis Piquot's journal.'

Outside night was falling. Owls hooted in the forest, dogs barked in the distance. Chris sat next to Laurent, so close their shoulders touched.

'Actually it's more a fantasy than a real travel journal,' Laurent started. 'Piquot wrote three stories about Bonnieux.'

He looked at his notes.

'"Will-o'-the-wisp" is about the shimmering lights that shine in the ancient woods between Manoir Coste and Bellefontaine several times a year – in the springtime particularly – and which are rumoured to be the guardian spirits of some ancient goddess.'

'I saw those lights ... twice,' Amy said. 'Madame Ducros, one of my guests, saw them too, not to mention many other people who mentioned them to me – Sophie Dessange, Madame Verdier, and Lily.'

Chris gasped. 'What could they be?'

Laurent gave her a reassuring smile. 'There's nothing to be afraid of. These are just stories, old tales and superstitions.'

He carried on.

'Another story, "The Devil's Mouth", refers to the temple in the woods. Piquot went to the temple, which he reported was only an empty shell with statues of a goddess standing guard on either side, like we see on the prints. Inside the temple was an altar and a gaping hole – the entrance to a tunnel supposedly leading to an underground chamber. Piquot didn't go in. He was afraid of getting lost on his own.'

'Renaud Coste mentions this in his diary,' Amy cut in. 'He wrote that locals called it "the gaping mouth of hell".'

Laurent took a sip of wine. 'Interesting.'

He put his glass down and looked at his notebook.

'The last story is a rather chilling one, and reminded me of that dream of yours. "The Forgotten Virgins" is all about young women found wandering in the woods in a state of utter terror.'

He cast Amy an uneasy glance.

'Go on.'

'Piquot reports that the poor girls apparently all ranted about being taken underground by masked and ghostly figures and being covered with human blood before being abused.'

He swallowed audibly.

'A handful also claimed they had seen a young man being killed and beheaded in front of their eyes.'

Amy started pacing the kitchen floor.

'So it may be true ... I can't understand how these atrocities were allowed to carry on for years – centuries – without anyone trying to put a stop to them.'

'Please tell me these are only fairy stories,' Chris said, a pleading look in her eyes.

Laurent again raked his fingers in his hair. 'Of course they are. I mean ... even if my research indicates that sacrifices did happen around here in ancient times, it is simply inconceivable that they should have carried on until Piquot's time, let alone now.'

Chris let out a long sigh. 'Thank God for that. For a moment, it looked as if you actually believed all this nonsense.'

Amy was sure Laurent was lying to reassure Chris.

'Right,' he said, rubbing his hands together. 'It's time I drew the Coste and Bruni family trees! I have dates and facts aplenty ... It's going to be a long night.'

Chris patted his forearm and stood up.

'I'll make you some coffee to keep you going.'

'I want to come with you tomorrow when you explore the tunnel with Fabien,' Amy decided. 'That way I'll know for sure if it leads to the cellar and how people crept into Bellefontaine at night.'

'Don't you think you're being a little paranoid? Even assuming there was an old tunnel under Bellefontaine, and it hasn't collapsed, why would anyone want to sneak into the house?'

'To scare me, drive me crazy, sabotage my business, force me to sell up and leave.'

She looked at her sister.

'I'm afraid I haven't been totally honest with you.'

She told them about the leaking taps, the television and radio being turned on all night, about the fire in the living room, the freezer defrosting – and the cellar door she'd find open in the morning when she was sure she'd shut it before going to bed.

'I thought I was tired and distracted, but I now believe someone was coming into the house to play tricks on me.'

'Poor Amy. You must have been so scared.'

Chris cast a nervous glance towards the hallway and the cellar door.

'I also believe the people involved in that cult – whoever they are – came in through the tunnels and the cellar to take me to the underground chamber I remember.'

'But if this was true – and I'm really not convinced it's the case – then why didn't you scream and fight your attackers off?' Laurent objected.

'I must have been drugged. I remember feeling something damp on my face – something that smelled of chemicals.'

Laurent frowned.

'Damn it, Amy. What if you're right and you didn't have a nightmare and sleepwalk into the woods after all? What if …'

'Oh my God,' Chris said. 'What if they come here and take Peter?'

'Don't be scared,' Amy said. 'I don't think anyone has sneaked into Bellefontaine since the burglary, and since Fabien gave me Michka. That puppy may be small but she sure can bark.'

Chris' face broke into a relieved smile.

'There you are! That's the proof you were waiting for, the proof that Fabien can't be one of the bad guys. He wouldn't have given you the dog if he and his associates needed access to the house to terrorise you, would he?'

Amy gasped. Chris was right. Fabien was innocent. He had to be. It felt like a huge weight was suddenly lifted off her chest.

She grabbed hold of her car keys and handbag.

'Where are you going now?' her sister asked.

'To see Fabien. I want to tell him everything, and apologise for my behaviour.'

She heaved a sigh. 'I've been so confused. So suspicious. So wrong. I even thought he had nailed that dead rabbit on my door, slashed my tyres, and planted that dead crow on my car.'

Laurent smiled. 'I have trouble picturing him doing any of that. Hurry, then. Chris and I will hold the fort.'

It only took half an hour to drive to La Bergerie. She stopped the engine, switched the headlights off, and got out of the car. The night was quiet, except for a warm breeze rustling through leaves and a river gushing nearby.

In front of her the cliffs stood, dark now against the starry sky. Amy walked to the youth hostel's reception where a middle-aged man was watching a game show on an old-fashioned television set behind a wooden counter. He directed her to the games room at the back of the building.

What should she tell Fabien? Amy wondered as she made her way to a wooden hut from where laughter and music drifted through the open door. She stood in the shadows and peered inside. The children played table football, ping-pong or darts. Frédéric sat slumped on a sofa, a beer bottle in his hand, a sports newspaper spread open in his lap. At the far end of the room Fabien played pool with a couple of older boys. He had changed into a pair of faded jeans and a black T-shirt. A lock of dark hair fell onto his forehead as he bent down to take aim at a ball.

He must have felt her gaze because he stopped and looked straight at her across the playroom. He put his cue on the pool table, said something to one of the carers, and walked towards the door.

She retreated into the shadows outside to wait for him. She still had no idea what she was going to say.

Suddenly he stood in front of her.

'This is a surprise. Has anything happened? Are you all right?'

'I need to speak to you, if you can spare the time.'

'Sure. Let's go by the river. We won't be disturbed there.'

He took her hand to lead her down a path that snaked down a slope. The noise of the waterfall rumbled a lot louder now. She breathed in the scent of the water. She could even feel the humid haze rising from the river like mist. Fabien stopped and turned to face her. The crescent moon lit his face.

'Go on. I'm listening.'

'There's so much to say. I don't know where to start.'

'Take your time.'

He gave her hand a light squeeze.

She took a deep breath and started talking very fast.

'First, I lied about the reason I pushed you away after the night we … the night I spent in your cottage. It wasn't because I didn't want a relationship, but because I needed time.'

'Time for what?'

Fabien lifted her hand to his mouth and turned it over to kiss her wrist, caressing her skin so softly with his lips that she shivered all over.

'Time to work out the truth about you. I didn't trust you. I was wrong, I know that now. You see, there are things I never told you about Bellefontaine, things that happened to me, and to others.'

Once she started, the words tumbled out.

'The night before you found me in the forest, I had a dream ... well, I thought it was a dream.'

She described the ceremony as best she could, with as many details as she could remember.

'So when I ran away from the cottage, from you, it was because the *salinum* on your shelf was the exact same one as I saw during the ceremony. I thought you were involved. I thought you were one of *them*. Then we found the ring ... and once again, it was the same one the man in the temple wore.'

'My father's ring,' Fabien said in a cold, harsh voice. 'I understand now. Carry on.'

Amy told him about Sophie Dessange, and explained that the woman had now contacted the gendarmes.

'Capitaine Ferri and Lieutenant Bijard came to see me on Sunday to tell me she wanted to come to Bellefontaine. I don't think she'll be happy to see Bijard there, since he was the one who didn't believe her years ago, the one who refused to take her statement and put her on the train back to Avignon.'

Fabien started.

'Bijard? He led the enquiry into my father's shooting accident. My mother often complained that he hadn't done a thorough job. Is there anything else you haven't told me?'

'There is. I found a trap door in Bellefontaine's basement. I'm sure it leads to one of the tunnels featured on the plans of Manoir Coste and that's the way people got inside Bellefontaine at night.'

She paused.

'I didn't dream the ceremony, Fabien. It really took place. As for Sophie Dessange, I believe her when she says she was hurt and her boyfriend was killed. I believe all of Chevalier's and Lily's stories about the goddess and the cult too. And I'm scared. We must stop these people, whoever they are.'

He let go of her. His eyes glinted in the moonlight.

'Nobody will hurt you ever again, I promise.'

Chapter Twenty-One

Anger twisted inside him. He wished there was something – or someone – to punch. Instead he bent down, grabbed hold of a large stone, and threw it as hard as he could against the cliff on the other side of the river.

How could he have been so blind to what was going on under his nose all this time? He'd always dismissed the stories about the goddess and her followers as fanciful gossip. If what Amy was saying was true – and he now believed it was – there was a gang of maniacs, rapists and murderers in Bonnieux, who might even have taken advantage of Manoir Coste's network of ancient underground passages to commit their crimes and evade justice.

Who the hell were they? Did he know them? Maybe he worked alongside them and talked to them every day. He would hunt them down, every single one of them. After all hunting was in his blood. But first he would get the man who stole his father's ring and abducted Amy, the man who had dared touch her in that underground temple of his. A primal urge to hurt, maim, and kill overtook him at the thought of what she'd experienced that night – and of what might have happened.

He was about to pick up another rock when he felt a light touch on his shoulder. Amy stood in front of him, so small and vulnerable his heart, his whole body, ached with the need to scoop her in his arms, take her away and keep her safe, always.

The moonlight cast a silver glow on her long hair, made her eyes look dark, and her blouse so transparent he could see the contours of her breasts under the thin fabric. His mouth dried up. She looked like a magical creature of the night, a very desirable creature. He almost groaned aloud as he remembered the feel of her skin and the softness of her body under him.

No wonder she'd been terrified. She was alone, with no one to rely on, no one to trust. He should have been there to protect her, and make sure she was safe.

And what had he done? He'd given her a puppy! A harmless, fluffy puppy! His whole body stiffened with rage once again, this time against himself.

'I didn't protect you,' he whispered in a hoarse voice. 'It wasn't your fault. You didn't know.'

She put the palm of her hand against his cheek in a soothing gesture.

'Didn't want to know, more like.'

What if that sordid family secret he'd uncovered a few months back whilst going through his father's papers in the library had anything to do with all this? What if his father – and his grandfather before him – had known about the temple all along? What if they'd been part of it?

He wrapped his arms around Amy's waist and pulled her to him. A low growl escaped from deep inside his throat as her lips parted to respond to him. His mouth demanded, his hands possessed, but it wasn't nearly enough. He wanted to drown himself inside her. He wanted to forget about that damned temple and its goddess, about the cult and those threatening the woman in his arms. He wanted to forget the world and give in to the need pulsing inside him.

'I think we'd better go back. I'm not sure I can behave myself if we stay out here.'

'Maybe I don't want you to behave yourself,' she replied in a breathless voice.

He needed no further encouragement. He bent down to kiss her again. His fingers slid down her stomach, impatient, when twigs snapped and stones rolled on the path nearby. He stilled, held his breath, listened. Someone was close by, spying on them.

'What was that?' Amy asked.

'Stay here,' he instructed as he sprinted up the path.

He ran as fast as he could but whoever had been there was either gone, or hiding in the bushes. It was far too dark to start searching.

Cursing he ran back down to the riverbank where Amy waited for him.

'It must have been kids,' he said with a frown. 'I couldn't catch them.'

'Are you sure they were children?' she whispered in a tight, frightened voice.

'Of course.'

It had to be kids from the Bergerie, who else would be hanging about here at this time of night?

'They probably wanted to mess about in the river, then stumbled on us and got an eyeful.'

He smiled and took her hand. It was icy to the touch. 'You're cold.'

He pulled her into his arms, and then he knew for sure.

It wasn't just lust. It was more – much, much more. Deep down he'd known for a while. He didn't care if it was the result of a spell or an enchantment. He'd fought it long enough. It was time he accepted it. He loved her, like he'd never loved a woman before.

He held her tight and rubbed her back until she was no longer trembling.

'Come on, let's go back to the Bergerie.'

They walked back to the youth hostel hand in hand.

'We'll go to my room first, then I'll get us some tea or coffee.'

The reception area was deserted and Fabien took his key from a hook on the wall, before leading Amy to his room, which was located on the ground floor and furnished only with a single wooden sleigh bed, a rickety old chair and a white sink.

'It's what people call rustic.'

He switched on the bedside lamp and a cosy, warm orange glow bathed the room, then walked back to her and put his arms around her waist.

She nestled against him.

His hands stroked her soft, curvy hips as he bent down to kiss the hollow at the base of her throat where her pulse beat fast, then the soft swelling of her breasts.

He pulled on the tie of her top to loosen it and peeled it off her, before unclasping her bra and letting it fall to the floor. Her skin glowed. Her breasts heaved with her every breath, inviting his touch. He stroked them slowly, revelling in the feel of the smooth, silky flesh.

Her body trembled and sagged in his arms. He held her more tightly as her fingers tangled in his hair, and pulled him closer. He heard her whisper his name, along with a string of words he didn't quite understand. She spoke in English, and the sound of her soft, breathless voice made him even wilder. He looked up, her eyes were unfocussed, her lips parted in surrender.

With an urgency he couldn't control, he unfastened her jeans and pulled them down together with her knickers. She kicked her pumps off. Her clothes fell to the tiled floor, and at last she stood naked in front of him. His heart drummed so hard against his ribs it hurt.

His hands slid along the round curves of her hips. She

moaned and gripped his shoulders harder as he touched and stroked, and his caresses became insistent, driving them both to the edge.

Why the hell was he still dressed? He wanted her against him. He wanted to feel her, all of her. Touch and take, and make love to her as the night grew deep and still.

He pulled his T-shirt over his head in a swift move and threw it on the floor. She raised her hands towards his chest. The touch of her fingertips on his skin as she slowly stroked him made him groan. Never before had he been so close to losing control, so he scooped her in his arms, lay her on the small bed and got rid of the rest of his clothing, before covering her with his body. Grabbing hold of her hands, he pinned her arms on either side of her head and looked deep into her eyes.

'You won't run away from me this time, will you?'

'No. I promise. Never again.'

Her eyes were unfocussed, her voice hardly a whisper. She was his. His heart felt about to burst as he drove inside her.

A loud knock on the bedroom door woke Amy up the following morning. They had fallen asleep only a couple of hours before, entwined in each other's arms in the small bed. She shook Fabien gently. It had no effect, so she kissed his chest and bit his shoulder lightly. His hands slid down her back, sending tingles of pleasure in her whole body.

'Hmm ... I want to wake up that way every single morning from now on.' He opened his eyes and smiled. '*Bonjour, Aimée.*'

'There's someone at the door,' she whispered.

'*Monsieur Coste. Il est sept heures,*' a man called from the corridor.

Unconcerned, Fabien pulled her on top of him and brushed her hair off her face.

'I'll be right there,' Fabien called back in a rough, sleepy voice.

He didn't move. Instead, his lips found hers, his fingers stroked a slow path down her back, rekindled delicious fires and aches inside her.

'We have to get up,' she said as he nibbled the side of her throat.

'They'll come back.'

He started making love to her and nothing mattered any longer.

He was right. Twenty minutes later, there was another knock on the door.

'The coffee's getting cold and the kids are getting restless,' the man said in a more pressing voice.

Fabien sighed. 'This time I'll have to get up. I want to take the children abseiling and be back at Manoir Coste to go down into the tunnel with Orsini this afternoon.'

He propped himself up on his elbow and looked down at Amy, who stretched languorously on the bed.

'*Mon aimée*, you look wild and wonderful.'

The warm, soft glow in his eyes made her heart beat faster. Had he just called her his beloved?

Self-conscious, she ran her fingers through her tousled hair. She wasn't the kind of woman a man like him could love. She wasn't sophisticated, wealthy, or from a posh family. She didn't ride – she didn't even share his passion for hunting! He was a wealthy aristocrat, who owned a luxury hotel and she ran a small, and far from successful guesthouse.

He was the mighty and powerful duc de Coste, and she was only the new lady of Bellefontaine.

Suddenly a feeling of dread spread through her chest and it was as if a black cloud filled the bedroom.

'What's wrong? You've turned pale all of a sudden, as if you've seen a ghost.'

She sat up, pulled the sheet up to cover herself and looked at him in dismay.

'Do you realise what we've done? We have repeated the pattern. A duc de Coste and a lady from Bellefontaine.'

She closed her eyes and recited the words engraved on one of the stones Laurent had found. *'The spell flows with the spring, binding hearts together until death tears them apart.'*

'You said that before, and I told you I didn't believe in spells.'

'It's not a spell. It's a curse, and it doesn't matter if we believe in it or not.'

'So what are you saying? That what I feel for you isn't real but an illusion? That I'm not really in love with you but under the influence of an ancient goddess who cursed my ancestors?'

'Well, put like that it does sound a little silly,' she admitted.

Then she gasped. 'Did you just say that you were …?'

'In love with you. Yes. I did, and I am, and I won't let you convince yourself, or me, that it's not real.'

She took a shaky breath, and pushed the immense joy of hearing him say he loved her deep inside her.

'Don't you understand? It's a curse! Laurent researched your family tree and he said nearly all the male heads of the family died young. Look what happened to Renaud Coste, to your grandfather … how many other Coste men had a liaison with a lady from Bellefontaine and suffered an early death?'

'What else did Orsini dig out about my family?' His voice turned cold.

'Nothing special. I only meant that I don't want anything to happen to you.'

'I've had enough of this nonsense. I'm going for a shower.' And he walked out, leaving her shaky and sorry she'd spoken out and made him annoyed.

She got up, splashed cold water over her face, combed her hair, and got dressed.

He opened the door a few minutes later, a sombre look on his face. Without a word he strode across the room, with the towel still tied around his waist, pulled her to him and kissed her hard on the mouth. His dark hair was wet, his chest still damp.

'Sorry about losing my temper before,' he said. 'This whole business is getting to me.'

'I know. Don't worry.'

She touched his hair, the side of his face, rough with stubble. He turned a little, just enough for his mouth to kiss the palm of her hand, sending shivers along her arm, her whole body. Her heart constricted almost to the point of hurting. Was it possible to love someone so much, and feel such a potent mixture of pleasure, joy and pain?

'I'd better hurry. It looks like it's going to rain, and I don't want to get stuck on the cliff top with the kids.'

He dropped his towel, looked through his bag for a grey T-shirt and sports pants, and got dressed quickly.

'Ready? Then let's face the mob.'

He finished lacing his trainers and took Amy's hand.

The dining room was like an old-fashioned school refectory, with long tables and wooden benches. Two dozen children and teenagers, and several carers from

Maison Espérance, were enjoying a hearty breakfast of hot chocolate, coffee, bread and jam, and pains au chocolat.

A young man waved to Fabien.

'There's space over here. I saved you some coffee,' he called. Then looking at Fabien and Amy in turn he added, 'I didn't know you had a guest.'

Frédéric sat at the far end of the bench. He looked awful, his eyes bloodshot, his face creased and pale. The man drank too much and it was starting to show.

When he saw Amy he sneered.

'Well, well, it looks like someone got lucky last night.' He licked his lips slowly.

A shiver of disgust ran down Amy's spine. She averted her eyes without answering and looked at Fabien.

'Are you sure you're fit to climb?' Fabien asked his cousin in a sharp voice.

'Of course I am, your lordship. I would happily race you to the top of the cliff.'

His hand shook as he poured a cup of coffee.

'I don't think that's a good idea. Let's concentrate on getting up there and back in one piece. I don't like the look of the sky.'

Unease tightened Amy's chest as she looked at the ominous grey clouds.

'Maybe you'd better cancel.'

'We'll be all right, don't worry.'

They looked at each other over the breakfast table – a deep, intense look that moved and churned intense emotions inside her. Then he smiled, and a line appeared on the corner of his mouth. She couldn't resist touching his cheek lightly. He caught her hand and held it for a second before kissing it. Was it real? Did he truly feel for her the same wild, burning love she had for him? She swallowed hard, and forced herself to drink her black coffee and take a bite of toast.

When breakfast was over, Amy followed Fabien, the staff and the children from Maison Espérance outside. Fabien was right. The weather was turning. The sky was the colour of lead, thunder rumbled in the distance. After weeks of dry, sunny weather, it looked like rain was coming at last.

Her mobile rang. It was Chris.

'You need to come back.'

'What's up?'

'I just had a call from the gendarmerie that they will be here at ten o'clock.'

'I'm on my way.'

Amy switched off the mobile and rubbed her temple with her fingers.

'It was my sister Chris. She is staying at Bellefontaine at the moment,' she told Fabien. 'I have to go back. The gendarmes will be there soon.'

Oblivious to the children and Frédéric gawking at them, Fabien drew her into his arms and brushed his lips to her forehead, her eyelids, her mouth.

'I'll drop by at Bellefontaine tonight after Orsini and I explore the tunnel,' he said. 'With luck we'll find that temple today.'

She looked up, her throat suddenly tight with anxiety.

'Can I come with you?'

'No. Absolutely not. I don't want you anywhere near the tunnel, or the temple.'

'Then promise you'll be careful. You never know what – or who – you'll run into.'

'Don't worry.'

He kissed her once more, then gave the order for the children to start on the rocky path at the foot of the cliffs.

As they disappeared into the trees, a sudden, irrational fear gripped her heart. Something was about to happen. Something terrible. She almost ran after Fabien to beg him to turn back. She forced a breath out and shook her head. She was being foolish and overanxious. He was an experienced climber and knew what he was doing. He would be all right.

Chapter Twenty-Two

She stopped in the village for fresh bread and a carton of milk and was back at Bellefontaine within the hour.

Chris opened the front door and smiled. 'Good morning, stranger. You look tired, but happy. I trust everything went well with Fabien.'

Amy smiled back and let out a contented sigh. 'Oh yes. It was … wonderful. Is Laurent here?'

'No, he went to Manoir Coste first thing this morning. He said there were things he had to check.'

Amy went up to her room to shower and change. Once dressed, she turned to the window and looked at the grey sky, still unable to shake the anxiety she'd felt as she watched Fabien walk up on the cliff path in Buoux.

What if it rained and he got stuck on the cliff face during a thunderstorm, or if he fell and got hurt? She shook her head and turned away from the window. Fabien would never compromise the children's safety. She had to stop worrying. He said he'd come round in the afternoon. In the meantime, she would keep busy.

Peter popped his head round the door.

'Auntie Amy. Mum sent me to tell you that the police are here. There's a woman with them.'

Capitaine Ferri, Lieutenant Bijard, and Sophie Dessange sat at the table in the kitchen. Capitaine Ferri got up to shake her hand. She nodded to Lieutenant Bijard and smiled at Sophie, taking in her haunted eyes and pale, drawn face, made even more strikingly white by the bright red raincoat she was wearing. It must be devastating to return to Bellefontaine and confront the past after all these years.

'If you don't mind, Mademoiselle Carter, we need access to the garden for Madame Dessange to show us where the alleged events took place,' Capitaine Ferri said.

'I don't mind, but you'd better hurry. It looks like it's going to rain.'

As she finished speaking, a mighty crash of thunder resounded in the dark sky above them. Huge drops of rain splattered onto the windows and long flashes of lightning streaked the sky.

'The worst of the thunderstorm is on the other side of the valley, towards Buoux,' Lieutenant Bijard remarked.

Amy's throat tightened once again and she glanced at the black storm clouds. Buoux. That's where Fabien and the children were.

Capitaine Ferri opened his notebook.

'Mademoiselle Carter, when we came to see you on Sunday we asked you if you had any knowledge of events taking place in or around Bellefontaine which could corroborate Madame Dessange's claims.'

He looked at her, his pale blue eyes serious but not devoid of sympathy.

'You were very vague, and refused to confirm or deny anything.'

'Tell them about your dream, please,' Sophie Dessange interrupted, joining her hands in a pleading gesture.

'Dreams? If the best you can offer is dreams, then we're wasting our time, just like we were twenty-six years ago.' Bijard adjusted his navy blue cap as if he was getting ready to leave.

Sophie's face became livid. 'You didn't listen to me at the time, Lieutenant. In fact, you refused point blank to take my statement. I was young and in shock. I did what you said. I went home, convinced myself that Mike had abandoned me, and tried to forget him. But I didn't forget. I know that something happened to him that night and, this time, you will take me seriously. I'm not an impressionable young girl any more.'

'Calm down, Madame Dessange. Nothing will be gained by you getting hysterical,' Lieutenant Bijard said.

Amy stepped forward, and had to clench her fists hard by her sides so strong was her urge to slap the man's smug face.

'I find your tone offensive, Lieutenant. You are here to conduct an investigation into a very serious crime, not to make fun of the victim.'

'Please, this is getting us nowhere.' Capitaine Ferri held his hands up in a calming gesture.

'Lieutenant, I would like you to go back to the gendarmerie and return in an hour's time. I am sure you will find some paperwork to keep you busy.'

'Very well.' Bijard threw Sophie an angry glance and muttered something under his breath but complied.

'Madame Dessange,' Capitaine Ferri said, 'could you show me where you were that night?'

'Of course.'

Sophie zipped up her red coat. Amy fetched a cagoule from the utility room, pulled a pair of wellies on and followed Sophie and Ferri out. Once on the terrace, Sophie paused a moment.

'The garden hasn't changed that much … Mike and I put our sleeping bags on the grass, somewhere around there. I remember we leaned against that tree over there while we ate our picnic. Mike made a fire.'

'Did you see anyone in the garden or the forest at all?'

'The place was abandoned, that's why we chose it, but I did see some lights in the forest before falling asleep.'

'Do you remember where you woke up the next morning?' Ferri asked.

'It was in the forest. I'm not sure I can find the place.'

They walked across the garden and onto the path between the cedars that swayed in the wind. Sophie stopped a few times to look around and touch the thick bark, as if they could communicate with her and indicate the way. They walked for twenty minutes before Sophie stopped. Her face was wet, a mixture of raindrops and tears.

'I'm sorry, it all looks the same to me.'

'It's a very large forest,' Capitaine Ferri agreed in a kind voice. 'I've been in Bonnieux for almost a year now and still haven't had the chance to explore it fully.'

Amy had an idea. What if she showed Sophie where she had woken up after her so-called dream?

While they were walking, she explained to Ferri what happened that night. Although he tried to keep a neutral expression, she could see incredulity in his eyes. Secret rituals were not the type of events gendarmes were used to investigating.

'This way.'

The path was getting narrower, winding between high trees. It was dark and there was a strong, pungent scent of pine.

'It was somewhere around here.'

She pointed to the place where she had woken up.

Sophie walked away from the path towards the ancient woodland Amy had discovered a few weeks before while taking Michka on a walk. Sophie stopped near the smooth, large rocks masking the entrance to the spring.

'This place looks familiar,' Sophie whispered. 'I remember large stones like these, and bright green light filtering through a thick canopy of trees. Oak and birch trees.'

Capitaine Ferri joined them. He had the pained look

of a man who is trying to show understanding but whose patience is about to run out.

He took a map out of his coat pocket.

'I think we're here.'

He pointed to an area on the map, halfway between Bellefontaine and Manoir Coste.

Was this where the lost fountain and temple had once stood? Amy could see no stonework but that may be because Gaston Bruni removed it all. Perhaps Laurent would be able to find something – such as the entrance to the tunnel that locals and Denis Piquot called 'the devil's mouth' – with his surveying equipment.

'I think we're done here,' Capitaine Ferri said as he turned back and marched ahead. Dark clouds had swallowed most of the daylight, heavy rain flattened the flowers and the tall grasses, and by the time they reached Bellefontaine the three of them were soaked.

Amy was surprised to see Adèle and Paul sitting at the kitchen table with her sister.

'I was starting to wonder where you got to.'

Chris stood up.

'It took longer than I thought.'

Amy greeted Adèle with a kiss on the cheek then looked at Paul, surprised to see that his face was pale and covered with a shiny film of sweat as he stared at something – or someone – over her shoulder.

Amy turned round. Behind her, Sophie pulled the hood of her red coat down and ran her fingers through her wet hair, and Capitaine Ferri wiped his black boots on the doormat.

'We didn't know you had company,' Paul said. 'I didn't see the gendarmerie van in the courtyard.'

'That's because Lieutenant Bijard drove it back to the village,' Amy explained. 'He's coming back shortly.'

'I told Paul about the trap door in the cellar. He's going to take a look at the basement,' Adèle said.

'There's nothing down there, Amy.' Paul's voice was strained. He took a white handkerchief out of his trouser pocket and wiped his forehead. 'I would have noticed any hidden passage or blocked tunnel when I resurfaced the floor.'

'Then why don't you go and have a look for yourself if you don't believe me?'

Amy took the basement key off a hook in the utility room and threw it over to him. 'Here is the key.'

A knock on the door announced the return of Lieutenant Bijard. Ferri told Amy she would have to come down to the station the following day to make a statement.

Sophie shook Amy's hand. 'Thanks to you, I hope they'll finally realise that I wasn't making anything up.'

'I forgot something in the van.' Paul rushed out.

Lieutenant Bijard said he would wait outside and followed him.

When he came back, a few minutes later, Paul went straight down into the basement. Amy bid Sophie and Capitaine Ferri goodbye, and watched the van from the gendarmerie leave, with Sophie sitting at the back since she had left her car in the village.

'I never liked Bijard.' Adèle pursed her lips and shook her head. 'He used to be a friend of Paul's. In fact, Paul, Bijard, and Marc Chevalier were inseparable when they were young – before we got married. They used to be a bit wild and get into all kinds of scrapes I was told, but they fell out one day, I don't know why. That's why I was so surprised when you said Marc recommended Paul for the renovation works here at Bellefontaine. As far as I know they haven't spoken for years.'

Remembering her encounter with Paul and Marc

Chevalier in the woods, Amy frowned. He and Paul did talk – a fact Paul obviously wanted to keep from his wife. She wasn't sure it was her place to say anything.

'Why were the gendarmes here?' Adèle asked. 'And who was that lady with them? She didn't look very well.'

'Sophie Dessange. I told you her story, do you remember? She is having the case re-opened.'

Amy offered Adèle a coffee and the two women talked while Paul was down in the cellar.

'Why did you pile up all that rubbish in the cellar?' Paul asked in a grumpy voice when he came back, wiping his hands on his blue overall.

'I was afraid the trap door led to a tunnel and I wanted to make sure nobody could get in,' Amy explained.

Paul shrugged dismissively. 'You're fretting for nothing. It's not a trap door but some kind of storage box for coal or grain, I'm sure of it.'

'Then why is there no ring or mechanism to open it?' Amy insisted. 'It seems to me that you can only open it from the other side.'

'How should I know? I'm telling you, there's nothing to worry about.'

He turned to his wife. 'Are you ready? I have things to do before lunch and I've wasted enough time here already.'

And he walked out of the front door without even saying goodbye.

'I'm sorry. He is in a foul mood again.' Adèle let out a heavy sigh and promised to call soon.

'I'm bored … What can I do?' Peter said when Paul and Adèle had left.

It was raining too much for him to go outside, and watching television was out of the question as long as the thunderstorm raged.

'I know!' Amy said. 'Let's explore the old barn. The last time I looked it was full of rubbish. Maybe we'll find some treasure.'

It would give her something to do while she was waiting for Laurent and Fabien to arrive. She searched the kitchen drawers for the key to the padlock. She had not been in that barn since visiting before Christmas. It was the only part of Bellefontaine she hadn't had renovated.

She located the padlock key, linked arms with her nephew, and together they ran to the barn. The large wooden door creaked as she pushed it open. And Amy stepped into the dusty barn filled with boxes, crates, and bags.

'Wow! That's great!'

Peter walked around, his eyes filled with excitement. They opened countless boxes, exclaiming in delight as they lifted dusty old ledgers, chipped ornaments, rusty tools, and bunches of keys. There was nothing of any value so it was no wonder it hadn't been claimed by the heirs to Magali Bruni's estate when they sold her the *bastide*. After a while, Peter asked if he could climb up to the mezzanine.

'Yes, but be careful. The ladder may not be very secure.'

He came back down five minutes later, holding a faded photo.

'There's nothing much upstairs but I found this stuck in the wooden floor.'

Amy glanced at the photo. It showed a very young, very beautiful woman in the arms of an older man. Amy's heart jumped. It was Serena Chevalier – a youthful, Serena. The man bore a striking resemblance to Fabien. He must be his father, Armand Coste. From the way that he held her, there could be little doubt the two were lovers.

Did Céline know that her husband had been involved with Serena? Did Fabien suspect anything?

So it seemed that Serena, Rosalie's adoptive daughter, had carried on with the tradition of Bellefontaine women having a liaison with a Coste. For the second time today Amy thought about the curse – the ducs de Coste dying a violent death after having an affair with a lady of Bellefontaine, and she suddenly felt the urge to speak to Fabien and make sure he was safe.

'Come on, Peter, let's go back.'

She was fastening the padlock onto the barn door when Chris called her from across the yard.

'Come quickly. It's Fabien. There's been an accident.'

Chapter Twenty-Three

'He has a mild case of concussion, a sprained shoulder, and a few bruises here and there.' Céline's voice was shaky as she spoke to Amy on the phone. 'He was very lucky.'

'Did he say what happened?'

'He said he was anchored to a boulder at the top of the cliff, parallel to the children who were abseiling so that he could abseil down with every child then climb back up for the next one. It started raining harder, so he decided to call it a day and was going back up one last time when his rope slackened and fell on top of him, tipping him off balance. Thankfully he fell onto a ledge and just about managed to get down before losing his grip and sliding down onto the ground.'

Amy felt the blood drain from her face.

She closed her eyes and swayed against the wall. She had been right to be scared. Fabien was hurt. He could have died.

'Will you call me when he gets home tomorrow?'

'Of course,' Céline promised.

'How is he?' Laurent asked, glancing up from the sheets of paper covered with names, dates, and question marks he'd been writing on.

'Not too bad, considering. He'll be out of hospital tomorrow.'

Amy's fingers trembled as she brushed her hair away from her face. She peered at the sheets of paper on the table.

'Are these the Coste and Bruni family trees?'

Laurent nodded. 'I went back to the late eighteenth century when Renaud Coste and Magali Bruni were born.

Renaud died at Waterloo in 1815 before his son Louis was born. Louis himself was twenty-two years old when he died, having just married, and his son, Jean, was born after his death, in 1837. As you can see, he too died young. However, Jean's son, Michel, lived to the ripe old age of sixty. He's the only duc de Coste to have done so.'

'How strange that three successive ducs died so young. Do we know what happened to them?' Amy asked.

Laurent flicked open his notebook. 'As required by French law, the death certificates were signed by a doctor and countersigned by the *Officier d'Etat-Civil* – the mayor's representative. Louis' death appears to have been caused by muggers in the woods. He was shot in the chest and died of his injuries. Jean died in an accident, although there is no detail about it.'

'What do we know about Michel de Coste – the one who lived longer than all the others?'

'He was the local *député* – that's member of parliament – for Provence. He lived in Paris much of the time, leaving the management of the estate to his cousin Victor, who happens to be Arsène's grandson and a direct ancestor of Frédéric Coste.'

Laurent looked through his notes.

'Michel was Philippe's father. Philippe, who we know was Rosalie Bruni's lover and was so obsessed with finding the temple that he ignored the most basic safety rules, causing not only his death but the death of his workers on his makeshift archaeological dig. That was in 1935. His wife gave birth to Armand, Fabien's father, two months later.'

'And Armand Coste himself was shot in a hunting accident,' Amy finished, tracing the Coste tree with her finger.

Thoughtful, she bit her lip as she remembered the photo

she'd found in the barn. If the man was indeed Fabien's father, then it looked as if he too had been romantically involved with yet another lady of Bellefontaine.

'Rosalie was the end of the Bruni line,' Laurent spoke next to her.

Amy shook her head. 'Not quite. Don't forget that Serena Chevalier is Rosalie's adoptive daughter. Serena is the last one.'

'Yes, but she isn't a Bruni.'

'It doesn't matter,' Amy objected. 'What matters is that she is a lady of Bellefontaine.'

She leaned over the sheets of paper again to study the names on the family trees.

'How strange. Ever since Béatrice's birth in 1814, the Brunis have produced girls whereas the Costes have had boys. Béatrice had a daughter called Nicolette ... I wonder if Béatrice was Louis Coste's lover, and her daughter became his son Jean's lover too. If so, we would have a romantic entanglement followed by an accidental death for every duc except Michel Coste, the member of parliament who lived in Paris.'

'Are you thinking that the Bruni women were somehow responsible for the death of the ducs de Coste?' Laurent smiled, clearly not taking the idea seriously.

'I don't know. No, of course not. It's impossible, unless ...'

She remembered what Adèle had said about the poor branch of the Coste family managing the estate every time a duc died young.

Yes, of course! It made sense. Maybe there was no curse, just jealousy and greed. If Michel lived until old age it was because he entrusted his affairs to his poorer cousin, who would therefore have no incentive to get rid of him.

What if the poorer line of Costes were somehow in

cahoots with the women of Bellefontaine? Magali, her daughter Béatrice, and granddaughter Nicolette. There would be strong links – family links – between them if Béatrice was indeed Arsène's illegitimate daughter, like Renaud hinted at in his journal.

It was a shocking, but plausible, hypothesis.

If it was true then Philippe had been killed in cold blood and not during a mud slide in his forest dig, and Armand's hunting accident had been a cover up for murder. Could Frédéric's ancestors and the Brunis women have orchestrated such an evil plan and kept it going over several generations?

What about Fabien? Maybe it hadn't been an accident at the cliffs that morning. She pushed her reasoning to its logical and terrible conclusion. Perhaps Frédéric had deliberately cut or loosened Fabien's rope so that he fell to his death.

Laurent gathered all his papers into a pile.

'Since Fabien is in hospital and I can't explore the castle tunnel today, I'm going for a walk in the forest. I have a theory I want to check out.'

He looked at the window. It was still raining. It hadn't stopped all day. Rising to his feet, he put his map and compass in a rucksack.

'What theory?'

'You may think it's ridiculous, and it might very well turn out to be, but when I examined the fountain at Manoir Coste this morning I realised that each of the lions looked in a different direction. It reminded me of an ancient building I once surveyed in Rome where the statues were positioned in such a way their fingers pointed to a location in town – a temple. And it got me thinking. What if the lions' eyes cross at one point in the forest?'

284

'So?' Chris asked, arching her eyebrows.

'So maybe the point where their eyes meet is the location of our temple, just like the statues in Rome.' Laurent turned to Amy and Chris with a triumphant smile.

Amy pulled a face. 'It sounds a little complicated.'

'I made some calculations on the map and now I want to check my theory out. Who is coming with me? I know it's raining but ...'

'I'll come, and Peter too.' Chris got up. 'We both need exercise and a bit of rain isn't going to stop us, we're Brits!'

Laurent beamed at her, as if it was exactly the response he had hoped for. Chris called Peter and the three of them geared up with boots and cagoules.

'I'll start cooking a hot meal for this evening,' Amy promised as she waved them goodbye.

She prepared a chicken casserole and a potato gratin and put everything in the oven before doing some tidying up.

The rain had stopped by the time she finished cleaning, so she decided to go for a walk. She clipped Michka's lead on and started on the main road. A van from the gendarmerie sped past all sirens blazing. Another road accident, she thought, as she watched it turn at speed around a bend in the road. The road to Bonnieux was notorious for its hairpin bends and its sheer drop down to the plain below. In the few months she'd lived at Bellefontaine there had been several crashes already.

She soon realised that she'd been right. An ambulance and the police van were parked at the side of the road, and a car lay on its side halfway down the hill. The paramedics were getting the driver out. Amy could see it was a brown-haired woman wearing a bright red coat, like the one Sophie had on that very morning at Bellefontaine.

Her legs suddenly weak, a sick feeling at the pit of her

stomach, she accosted the gendarme who stood guard next to the van.

'Can you tell me if the lady driver is badly hurt? I think I know her.'

'I'm sorry, mademoiselle. The medics couldn't do anything for her.'

'You mean she's dead?'

'I'm afraid so. You look like you're about to faint,' the policeman said in a kind voice. 'Would you like to sit in the van for a moment?'

'No, thank you. I'll go home now.'

A car stopped by the side of the road. The driver wound her window down and leaned out. It was Armelle Capitelli, the journalist from the local newspaper.

'Good afternoon, officer, I just heard the report of a fatal road accident. Can you help me establish the facts for my article?'

The gendarme remained impassive. 'A statement will be issued later.'

'Come on, officer, I only need a name, and a few details,' the reporter said in a cajoling voice.

'I gave you my answer, madame. Now please leave. The medics are bringing the victim up.'

Oblivious, the journalist turned to Amy. 'Did you see what happened, Mademoiselle Carter? You look upset. Maybe you knew the victim?'

'Somebody just lost their life. Isn't that reason enough to be upset?'

'Yes, I suppose you're right. By the way, I thought of a few headlines for my article about Bellefontaine. I quite like, "Book a room and meet your doom", or "Bellefontaine, a room there will give you nightmares".

What do you think?'

Amy's voice shook when she answered. 'I think that if you ever dare print any such rubbish, I'll sue your paper.'

Pulling on Michka's lead she walked away before the journalist could see the tears stream down her face.

She took her time walking back, and when she finally opened the *bastide*'s front door she was greeted by sounds of Chris, Peter and Laurent laughing.

She wiped her face, took her jacket off and steadied herself with a few deep breaths before making her way to the kitchen.

'Auntie Amy, we had a great time in the forest. Look how muddy we are.'

Peter's wet hair was plastered on his head. Water dripped down his coat and trousers to form a puddle on the tiled floor.

'Did you find anything?' she asked Laurent.

'No, but I'll go back tomorrow,' he replied. 'I'm sure that I'm right about this, it's just a matter of adjusting my calculations.'

'Well, it was fun but I think we'd better get changed or we'll catch a cold.' Chris took Peter's hand and oblivious to his protests pulled him towards the stairs.

Amy turned the oven back on to warm up the casserole and the gratin and set the table. She would tell Chris and Laurent about Sophie Dessange's accident after the meal, once Peter was in bed.

Chapter Twenty-Four

Not only was it still raining heavily the next morning, but the wind had picked up too. It blew and howled and made the cedar forest move like a wild, angry green sea. Cold raindrops pricked Amy's face and arms as she opened her window and hooked her shutters securely onto the wall. She stared at the sky where dark grey clouds churned and swirled. The weeks of heat and drought were well and truly over.

After a quick shower, she got dressed in a pair of jeans and a red jumper, tied her hair in a ponytail with a red silk scarf, and slipped a pair of trainers on. She knocked on Chris' door to wake her up since her sister had offered to help with the shopping this morning, and Laurent said he would babysit.

The road to the village was partly flooded, with some sections covered with a layer of mud and scattered with rocks and broken branches. The windscreen wipers struggled to keep up with the torrential downpour and Amy had to focus hard to zigzag between the obstacles. They reached the spot where Sophie Dessange had lost her life the previous day, and Chris sighed.

'Poor woman. When I think she was with us yesterday morning ...'

'By the way,' she started again after a moment of silence, 'your friend the builder has quite a temper. He had a massive argument with one of the gendarmes yesterday.'

'Really? Which one, Bijard or Ferri?'

'The older one with the nasty smirk and the grey moustache,' Chris answered. 'He told your friend he'd better sort things out, or else. They were both growling at each other so much I thought they were going to have a fight.'

'I wonder what they were arguing about.'

Once in Bonnieux, they went to the bakery and the mini-supermarket to buy what they needed for the next few days, but it was early and a couple of shops were still closed.

'Let's go to the café while we're waiting,' Chris suggested.

'Good idea.'

Amy pushed open the door to one of the cafés on the main square, and they sat at a small table in the window.

'We'll have coffee and croissants,' she decided.

A waiter came to take their order, and she looked around, aware of the sudden silence in the café as people stared in her direction and conversations stopped.

'Why is everybody glaring at us?' Chris whispered.

'I don't know.' Amy tried to smile.

A copy of the *Journal du Luberon* lay folded up on the table. She opened it and glanced at the headlines while they waited for their order. The front page covered the threat of floods in the region.

She turned to the inside page. The headline jumped at her. So this was why the café patrons had been staring.

'I hate that woman!' she hissed.

'What woman?' Chris looked at her as if she'd gone mad.

'That journalist – Armelle Capitelli. She was threatening to write a story about Bellefontaine's mysteries ... well, now she's done it. Listen to this. "Hotel Bellefontaine, will you get out of there alive?"'

Amy started reading the article and translating for Chris. The journalist recalled Amy's sleepwalking episode in the forest and her rescue by Fabien. She then declared that staying even one night at Bellefontaine could seriously affect one's mental health, giving Eva's nightmares in example –

'the young woman suffered nightmares so severe that she had to cut short her honeymoon and return to England.'

To finish the reporter mentioned Sophie Dessange, who had 'experienced a mental breakdown while camping with her boyfriend in Bellefontaine's gardens years before' and who had visited Bellefontaine the very morning of her accident and ended up dead when her car skidded off the road.

To finish, Armelle Capitelli warned readers about Bellefontaine's negative aura. '*Beware... booking a room at Bellefontaine could be the last thing you ever do.*'

'What a lot of rubbish! The newspaper shouldn't be allowed to get away with it,' Chris exclaimed, slamming her hand on the small table's marble top. 'It sounds like she has something personal against you, that she wants to ruin your reputation and your business or something.'

Amy folded the newspaper and put it down as the waiter came to place their cups of coffee and a basket of warm croissants, small pots of jam, and a dish with curls of butter on the table.

What if her sister had a point? As well as the dead rabbit nailed to the front door, the slashed tyres of her car, the aborted fire or her appliances being switched on at night, there had been other incidents she had blamed purely on bad luck. The breakdown of the butcher's delivery van the morning of her garden party, for example. The mix up at the tourist fair at Apt. Bellefontaine's bookings that kept going wrong at Bonnieux Tourist Office. And Monsieur Garnier refusing to grant Bellefontaine even one star on the grounds that she was a drunk.

'Wow, so much bad luck is spooky,' Chris said before biting wholeheartedly into a croissant smothered with jam and butter.

'Unless it's not bad luck at all ...'

Thoughtful, Amy drank a sip of her hot black coffee.

'The link between the butcher's and the Tourist Office is Jacques, a young man who also works for Manoir Coste.'

She pictured the young man's sullen face as he stood behind the counter at the Tourist Office – the Tourist Office with its bright red painted walls. The red paint was the same colour as the paint splattered on her car bonnet. What if Jacques was the one who had slashed her tyres, spread paint all over her bonnet and killed that poor bird? What motive could he possibly have to want to scare her? Then she remembered something else Monsieur Verdier had said.

'Amy, what's the matter?'

'Apparently Jacques is so besotted with Claudine Loubier he'd do anything she asked him to.'

'You think Claudine asked him to fake the breakdown of Monsieur Lefèvre's van to ruin your garden party, and mess up Bellefontaine's bookings? Why would she want to do that?'

Amy pulled a face. 'I have no idea but her mother owns an antique shop in the village and I am convinced she gave poor Eva Barlow the fluorite crystal and filled her head with tales of secret ceremonies and human sacrifice, then alerted the reporter. Maybe she is a friend of Serena Chevalier who wants me out of Bellefontaine so badly.'

Amy stared out of the window. The rain was still falling in sheets. People ran in between the shops, their umbrellas offering little protection.

'This weather reminds me of Manchester.'

Chris picked up another croissant. 'But it's wonderful to be here. You were right all along, sis. I feel a lot better for having left Toby.'

'Good. And I am glad you're here.' Amy finished her

coffee. 'Come on. The shops must be open now, and I want to get back.'

She glanced at the bill, left a handful of euros on the table, and stood up.

'Sweets dreams, ladies of Bellefontaine,' a man called as she pushed the door to get out, 'or should it be sweet nightmares?'

A chorus of laughs filled the small café. Startled, she turned round. The men stopped laughing, but not one would meet her eyes.

They drove back to the hotel in silence, looking in dismay at the destruction the rain and wind had already caused. Amy's fingers gripped the wheel tightly, and she heaved a sigh of relief when they finally arrived at Bellefontaine.

Laurent and Peter were playing cards on the kitchen table.

'Care to join us for a game?' Laurent asked Chris.

'Nobody's playing any more,' Amy replied. 'I want the three of you out of here for the day. Go to Arles, or Aix … anywhere, but don't come back until I tell you to.'

Laurent looked up at her, surprised. 'What's up?'

'A feeling I have. Call it a premonition. Please do as I ask.'

Maybe it was Sophie Dessange's car accident, or Fabien's fall. Or maybe the events of the last few weeks and the discoveries about the entangled pasts of Bellefontaine and Manoir Coste preyed on her mind, but she couldn't help the feeling that something was about to happen, here, today, and she wanted her sister and nephew out of harm's way. As for her, she had no choice but to stay at home. She didn't want to miss Céline's call to tell her that Fabien was out of hospital.

'Let's to go Arles,' Chris told Laurent. 'You said it was a wonderful city. You can show us round.'

The archaeologist got up. He seemed troubled.

'I don't like the idea of leaving you here on your own,' he told Amy.

'I'll be fine, don't worry,' she replied with more confidence than she felt. 'And I have Michka to keep me company.'

After Laurent, Chris, and Peter climbed into Laurent's van and drove off Amy stood for a while in front of the window and watched the rain and the wind beat down the flowers and bushes in the garden.

Even though she wasn't hungry, she made a cheese sandwich and some coffee for lunch, and ate at her desk while working on her accounts, updating her website, and replying to enquiries. By two o'clock, the sky was so dark she had to switch on the lights.

The wind rattled the shutters of the study so hard they banged against the outside wall. She opened the window to hook them up, but the window lock got stuck and she had to leave the window ajar on the latch.

It was quiet in the house. Too quiet. She realised it had been a while since she'd last seen or heard Michka. She called, walked around the house, but the puppy was nowhere to be found. Where was she? Not in the garden since the patio doors and the kitchen door were locked. The dog must be asleep on the bed in her room, as usual. Amy walked into the hallway to get to the stairs and gasped.

The cellar door was ajar.

She had been too distracted by news of Fabien's fall and Sophie's accident to make sure that Paul had locked the door. She stood on the threshold, and called the puppy. Sure enough, Michka barked back in reply. Amy called again, and waited, but the puppy didn't come. She would have to go down and get her. With great reluctance, she switched on the light and climbed down the staircase.

Her heart skipped a beat when she reached the bottom of the stairs and saw that the trap door was open onto a deep, black hole. How was this possible? What had happened to all the boxes she had asked Paul to put back? Another bark echoed from inside the hole. This time it sounded more distant.

Amy knelt down and stared into the dark pit.

'Michka! Come back.'

A long way down, the dog barked in response.

'Don't worry, sweetie, I'm coming to get you,' she said.

The hair at the back of her neck prickled, and she shivered. Someone was standing behind her. Watching.

She tried to scramble to her feet but hands grabbed her from behind. A wet cloth smelling of chemicals was pushed against her mouth, making her retch. She remembered that smell – that feeling against her face. She had first experienced it the night of the break-in.

She tried waving her arms about to wrestle out of her attacker's grasp but she soon couldn't breathe. All the strength slipped out of her body, leaving her as weak as a rag doll, and she fell to the ground.

Helpless, she heard the man walk to the entrance of the cellar and switch the light off. He came back and eased himself into the hole. When he was down to his shoulders he grabbed Amy's legs and pulled her downwards so that she rested against him.

'There you are, my lovely. Now we can begin,' he said before closing the trap door.

Chapter Twenty-Five

She was hot, so hot. Her heart drummed and her head throbbed. Her mouth was parched, her body felt so heavy and numb even opening her eyes was an effort, and then all she could see were shadows and hazy lights.

She tried to focus on her surroundings. She was sitting on a hard stone floor, with her back against the rough wall of a cave which was lit by dozens of tiny flickering flames, and in the surrounding shadows dark and silent figures stood guard.

She squinted – even though her vision was still blurry, she could make out that the candles reflected into pure white crystals at the centre of the chamber, and that it wasn't people staring at her from the shadows, but statues. On either side of the chamber were two darker openings, no doubt leading to underground passages.

So *they* had taken her again. The goddess' followers, the cult – whoever they were. How long had she been down there? She looked at her watch but the numbers were too hazy for her to see the time. She let out a sigh of despair. If only she didn't feel so tired …

Her eyes closed again and she drifted back to sleep.

When she next woke, her brain was less fuzzy, her sight a little sharper. She tried moving her arms and this time managed to lift them off the ground. Her legs however still felt as heavy as blocks of concrete.

Men's voices echoed into the chamber from one of the tunnels, coming her way. Amy recoiled against the uneven stone wall as two ghostlike figures wearing masks and long white robes glided towards her.

'She's awake,' one of them said.

He knelt down next to her, slid his fingers along Amy's face and throat, brushed against her breasts. She tried to raise her arms but was powerless to fend him off.

'See, lovely Amy? You can't resist me,' he whispered. She knew that voice, even if it was distorted by the mask but she couldn't quite place it.

'Enough!' the other man ordered in a curt voice. 'We don't have time for any of that. You can do whatever you want with her after the ceremony. For now, we must bring the boy in here and prepare. It's getting late and the others will be here soon.'

They left. When they returned they were carrying the body of a young man who they dropped unceremoniously onto the ground. Amy couldn't see his face, only that he had brown hair and was tall and slim.

'Give them both more draught and meet me in the temple in five minutes,' the man who appeared to be in charge instructed.

The other waited until he'd gone out to produce a vial and force some liquid into the boy's mouth. He then lifted Amy's head.

She clenched her teeth and tried to turn her face away

'Don't worry, I won't give you much. I want you awake. I want you to enjoy everything I do to you.'

She shook her head and pressed her lips together.

'Damn you! Will you open your mouth?' he growled.

He pulled on her ponytail to yank her face upward, pinched her nose until she gasped for breath. Swiftly he then inserted the vial into her mouth. A bitter, salty liquid trickled down her throat, making her cough.

Immediately the room started spinning and she was sucked into the shadows again.

Next thing she knew, someone was giving her shoulder a shake.

'Amy, wake up. Please, wake up.'

A hard slap stung her cheek. She cried out in shock, her eyes flung open and she stared in disbelief at the boy sitting next to her.

'Stéphane?'

'Thank God you're awake! Sorry I hurt you, but I didn't know what else to do. I've been trying to wake you up for ages. We must leave before that weirdo Frédéric Coste and his friend come back.'

'Frédéric Coste? Are you sure it's him?' Her voice was slurred, every word an effort.

'Positive.'

So it had been Frédéric all along. It all made sense, of course! He had access to the Manoir, the tunnels and Fabien's cottage. He had stolen Fabien's ring, and he was the man who had performed the ceremony.

'What are you doing here?'

'I got a text from my dad earlier today asking to meet up in the old village, but when I got there, his van was parked on the path and he was nowhere to be seen. Then I don't know...'

He rubbed his hand over the back of his head. 'Someone hit me from behind and knocked me out.'

Amy glanced towards the two tunnel entrances.

'Can you remember which way you came?'

'That way,' Stéphane replied without hesitation. 'I woke up as Coste and the other guy carried me along but I played dead. And when Coste gave me some of his drug, I pretended to drink and spat it out as soon as he turned his back.'

He pulled on her arm again. 'Come on now. We must go.'

'I can't move.'

There was no way she could stand and walk, let alone run.

'Listen, Stéphane, you have to escape alone and raise the alarm.'

He shook his head. 'I'm not leaving without you.'

'You must, or we'll both get caught. Can you see anything I could use as a weapon against Frédéric and his accomplice when they come back?'

Stéphane rose to his feet and walked around the room. He picked up a fluorite crystal.

'Will this do?'

He handed it to her. It was heavy, with a sharp spine down its middle. She could hardly hold it.

'That's fine. Now please untie my hair.'

She placed the crystal on the ground next to her and hid it under her red scarf.

'Before you go, pull one of the statues down, drag it into the darkest corner of the room, and cover it with your sweatshirt so that it looks like you're still asleep.'

He did as she said, then turned to her.

'Now what?'

'Now you run. Hurry.'

For a minute she feared he would change his mind and stay.

'I'll get help, you'll be all right, you'll see,' he said in a choked voice at last. He pecked a kiss on her cheek, jumped to his feet, and dashed out.

Even though she wanted to stay awake, Amy couldn't help her eyes closing and she dozed off again. The sound of approaching footsteps woke her up. Terrified, she pressed her back against the wall and put her hand over the crystal.

Frédéric knelt down at her side. He had removed his

mask. His face was flushed, his eyes feverish, the pupils black and enormous as if he too had taken drugs. Hopefully this meant he wouldn't be thinking straight and would fall for what she had planned.

'It's time,' he said in a fast, breathless voice. 'Time to take you to the ceremony.'

'What are you going to do with me?'

She forced a smile and added in a voice she hoped he would find husky and cajoling, even though it sounded croaky to her own ears, 'I'd much rather you and I stayed here, on our own.'

Gritting her teeth she put one hand on his knee through the silky fabric of his robe whilst gripping the crystal hidden under her scarf with her other hand.

'They say I have to wait,' he said, 'but they're wrong. What harm will it do if we have a little fun now? I can see you want it as much as I do.'

With a growl, he bent down to kiss her, pushed his tongue between her lips.

She gripped the crystal harder. She would only have one chance at this. She mustn't waste it.

Summoning all her strength, she lifted the crystal and bashed it at the side of his head.

He grunted with pain and looked, stunned, at her. She gave him another, stronger, blow on the forehead and he went limp on top of her.

She wriggled free from under him but he was heavy and it took several attempts before she could push him aside. She had to get away. He may not be unconscious for long. At last she sat up and pushed herself up against the wall. Breathing hard, she took a few unsteady steps.

After a last look at Frédéric's unconscious form, she started down the tunnel Stéphane had disappeared into earlier. Faster. Faster. She urged herself as she stumbled in the darkness, holding onto the slimy stone wall for support. Her shoes sank into the muddy ground. Water dripped from the walls and the ceiling. The patter of raindrops echoed inside the tunnel, louder and louder.

She frowned. How odd. It was raining inside.

No, the tunnel was flooding! A wave of water, mud, and debris rushed towards her with a loud, gushing sound that echoed in the tunnel. She'd never be able to get out that way. She had to turn back and try the other tunnel.

Frédéric was still unconscious in the cave, but for how long? She forced her wobbly legs to move faster.

The second passageway was still dry. She counted about fifty steps before she saw an orange light glowing in front of her, and another thirty before she entered the next chamber. Her throat tightened. This was where she'd been before.

The first thing she saw was the statue dominating the shrine. Like the one she had found in the garden at Bellefontaine, it had a crown of oak leaves and slithering snakes. A thin black ribbon coiled around the pale grey column of her throat. In the flickering candlelight it looked like a slithering snake, and it reminded her of Serena Chevalier's and Rosalie Bruni's necklaces.

She looked at the carving on the pedestal – Ρσκλίσίᾱ. Bona Dea's Greek name that Laurent had translated into 'The Good Listener' or 'The Wish Granter'.

All around fluorite crystals glittered and four *salinum* engraved with lions and snakes were filled with white powder – salt, probably. This must be where Anne Loubier had taken Fabien's *salinum* from. Was she part of the cult too, like Frédéric? What about Claudine ... Just how many more people she knew were involved?

Shadows shrouded the far end of the chamber where

niches dug into the rock appeared to display small, round objects. Amy stepped forward and just as quickly stumbled back. These were skulls, with their empty sockets staring straight at her.

She bumped into a stone table standing in the middle of a triangle painted on the ground. It was the table she had been lying on during the ceremony. She now saw that it was hollow at the centre and splattered with reddish brown stains – the colour of dried blood.

Terror made her heart thump against her ribs. So this was what awaited Stéphane! He was the young man the cult followers wanted for their ceremony. They meant to kill him, and rape her. Only now she knew Frédéric was one of them, they would never let her live … There was only one other exit from the chamber. She had to risk it, and hope she wouldn't meet anyone coming the other way.

'There you are, bitch!' It was Frédéric's voice behind her.

She willed herself to run into the narrow, winding passage. She didn't get very far. As she turned the first corner, she bumped into a masked and robed man.

Behind him were others.

The man grabbed her.

'Let me go!' She tried to kick him.

Another stepped forward and slapped her, knocked the breath out her and she stopped moving.

'Good. You got her,' Frédéric said as he caught up with her.

'How on earth did she escape? And where is the boy?' the man asked.

'He got away.'

Frédéric rubbed the bloodied bruises on his forehead and looked at Amy with undisguised hatred.

'You will pay for that, just you wait and see.'

A woman stepped forward. Like the others, she wore a mask, but the strands of red hair curling under her white hood, and the black ribbon snaking around her neck gave her away. It was Serena Chevalier.

'Then it's hopeless,' she said. 'Without the sacrifice, I won't be able to read the oracle.'

Another woman spoke.

'You promised we would perform the ceremony tonight. You promised to tell us who would be the next priestess. Never mind the boy. Can we not use her?' She pointed to Amy.

They were going to kill her! Frantic, Amy tried to wriggle free of the man's grasp.

'Reading the oracles requires a young man's blood,' Serena Chevalier retorted. 'You should know that by now. I suppose I'll have to try without it.'

Amy struggled again.

'Stay still or else,' the man growled, tightening his grip.

Or else what? It didn't matter any more. She had nothing to lose. She kicked the man, elbowed him in the stomach, and tried to bite his hand. It wasn't enough.

'I said to keep still.'

He gave her a hard shake, lifted her in his arms, and carried her into the temple where he slammed her down onto the table. Her head bumped against the stone. Pain flashed through her skull.

'She needs more draught,' someone said.

As he bent down to administer the sedative, Amy recognised the icy blue eyes of Marc Chevalier staring at her through the mask. She clamped her teeth together, pressed her lips firmly shut, but once again he held her nose and when she had to breathe he poured some drug into her mouth.

Her last thought before she lost consciousness was for Stéphane. Thank heavens he'd got away. At least *he* was safe.

The dull beating of drums echoed the pounding of her heart. Ghostly shadows danced on the walls. A woman's voice chanted words she didn't recognise.

'*Sum periculi ... sum periculi.* I beseech you, earth mother, Gallia, Merciful Listener. Fly to me, touch me with your wand. Inspire me with the true will of the gods and tell me who will be your next priestess. I have no blood to offer you tonight but I pray you can let me hear your voice.'

Serena Chevalier placed her hands over her head and followed the shape of her body. Amy realised that her clothes had been removed and she now wore a white muslin gown that barely covered her. She tried to move away from the woman's touch. Her body didn't respond. 'I beseech you, Goddess.'

Serena threw her head backwards and stood still as the dull, hypnotic beat of drums echoed into the temple for what felt like an eternity.

'The Goddess spoke to me and chose the next priestess,' Serena spoke at last.

She pointed to Amy. 'She shall be my successor.'

'No!' a voice shouted in protest. A voice Amy recognised. Anne Loubier's. 'You promised it would be me.'

Serena shook her head. 'She is the chosen one. We tried to scare her, hurt her, make her go away so that Bellefontaine would be empty once again and we could pursue our activities without fear of being seen. We were wrong. I should have understood it before. She is the new lady of Bellefontaine. She will keep our Goddess alive and our treasure safe. She is our future.'

'You're ill, Serena, you're not making sense,' Anne Loubier protested. 'You promised me the key to the treasure.'

Serena placed a crystal on Amy's stomach. 'She is with child. A daughter. She will be the first of a new bloodline of Bellefontaine's priestesses.'

She took a deep breath and raised her arms in the air.

'And so I have carried out the Sacred Act. The Goddess has spoken and has now withdrawn from her temple.'

She removed her mask and slumped forward, as if all her strength suddenly left her. Anne walked over to her, grabbed her shoulders and gave her a violent shake.

'Listen, you! For years you told me that I would be your successor. My daughter and I were the future, you said. You can't change your mind now and pick her. She isn't one of us.'

'Take your hands off her,' Marc Chevalier warned.

Serena straightened up and faced Anne Loubier.

'You must obey. I am not giving up my duties just yet, but when I do, Amy Carter will be our next priestess.'

'I don't understand. What are we doing now?' a man said from the back of the chamber. 'It's far too early to finish. Are we not having our usual session?'

Serena shook her head again. 'Not tonight. Everybody must leave now. I will contact you in the usual way when it's time for us to gather again.'

The music stopped. People left the cave one by one.

Soon only Anne and Frédéric remained with the Chevaliers.

Anne removed her mask and threw it on the ground.

'I won't give up, Serena. You always said *I* would have the key to the treasure.'

Serena let out a bitter laugh. 'I'm starting to think that's all you were ever interested in.'

'So what if it was?' Anne snapped. 'Oh don't get me wrong. I did enjoy your ceremonies – the drama of it, not to mention the drugs and the sex. I wasn't so keen on that blood ritual you performed after Rosalie died and you became our priestess – far too gruesome for me. In fact, I'm rather glad the boy escaped tonight and we were spared any more of that, and I know I'm not the only one.'

She jabbed her finger into Serena's chest.

'Why do you think people come to our little gatherings? Well, I'll tell you why. It's not for the love of your earth mother or to listen to you rant in Latin or Greek or whatever language you use to address your stupid goddess. Sex and the added excitement of performance enhancing drugs, that's why! I've been loyal to you for years. You owe me the key to the treasure.'

The two women faced each other, the tension between them palpable.

'Loyal? I always knew you stole precious objects from our temple from time to time,' Serena replied in a weak voice. 'I didn't say anything because I thought you were sincere in your devotion to our goddess. Now I can see you were never worthy of the treasure. My decision is final.'

'We'll see about that! I need the treasure. I need money or my business is finished!' Anne stormed out.

Frédéric had remained silent all this time. Now he put his hand on Amy's shoulder.

'What are we doing with her? You said I could have her after the ceremony.'

'That was before the goddess spoke to me. We need her alive and well. I told you, she is our next priestess.

You can't touch her. I forbid it!'

Frédéric tightened his grip. 'I'll do what I bloody well like. You can't stop me, you're half dead already.'

His voice was full of spite.

'How dare you speak to my wife that way?' Marc Chevalier cut in.

He too had now removed his mask.

'You've done enough damage already. You let the boy escape, and yesterday you tried to kill Fabien on the cliff. That was bloody stupid.'

'I had to do it. He was going to go into the tunnel with that archaeologist and they would have found the temple.'

'There were other ways of stopping him ... You really are hopeless. Just leave, will you?' Marc Chevalier said.

It happened very fast. Metal glinted in Frédéric's hand as he lifted his arm and plunged a knife into Marc Chevalier's chest. The knife slurped as he pulled it out. Marc gasped and looked down as a red stain grew and spread on his white robe. He pressed a hand to his heart and collapsed onto the ground.

'Marc!' Serena's cry echoed in the cave as she dropped to her knees, oblivious to the water, which now started to pool into the temple.

'You killed him!' she howled, cradling her husband's head in her lap.

'Shut up,' Frédéric shouted back. He hit her across the face and she crumpled to the ground.

'That leaves just you and me.'

Frédéric gave her a crazed look, put his hands around her neck and squeezed until Amy struggled for breath.

'I feel like playing with you a little,' he whispered.

'How does that feel, my lovely?'

There was the stomping of running feet at the entrance of the cave.

'And how does *that* feel, you worthless bastard?'

Fabien shouted as he threw himself at his cousin from

behind. He grabbed his shoulders, pulled him off Amy and threw him across the room.

'Fabien,' Amy whispered, overcome with relief.

Her joy however was short-lived. With a savage growl, Frédéric lunged at his cousin, pushed him against the shrine, and lifted his knife once more.

'Now I'll finish off what I started at Buoux,' he snarled, holding the blade to Fabien's throat. 'What I should have done a long time ago.'

She had to do something to help Fabien. She touched the crystal Serena had placed on her stomach. Her fingers curled around the stone and she threw it as hard as she could towards Frédéric.

Her pathetically weak shot didn't even reach him but hit the statue with a clanking sound. Frédéric slackened his hold on Fabien to cast a surprised glance behind him.

Fabien grabbed hold of his arm, twisted it behind his back, and bashed his hand on the shrine so that he let go of the dagger. It dropped onto the ground and sank in the muddy waters that now filled the temple.

Fabien smashed his fist into his cousin's face, slammed him against the wall and Frédéric slid down to the floor.

Rushing to Amy's side, Fabien lifted her from the stone table and cradled her in his arms.

'Thank God I wasn't too late. I thought I'd never find you.'

He stroked her face, kissed her lips.

'We have to get out. The tunnels are getting flooded.'

'They drugged me. I can't walk. I can hardly move.'

'Then I'll carry you.'

'What about Frédéric and the Chevaliers? Are we leaving them here?'

'Bijard and his men are on their way. They'll deal with them.'

He lifted her in his arms. Amy rested her head on his shoulder.

'How did you know where I was?'

'Stéphane told me. I was discharged from hospital tonight. My mother was driving back to the Manoir when we almost ran him over on the main road.

'We drove to the old village. Stéphane helped me find the entrance to the tunnel, and I phoned the gendarmerie to let Bijard know what was happening. He told me to wait for him, but knowing you were in there was driving me mad, so I left my mother and Stéphane in the car and went into the tunnel. Thankfully I managed to find you.'

He stopped and looked at the skulls nailed to the wall.

Amy felt his muscles contract, his body shudder.

'What are they?'

'Sacrifices to the goddess,' she answered in a quiet voice. 'If Laurent is right, most of them date back from the time before the Romans came to Provence ... others, unfortunately, could be more recent.'

'So it was true. It was all true!' He shook his head in disbelief. 'There really was a cult. They killed and hurt all these people. And Serena was their priestess.'

'That's not all, I'm afraid.'

As Fabien started through the tunnel, she told him about Anne Loubier being involved too and wanting to be the next priestess.

'I suspect what she's really after is the treasure you once told me about. Serena is keeping its location a secret. She said only the priestess has the key to it.'

Suddenly, she blushed, remembering some details of the ceremony.

'Serena chose me ...'

Fabien looked down. 'For what?'

'As the new lady of Bellefontaine, she said I was the best placed to keep the goddess' cult alive. She said something else too.'

'What?'

'She said I was pregnant and that I would have a baby girl,' she said quickly. 'But she's wrong. I mean, how can she possibly know that?'

Fabien didn't reply but he held her more tightly against him, so close the drumming of his heart reverberated inside her.

By the time they reached the first chamber and started into the tunnel, the water level reached up to Fabien's thighs.

'We'll soon be back at the old village, don't worry,' he said.

'I'm so sorry you have to carry me,' she apologised. 'You've just been injured.'

He bent down and kissed her lips. 'I'm just glad I got there before Fred hurt you.'

'Did you hear what he said about the climbing accident?'

He nodded. 'It was no accident.'

They came out of the tunnel at last and into the cold, pouring rain. Shivering in her flimsy white robe, Amy nestled closer to Fabien.

The village of Bories was dark and silent.

'This is strange. Where is everybody? Bijard and his men should be here too by now. And where are my mother and Stéphane? The Range Rover is still there but it's empty.'

He carried her to the car, flung the passenger door open, and helped Amy sit down before getting in. He had just closed the door when there was a beeping sound. He pulled his mobile out of his pocket, stared at the screen in disbelief and let out a muffled curse.

'Someone sent me a text,' he explained, turning to Amy.

'It says my mother and Stéphane are at Bellefontaine and I am to make my way there immediately if I want them to be safe. What the hell does this mean?'

'Maybe Anne Loubier sent it,' Amy suggested. 'She went out of the temple just before you arrived.'

'And there are so many tunnels, it's no wonder I didn't see her – or any of the others. What I'd like to know is where the bloody hell the gendarmes are. They should be here—'

'Unless Bijard is one of them, and he didn't alert Ferri and his men,' she finished in a grim voice.

'Damn it, I think you're right. Remember what I told you? My mother thought he had rushed the investigation into my father's accident, all those years ago. You said he refused to take Sophie Dessange seriously and practically forced her out of Bonnieux.'

'He is – or was – a close friend of Marc Chevalier,' Amy added.

Fabien let out a sigh, rubbed his face with both hands, and looked up.

'I'll call Ferri now, and tell him to get Frédéric and the Chevaliers out of the tunnels, even if the prospect of leaving them all down there to drown seems very attractive right now.'

Amy put her hand on his forearm. 'Wait! What if Bijard has other accomplices at the police station?'

Fabien closed his eyes and leaned against the headrest.

'Then I'll go to Bellefontaine on my own and sort this mess out. We should get changed first. You can't stay like this, and I'm soaked through. Thankfully I left some stuff from the climbing trip in the car.'

He turned round and rummaged through a bag on the back seat. He pulled out a sweatshirt, stripped down to the waist and cast away his wet shirt. In the crude glare of the overhead light, she saw the large purple bruises and deep scratch marks on his chest, shoulders and arms. How on earth had he managed to fight Frédéric then carry her through the flooded tunnels earlier?

He handed Amy a jumper and a pair of woollen socks.

'I'm afraid that's all I have left but it should keep you warm for now.'

They didn't talk during the fifteen-minute drive to the *bastide*. Amy kept flexing her fingers and toes, glad to be regaining some feeling in her arms and legs. Fabien parked on the side of the main road, a hundred metres or so before Bellefontaine's gates. As soon as the car stopped she put her hand on the door handle to get out.

'The effects of the drug are wearing off. I'll be able to walk, I think.'

He turned to her, an almost savage expression in his eyes. 'You're not going anywhere. You're staying here and you're waiting for me. Is that clear?'

'I want to help you,' she protested.

He put his hands on her shoulders so that she faced him. 'Will you do as I say? I want you to be safe. You've just escaped from a bunch of lunatics and murderers – from my cousin who wanted to ...'

He took a ragged breath, leaned over and kissed her deep and hard.

'You stay here. I'll come back for you.'

And he got out of the car.

Chapter Twenty-Six

Amy checked the digital clock of the Range Rover once again. It was over half an hour since Fabien had left. Enough was enough. Never mind his instructions not to leave the car, she wouldn't stay here a minute longer.

She let herself out. The rain soaked her in seconds as she crept along the flooded road and into the courtyard but she hardly noticed. Two cars were parked next to hers – a Mercedes coupé and a police van. So Bijard was there ...

She stood in the courtyard for a minute, indecisive. She had to find a way to get in, but knocking on the front door was out of the question. She remembered the window she'd left open that afternoon while working in the study. Hopefully no one had noticed it.

She was in luck. The window was still open. She placed her hands on the wooden frame, stood on her tiptoes and climbed into the dark and empty room.

Muffled voices drifted from the living room. Holding her breath, she pulled the handle down and opened the door slowly. Please don't creak, she prayed.

Frédéric was shouting. 'Let me finish him off, I don't understand why you want to keep him alive.'

So he was there too. No doubt he had followed one of the tunnels and got in through the trap door in the basement.

'Because we need him,' Bijard answered in a calm voice. 'He'll give us the money to get away if Serena doesn't tell us where the treasure is. All we'll have to do is get a bit rough with his dear mother.'

'You're wasting your time,' Serena said in a breathless voice. She must have followed Frédéric out of the tunnels.

Anne Loubier was probably there too, but Amy couldn't see into the living room from where she stood.

'I will never tell you where the treasure is,' Serena carried on. 'It belongs to the goddess and her priestess.'

'Then you are crazier than I thought,' Bijard retorted.

A woman was crying – Céline, probably. Filled with dread, Amy slid along the wall in the corridor and into the kitchen. Who else was there, and why couldn't she hear Fabien's voice? As for Chris, Peter and Laurent, she hoped they were still in Arles ...

'Where's my dad?' Stéphane asked then.

'At the bottom of a pit in the old village,' Bijard answered coldly. 'The fool wanted to give himself up and tell Ferri everything, including how we rammed that nosy cow Sophie Dessange off the road in his van yesterday. He completely lost it when he saw her at Bellefontaine. Kept saying she was the ghost from his past, the young woman he raped when he was high on drugs the night we helped Serena perform her blood ritual. Now she'd come back, he was sure she'd recognise him – recognise us all.'

'You're lying! My dad would never hurt anyone.' Stéphane started sobbing.

'You can believe what you want, kid,' Bijard said. 'Whether he liked it or not, your father was in it with us up to his neck ... I got rid of him, then used his phone to text you to meet him at the old village so we could get hold of you for Serena's sacrifice.'

Amy pressed her hand against her mouth. How could Bijard be so cold about killing a young, innocent boy?

'A sacrifice? You mean, you wanted to kill Stéphane?' Céline asked in a choked voice. 'Why?'

'Ask her, she's the priestess,' Bijard sniggered and Amy guessed he must be pointing to Serena.

'It was time for me to pass on my duties, and the goddess requires the blood of a young man to read the oracles every time a new priestess is to be chosen,' Serena answered calmly. 'It's tradition.'

'And how many boys did you and your accomplices murder for your so-called goddess?' Céline asked.

'Only one, when the goddess chose me to succeed my mother.'

'You are crazy.'

'Tell me about it,' Bijard spoke again. 'Serena, my patience is running thin. We want the treasure and you're going to lead us to it before the tunnels flood completely. Ferri might be an outsider and quite new to Bonnieux, but he isn't a complete fool. It's only a matter of time before he figures everything out, and Anne and I want to be a long way away when that happens.'

'Why should I help you? My husband is dead, murdered by that drunken, useless fool over there. The doctors say I only have a few weeks to live. The people I considered my friends and disciples betrayed me. I'm not afraid of dying tonight. In fact, it would be a blessing.'

'Then you'll get your wish. I'll kill you, and the others too,' Bijard said in a cold voice.

'Go ahead. I don't care.'

Amy repressed a gasp. She was the only one Serena cared about. If she convinced her to reveal the location of the treasure, maybe Bijard, Anne, and Frédéric would leave. It was a gamble, but it was the only chance she had.

She stepped out of the safety of the corridor.

'If I am to be the next priestess, then I need to know where the treasure is,' she said, trying to remain calm as she walked into the living room.

'You!' Frédéric sprung to his feet and grabbed her arm.

His face was bruised, his nose bloodied and swollen, probably broken. His white robe was ripped and covered with blood and mud stains.

'Let go of her, you idiot.'

Bijard waved a gun and Frédéric stepped aside.

Faint with fear, Amy took in the scene in the living room. Her eyes were drawn immediately to Fabien's unconscious form lying in front of the fireplace.

'What have you done to him?'

'Frédéric hit him from behind, the coward, as Fabien tried to negotiate our release,' Céline replied.

She sat on the sofa, a protective arm around Stéphane.

'And I'd do it again, and more,' Frédéric snarled.

'Be quiet, will you? You're not helping,' Anne Loubier said.

She sat next to Serena. Both women still wore their white ceremonial robes, now dirty and muddy like Frédéric's.

'Fabien Coste will die, you know.' Serena looked at Amy. 'If not tonight, then soon. As our next priestess, you must do your duty.'

'What duty?' Amy asked, her throat tight.

'It's the duty of the ladies of Bellefontaine to punish the ducs de Coste for destroying our temple.'

Serena turned to Frédéric. 'Your side of the family always helped us. It was their revenge for being deprived of inheritance, and it gave them a chance to manage the estate to their advantage.'

So she'd been right about that. Something however didn't add up. 'But Philippe Coste died during the flood. It was an accident.'

'It was no accident. My mother drugged his and his men's drinks. All she had to do was to wait until they became drowsy, push them into the pit and watch as they drowned in the mud one by one.'

There wasn't a trace of compassion in her voice. Amy swallowed hard, and hesitated as she glanced at Céline.

There was something else she wanted to know.

'What about Fabien's father?'

Serena smiled. 'He was mine ... Coste men can never resist the ladies of Bellefontaine, and Armand was no exception. He adored me. We were lovers for a long time, even after he married *her*.' She pointed at Céline.

'Rosalie said he had to die, like the others.'

'So you shot him in the forest,' Amy said.

'Frédéric's father helped me. He had gambling debts to pay off, and needed to be in charge of the Coste estate.'

'You killed my Armand, you crazy, heartless monster!' Céline's face was pale, her eyes open wide in shock. She glowered at Bijard. 'You knew all along, didn't you?'

'That's right, ma'am.' Bijard walked over to Amy, and pointed his gun to her forehead. The cold metal against her skin made her gasp.

'Anyway, that's enough talking for now. Serena, if you value your new priestess' life, I suggest you get up and show us where that damned treasure is.'

Serena's face turned livid, and her lips grey. 'Please don't hurt her. I'll show you the way.'

Bijard stepped back and Amy let out a breath of relief.

'I need my wellies to go down into the tunnels,' she said. 'They're in the kitchen.'

'Hurry then.' Bijard followed her into the utility room as she put her boots on.

Once they were back in the living room, Serena took Amy's hand, and squeezed.

'I suppose it doesn't matter any more if Bijard or Anne get the treasure, as long as you are safe. You're the only one who matters now. All right. I will take you to the treasure.'

'What about me?' Anne protested. 'I deserve something for putting up with you all these years.'

'You and Frédéric deserve nothing,' Serena snapped as she rose to her feet. 'You betrayed me, and *he* killed my husband.'

'Watch it, Bijard,' Anne warned then, pointing at Fabien. 'Fabien is waking up.'

Fabien let out a groan as he sat up and rubbed the back of his head with his hand. Immediately, he glared at Amy.

'What are you doing here? I asked you to stay in the car.'

Amy rushed to his side. 'Serena is going to show us where the treasure is, so that the others can get away.'

'You want to go back down there?' Fabien got up, winced in pain. 'The tunnels might be completely flooded by now.'

She shrugged. 'Not really, but I have to.'

'Then I'm coming too.' Turning to Bijard, he said in a voice that suffered no contradiction. 'You'll need someone who can carry heavy bags of ... whatever we'll find.'

Bijard nodded. 'Good thinking.' Turning to Frédéric and Anne, he added, 'You watch the kid and Céline Coste whilst we're gone, and make sure they don't cause any bother.'

Amy found two electric torches in the kitchen and a roll of heavy-duty bin bags, and Serena led them down into the basement, where the trap door was wide open. This must be the way Anne, Frédéric and Serena had come in earlier from the temple.

Serena lowered herself down through the trap door, followed by Amy and Fabien.

The tunnel was dark, so Bijard gave Serena a torchlight to lead the way and kept one for himself as he walked at the back.

After a steep incline the tunnel forked into two passages. Serena turned right, seemingly oblivious to the water level that now reached up to her knees.

317

'How long until we get to that bloody treasure?' Bijard hissed. 'It's freezing in here.'

'We're almost there,' Serena replied.

A few minutes later she asked Fabien to hold her torch, placed her hands inside two holes in the wall, and pushed forward. The wall receded, and the floodwater gushed through the opening. A strange blue light glowed faintly. It looked just like the blue light Amy had dreamt about. Serena led the way down a flight of steps roughly carved out of the rock.

Fabien grabbed hold of Amy's hand. 'Take care, it's slippery.'

They saw the lake as they reached the last few steps. Its clear waters cast a luminous, eerie blue green on the cave all around.

Bijard whistled between his teeth. 'What is this place?'

'This is the source of our sacred spring where the Goddess was born,' Serena answered. 'Her spirits light up the lake, and when *She* wants to talk to us, *She* sends the lights into the woods. This is the way it's always been, the way it'll always be.'

'So this is the very first temple.'

Even Fabien sounded in awe. He walked to the edge of the turquoise water and knelt down.

'The temple and the Roman fountain were built just above us.' Serena nodded. 'But the temple was a decoy, an empty shell hiding the real entrance to our secret worshipping chamber.'

The cave glittered with hundreds of stalactites made of shiny white and purple crystals.

'The whole place is full of fluorite crystals,' Amy whispered.

'They're the Goddess' magic stones.'

'Why did you give me one?'

'I wanted to unsettle you, scare you away. It worked. You did have vivid dreams, didn't you?'

Amy nodded.

'Who organised the burglary at Bellefontaine?'

'Frédéric and me,' Bijard replied. 'We couldn't let the archaeologists take away the artefacts and show that there was indeed a Gallic temple to be found in the forest. We returned to Bellefontaine later that night, drugged you and took you down to the temple.'

'We only meant to frighten you,' Serena said, 'so that you'd go away and Bellefontaine would be empty once again ...'

'And then your husband would have been able to buy it.'

Serena winced. 'That's right. Marc only agreed to take on the sale of Bellefontaine because he thought he could put off any potential buyer. The plan was to wait for two years, then put in an offer ourselves. But you came along ...'

'All right, ladies, enough chatting. Where's that treasure?' Bijard sounded edgy, perhaps even a little scared.

Serena sighed. '*Le trésor*. Follow me.'

They walked up to a recess at the back of the cave. Serena turned a ring hidden inside the wall, which slid to one side.

'The treasure is inside.'

She stepped into the cave, closely followed by Bijard who darted his beam of light around and gasped in shock. There were statues, gold and silver vases, goblets and plates, caskets full of glittering coins and gems, piles of golden jewellery, swords adorned with precious stones, together with ancient shields and helmets.

'Ça alors! This is incredible.' Bijard shook his head in awe, before gesturing at Fabien and pointing to the bin bags. 'Come on. We have to fill them up. Hurry!'

He started grabbing anything he could lay his hands on to fill the bags.

'We'll have to come back. There's so much.'

Amy stopped in front of a statue, which looked like an earlier version of the Goddess' head she had found in Bellefontaine's garden. The stone was roughly carved, the eyes and nose just an outline, yet the crown was unmistakably the same with oak leaves and snakes.

'Is that the Goddess?'

'Our Gallic mother. The one who listens to women, later known as Bona Dea or Fauna. The Romans adopted her but in doing so they betrayed her. Only *we* remained true to the real Goddess throughout the centuries.'

'No one cares about your stupid goddess, Serena,' Bijard interrupted. 'Right, we're done for now. Let's go back to the house.'

He heaved a bag over his shoulder, but as they returned into the main cave they saw that water now gushed down the stone steps like a waterfall.

'*Merde* … Is there another way out?' he asked, but Serena wasn't listening. She stood near the edge of the underground lake, as if in a trance. Slowly she pulled a dagger from the folds of her tunic, held it with both hands, and extended her arms in front of her.

'No,' Amy cried out. 'Fabien, stop her!'

She stepped forward but Fabien yanked her against him just as Serena plunged the blade into her chest and collapsed on the ground.

They both rushed to her side. The dagger stuck out of her chest at an odd angle, blood gushed out from the wound onto her tunic. Her eyes stared blindly at the cave's glittering roof.

'Hell, now what?' Bijard paced the cave, frantic.

'Now we look for an exit,' Fabien said calmly. 'Put your bag down and search on that side. Hurry, the water level is going up.'

Despite the loud gushing of the water in the cave, Amy thought she could hear something else – men shouting, and a dog barking on the other side of the cave wall. Hope surged inside her. Could it be Michka? She walked up to the wall and called as loud as she could. The dog barked in response. Suddenly rocks tumbled and crashed around her as a side of the wall collapsed and half a dozen gendarmes wearing Special Branch dark blue uniforms stormed in. Amy stepped back with a shriek.

'Throw your weapon to the ground and put your hands up. Now!'

The gendarmes pointed their guns at Bijard, who swore as he dropped his gun and held his hands up in the air. He was quickly surrounded by several gendarmes who handcuffed him and took him away. Michka jumped above the rubble and yelped excitedly as she raced towards Amy.

'Oh, sweetie, I'm so glad to see you.'

Amy bent down to stroke the puppy's fur and scratch behind her ears.

'We found her in the woods earlier this evening,' Capitaine Ferri explained as he carefully stepped over the pile of rocks.

'Mademoiselle Carter,' he added, 'it's a relief to see you're safe and well...' He glanced at Serena's body. 'What happened to Madame Chevalier?'

'She killed herself a few minutes ago in front of us, Capitaine,' Amy said with a shaky voice. 'We could do nothing to stop her.'

'I see ...' The gendarme walked away, crouched down

next to Serena's body, and gave his men orders to get the forensic team.

A slightly dishevelled man then stepped into the cave.

'Laurent!' Amy cried out. 'What are you doing here?'

Laurent stared open-mouthed at the glittering cave and the turquoise underground lake.

'Where are Chris and Peter?' Amy asked.

'They're fine, don't worry,' the archaeologist spoke at last. He looked around and whistled between his teeth. 'What an amazing place.'

'You haven't seen everything yet. You're definitely going to be as famous as your colleague from the museum after tonight. This way to the treasure, Professeur Orsini.'

Laurent's eyes widened. 'A treasure? For real?'

He didn't wait for her answer but ran across the cave, almost bumping into Fabien on the way.

'We can't stay here for much longer,' Capitaine Ferri said as he came back. 'The water levels are rising, the cave and tunnels will soon be flooded.'

'I must return to Bellefontaine immediately,' Fabien urged. 'My mother is there with Stéphane Michon. They are being held hostage by Frédéric and Anne Loubier. They were all members of a sect involved in murders and rapes, a sect led by Serena Chevalier.'

'Don't worry about your mother and Stéphane,' Capitaine Ferri said. 'They're both safe. We stormed into Bellefontaine one hour ago, and arrested your cousin and Madame Loubier. We tried to follow your steps down the tunnel from the basement but it was flooded so we had to find another way to get to the temple. Fortunately Professor Orsini was at hand. He said he knew how to find the location of the temple in the forest. Once there, we made our way down the tunnel.'

Capitaine Ferri shook his head and looked around again. 'This is quite a story.'

'There is more, much more,' Amy said grimly, shivers running up and down her spine as she remembered the skulls nailed to the wall and the bloodstained stone table.

'Bijard confessed to killing Paul Michon and Sophie Dessange,' she added.

Ferri shook his head and sighed. 'I can't believe Bijard led a double life and fooled everybody for so long.'

He left them again, this time to arrange for the removal of Serena's body and make sure the treasure was secure, and as soon as he walked away, Fabien put his hands on her shoulders and drew her against him.

She nestled in his arms and breathed a long sigh of relief. The nightmare was over.

'I think we deserve a rest,' he said, stroking her hair.

'What do you say to disappearing for the next few days?'

'I say it's an excellent idea,' she replied.

Forgetting the past twenty-four hours would be difficult but as long as she was with Fabien, she would do her best to try.

Chapter Twenty-Seven

Fabien's lips lingered on Amy's shoulder, trailed up along the curve of her neck to nip at her earlobe. She stirred and muttered something in English, then turned round to face him and curled up into his arms. This was where she belonged. He never wanted to be parted from her again. He *would* never be parted from her again.

'You must get ready for the party,' she said.

'The only place I have to be is right here, with you.'

He kissed her, tender at first then hard and urgent. And when he took her, they were lost to the world again.

All too soon golden sunlight filtered through the half-closed shutters onto the walls and the tiled floor of his bedroom. It was sunset, on the last day of April. Manoir Coste's celebrated Fête des Lumières was about to start without its host and he didn't care. He had delegated much of the organisation of the evening to his head of staff and a couple of personal assistants.

Come to think of it, he had delegated much of the running of the hotel since Amy had come to live at the cottage, a week before. He knew what his staff whispered behind his back and it made him smile.

'*Monsieur le duc est amoureux.*'

They were right, even if *amoureux* was too meek a term for the passion, the tumult and the sweet madness of his feelings for Amy. He, who'd always been driven to the point of obsession by his need to turn Manoir Coste into a thriving business, had only paid sporadic visits to the office this last week, and even then he'd been so distracted he couldn't focus on any of his work. Yet there was much to be done. He had to appoint a new PR, for a start.

Claudine had resigned and now lived at her mother's house, pending the end of the police investigation. She had broken down during her interrogation by Capitaine Ferri and blurted out all she knew. The ceremonies her mother had forced her to attend. The affair she was having with Fred, as a solace for Fabien's indifference towards her. Then there was the sabotaging of Amy's budding guesthouse business ordered by her mother and Serena Chevalier that she had helped carry out by using her position at Manoir Coste and her business contacts, including Garnier, the inspector from the Tourist Board and Monsieur Verdier's assistant Jacques.

The young man had been the one who had nailed that dead rabbit on Bellefontaine's door when Amy had first arrived. After vandalising Amy's car the morning of the garden party, Jacques had pretended that the butcher's van had broken down on the way to Sisteron. He had later interfered again and again with the Tourist Board's database and computer booking system.

'Mademoiselle Claudine told me that she wanted the English woman out of Bellefontaine and that she'd make it worth my while if I managed to scare her away,' was all a remorseless Jacques told the gendarmes.

He had, however, denied ever sneaking into Bellefontaine at night. The taps and appliances turned on and off during the night, the fire in the living room, the freezer door left open had all been orchestrated by Frédéric, Bijard and Marc Chevalier. Frédéric had also confessed to spiking Amy's drink at Manoir Coste, to 'teach her a lesson' after he'd seen her on the terrace with Fabien.

And Fabien had never suspected a thing. What a blind fool he'd been.

Claudine would never work for any of his contacts in the

hospitality industry, Fabien would make sure of that, and she'd better leave Bonnieux for good too ...

If Ferri didn't believe that she had done enough to be placed in custody, it was another matter altogether for her mother. Anne was detained at Cavaillon jail, charged for now with complicity in kidnapping Stéphane and Amy and with Paul son's attempted murder. Fabien had no doubt the list of her crimes would grow with time. Together with Bijard, Fred and the Chevaliers, she had been at the core of the Bloody Bonnieux Sect, as the local and national press now referred to it.

Now that the Chevaliers were dead, the police relied on Bijard and Anne Loubier to help them identify the other members of the sect, but they weren't being forthcoming with information. A search of the Chevaliers' house had produced notebooks full of codes and numbers, which the gendarmes were unable to decipher.

Bijard had been transferred to a high-security jail in Lyon, the charges against him being more serious than the ones against Anne. Not only had he admitted to Paul Michon's and Sophie Dessange's murders but he was also charged with Sophie Dessange's rape and with killing her English boyfriend. There was also the matter of the murder of Fabien's father that he had helped cover up as a hunting accident and of obstructing the course of justice.

As for Fred, he had suffered some kind of psychotic episode shortly after his arrest. His lawyer claimed that his drink and drug habit had impaired his mental faculties, and that he would be unable to stand trial for the numerous offences he was charged with, among which was the attempted murder on his person at the Buoux cliffs. The examining magistrate had agreed to detain him in a mental hospital in Apt to be assessed.

Lock him up and throw away the key. Or better still, let him deal with him.

Fabien took a few gulps of air, willing the knot of anger twisting inside him to loosen. He never wanted Amy to lay eyes on these monsters again. He knew, however, that they would both be called as prosecution witnesses during the trial in a few months' time.

He let out a sigh. Guilt tugged at his heart. He hadn't been completely honest with her. It was time to tell her the truth.

Amy shifted in his arms and opened her eyes.

'What's the matter? You look preoccupied.'

'There's something I need to tell you. Something I should have told you before. It's about my father and Serena Chevalier. What she said that night at Bellefontaine, about their affair ...'

'You heard what she said? I thought you were still unconscious. I'm so sorry you had to find out like that.'

'The thing is, I already knew.'

She propped herself up on her elbow, gazed into his eyes. 'You did?'

He nodded. 'Shortly before you bought Bellefontaine, I found letters from Serena addressed to my father stuffed into a folder in the library – letters that left no doubt in my mind that they'd been having a liaison over several years, even after he married my mother.'

He felt again the anger, the shame harden into a fist inside him.

'What was my father thinking of? From what she wrote, he was the one doing all the chasing, the one who behaved like a love-crazed fool – or rather a lust-crazed fool – and the one who indulged in all sorts of ... sexual activities with Serena, and their friends.'

Compassion filled her eyes and she touched his face with the tip of her fingers. He took hold of her hand, brought it to his mouth, and kissed the inside of her wrist.

'I made a promise to myself then,' he carried on. 'To protect my mother, make sure she'd never find out. And to protect Manoir Coste. If I was unpleasant, hostile even, towards you at first, it's because I wanted Bellefontaine to remain empty and disappear into overgrown thorns and weeds. It was where my father would meet Serena, where he betrayed my mother time and time again. And where there might still be proof of their affair. I was afraid you'd find something and—'

'I did ... There was an old photo of Serena and your father in the barn, but I would never have told your mother, or anyone else. I would never have caused her, or you, any pain.'

'I know that now. I'm just sorry I didn't tell you before. It's been eating at me. I was determined not to let any scandal break out, compromise my family name, and Manoir Coste, of course.'

He let out a bitter laugh. 'And look how it all turned out. The scandal is far worse than I could ever have imagined.'

He held her tightly, kissed her lips, aroused once again by her warmth, her softness, and the irresistible scents of vanilla and woman lingering on her skin.

'I love you, *mon Aimée*.'

'I love you too, more than words can say. But for now, you must go to the fête.'

He shook his head. 'I told you, I'm not going anywhere.'

She pulled a face. 'What if I want to go? I heard so much about it, I want to enjoy the lights and the fireworks too.'

'Are you sure you're up to it? There'll be journalists, people will stare at you ...'

'You'll be there. That's all that matters.'

'In that case, I suppose I'd better get ready.'

He kissed her and got up. She heard him turn the shower on, hum a French song. This past week was a blur. The torrential rain had stopped as suddenly as it had started, and the weather had turned warm and sunny again. Fabien had taken her for days out to secluded *calanques* on the coast where they sat on small rocky beaches, gazed at the turquoise blue sea, and tried to forget the terror of the events in the underground temple.

Bellefontaine was sealed off by the gendarmes as their investigation carried on. Amy had only been allowed back to get some clothes and personal effects. Chris and Peter had gathered their belongings too before checking into Manoir Coste, courtesy of Fabien. They were joined most evenings by Laurent, who rented a house nearby with Ben, Patricia and other archaeologists from Arles.

Laurent expected to stay in Bonnieux for the foreseeable future to catalogue the treasure, which had thankfully been saved from the flooding, explore the tunnels and secret chambers of the Gallic Goddess and map out the network of underground passages which criss-crossed the hill underneath the forest.

'I found the missing link between the two most important goddesses of the ancient world,' he had told Amy and Fabien earlier. 'Cybèle, the Magna Mater of the east, and the Gallic Goddess of Bonnieux who was the Magna Mater from the west and was here in Provence all along.'

The interest from the national and international press had been extraordinary since the story first broke out. All the hotels and guesthouses in Bonnieux and surrounding villages were full of journalists, television crews, historians, and researchers hoping to catch glimpses of the cave, the treasure, or of Bellefontaine.

Amy was glad to be staying with Fabien at the cottage. She had temporarily closed her business and cancelled the few reservations she'd taken for the summer. She had no idea when she would be allowed to re-open Bellefontaine as a guesthouse. More to the point, she had no idea whether she ever wanted to live there again.

Fabien came out of the bathroom and proceeded to get dressed in a crisp white shirt, black trousers, and black smoking jacket. He fastened his bow tie in front of the full-length mirror against his wall, turned round and smiled. And her heart missed a beat. He might look tall, dark, and powerful, a worthy descendant of the proud warrior line of Costes, but he was only a man and she had come very close to losing him.

'Are you sure about this?' he asked.

'Positive. I'll be with you very shortly.'

He bent down over her and kissed her slowly, his fingers trailing along her arms, then up and down her back.

'You'd better go,' she said, putting her hands on his chest and pushing him away gently.

He sighed. 'I'll see you later.'

She heard his footsteps descending the staircase and the front door closing. She wanted to go to the fête tonight. She couldn't hide in the cottage forever. Besides, if she was with Fabien, she could face anything and anyone. Chris and Peter would be there too and she looked forward to spending some time with them before they left for Manchester. Chris wanted to finalise her separation from Toby and her move to Provence as soon as possible. Her eyes shining with happiness and excitement, she had told Amy that Laurent had asked her and Peter to live with him and that they were madly in love.

She ran a bath and poured some vanilla essence in the hot

water. In the bath she placed her hands onto her stomach, remembered Serena's words, and smiled. It was still too soon to know if she was indeed pregnant, but something inside her whispered that, as strange as it may seem, the woman had been right.

It didn't take long to get ready. She slipped into her black evening dress and a pair of slingback shoes, brushed her hair, and put a little make-up on.

Glancing out of the window she drew in an astounded breath. Hundreds of glittering lights turned the garden into a fairy tale, and tea lights in coloured glass containers shimmered on every windowsill of the three-storey castle.

Amy felt a twinge of sadness as she thought about Adèle and Stéphane. They should have been here tonight, together with Paul. Amy had gone to Adèle's house earlier on in the week to offer her support but her friend hadn't invited her in.

Poor Adèle. She wasn't only grieving the loss of her husband. She was also reeling from the horror of discovering he'd been involved in a criminal organisation for almost as long as she had known him. In his statement to the police, Bijard had confirmed that Paul had taken part in the rape of Sophie Dessange in the underground temple years before, but admitted that Paul had been high on drugs at the time. He had looked on, as Serena and Marc Chevalier had carried out the bloody ritual of killing and mutilating Sophie's boyfriend as a rite of passage for Serena to be ordained the new priestess.

Paul had then tried to sever his links with his former group of friends, but they hadn't let him, calling on him for various favours over the years, reminding him that whether he liked it or not, he was one of them and threatening to hurt his family if he refused to help or tried to expose them.

When Amy had purchased Bellefontaine, Marc Chevalier had asked Paul to make sure the trap door in the cellar would be left intact so that it would still be possible to gain access to the *bastide* from the tunnels.

Amy couldn't even begin to understand how Adèle and Stéphane would manage to reconcile the memories they had of Paul with the revelations about his past. She could only hope time would heal their pain.

She turned away from the window and was about to go down when she heard the front door open. Fabien must have forgotten something, or maybe he was coming back for her. Michka barked, then yelped in pain. Heavy footsteps climbed the staircase. Her blood froze, and her heart started beating fast and wild.

Whoever was coming up the stairs wasn't Fabien.

A tall silhouette shadowed the doorway to the bedroom. 'Frédéric.'

'Surprise, my lovely!' he said in a throaty voice. 'We have some unfinished business, you and I.'

His lips stretched into a thin smile, a malicious glint shone in his eyes. He was wearing dark blue trousers and a white shirt, probably the uniform of the mental hospital he had been admitted to a few days before.

'What are you doing here? How did you get out of hospital?'

He laughed. 'Bijard wasn't the only gendarme who enjoyed Serena's kinky sessions in the temple. You upset a lot of people when you wrecked our little sex club, you know. It used to provide a most enjoyable way of passing an evening. Drugs, sex, and a show with Serena performing her loony priestess' act ... But now it's all over, thanks to you.'

He was blocking the doorway so Amy moved towards

the window, grabbed hold of the latch and frantically tried to pull it down. She had to open it, shout for help.

'Move away from the window and come here.'

He walked to the unmade bed and patted the sheets. 'This time, nobody will come between us.'

Amy pressed her back against the wardrobe.

'I said come here!' he said, his voice edgy now as he produced a knife from his trouser pocket.

Amy didn't move.

'Don't force me to do unpleasant things, Amy,' he warned. 'At least, not just yet.'

The phone rang downstairs, shrill, resonating in the empty cottage. It stopped after about twenty rings, only to start again. Her mobile started chiming too from the bedside table where she had left it.

'Shall I answer?' Amy moved towards the bedside table.

'Leave the damned phone and come to me.' Fred sat on the bed and stared at her.

Amy didn't move. Her legs shook so badly she feared they might give way under her. She had to gain time. Surely, the hospital staff had noticed that Frédéric was missing. Wasn't he supposed to be detained in a secure unit?

'Take your dress off,' he ordered.

'No.'

Frantic, Amy tried to think of something she could use as a weapon. Behind her on the shelves were a couple of vases and sculptures, but they were too far for her to reach.

'Fine, I'll do it for you.'

He licked his lips, rose to his feet, and walked around her, slowly. Reaching out, he unzipped the dress and pulled it down until it billowed onto the floor.

'Now we'll take the rest off, won't we?' He took her hand, pulled her to the bed, sat down.

'No wonder my bastard of a cousin likes you. You're beautiful. And very soon, you'll be mine. All mine.'

He pointed the blade of the knife onto her stomach and traced a line down to her knickers.

Amy heard the front door open with a crashing noise and footsteps climb the stairs four by four.

'Amy!'

Frédéric sprung up, grabbed hold of her and held her tightly in front of him like a shield. The blade of his knife pushed against her throat.

'Amy!' Fabien shouted again. 'Ferri just called me. Fred's escaped and—'

He stopped in the doorway. He had his hunting rifle in his hand.

'Hello, cousin, your girlfriend was showing me how lovely she is.' Frédéric sniggered and pressed the knife harder to her throat.

'Let her go,' Fabien ordered calmly. 'This was always between you and me.'

'I'll never let her go. In fact, you're going to watch me kill her right now.'

The blade nicked Amy's skin. A little blood trickled out and dripped onto Frédéric's shirt.

Fabien lifted the rifle to his shoulder, took aim.

'This is your last chance. You know I never miss.'

Frédéric laughed – the high-pitched cackle of a madman – and pulled Amy even further back into the room.

'Say bye bye to his lordship now, Amy.'

The room spun and darkened, she struggled to breathe. She was going to die. There were so many things she wanted to tell Fabien, but only a whimper escaped from her lips.

A flash of light blinded her and an explosion thundered inside the room. Frédéric relaxed his grip and dropped to his knees. His body crumpled onto the floor in front of her. Half of his head had been blown away.

She screamed.

Dropping the rifle to the floor, Fabien strode to her and pulled her to him.

'I'm so sorry, *mon Aimée*. It's my fault. I should never have left you alone.'

He held her tight, rocked her like a child in his arms, kissed her forehead, her hair, her lips.

Her teeth clattered, her whole body shook.

'You're cold.'

He took his jacket off, wrapped it around her shoulders.

Suddenly men's voices shouted downstairs, footsteps echoed inside the cottage and half a dozen gendarmes burst into the bedroom.

'How is she?' a gendarme asked.

'She'll be fine,' Fabien answered, holding her against him. 'I shot him,' he added in a tight voice. 'I shot my cousin.'

'So I see. You'll have to come with us, monsieur le duc,' one of the gendarmes said. 'We're going to need a statement from you. And from you too, mademoiselle, but we'll get a doctor to take a look at you first.'

Amy wiped the tears from her face. Her hair felt wet and sticky too so she ran her fingers through it, then looked down at her hand. It was covered with blood.

'I'm going to be sick,' she mumbled. Her hand clamped on her mouth, she rushed to the bathroom.

When she came out again, Fabien reached out for her.

'It's over now,' he said. 'This time, the whole thing is over.'

Chapter Twenty-Eight

One year later

'Is Clémence asleep?' Fabien took Amy's hand and brought it to his lips.

She nodded. 'Fast asleep. Your mother ordered me not to come back to the cottage before midnight. She said she only wants Michka to keep her company tonight.'

'She's right. Tonight is for us.' Fabien smiled. 'You look beautiful. Are you ready to dance and enjoy yourself with your husband?'

Amy had dressed with great care for her first evening alone since giving birth to her baby daughter, and she knew she looked good, if a little curvier than before. The deep blue dress was the colour of her eyes, and the large oval-shaped sapphire necklace – a wedding present from Fabien – sparkled against her skin. Her hair hung soft and loose on her shoulders. But more than designer clothing and expensive jewellery it was love and happiness that made her eyes glitter and her smile so radiant.

Fabien got up from behind his desk, and her heart skipped a beat as he walked to her and took her hand.

'Shall we go?'

She nodded. They walked out of the study and followed the corridor towards the ballroom. It was lit with candles, and already packed. Oblivious to the crowd, Fabien led Amy across the dance floor, encircled her waist with his arms and they started dancing, slowly, as if they were alone.

Outside, night was falling. Hundreds of tea lights trembled on the windowsills of Manoir Coste and on the balustrades of the terrace. Garlands of coloured lights and lanterns stretched between trees in a magical display. Manoir Coste's Fête des Lumières had started. This year, however, there would be no fireworks at nightfall. Fabien had announced that he didn't want the noise to frighten his baby daughter.

After a few dances, Fabien led Amy out onto the terrace, he wrapped his arm around her waist and they stood, side by side, in the fading daylight.

'*Je t'aime, mon Aimée,*' he whispered, staring down at her.

She leaned on his arm, moved to tears. They had come so close to losing each other, one year ago, engulfed in the madness and violence of Serena Chevalier, Frédéric, and their acolytes, that she would never take happiness for granted ever again.

She turned her head towards the cedar forest. It may look dark and mysterious for now, but during the day it echoed with the excited cries and laughter of children cycling, running or taking part in the many activities organised by the new charity she and Fabien had established and which they had based at Bellefontaine.

The *bastide* had been turned into a holiday and activity centre for disadvantaged children and teenagers, and nature and cycling trails now criss-crossed the forest. Both Fabien and Amy volunteered there as often as they could, and Adèle and Stéphane helped out too. It gave Amy's friends comfort and purpose to make a positive contribution to the village after the trauma of the trial and the revelations about Paul.

Six months before, Bijard and Anne Loubier had been tried at the Assizes Court of Lyon, amongst a frenzy of national and international media coverage. As key witnesses for the prosecution, Amy and Fabien stayed a few days in the town, in a hotel in the old quarter where the Palais de Justice stood, overlooking the river Saône.

There, in the oak-panelled courtroom, Amy had relived in minute details her ordeal when Frédéric had abducted her from Bellefontaine and taken her to the underground temple, and later when he had escaped from hospital and burst into Fabien's cottage to pursue his revenge.

She had watched Bijard's arrogance slowly crumble and Anne Loubier lose her haughtiness as the sentence was read out to them – Bijard had been condemned to a life sentence and Anne to twenty-five years in jail. Since neither of them had given away the names of the other members of their group, and the gendarmes had been unable to decipher Serena's notebook, they would bear sole responsibility for the horrors committed in the name of the ancient Gallic goddess now known as 'The Bloody Goddess of Bonnieux'.

There were still mysteries surrounding the goddess and her followers, mysteries which might never be explained. Serena's knowledge of her pregnancy, for one.

'What are you frowning about?' Fabien whispered next to her. 'Tonight is for joy and happiness, not for sombre thoughts.'

He put his arm around her shoulders when Amy's attention was drawn once more to the forest.

'What is that?' she cried out. 'Can't you see, over there? There are lights in the forest.'

But as quickly as they appeared, the lights vanished.

Fabien shook his head.

'I can't see anything. But don't worry, it was probably only kids from Bellefontaine, enjoying a night walk with the youth workers. Come on, *mon Aimée*, let's go back inside.'

Amy peered into the darkness again, but whatever had been there had gone. Fabien was right. The ghosts had forever left Bellefontaine, and there would only be joy and happiness from now on.

Thank You

Dear Reader,

Thank you so much for reading *Escape to the Little Chateau*. I loved writing about Amy's adventures in Provence and the romance between her and Fabien. I first got the idea for the story during a summer family holiday in Provence, a part of France I always loved. 'Water is gold' says an old Provençal saying, and true enough, there are fountains everywhere – some are very grand like in Aix-en-Provence, others a plain stone trough with only an old tap spurting fresh water. One fountain in particular captured my imagination. It was in Cassis, where we had stopped for an impromptu picnic. As soon as I saw it and read the inscription in Latin, I felt I had the basis of a plot …

If you did enjoy the story, then I would be very grateful if you could take a few minutes to leave a review. It is a wonderful feeling for an author when readers let you know that they loved your story and your characters. Reviews are invaluable, not only to raise a book's profile, but also to encourage the author to keep writing, especially when self-doubt creeps in.

Please feel free to contact me on Facebook or Twitter. You can find the details on my author bio on the following page.

Marie

x

About the Author

Originally from Lyon in France, Marie now lives in Lancashire with her family. She works full-time as a modern languages teacher, and in her spare time loves writing romance and dreaming about romantic heroes. She writes both historical and contemporary romance, and best-selling *Little Pink Taxi* was her debut romantic comedy novel with Choc Lit. She is a member of the Romantic Novelists' Association and the Society of Authors. Her native France, as well as her passion for history and research, very much influences her writing, and all her novels have what she likes to call 'a French twist'!

For more information on Marie, visit:
www.twitter.com/MarieLaval1
www.facebook.com/marielavalauthor/

More Choc Lit

From Marie Laval

Little Pink Taxi

Take a ride with Love Taxis, the cab company with a Heart …

Rosalie Heart is a well-known face in Irlwick – well, if you drive a bright pink taxi and your signature style is a pink anorak, you're going to draw a bit of attention! But Rosalie's company Love Taxis is more than just a gimmick – for many people in the remote Scottish village, it's a lifeline.

Which is something that Marc Petersen will never understand. Marc's ruthless approach to business doesn't extend to pink taxi companies running at a loss. When he arrives in Irlwick to see to a new acquisition – Raventhorn, a rundown castle – it's apparent he poses a threat to Rosalie's entire existence; not just her business, but her childhood home too.

On the face of it Marc and Rosalie should loathe each other, but what they didn't count on was somebody playing cupid …

Visit www.choc-lit.com for details.

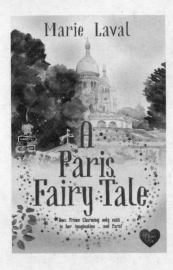

Marie Laval

A Paris Fairy Tale

Is Paris the city of happily ever afters?

Workaholic art historian Aurora Black doesn't have time for fairy tales or Prince Charmings, even in the most romantic city in the world. She has recently been hired by a Parisian auction house for a job that could make or break her career. Unfortunately, daredevil journalist Cédric Castel seems intent on disrupting Aurora's routine.

As Aurora and Cédric embark on a journey across France, they get more than they bargained for as they find themselves battling rogue antiques dealers and personal demons, not to mention a growing attraction to each other.

But with the help of a fairy godmother or two, could they both find their happily ever afters?

Visit www.choc-lit.com for details.

Bluebell's Christmas Magic

A flick of a feather duster and a sprinkle of Christmas magic …

Cassie Bell is used to mess. Her cleaning business, Bluebell Cleaning, is well known in the Cumbrian village of Red Moss. However, now it's almost Christmas and Cassie has a slightly messier situation to deal with than she's used to.

She's been hired to help Stefan Lambert, an injured army helicopter pilot who's staying at the local Belthorn Manor whilst he recovers. Stefan resents Cassie's interference and is definitely not looking for Christmas cheer. But Cassie prides herself on sparkling surfaces – so, can she bring some festive sparkle to Stefan's life too?

Visit www.choc-lit.com for details.

Angel of the Lost Treasure

An ancient secret hidden within a mother's song …

When young widow, Marie-Ange Norton is invited to Beauregard in France by the mysterious Monsieur Malleval to collect an inheritance, she has no choice but to accept.

But when she embarks on the voyage with her fiery-tempered travelling companion Capitaine Hugo Saintclair, little does she know what waits for her across the sea in turbulent nineteenth-century France on the eve of Napoleon's return from exile. When she arrives, she is taken aback by Malleval's fascination with her family – seemingly inspired by his belief they are connected to a sacred relic he's read about in coded manuscripts by the Knights Templar.

As it becomes clear that Malleval's obsession has driven him to madness, Marie-Ange is horrified to realise she is more the man's prisoner than his guest. Not only that, but Hugo is the only person who might be able to help her, and he could represent a different kind of danger …

Visit www.choc-lit.com for details.

Happy Dreams at Mermaid Cove

From the big city to a little yellow mobile library on the Isle of Skye ...

Workaholic art historian Aurora When Jenna Palmer agrees to the new position of mobile librarian on the tiny Arrandale peninsular of the Isle of Skye, she knows she's signing up for difficult working conditions and mediocre wages. But Jenna needs to get away, and a little yellow mobile library called Buttercup could be her escape to happier dreams ...

However, whilst Jenna can get to grips with foggy island roads, local mermaid legends and even big purple monsters, she never expected to have to contend with a boss as grumpy as Daniel McGregor, or a young book lover as enthusiastic as his niece, Katrina.

Arrandale might represent Jenna's safe port in a storm, but could she and Buttercup also become a beacon of hope to Daniel, Katrina and the entire island community?

Visit www.choc-lit.com for details.

Introducing Choc Lit

We're an independent publisher creating
a delicious selection of fiction.
Where heroes are like chocolate – irresistible!
Quality stories with a romance at the heart.

See our selection here:
www.choc-lit.com

We'd love to hear how you enjoyed *Escape to the Little
Chateau*. Please visit **www.choc-lit.com** and give your
feedback or leave a review where you purchased this novel.

Choc Lit novels are selected by genuine readers like yourself.
We only publish stories our Choc Lit Tasting Panel want to
see in print. Our reviews and awards speak for themselves.

Could you be a Star Selector and join our Tasting Panel?
Would you like to play a role in choosing which novels
we decide to publish? Do you enjoy reading women's
fiction? Then you could be perfect for our Tasting Panel.

Visit here for more details…
www.choc-lit.com/join-the-choc-lit-tasting-panel

Keep in touch:
Sign up for our monthly newsletter Spread for all the latest
news and offers: www.spread.choc-lit.com. Follow us
on Twitter: @ChocLituk and Facebook: Choc Lit.

Where heroes are like chocolate – irresistible!